UNWRITTEN RULES

Rules of the Game: Evanston River Otters

BRIGHAM VAUGHN

Two Peninsulas Press

This is a work of fiction. Names, characters, businesses, places, events and incidents are either the products of the author's imagination or used in a fictitious manner. Any resemblance to actual persons, living or dead, or actual events is purely coincidental.

Editing by Rebecca Fairfax

Formatting by Brigham Vaughn

Cover design by Brigham Vaughn

Cover Images:

© Globalstock/iStock

© patrimonio designs ltd/AdobeStock

© alswart/AdobeStock

Printed in the United States of America

First Printing 2022

AUTHOR'S NOTE

I hope you enjoy Jamie and Taylor's story. I loved exploring the world of figure skating and how that overlaps with hockey. And, of course, I had a side character or two who tried to steal the show!

I loved returning to the Otters team and it was fun to see more of the characters I'd established in the previous books as well.

I had so much fun with Zane and Ryan's story and it is available for FREE through Prolific Works as part of a huge giveaway, so please take a moment to check out *Road Rules* if you haven't already.

Gabriel and Lance's story is featured in *Changing the Rules* and it is available on Amazon. The books are best read in order.

Writing about NHL players and pro hockey certainly comes with its own challenges but I've really enjoyed the research and have accidentally became a big hockey fan in the process!

Thank you to Helena Stone, DJ Jamison, and Allison Hickman for your excellent beta feedback. Thank you to Marie-Pierre

D'Auteuil for making sure my Quebecois is spot on. I appreciate you all so much. And a huge thank you to Lynnette Brisia for your hockey-specific feedback as well. I really, really couldn't do this without you. Thank you for being endlessly patient with my hockey questions.

Huge thanks to Rebecca Fairfax for your fantastic edits and proofreading, thank you to Melissa Womochil, Julie Fouts Hanson, Rebecca Fairfax, and Sandy Bennett for your amazing proofreading. Thank you to Marie-Pierre D'Auteuil for your expertise on everything French-Canadian.

I would be a disaster without all of your hard work!

As always, enormous thanks to DJ Jamison for helping me stay on track (seriously don't know what I'd do without you). You're the best!

And most of all, a big thank you to all of you readers who make this possible. Without you, I wouldn't be living my dream of being a full-time author.

Happy Reading! -B

BOOK BLURB

Rule #1: Don't fall in love with your family's sworn enemy

Taylor Hollis brought home gold at the Olympics, then quit competitive skating at the height of his career.

Four years later, he lives a quiet life teaching figuring skating classes and looking for the perfect guy to settle down and build a family with.

When the Evanston River Otters hire Taylor to take part in a feel-good media piece, he'll have to defy his father and work with the son of the man he detests.

And his one weakness is a hot older guy who's good with kids.

Rule #2: Choose your loyalties wisely

Last season, Jamie Walsh left the Chicago Windstorm after a nasty divorce and falling out with his linemate.

Now he's getting settled as a new forward for the Otters.

His biggest priority is his five-year-old daughter, Ava, but he can't ignore how attractive he finds her skating teacher.

The only man he's ever been interested in.

The more time they spend together, the harder it is for Jamie to ignore his feelings.

Too bad Taylor's father has always blamed Jamie's dad for ruining his hockey career.

Jamie and Taylor are perfect for one another but they'll have to ignore both of their families' unwritten rules if they let themselves fall in love with the enemy.

TRIGGER WARNING *Unwritten Rules* includes frank discussion of eating disorders and past infidelity by secondary characters.

TEAM INFO & GLOSSARY

The *Rules of the Game* Series is set in a fictional universe.

Although real life hockey teams and players are mentioned in passing, all of the teams shown on page are fictional.

While I have done my very best to stay true to the rules and schedules of professional hockey, some minor creative license was taken writing these stories.

While not an exhaustive list of hockey terms and slang by any means, here are some used in the series that you might not be familiar with.

Biscuit - A slang term for the puck.

Black Ace - Extra players added to a roster for a team's playoff run after their own season is over in the minor-leagues or elsewhere. The Black Aces practice with the team and are expected to be ready to step into the lineup if any of the regular players in the lineup are unable to play.

Breezers - Hockey pants. Knee-to-waist protective gear that carry a variety of padding depending on whether they are worn by goaltenders or skaters. The pants are traditionally a one-piece garment with a lace-up fly augmented by a strap belt. This slang term is most commonly used in the Midwest.

Celly - Slang for "celebration". The expression of joy after a player scores a goal. Often unique to each player/team.

Corsi - An advanced statistic used to provide an indication of the time a team spends in the offensive zone, versus time spent in their defensive zone. This includes shots on goal, missed shots on goal, and blocked shot attempts towards the opposition's net minus the same shot attempts directed at your own team's net.

Crease - The shaded area directly in front of a hockey goal is called the crease. This is where a hockey goalie stops goals, and where opposing players are prohibited from interfering with the goalie.

Deke - A deke feint or fake is a technique where a player draws an opposing player out of position or is used to skate by an opponent while maintaining possession and control of the puck. The term is a Canadian abbreviation of the word decoy.

EBUG - Emergency backup goaltender. The NHL

requires its clubs to have an emergency back-up in attendance at every home game in case either team loses both of its goalies to injury or illness. If both goaltenders on an NHL roster are unavailable, the designated EBUG will dress for the game and either sit on the bench or, more rarely, play.

Fluff(ed) - Miss a shot.

Hatty (Hat Trick) - When a player scores three goals in a game, usually earning him a cascade of hats thrown onto the ice by fans (especially if the player is on the home team).

A natural hat trick is when a player scores three consecutive goals in a game.

A Gordie Howe Hat Trick is when a player gets a goal, an assist for a goal, and participation in a fight, all within a single game.

KHL - The Kontinental Hockey League is an international professional ice hockey league founded in 2008. It comprises member clubs based in Belarus, China, Finland, Latvia, Kazakhstan, and Russia for a total of 24. Based in Moscow, Russia.

Liney - An affectionate term for a player's linemate. Also sometimes used to refer to the linesman who works along with the referee calling offsides and icings and dropping the puck for face offs.

Pipes - The pipe-like bars that make up the frame around the goal.

Poke Check - When a player uses his stick in a poking fashion to knock the puck away from an offensive player. The most commonly used of all the stick check techniques and can be used by any player in any zone of the ice.

Rocket - An extremely good looking woman.

Salary Cap/Cap Space - The NHL salary cap is the total amount that NHL teams may pay for players. The amount set as the salary cap each year depends on the league's revenue for the previous season. The cap space is the amount of money that a professional team has available to spend on players' salaries.

Spitting Chiclets - Spitting out teeth that have been knocked loose in a fight.

Tape - A slang term for video footage of a hockey game.

Tendie - Goaltender. Also known as a goalie.

TOI - Time on Ice. The minutes and seconds a skater plays during a game or season.

Two-Touch - a common warmup before a hockey game. Players stand in a circle and the goal is to keep a soccer ball up in the air. The ball can be touched once or twice on each attempt, but should be passed in the air to a teammate. Players are eliminated until there is one final winner.

UNWRITTEN RULES

JAMIE & TAYLOR

"Hockey is figure skating in a war zone."

- ***Author Unknown***

PROLOGUE

FOUR YEARS AGO

"Hey, wanna come with me to the rink?"

Jamie Walsh looked up from his phone to squint at his teammate. "We had practice this morning and I'm still wiped from the flight. Call me lazy but I don't want to get any more skating in now, thanks."

Dustin Fowler laughed. "No, not the hockey rink, dude, the figure skating rink. Weren't you listening to anything I said?"

"Uh, no," Jamie said guiltily. "I was texting Kara. Sorry."

Fighting is more like it but what else is fucking new?

Fowler waved it off. "You're good. I get it. Wives take priority."

Jamie stifled a hollow laugh. *Priority*. Yeah. That was the damn problem. Kara didn't think Jamie was making their relationship enough of a priority.

And yes, Jamie definitely felt guilty jetting off to the Olympics for two weeks when she was home with their baby girl. But this had been a lifetime dream of his and he was thirty years old. This was his first and probably last shot at winning gold with Team USA.

Why couldn't she understand how important that was to him?

"Nah, it's okay. Kara left to put Ava down for a nap anyway. She's been fussy all day." Jamie sat up with a groan. "So you want to go check out the figure skaters? You trying to pick up or something?"

Jamie was cool with playing wingman while his single friend found a hot figure skater to hook up with but he prayed he wouldn't have to vacate their shared room later so Fowler could get some action.

Fowler chuckled. "No, dude. *My sister* is a skater. Her performance isn't until tomorrow but it's at the same time as our game against Finland. I wanted to swing by practice tonight and at least show a little support. Thought you might want to tag along."

"Oh," Jamie said. Damn, he really hadn't been paying attention.

Fowler scratched his head. "No biggie if you want to stay here and have some alone time with your wife once your little one is napping though. I won't be offended."

Jamie managed a wan smile in response. Even if Kara wasn't pissed about him leaving for the Olympics, they hadn't had sex in a long time, much less via Skype. They'd Skyped a lot in the past when he was traveling with the Chicago Windstorm but of course, that was before they got married and had a kid.

"Walsh?" Dustin stared at Jamie like he needed to go through concussion protocol.

Jamie shook his head to clear away the depressing reality of his marriage and stood. "Yeah, let's go. Watching some skating sounds fun."

Better than sitting around their tiny room and moping, anyway. He stuffed his phone in his pocket and put all thoughts of his relationship aside.

He was here at the Olympics and he was going to make the most of it.

But when they left the Olympic Village and arrived at the rink, there were men on the ice.

"Umm," Jamie said, looking around at the figure skaters.

Fowler laughed. "I got a text from Em saying the guys are nearly done with their run-through. The women will be up next."

"Got it." Jamie grinned at him.

"C'mon, man, let's find a seat." Fowler nodded to the stadium-style seating.

The stands were maybe half filled, and more people were trickling in.

Fowler waved to a couple sitting partway up and Jamie followed. He greeted Dustin's parents warmly. He hadn't seen them in years but he and Dustin had hung out a lot when they'd played together in Juniors and it was great to see his family again. They caught up for a minute before Jamie turned to face the ice.

There were half a dozen guys going through their full routines simultaneously. The controlled chaos wasn't so different from warmups before a hockey game but Jamie was still amazed no one crashed into anyone else while executing complicated jumps.

The skaters were all incredible. They appeared to defy gravity when they leapt and spun, graceful and strong all at once. It was so different from the hard physicality of hockey.

Jamie's attention was drawn to one in particular. It must have been the way he moved, every motion controlled but fluid. Effortless and graceful but still so damn *powerful.*

As he landed another complex-looking jump, Jamie let out the breath he'd been holding. "Damn," he muttered.

"They're good, huh?" Fowler said with a grin.

"Seriously. I'm envious of their footwork."

"You should try training with them sometime. It'll definitely help."

"Oh?"

"Yeah, during the off-season I work with a figure skating coach along with a private hockey coach and trainer. Really helps with my edgework and agility."

Well that explained why he was so damn good. "I'll have to look into it."

Jamie turned his attention to the ice again, his gaze immediately landing on the dark-haired guy he'd been watching before.

Jamie leaned forward, studying the lines of his body, watching a tightly controlled spin segue into a graceful glide. His heart beat a little faster and he felt oddly flushed as the routine built in intensity.

Jamie watched, lips parted, when the guy landed with a final dramatic flourish, the last to finish his performance. Jamie was on his feet clapping before he could stop himself, but many of the other people in the stands did too.

"Hey, who is he, anyway?" Jamie nodded toward the ice as the skater acknowledged the applause with a little wave and glided toward the boards.

"The favorite to win gold for the US this year." Fowler took a seat. "Taylor Hollis."

"Oh shit," Jamie whispered. He dropped into his seat with an audible thump, his knees taken out from under him like he'd been slashed by a stick.

Fowler gave him a puzzled look. "You know him or something?"

"Uh, not personally," Jamie said with a grimace. "But, um, you remember who my dad is, right?"

"Yeah, Adam Walsh. Former Chicago Windstorm center …" Fowler's eyes went wide. "Wait …"

"Yeah." Jamie slouched in his seat. "His rivalry with Rick Hollis was pretty legendary and Taylor is Rick's son."

"Shit. They had *beef* back in the day."

"They did," Jamie said tightly.

"Huh." Fowler considered the idea. "I'd never put two and two together."

"I vaguely knew Taylor Hollis was a figure skater but I had no idea he was here at the Olympics this year." Jamie scrubbed his hands over his face.

Shit.

The rivalry between their fathers had begun early in their careers and Jamie been seventeen when the accident happened. He'd spent his pro hockey career defending his father against the people who'd accused him of being a talentless goon.

The last thing Jamie wanted was for their history to be discussed in post-game interviews. He was under enough pressure already.

"Hey, there's Em," Fowler said with a nod as a young woman skated onto the ice, followed by a few other skaters.

Jamie watched Emily's routine while Fowler caught him up on her career and training, his face glowing with pride. Her routine was flawless, and Jamie enthusiastically clapped for her.

After practice was over, Jamie followed Fowler down to the ice and into the back hallway where they waited for Emily to finish talking to the press.

Jamie leaned against the wall, hoping he wouldn't run across Taylor while he was back here. He had a vague memory of seeing Taylor in the news over the years but he couldn't remember what he looked like and he hadn't been sitting close enough to the ice earlier to get a good look at his face.

He surreptitiously googled Taylor's name to check. *Huh.* Definitely the kind of guy who would stand out in a crowd, so he should be easy to spot. Jamie kept scrolling Taylor's bio, surprised to see he was a decade younger than him since their fathers were roughly the same age.

Of course, Jamie's parents had been young when they got married and had kids. The Hollises must have been older.

"Great job, Taylor!" Mrs. Fowler called out and Jamie's head snapped up.

Oh shit. Here we go.

"Oh, thank you," a light, clear voice replied.

Jamie nearly dropped his phone in his haste to get it tucked into his pocket. When he looked up, Taylor Hollis stood a few feet away. Yeah, definitely easy to recognize with his big blue eyes, pale skin, and flushed cheeks.

A weird tension settled in the pit of Jamie's stomach.

"Great to see you, Sue," Taylor said, beaming. He leaned in to kiss her cheeks. "You're here to see Emily?"

"Yes. We're so proud of her. And you of course. You were marvelous earlier."

"I knew I liked you for a reason."

They laughed together and Jamie shot a confused look at Dustin. "You *know* Hollis?" he hissed under his breath.

"Me personally? No, but he and Emily train at the same facility in Chicago so our families know each other," he said quietly. "Why?"

"I was just surprised."

The Fowlers and Taylor made small talk for a little while and Taylor flicked a few curious glances in Jamie's direction. His gaze was bold and assessing as it raked over Jamie's body but nothing indicated he knew who Jamie was. Good. That was for the best. The last thing Jamie wanted was to drag the Fowlers into their messy family history.

When Emily appeared, Dustin and his parents drifted away to talk to her, and Jamie and Taylor were left alone.

Taylor tilted his head back and smiled up at Jamie. He'd exchanged his skates for shoes and he was a good five or six inches shorter than Jamie.

"Well, *hello* there. I don't believe we've been introduced."

Taylor stuck out a hand and Jamie smiled as he shook, helpless to do anything else in the face of his bright grin. "Hello to you too. Great performance tonight."

Taylor made a face. "Ugh. I totally flubbed my last triple toe loop but thanks."

"It's definitely easier to see the mistakes instead of the successes," Jamie pointed out with a shrug. "But you can't focus on only the negative. Gotta take the wins along with it, right?"

Taylor's gaze raked across him again, landing on the Team USA hoodie he wore. "You're competing?"

"Yeah, I'm—"

Taylor held up a hand. "No. No. Let me guess." He narrowed his eyes and scrutinized Jamie closely. The attention made Jamie warm. "Snowboarder? Freestyle skier?"

Jamie's smile widened. "Neither."

"Luge."

He chuckled. "Nope."

"Darn. I was hoping I might get a chance to see you in spandex." Taylor winked.

Jamie laughed. "I've been known to wear spandex." Though it was usually buried under layers of padding.

"Hmm." Taylor's gaze trailed down to linger on Jamie's thighs. "Speed skater, then. You have *great* quads."

The back of Jamie's neck got warm again and he wasn't sure if he was glad or sorry he'd given in to Fowler's heckling and changed from sweats to jeans before they left. "Nope, but you're closer."

Taylor let out a little huff. "Hmm. You aren't a hockey player, are you?"

"Hey," he protested. "What's wrong with hockey?"

"Nothing! My dad was a hockey player. I can't believe I missed the obvious choice."

Jamie's stomach sank and he rubbed the back of his neck. Well, now he'd be an asshole if he didn't acknowledge their connection. "Uhh, yeah. I kinda knew about your dad. I'm, uh, Jamie Walsh. My dad's a former player too."

The look of horror on Taylor's face when he made the connection made Jamie wince.

"Yeah, sorry. I should have led with that, I guess," he mumbled. "I didn't want to make things awkward in front of the Fowlers. If you want me to go, I can—"

"No." Taylor shook his head. "No, don't go."

"Well, I get the situation with our families is, um, a little complicated."

Taylor sighed. "That's putting it mildly."

"But uh, maybe it would be good if we cleared the air before the media got wind of us both being here? I know my dad felt really horrible about what happened between them and—"

"Felt really horrible?" Taylor's voice turned incredulous. "He fucking should. He nearly paralyzed my father."

"It wasn't intentional," Jamie said bristling. "It was an *accident.* If Tucker hadn't plowed into my dad, it never would have happened."

Color rose in Taylor's cheeks, and he crossed his arms, glaring at Jamie. "He was *already* going after my father before Tucker slammed into him and—"

"That's bullshit," Jamie said, glowering. "And this is a ridiculous grudge to hold after so long."

"You didn't watch your father get wheeled off the ice on a stretcher," Taylor snarled, poking at Jamie's chest with his index finger. "You didn't see the look on his face when he realized his career was over."

Jamie batted his hand away and stepped closer, scowling down at him. "You were what, *eight* at the time? Maybe you misunderstood the situation."

"I was seven but I understood *plenty*." Taylor didn't back down an inch, jutting his chin up, his full lips flattening into a scowl. "My father nearly gave up on *everything* because he'd never be able to play hockey again. Because the doctors told him he might never walk again. So fuck you, Walsh. Fuck you *and* your father."

Taylor turned away, anger radiating from every line in his slim body as he swept past the Fowlers.

"It was great to see you but you might want to rethink the people you spend time with," he sneered, with one backward venom-filled glance at Jamie.

Hollis/Walsh Feud Reignites at the Olympic Games

The on-ice rivalry between Rick Hollis and Adam Walsh in the early 2000s was the stuff of legends.

It sold tickets and pumped up fans on both sides but the hotly contested fight for a playoff spot between the Chicago Windstorm and the Detroit Auto Wrenches quickly turned ugly.

A hit from Adam Walsh led to Rick Hollis being taken off the ice on a stretcher, ultimately ending his career.

Although Walsh was cleared of any wrongdoing by the league after Hollis's injury, Hollis has never held back about his feelings for Walsh's style of play.

What's equally clear is that there's no love lost between the younger generation either. Neither Jamie Walsh nor Taylor Hollis commented on a reported altercation at the Olympic practice rink last week but Taylor Hollis ended his silence yesterday.

The recent USA vs the Czech Republic game was marred by an altercation between ice hockey forward Jamie Walsh and the Czechian center that left Jakub Svoboda limping to the trainers.

When asked about it, figure skater Taylor Hollis echoed his father's words about there being no place in the game for unsportsmanlike behavior.

"I'd hoped there had been changes made since my father's day," the younger Hollis said. "It's disappointing to still see goon-like behavior not only being allowed but rewarded."

Despite the rivalry between their families, Jamie Walsh and Taylor Hollis both brought home a combined total of four gold medals for Team USA in the Olympics this year.

Jamie Walsh has been unavailable for comment.

CHAPTER ONE

PRESENT DAY

Taylor Hollis grimaced as he lifted his phone to his ear, bracing himself for the lecture he was about to get. They'd been arguing for weeks, and Taylor was exhausted. "Hi, Dad."

"Please tell me you're not going through with it." The disapproval in Rick Hollis' voice cut straight through Taylor.

"I am."

"I still can't believe you agreed to work with Jamie Walsh."

"He is *one* member of the team, Dad."

"Yeah, well, watch your back. You can't trust him. You know what he did at the Olympics—"

Taylor winced. He still felt guilty about the comment he'd made to the media four years ago. He'd been in a rough place in his own life and pissed at Walsh's dismissal of the accident, but he'd been out of line when he commented to the press. "Dad, can we not rehash this *again*? I know how you feel about me working with the organization—"

"I have no problem with the River Otters. They're a solid team. But Jamie Walsh—"

"Is not someone I want to talk about," Taylor said firmly.

"Don't pull the media tone on me, son."

Taylor squeezed his eyes shut. "Dad, I love you but you have *got* to stop. What happened with Adam Walsh was fucking awful and you have every right to be pissed at him but I'm tired of getting dragged into it over and over again." He leaned against the kitchen counter. "I signed a contract to work with the team. I'm going to be on my best behavior and so will Jamie Walsh."

Rick sighed. "I love you too, son, I just don't want to see you get hurt."

"I *won't*."

"Promise me you'll watch your back around him at least," Rick muttered, hanging up without another word.

Taylor resisted the urge to throw his phone across the room.

He yelped at the sight of the pan of oatmeal he'd left sitting on the hot burner. *Fuck*. Darting forward, he turned off the gas and rescued it. He stirred the oats forcefully, letting out a sigh of relief they hadn't scorched.

Taylor's phone buzzed on the counter beside him again. He squinted at the screen and saw it was his mom's cell calling. He answered cautiously, setting the oatmeal on a cool part of the stove. "Hey, Mom. What's up?"

"I want to apologize for your father."

Taylor rolled his eyes. "It's not your job."

"I know. But he means well."

"He does but he's still pissing me off." Taylor pulled out bowls, then scooped the oatmeal into them.

"He's worried about you."

"Can we not get into this?" Taylor said. "I love you both but this is my choice to make. I'm teaching a bunch of hockey players to skate. I'm not joining the fucking team. I'm going to be a professional and so is Jamie Walsh. Samantha promised me he'd be on his best behavior. Neither of us want bad press right now so we're going to suck it up and play nice for a month and a half and at the end, he and the rest of his team will walk away with better footwork and I'll walk away with an amount of money I'm in no position to turn down."

"I still don't know why you quit competing, Taylor. You—"

"Mom, *no*." He dumped blueberries into the bowls with a little more force than necessary. "I'm done with competition. I am doing this media campaign with the River Otters. I respect the opinions you and Dad have but I'm a grown-ass adult who can make his own decisions. Period. End of story."

"You're twenty-four, Taylor. In the scheme of things, that's barely grown."

Taylor swallowed back a huff of frustration that would make him sound like the teenager she still seemed to think he was. It was ridiculous. He'd been competing as long as he could remember.

He'd spent his entire life being praised for being mature and responsible by everyone around him but ever since he ended his Olympic career, his parents had treated him like a rebellious kid acting up.

They couldn't seem to understand quitting was the best choice he'd ever made.

"—are you listening, Taylor?"

"I have to go, Mom. I'm about to have breakfast with Charlie." He flicked on the electric kettle.

"How is that sweet boy doing?" Her voice softened.

"Better. A lot better, actually," he said around the sudden lump in his throat. "Gotta go though. Love you."

He hung up before she could respond, then stared blankly at his oatmeal for a moment before letting out a sigh. He hated the way his parents always wound him up. He loved them to bits but some days he wished he'd left Chicago completely.

Oh well, nothing to do but move forward and prove them wrong. Which was pretty much his entire motto in life.

"Oatmeal's ready!" Taylor called.

"Be there in a sec," Charlie answered from down the hall.

Taylor stirred his bowl of oatmeal, absently blowing to cool it as he stared out the kitchen window at the brick wall of the apartment next to them.

Thank God they hadn't paid for the view in this place.

A few moments later he heard soft footfalls before Charlie slid a hand along Taylor's waist, pressing a kiss to his cheek. "Thanks, babe."

"Happy to make it," Taylor said, pouring boiling water into two mugs.

"Yum, blueberries today, huh?" his roommate asked, reaching for his bowl and mug.

Taylor smiled down at his oatmeal as he carried it to the small kitchen table. That was progress. This time last year, Charlie would have grimaced and nibbled around the berries, claiming he was "too full" when the truth was, he was worried about the calories.

Charlie had come a long way in the past year, going from dangerously underweight to thin and willowy but healthy. There was a warm flush to his cheeks and his blue eyes sparkled again.

Taylor set down his bowl and mug of tea, crossing his legs before he spooned up a bit of the cinnamon-flavored oats.

"Are you terrified about what the Evanston River Otters have in store for you today?" Charlie took a seat on the other side of the table.

Taylor snorted. "No."

Many figure skaters—particularly the male queer ones—were not fans of hockey players. They'd spent too many of their formative years getting stuffed into lockers and called all manner of vile things by them.

But as the son of a retired NHL player, Taylor had known that under the aggressive male posturing often lay guys as insecure as anyone else.

Spending the next month or so with a dozen of them was a bit daunting though, even if he was twenty-four now and not afraid of anything.

Except centipedes. He shuddered delicately. So many legs. *Blech.*

"If I can wrangle children, I can whip some pro hockey players into shape."

"Mmm, kinky." Charlie batted his eyelashes.

They were thick, dark and glossy. Definitely not his natural lashes but he was one of the most talented makeup artists Taylor had ever met, though he currently had an internship as an interior decorator.

Charlie had done Taylor's makeup for the shoot today and Taylor kept preening every time he caught a glimpse of himself in the mirror.

"Not whip them into shape like *that*. I just mean I'm not afraid to push back, you know? I don't care if they're multi-millionaires with houses that could easily hold our entire apartment in one of their seven bajillion bathrooms. I'm not letting them cow me."

Not even Jamie Walsh.

"I know. You're no one's doormat." Charlie smiled at him. "Oh! By the way, I snuck a peek at some of them on the team's Insta the other day to scope them out and *damn*, girl."

Taylor smirked. He'd checked out the Instagram account too and Charlie wasn't wrong.

The eye candy was no joke.

The previous media relations person for the team *had* been a joke though, barely updating with any content.

Now that Taylor's friend Samantha McCoy had taken over, it was greatly improved.

The feed was now chock-full of player profiles, videos of practices, game highlights, suit porn from before games, and Taylor's personal favorite, sweaty workout shots. *Rowr.*

"What they're paying me isn't the only perk," he admitted.

"And queer players!" Charlie's eyes went wide. "Who'd have thought?"

Taylor laughed. "Wild, isn't it?"

The sudden rise in bi and gay pro hockey players had left Taylor absolutely gobsmacked. Taylor had assumed he'd be old and gray before the first guy came out, but it had happened a few years ago.

"The captain and his winger came out two seasons ago, right?"

"Mmhmm." Taylor took a sip of his ginger spice tea. "Zane Murphy and Ryan Hartinger. Best friends who suddenly realized they were in love with each other, I guess. It was an adorable story."

"Think that'll ever happen to us?" Charlie fluttered his lashes at Taylor.

"Unlikely."

"Ouch." Charlie clutched his chest. "Damn, honey, you don't have to be so cruel."

Taylor rolled his eyes. "If I ever confessed romantic feelings to you, you'd run screaming in the other direction. Besides, you like them big and brawny, and I am neither." He gestured toward his lithe body. They were both athletic but on the twink-y side of things.

Charlie shrugged. "You're big enough where it counts."

Taylor sputtered, trying not to inhale the tea. "Excuse me?"

"Come on. I've seen you undressed enough times to tell."

"*Aannyy*way," Taylor said, choosing to ignore the comments because that would only encourage Charlie, which he absolutely did not want to do. He'd learned that lesson the hard way. "Love you as a roommate and bestie but I am not your type, and you don't want kids, so I don't think we're destined to spend the rest of our lives together or anything."

"Yes." Charlie let out a dramatic sigh. "You're going to meet a man and fall in love and have sixteen babies and leave me eventually."

"Two, *max*," Taylor protested. "And I'm not opposed to adopting older kids."

"I know, I know." Charlie shot him a look, clearly over the topic. "But you do want a man and children and a cute little house in the 'burbs."

Taylor shrugged. "More or less but you don't have to sneer about it."

He'd been given more than enough shit in his life for his aspirations, and he could do without it from his best friend.

"Sorry, sorry." Charlie held up his hands in supplication. "Just because the thought of settling down with any man gives me the heebie-jeebies doesn't mean I should knock your choices."

"Damn straight." Taylor spooned up another bite of his breakfast.

"More like damn *homo*," Charlie teased. "Speaking of which, isn't there another homo hockey player on the team? The pretty one with the long hair, yeah?"

"Mmm, yes. Gabriel Theriault," Taylor said. "He's dating the silver fox coach."

According to the gossip floating around, the player and coach had fallen in love and dated secretly until photos of them surfaced on the *JockGossip* website.

At the time, neither of the guys had been out of the closet publicly and Taylor knew exactly how uncomfortable it was to have the sports world discussing one's every move.

Taylor had never hidden his sexuality, but figure skating was a very different world than pro hockey. People assumed most, if not all, male figure skaters were gay, and many guys had trouble getting people to believe they were straight.

Charlie continued. "Well, I'd be worried about you spending the next six weeks with them if it weren't for the queer thing they have going on."

"I'd be fine anyway," Taylor protested. "I can handle myself."

"Yes, yes, you're absolutely terrifying." Charlie's expression turned serious. "What about Jamie Walsh? How do you feel about that situation?"

Taylor sighed and chased a lone blueberry with his spoon. "Weird. I mean, I don't know what the fuck the moment between us at the Olympics was about. I think maybe I read something into it that wasn't there." Initially, he'd thought Jamie was flirting with him and then he'd been hit in the face with the news of who he was.

"I'm still Team *Bi-curious Hockey Player Who Isn't Out of the Closet.*"

Taylor snickered. "I know you are but I'm pretty sure I misread the signals. Either way, he turned out to be a married dude who my family *loathes*. I shouldn't have said what I did to the press and now it's gonna be horribly awkward to deal with each other."

"Pretend like none of it ever happened," Charlie said breezily. "That's what I do."

"You *don't*. Or your therapist and I will both smack you."

"Ugh. Fine. But I don't think it has to be a big thing. Unless you want it to be a big thing."

"No. I want to get through the next six weeks without any bad press."

Charlie snickered. "Too bad. I thought you liked big things." He waggled his eyebrows suggestively.

Taylor ignored him but Charlie forged on.

"So fine, perhaps *Mr. Maybe Bi-curious* is a bad idea but are you going to handle any of the other hot, hunky hockey players on the team? Some private tutoring perhaps?"

"Uh, no," Taylor said with an emphatic shake of his head and final scrape of his spoon against the bottom of his bowl. "Definitely not. I am a *professional.*"

Charlie giggled and pushed away his own dish. "You can always be a professional slut."

"That's your gig, not mine," Taylor joked before his mood plummeted. "Besides, we know how well it's worked for me in the past."

Charlie winced. "Sorry, babe, I didn't mean to hit a sore spot."

Taylor sighed. "It's … whatever. I just don't think it's a good idea to get involved with any more pro athletes. They can never give me what I want."

He stood and reached for Charlie's bowl, pleased to see he'd eaten it all, down to the last blueberry.

Taylor didn't like to monitor what Charlie ate but it was hard not to. It had hurt Taylor's heart to see him frail in a hospital bed with a feeding tube down his nose.

"Good job, babe," Taylor whispered, pressing a kiss to the top of Charlie's head.

Charlie's recovery had been slow and there was always the chance of a relapse.

Charlie beamed, tilting his chin up to look at Taylor. "Thanks! I don't even feel stuffed or anything. I think I'm finally getting used to this."

This being eating enough food to sustain a human being.

Sometimes, Taylor missed the days when he and Charlie were Olympic figure skaters. But most of the time, when he thought about the toll it had taken on both of them, Taylor was damn glad they'd gotten out of that world.

Performing in skating shows and teaching classes was perfect for Taylor. He didn't have to stress about every ounce he gained and claw and fight his way to success. He was much happier now.

Taylor let out a wistful little sigh as he carried the bowls to the dishwasher.

Of course, finding a man looking for the quiet married life he dreamed of was proving more elusive than Olympic gold.

He had several medals to his name but zero romantic prospects in sight.

CHAPTER TWO

"Daddy, Daddy, Daddy! Get up! Get up!"

Ava's excited yell and the muffled whomp on the bed beside Jamie's hip dragged him away from the lingering clutches of sleep.

"Nooo," he groaned. "Too early. It's still sleepy time."

With one eye half-open, Jamie reached out, intending to drag his daughter close and pretend to sleep, but she giggled and scampered out of reach.

"No, it's time to get up!" She turned on the lamp beside the bed and he squinted at the sudden brightness. "You gotta go to the rink. It's *important*."

"Mmm, thank you. What would I do without my favorite talking alarm clock?" he muttered when she scrambled closer, though he didn't have a clue why she was so excited this morning.

When Ava was finally close enough he could snag her, he wrapped an arm around her and hauled her close until she giggled against his shoulder, squirming playfully as she pretended to get away.

He pressed a kiss to her blonde curls and breathed in her scent. He missed the new baby smell she'd had when she was born, but she was five now and her hair smelled of berry shampoo and something uniquely Ava. Or possibly Play-Doh.

"Love you, Ava-Bear," he murmured.

She giggled more and tugged ineffectually at him. "Come onnnnnnnn. You're gonna be late."

He squinted at her in confusion, then groped for his glasses on the nightstand. While Ava waking him up wasn't exactly unusual, she wasn't so insistent that he get up immediately. There was typically more begging to lie in bed with him and watch videos or play games on his phone. Anything to get more screen time.

And he was never late for practice especially now that he was with the Evanston River Otters.

He'd left the Chicago Windstorm at the end of last season, disillusioned by pro hockey and his place in it, but by the time training camp with the Otters had finished, he'd fallen in love with the game again, even if it did take him away from his baby more than he'd like.

The last thing Jamie wanted to do was mess up his chances with the best team he'd ever played for.

"What's the hurry?" he asked with a yawn.

Ava squirmed out of his grasp and popped up to her knees, staring at him with a shocked expression. "Don't you *memember*? You're skating with Taylor today!"

Jamie smiled at her pronunciation before the words hit. He groaned and covered his face with his hands as if it would block out the truth.

Damn it, he'd almost forgotten that was today. He could have done without the team's latest training plan. Six weeks of working with an Olympic figure skater to improve their footwork. He was all for cross-training but Jesus, a month and a half was *ridiculous*.

And there was that little issue of it being Taylor Hollis he had to work with …

"You're gonna have so much fun," Ava gushed. "I love my classes. Taylor is sooo funny and he's a really good teacher."

Jamie dropped his hands to smile at her. "I'm glad to hear that, baby."

She'd been talking non-stop about Taylor ever since her lessons started last fall.

Kara had enrolled Ava in small group skating lessons. Ava had been over the moon with excitement about it and Jamie had initially signed off on it without realizing exactly who the teacher was. But the minute Ava came home raving about how excited she was to have Taylor Hollis for a teacher, Jamie had blown up at his ex-wife.

Kara had pretended to be surprised but no matter how much she widened her eyes, batted her lashes, and feigned total ignorance of the connection between the Walsh and Hollis families, Jamie didn't believe a word of it.

She *had* to have known.

In the end, Jamie was glad Kara had done it. Ava had gone through a rough time during the divorce last year and he loved that she was finally back to her usual bouncy, excited self. Small group lessons with Olympic gold medalist figure skaters didn't come cheap but Jamie would have happily paid a hundred times that to see her smile when she talked about Taylor.

"We should watch one of Taylor's videos now." Ava poked her tongue out of her mouth as she stretched to grab his phone on the nightstand.

"I thought I was supposed to get ready and go to the arena? I can't do both at the same time, can I?" he teased.

"Hmm." Ava settled back on the pillow beside his head, phone clutched in her little hands. "Maybe I can watch, and you can get ready."

He hid a smile. His daughter was a skillful maneuverer.

"Sounds like a good compromise." He reached for his phone, tilting the screen away so he could enter the password. "Need me to pull up a video on YouTube?"

"I can do it."

He didn't doubt it, so he handed the phone back. "Okay, baby. You watch while I get ready. Phone goes off before breakfast though. And then Grandma will be by to watch you while I'm at practice."

"'K," Ava said happily, staring at the screen with an intent gaze.

Whether or not that had actually sunk in was debatable and he crossed his fingers that she wouldn't have a meltdown when he asked her to eat without her nose buried in a screen, but he'd be the first to admit he was a bit of a pushover when it came to Ava. His mother and his ex-wife were on him constantly about limiting screen time but after the year she'd had, he had a difficult time refusing her anything.

He flung back the covers and clambered out of bed, wincing at the pull across his left shoulder.

Last night's game against Los Angeles had been a chippy one and Jamie had made a diving save to knock the puck out of the crease as it ricocheted off their goalie's pads. He'd prevented Los Angeles from getting the rebound, and set his teammate up to get possession, but he'd strained something in the process.

His shoulder was a nagging issue for him, but this strain wasn't anything the trainers had been particularly concerned about, so Jamie had spent the better part of the evening lying on an ice pack and wishing he had someone to kiss it better.

He'd have to do a better job stretching before this morning's practice.

Now, he shut the bedroom door long enough to pee and quickly rinse off in the shower, trying to keep his hair out of the spray since it was clean and took forever to dry.

After Jamie was dressed, he opened the bathroom door and peeked out.

Ava was still sprawled on the big bed, watching the video and he heard the voice of an Olympic announcer over the sound of classical music.

"Ten more minutes, Bear," he warned her, grimacing at his reflection in the mirror. He looked a little scraggly so he reached for his beard trimmer. If he was going to be on video today, he needed to neaten up his facial hair.

"Okay," she called back. "*Ooh*, I like this part."

Jamie wasn't sure if the last comment was meant for him, but he tried to listen the best he could over the buzz of the trimmer while she narrated the performance. It was mostly pleased and excited noises like she was watching fireworks. Lots of *oohs* and *ahhs*.

When Jamie's beard was short and neat again and he'd smoothed it down with some balm, Ava was still going, chattering away about the skater's costume.

Jamie fixed his hair while making the appropriate listening noises so she'd know he wasn't ignoring her.

No one deserved to feel ignored, least of all Ava.

In the mirror, Jamie watched her flip on her stomach, her bare feet poking out from her purple pajama pants as she wiggled her legs back and forth excitedly. He smiled. God, she was getting so big. He could hardly believe she was the baby he'd held moments after her birth.

He'd loved Ava from the moment he laid eyes on her squished little crying face, and he'd felt such love for Kara in that moment too.

They never should have gotten married. But he'd been so pleased when Kara told him she was pregnant. Shocked because he'd thought they were being careful, but he'd immediately been happy about the news. He'd always wanted kids, and this merely moved up the timeline. Kara had sounded happy too, and proposing to her had seemed like the only thing to do.

Jamie had convinced himself to ignore all the red flags and they'd had a lavish beachside wedding during the off-season, Kara's belly starting to grow round under her white dress. He'd said his vows with all the hope and enthusiasm a groom should have at a wedding

Things had been rocky in the months leading up to Ava's birth, but he'd chalked it up to the pressures of the season and adjusting to the pregnancy and marriage.

And he'd fallen in love with Kara all over again while she clutched his hands and labored to give birth to their daughter. He'd truly believed those shared moments had solidified their marriage and made them both realize what a team they were. How important their family was to both of them.

What a naïve idiot he'd been.

Jamie's mind twisted away from those thoughts, and he tuned back in to Ava's far more pleasant stream of chatter. "—pretty. I think Taylor is the prettiest boy *ever*. Don't you, Daddy?"

Jamie tried not to flinch.

Taylor Hollis was, in fact, pretty.

Far too pretty.

Too pretty for Jamie's good, that was for damn sure.

Jamie mumbled his agreement like he always did when his daughter asked him questions like that, because answering it out loud might make it a little too real.

It had been four years since Jamie had seen Taylor in person and he was no more prepared for it than he had been after his Olympic practice.

And he was about to spend the next six weeks working with the skater who hated his guts.

The one and only man he'd ever been attracted to.

The practice facility was quiet when Jamie arrived. Despite Ava's concern and the mid-January dump of snow they'd gotten overnight, he was there plenty early. He waved at a security guard and a couple of the equipment guys, then nodded hello to

Lance Tate when he passed his open office door. The offensive position coach was on the phone, so he waved distractedly, and Jamie didn't bother him.

The doors to the rink were open and Jamie glanced down the hall as he passed. He stopped immediately at the sight of someone on the ice. Someone dressed in black who darted and whirled. Definitely not one of his teammates.

He turned and walked down the hall, once again mesmerized by the graceful movements.

Most of the world had been in love with Taylor after watching him win gold at the Olympics four years ago.

But Jamie didn't like to think too closely about how it had felt to watch Taylor's sinuous body twist in a sparkling skintight black skating costume as he flew across the ice in the Olympic arena.

Jamie also didn't like to think about how many times he'd watched the performance on video since. It was almost better to watch the recording, the camera panning in at the end to show Taylor's heaving chest, sweat trickling down his flushed cheeks, a brilliant smile on his face.

Of course, Jamie now had a perfectly good excuse to watch endless Taylor Hollis performances since Ava was obsessed with the skater in the way only a five-year-old could be. Hell, Jamie had to stare at Taylor's poster on Ava's wall when he tucked her into bed at night.

But that didn't excuse why he sometimes watched them *alone.*

Or why he felt … *things* when he watched them.

Actually, he damn well knew why. He wasn't an idiot. But that didn't make it easier to face.

So far, Jamie had been able to avoid Taylor. Ava's lessons were often on game days around the time he napped and either Kara or Jamie's mom took her. Which meant today was the first time in four years they were actually interacting in person.

Jamie's stomach knotted.

Hopefully, he and Taylor could remain professional and ignore the animosity between their families.

"He's incredible, isn't he?"

Jamie turned to face his captain, Zane Murphy, his heart racing at being caught staring.

"Uh, what?" Jamie managed to sputter out.

"Taylor Hollis. He's talented as hell, isn't he?"

Jamie pulled his brain together enough to nod. "Um, yeah. I can definitely see why they hired him to teach us footwork."

Murphy snorted, raking a hand through his thick dark hair. "Let's be honest, it's good PR."

"Well that too," Jamie admitted. He stole another glance at Hollis who was still on the ice, skating like he was performing for an invisible crowd.

The team could definitely use a PR boost. Jamie had been pretty shocked to find out one of the team's assistant coaches was involved with a player. Of course, he'd also been shocked to find out about his wife's infidelity too, so maybe he was just an oblivious idiot.

If he never got called a cuck by another online commenter, it would be too fucking soon.

Hopefully, some feel-good media showing hapless hockey players trying to learn footwork from an Olympic gold medalist figure skater would improve the franchise's image.

"Think it'll work?" Jamie asked Zane, who had been staring across the ice at Taylor's leaps and spins with a thoughtful expression.

"Honestly, I don't know." A frown crossed Zane's handsome face. "I really don't. But I do appreciate you volunteering to take part in the filming. I know that change was last minute."

The lessons were mandatory but Jamie had *not* volunteered to be filmed. At least not initially. But when one of their rookies went out with an injury, Zane had begged Jamie to take his place. Jamie was grateful for his spot here, so he felt an obligation to do it for the team. Samantha had also assured him they had no desire to play up the Hollis/Walsh rivalry, so Jamie had reluctantly agreed to take part.

The Otters had always lagged behind most teams in terms of their online media presence and once the scandal broke, they hadn't wasted any time hiring a shiny new Director of Marketing and Digital Media.

It had only been a few weeks since Samantha McCoy had joined the team, but she'd clearly laid out the entire idea for the campaign ahead of time. That or she hadn't slept at all since she was hired. All of a sudden there were PR and social media people everywhere and Jamie couldn't eat after practice without it being recorded.

"Good to see you here so early, gentlemen," a woman called out, her voice echoing around the rink.

Jamie and Zane turned in unison to face her.

Jamie wasn't even sure how Samantha moved so fast in such high heels on the rubberized flooring around the practice rink while wearing a narrow skirt.

"I figured I'd get here early in case you need any help getting the guys wrangled," Murphy said with an easy smile

She grinned, her blue eyes lighting up. "That's great to hear. Thank you both."

Jamie nodded. He wasn't about to explain he'd arrived early half-hoping to sneak a glimpse of the attractive skater across the ice, not because he was a thoughtful guy like Murphy.

Then again, there was probably a reason Jamie had never been named a team captain. Plus, his former teammates hadn't respected him. Or at least, one in particular hadn't.

Jamie ground his teeth together at the thought of Boyd Marsh.

"We have a busy morning ahead of us," Samantha said, her tone turning businesslike. "I hope you're ready for a lot of camera time."

"Sam! There you are!"

Damn it. Jamie wasn't mentally prepared to face Taylor in person yet.

But he turned and pasted a smile on his face as Taylor skated up to the boards. Even in skates he seemed small. Five inches shorter than Jamie, to be precise. Of course, the fact that Jamie knew he was 5'7" pointed out just how much reading up on the skater he'd done.

Taylor was even prettier than he'd been four years ago. His eyes were more striking than Jamie had remembered. Irises the color of the winter sky with deep blue rings around the outside, all framed by thick lashes, dark against his pale skin.

Holy shit, Taylor was wearing makeup, wasn't he?

That really, really shouldn't make Jamie's mouth go dry.

Taylor's gaze skimmed over Jamie, and he nodded dismissively before he stepped off the ice and walked toward Samantha.

Ouch.

That shouldn't have been a blow to Jamie's ego, but he felt it square in his chest and he rubbed absently at the spot. He supposed indifference was better than outright hatred. Of course, the entire organization was aware of the Hollis/Walsh feud and both of them had promised to be on their best behavior. It was in the agreements they'd signed to do this media campaign.

Taylor gripped Samantha's elbows and pressed kisses to her cheeks. "Hey. Good to see you. You look gorgeous as always."

Samantha was quite tall, with long legs and a sweep of strawberry blonde hair, blue eyes, a strong chin, and a faint smattering of freckles across her nose. In theory, Jamie should have been attracted to her, but he struggled to muster up more than a flicker of interest in her leggy beauty when Taylor was standing there with his slender body and sharp jawbone.

Damn it, this was going to be a problem.

Jack Malone—one of their D-men—had grumbled about them being the queerest team in the league, and well, he wasn't *wrong*.

He was also the one guy on the team who set Jamie's teeth on edge but that was beside the point. The Evanston Otters now had three openly LGBTQ+ men on the roster.

And Jamie had to be sure he kept his interactions with Taylor brief or he was going to prove Malone right by making it four.

Samantha smiled at Taylor, returning his greeting and compliment. "You look gorgeous too."

Taylor scoffed, gesturing toward his outfit. "I feel so plain. Not a sparkle in sight."

For a figure skater, he was dressed rather conservatively in all-black leggings, an oversized sweater, and gloves. The color made his pale skin glow though and Jamie tried not to let his gaze linger on his very high and firm ass.

Fuck.

"You could never be plain," Samantha said with a laugh, then tucked her arm into Taylor's. "C'mon, let's go get set up."

Jamie wasn't sure if he should follow or not but when Murphy fell into step behind Taylor and Samantha, he did too.

For the next twenty minutes, Jamie did whatever he could to help the social media crew and interns set up the small media interview room and the larger adjoining press room.

Players trickled in and the noise levels rose as they arranged the room to their liking.

A few of the single guys rushed in to help with setup too, presumably hoping to impress Samantha. There'd been plenty of talk in the locker room about how hot she was, but Murphy had quickly shut it down, reminding the guys to be respectful.

At precisely nine a.m. Samantha cleared her throat. Everyone obediently fell silent.

"Welcome. Thank you for volunteering to take part in this media campaign. We'll start by filming the introductions and short interviews. Please line up in the hallway and I'll call you in individually. After, we'll talk more about the plan for the day, go through your regular warmups, then dress for practice."

Her gaze swept across them as they nodded like bobbleheads.

"We'll start with our captain."

Murphy took a seat in the chair in front of the camera and lights, and Jamie escaped into the hall with the half of the team who'd volunteered to make fools of themselves. The rest of the guys on the team would still be doing footwork lessons. They just weren't going to be filmed doing it.

Their Swedish center, Anders Lindholm, wound up in front of Jamie in line.

"Looking forward to this?" he asked.

Jamie shrugged and gave him a tight little grin, leaning against the cinderblock wall in a show of feigned nonchalance. "That might be stretching it, but it should be entertaining at least."

They spoke about the team and the upcoming game while they waited for Murphy to finish. When Hartinger got called into the room, Jamie turned to look at their Canadian winger, Dean Tremblay, who was talking with Gabriel Theriault and Kelly O'Shea, their top defensive pair.

"Hey, Walsh," Tremblay said when he caught Jamie's gaze. "We're laying bets on who falls on their ass the most. You in?"

Jamie chuckled. "I'd probably put my money on *myself*, to be honest."

Tremblay laughed and they joked around for a while, but when his attention turned to the other guys, Jamie's thoughts returned to Taylor, his anxiety growing.

The door swung open to let one of the social media interns through and Jamie caught a glimpse of Taylor mid-stretch, his sweater lifting to show off his flat abs, toned thighs, and bubble butt, his mouth parted in a yawn as he reached for the sky.

Nope.

Forget anything Jamie had thought earlier, it was going to take a miracle for him to not embarrass himself by staring at Taylor's tight body and full lips.

In front of cameras, nonetheless.

"I'm so fucked," Jamie muttered under his breath.

CHAPTER THREE

"Hellllоооо, handsome," Taylor muttered under his breath to Samantha when Zane Murphy took a seat in the interview chair.

Okay, maybe Charlie had a point about the hunky hockey players.

Samantha snickered. "That one's taken."

"Bi though," Taylor countered with a smile. "That's something."

"Down, boy," Samantha said. "We don't need any more scandals."

He gave her a sympathetic look. Poor thing. She'd been yanked in to handle the mess left in the wake of the coach-player scandal and now she had to wrangle these guys into being on their best behavior. The last thing she needed was him causing problems.

"I'm just looking," he protested quietly. "I'm allowed to, right?"

"*Carefully*," she said.

"Aye, aye, Captain," he said more loudly, his sketchy salute earning him an eye roll from Sam and a perplexed look from the handsome hockey player nearby.

"Not you," Taylor called out to Zane. "Just teasing Sam."

Zane merely chuckled, then sat quietly while a stylist fussed with him for a few minutes, blotting any shininess on his skin, dusting him with powder, smoothing his beard, and tweaking his thick dark hair to lay right.

Damn it, he really *was* gorgeous.

"I'm still impressed with how quickly you pulled this whole thing together," Taylor said.

Samantha shrugged. "It's what I do. I'm excellent at my job and they needed the best."

"Hey, I'm glad it worked out," he said with a smile. "It'll be great for both of us."

Zane's intro and interview went quickly enough and a few minutes later, his boyfriend Ryan was ushered in.

Shit, he was nothing to sneer at either.

Ryan plopped onto the chair, his big body sprawling comfortably. "Okay. Make me pretty," he said to Jenny, the stylist.

She chuckled and brushed a bit of powder across his face. A little product in his hair to tame some of the frizz in his blond curls and then he was done. "There. All set."

"Oh damn. That was easy." He grinned, his blue eyes sparkling. "Guess it helps when you're already so good-looking, huh?"

He threw a wink in Taylor and Samantha's direction, and Taylor laughed aloud at the brazen confidence. Ryan was going to be *fun* on camera.

They made it through his interview with no problem and Samantha called out the next name from the list on her tablet.

"Jamie Walsh."

Taylor tensed when Jamie re-entered the room. *Damn.* Talk about good looking.

Taylor had seen Jamie watching him earlier, but he'd tried to ignore it, funneling his attention into his skating.

But now, Taylor had a good excuse to look his fill.

Jamie was quite a bit older than Taylor. Thirty-four, if Taylor remembered right, and blessed with thick, wavy hair in a sun-kissed golden-brown hue that perfectly complimented his warm skin tone, dazzling blue eyes, and bright smile.

Not that Taylor had spent any time leading up to this media event watching footage of Jamie and feeling guilty about it or anything.

After Jamie was fully prepped for the interview, Samantha asked the first question.

Jamie's voice was clear and strong. "My name is Jamie Walsh. I'm a forward with the Evanston River Otters. I'm a single dad and my daughter Ava is the center of my world. In my spare time, I love to play video games and hike."

"How do you feel about learning to figure skate?"

"A little nervous." Jamie gave a lopsided grin, his body language easy and relaxed. He must not be *too* nervous. "I'm pretty sure I'm going to make a fool of myself but it's all in good fun."

"Tell us a little bit more about your history as a player, Jamie."

"Well, after college, I played in Sweden for two seasons with Karlstad, then signed with the Chicago Windstorm. I played with them for eight years, and this is my first season with the Evanston River Otters."

Taylor chewed his lip while he listened to Samantha lob a few more questions at Jamie.

Since the Olympics, he'd kept half an eye on Jamie Walsh's career. Other than the minor injury the Czechian skater had suffered, Jamie had been a model player.

Ugh. Why had Taylor let him get under his skin?

It had been stupid.

Yeah, the shit between their fathers was ugly. There was no denying that.

Hearing Jamie talk about it had made his blood run hot. Assaulted by memories of his father lying in the hospital bed, clutching Taylor's mom's hand, while they listened to the doctor say the imaging was inconclusive. Only time would tell if it was damage to his spinal column or swelling compressing his spine.

It might take days or weeks to learn if he'd ever walk again.

Taylor had only been seven at the time but he remembered how fiercely he'd hated Adam Walsh.

And watching Adam's interviews as an adult, listening to him say he was relieved by the news Rick Hollis could walk again and that the incident had been 'an unfortunate accident,' had made him see red.

But how much of the anger was really his own?

Now that he and Jamie were working together, Taylor had no idea how to apologize. Or if he even should.

What if he made it *worse*?

What if he messed up his chance to pay off some of the bills hanging over his head? If Taylor didn't play nice with Jamie Walsh, he could lose this job and he couldn't afford to.

The interest on the loans he'd taken out was adding up fast and Taylor had barely made a dent in them.

So all Taylor could do was pretend like everything was hunky-dory with Jamie Walsh.

And ignore the number of times in the past four years he'd fantasized about rubbing his dick against Jamie's incredible thighs.

"Okay, gentlemen." Samantha bustled into the gym as they finished their exercising. "I hope you are sufficiently warmed up."

"Damn, I'd like to warm her up," Benny Dixon, their backup goaltender, muttered under his breath.

"Dude—" Jamie began but Murphy beat him to it.

"Cut it out." He leveled the rookie with a look. "Give her some respect."

Samantha's gaze didn't even flick in their direction, so she was either choosing to ignore Benny's comment or hadn't heard it. The cameraman who had been filming their warmup was on the other side of the room so hopefully he hadn't picked it up either.

"Sorry," Benny muttered.

He was generally a good kid but *damn* he seemed young. Maybe because the Otters' team was a bit older than Jamie's previous one. The Otters' roster was filled with veteran guys so the ones fresh out of juniors or NCAA hockey seemed painfully immature.

Or maybe it was because this past year had made Jamie grow up in a way he never could have anticipated.

Murphy finished his stretch and glanced around the room. "Everyone ready?"

The guys nodded or called out a 'yes' and rose to their feet.

Samantha cleared her throat. "Next, you'll put on the gear laid out for you. After, we'll hit the ice."

A cheer went up and Jamie smiled, giving his shoulder one final gentle stretch. He didn't want a repeat of the strain he'd had the other night.

"Okay, let's get started, boys." Taylor sashayed into the gym with a big smile on his face. "Follow me to the dressing room, please."

The guys trooped after him and Jamie smiled at the sight of the group of big sweaty hockey players following the petite ice skater. He was pretty sure Taylor could hold his own at any size though. He certainly hadn't hesitated to rip Jamie a new one.

Taylor stepped into the dressing room and turned to face the team, throwing his arm to the side with a flourish. "Voilà!"

Collective groans went up from the team at the sight in front of them.

Jamie's jaw dropped. "*Shit.*"

Hartinger groaned. "You're telling me. Figure skates, man? I am going to fall on my face."

Murphy shook his head fondly. "First challenge and you're all already whining. Not a good look, boys."

Hartinger grumbled and bumped shoulders with his boyfriend as they walked toward their stalls. "You can't tell me you're happy about this."

"No, but I'm not a big baby who complains about everything."

"Hey!" Ryan protested but he was laughing. "Love you too."

Taylor chuckled, surveying the room of grumpy hockey players with a delighted smile on his face. Jamie *wanted* to be mad but even he could agree this was pretty funny. He should have seen it coming.

Samantha motioned to the guys with cameras, and they stopped filming.

"Good news, gentlemen," Taylor said, raising his voice. "We're not *complete* sadists. We will be heat molding the boots for you. It turns out your feet are important for the game or something and the head office didn't want to risk damaging their very expensive investments."

He brushed a lock of black hair off his forehead, his grin wide and genuine. "So, sit tight. The skates at your stall are props and the equipment guys will be bringing out warm boots to fit on you. It'll be the same as fitting new hockey skates."

"Oh, thank God," Cooper muttered.

While Jamie waited for his boots, he strapped on the pads they'd given them. Just light protection for their knees and elbows, and when the equipment guy came around with skates for him, he slipped his feet into the warm boots, wiggling until he was sure they were properly seated.

"Careful with your lacing," Taylor called out. "Pull outward, not up, so you don't end up with popped rivets."

After their skates were laced, Jamie walked around the dressing room, allowing the boots to cool and mold to his feet.

They felt … strange, there was no denying that. But they were better than Jamie had expected. And though it was a tedious process to let the boots cool, unlace them, hand them over to the equipment manager to have the blades attached, and re-lace them, they had a pretty good system going.

Still, it was a relief when they finally took to the ice.

Until his feet actually hit that ice.

"Whoa," Jamie said, wobbling a little. "This feels weird."

"The fuck?" Hartinger muttered, gliding out behind Jamie. He glanced over at Samantha. "Shit. Can I swear on camera?"

Samantha laughed, one of those full belly laughs that made Jamie smile because it sounded so genuine. "Yeah, you can swear. We'll bleep it out if need be."

"All right, boys," Taylor said, clapping his hands to get their attention.

Jamie wondered if he did that in the kids' classes too and his smile widened. Ava was going to *love* watching these videos of him making a fool of himself while Taylor ordered him around.

"We'll start with a few laps to get the blood flowing and get you used to figure skates," Taylor continued. "C'mon. Move it, boys."

Jamie wasn't sure if he'd *ever* get used to them. "These feel fucking weird," he muttered.

"They really do," Dean Tremblay said with a frown as he skated next to Jamie. "Not a fan."

But it did get a little easier after a couple of laps and it was funny to watch the guys who struggled. Behind him, Theriault cursed up a blue streak in French and ahead of him, Cooper belly-flopped onto the ice when he caught his toe pick.

Laughing, Jamie had to skate around him to keep from running him over.

After they were done with laps, Taylor instructed them to form a kneeling semi-circle around him. "We'll begin with arabesques. I know you have speed, strength, and agility, but you need to learn grace as well."

Arabesques sounded fancy but when Jamie watched Taylor demonstrate, they seemed pretty simple. Taylor pushed off, moving backward, lifting his arms like a bird flying as his left leg moved out and behind him.

"Now, you try," Taylor instructed. "We'll go one at a time. Make sure you engage your core and lift from there."

Hartinger and Murphy both did okay on their first time, but Taylor called out a few instructions to them anyway, refining their technique.

"Holy crap, this is harder than it looks," Hartinger said, wobbling a little when he tried to lift his back leg higher.

Taylor gave him a pleased little smile.

When it was Cooper's turn, he promptly fell flat on his face and had to try a few times before he got the hang of it, grumbling the whole time.

Jamie made an attempt, but he wobbled, surprised to realize how difficult it really was. "Damn," he muttered under his breath.

"Lift your arms and your chest," Taylor called out. "Strong abs so you're not leaning too far forward. Your back leg extends behind you."

When Jamie tried it, it helped with his balance, and he was able to glide for a short distance.

"Nice!" Taylor called. "Now, point your toes."

That of course totally unbalanced Jamie and he landed with a whomp on the ice on his chest, the air knocked out of him for a second. A little winded, he laughed and got to his feet with a rueful grin.

"Nice one, grace!" O'Shea yelled.

Jamie suppressed the urge to flip him off. At Taylor's prompting, Jamie tried the move again and even managed to point his toe this time.

Tremblay went next, then O'Shea, and they went down the line with varying degrees of success.

"Nice extension, Hajek!" Taylor called out.

Fucking goalies.

They practiced a few more times as a group and Jamie was almost sorry when they moved on to the next thing.

"Next up, we have a spin," Taylor explained, walking them through the steps verbally.

He waited until the groaning died down. "Let me demonstrate first."

The demonstration was definitely worse.

O'Shea muttered, "Oh hell, I'm gonna puke trying that," as Taylor twirled in circles, finishing with a flourish of his arms.

The groans deepened when Taylor talked them through each step. "Left hand straight out in front of your face, right arm extended to the right. Bend both knees, turn to your left and send your right toe out."

The guys tried it as a group and once again, Cooper promptly fell on his face.

Whistles, clapping, and plenty of chirps followed.

"I hate you all," he muttered, getting to his feet again. "At this rate, I am going to be more bruised than after a fucking game."

"Maybe because you're not working hard enough during the games," Tremblay teased.

Cooper's look was withering.

They went through the line again, each of them trying the rotation, most of them struggling. Jamie did okay,lead not great, but his ego could take it.

It was hilarious to watch and despite the bitching and moaning from the team, everyone seemed to be having fun.

Taylor continued. "Next, we'll make one more rotation, bringing our arms in against our chests, both feet together."

Jamie nearly bit it again when he tried, but he managed to stay upright at least.

The next step was to lift one foot while they spun.

That, of course, went over like a lead balloon and once again, Cooper and Hartinger wound up on the ice, this time on their asses.

"My butt is going to be so bruised," Hartinger grumbled. "Fuck my elbows and knees, my ass needs more padding."

Murphy said something too low for Jamie to hear but it made Hartinger laugh. Probably some joke about kissing it better when they got home or something.

Jamie focused back on the lesson and listened intently while Taylor described how to put all the moves together and end with a final flourish of their arms.

Jamie gave it a try and was vaguely queasy after a few spins but he got the hang of it okay.

"Nice job, Walsh," Taylor said, skating closer, his gaze warm. "You're doing very well."

Taylor's praise made heat fill Jamie's body as their gazes locked. Oh hell. He was in trouble, wasn't he?

But the spell was broken when Taylor turned away.

Jamie ruthlessly put all thought of Taylor from his mind and focused on his skating.

By the time they were done, and their post-skate wrap-ups were filmed, Jamie was exhausted.

"How the fuck do Hajs and Lindy look so damn good?" Hartinger muttered as they left the ice.

"Well, I learned in Sweden when I was small," Lindholm said with a tiny smile.

"Am goalie," Hajek said with a shrug. "Good at everything."

Jamie let out a little snort and made his way to the dressing room to get the damn figure skates off and get his cooldown workout in before he showered.

To his surprise, there were two familiar faces waiting for him when he stepped out of the dressing room an hour later.

"Daddy!" Ava squealed and launched herself at him.

He caught her, wincing at the pull in his shoulder but too busy smothering her face in kisses to care. "Hi, Ava-Bear. What a nice surprise."

He smiled at his mom and leaned in to kiss her cheek a little more sedately. "Thanks."

"How was practice?" Jodi Walsh laid a peck on him too.

"Okay. We've started working with Taylor Hollis on our footwork." He shifted Ava to his other hip to take the strain off his joint.

"Yes, I know," she said drily. "I heard all about it from Ava."

Jamie chuckled and stroked Ava's hair. She had her head buried in his neck, surprisingly quiet. Probably still a little sleepy from the drive over. "I'm sure you did."

"So, how was it?" His mom stared expectantly at him.

"Oh, fine." He shrugged. "Nothing I can't handle."

"Did they bring up the incident?" she asked quietly.

"The incident" was how his family had always referred to the game where Rick Hollis was injured.

"No. The plan is to ignore it like it never happened."

"Your father still feels so guilty."

"He needs to let it go," Jamie said with a tired sigh. "I know he feels guilty, but it wasn't like he did it on purpose. Accidents happen in hockey."

"Well, yes, which is why we both tried to talk you into baseball."

Jamie shrugged. He'd played both well but he'd loved hockey more. "Nothing is foolproof," he pointed out. "I could be an *accountant* and get hit by a bus on the way to work."

She gave him a mildly exasperated look. "Yes, you could. But that isn't my point."

"I know." Jamie yawned, leaning back against the wall.

"Aww." She laughed. "Did that little skater wear you out today?"

Jamie ruthlessly stomped down the mental images that conjured up. "No, but Ava did wake me up early." He ruffled her hair and she let out a giggle against his shoulder.

"She's good at that." His mom smiled at them both. "Now. What do you say to lunch?"

"Yes, please." He pushed himself upright. "I'm starving."

"So, nothing has changed since you were seven?" she asked with a laugh.

"*Exactly*." He looked at Ava while they walked toward the exit. "What are you in the mood for, squirt?"

She sat up and chewed her lip thoughtfully. "Pizza."

Jamie smothered a snort in her hair. *Shocker*. Just like the last 437 times he'd asked her.

"Pizza it is." He exchanged an amused smile with his mom who rolled her eyes, then flipped Ava's hood up to cover her hair. She was already bundled up in a puffy winter coat and it had been snowing this morning when he drove to the rink.

Thankfully, there was a great little place nearby that made individual pies. There were only so many times he could eat the pepperoni, olive, and pineapple combo Ava begged for every time. What five-year-old liked olives? *His* kid, apparently.

"Wait!" Ava called and Jamie rocked to a stop. "I wanted to say hi to Taylor." Her lower lip quivered a little.

"I don't know if he's still here, Bear," he said gently. "Besides, you have practice this afternoon. You'll see him then."

"Oh." She let out a disappointed sigh, her lip pushed out a little and her eyes very big. "Guess that's okay."

"Good. Because I am *starvinggggg*," he said dramatically. "If I don't get fed soon, I'm going to eat you!"

He playfully pretended to chomp at her hair, and she giggled the whole way out of the building.

CHAPTER FOUR

"Oof," Taylor muttered under his breath as he watched Jamie Walsh carry his daughter through the door.

Taylor hated that guy, right?

He thought he did, anyway. He had a vague recollection of that.

But it was incredibly difficult to remember when his head was filled with images of a sexy hockey player being cute as hell with his kid.

The kid Taylor adored.

Ava was his absolute favorite student in his class. And now Taylor knew who her father was.

Shit.

Taylor felt a little stupid for not figuring out that Ava Walsh was the daughter of Jamie Walsh, but there were probably hundreds, if not thousands, of people in the Chicago area with that last name. And she'd always been dropped off by her mom, Kara, or her grandmother, Jodi, who had been nothing but lovely to Taylor.

So Taylor was pretty much gobsmacked right now.

And maybe drooling a little. Because the one thing that always made him turn to mush was seeing hot guys being cute with kids.

Jamie and Ava Walsh were top-notch adorable together.

Thinking about Jamie effortlessly lifting Ava into his arms made Taylor feel a little dreamy. Her squeals of laughter when he playfully kissed her were so *cute*.

Jamie's tight ass under a pair of team sweats hadn't hurt either.

Taylor hadn't meant to stare like a weirdo, but he'd been in Samantha's office waiting for her to return and had the perfect view. How could he not?

"You might want to wipe up that drool," Samantha said drily. She pulled the door tightly shut behind her.

Taylor flushed and immediately pressed his hands to his cheeks to hide the color there.

"I thought I was going to have to worry about you two being at each other's throats." She shot him an amused glance as she took a seat behind her desk. "Guess not, huh?"

"He's … attractive," Taylor said primly.

"If that's your type."

"He's not yours?"

"No, I go for nerdy guys. Went on a date with a physics professor from U of C last night and let me tell you, he was hot talking about particle research." She fanned herself. "Jamie Walsh is objectively very attractive but none of the guys here do it for me. Thank God. We don't need any more complications."

"I feel like today went well though," Taylor offered.

"It did," Samantha said with a little smile. "We're off to a good start. Thanks for agreeing to do this. I know you had your reservations."

He shrugged. "I did, but it seems like Walsh and I will be able to work together, which was the big concern."

"Plus, you find him hot."

Taylor gave her a sheepish glance and held his fingers close together. "Just a little bit."

But hot or not, Taylor and Jamie had way too much family baggage to ever consider being more than cordial.

Even if Jamie had been sexy as fuck when his brow furrowed and he sank his teeth into his lip while he attempted to learn the figure skating moves. He'd been pretty good actually. Very focused. Very willing to try.

Which also turned Taylor's crank in a way he hadn't expected.

Samantha cleared her throat. "I'm glad you're getting along well because I want to run an idea by you."

Taylor groaned. "Why do I feel like I am going to hate this?"

"Because you're a horrible cynic?"

"Am not!" he protested with a laugh. "Just a realist. Anyway, what is this idea?"

"Individual lessons. One-on-ones with the team members."

Taylor raised an eyebrow. "With the *entire* team? That sounds like a huge time investment."

"We'd up your pay."

"The franchise signed off on that?"

"Taylor, have you noticed what they're paying these guys to play hockey? Their concern is getting fans in the seats to watch games. The quick teasers we posted for this are already blowing up. The head office gave me a generous budget for this media campaign and how it's used is at my discretion. I think one-on-ones will go over incredibly well with the fans and it's good for the team's skill development."

Taylor's stomach knotted at the thought of being alone with Jamie Walsh. Well, not alone. There would be a camera crew around and Samantha maybe, and all sorts of other people.

But still. He didn't like the way his old hang-ups about Jamie Walsh mingled with the flare of attraction he'd felt earlier. And the thought of that playing out on camera …

"Can I think about it?" He looked up at Samantha. "I want to do what I can for the team but honestly, given the history, I'm a little wary."

Samantha's gaze softened. "Of course. Take a few days. The guys are going on the road tomorrow anyway so you won't have another lesson with them until later this week. Let me know when you make a decision. And if the answer is no, I'll understand."

"Thank you. That sounds fair," Taylor said with a smile, grateful for his friend's understanding. "Okay, I'm going to go run some errands before I have to be back here to teach this afternoon."

Samantha smiled brightly at him. "Sounds good."

Taylor said goodbye to Samantha. Outside, Taylor took a deep lungful of wintry air, surprised by how sunny it was, the light glinting off the fresh snow.

This morning had gone far better than he'd expected. He and Jamie had gotten along well enough. He was pleased they'd both acted like professionals.

The thought of working one-on-one with him still made Taylor nervous though. Maybe he should talk to Jamie about it directly. Maybe it would be better if they cleared the air. It still didn't feel right that he hadn't apologized for the way he'd acted at the Olympics four years ago and the comment in the press.

Or maybe Taylor should run all of this by Charlie and see what he thought.

Of course, Charlie would probably suggest Taylor fuck him.

Taylor let out a little snort, then shook his head as he walked to his car.

Yeah, no.

Hot or not, Taylor was definitely not going to fuck Jamie Walsh.

Jamie spent the next two days on the road. They lost to Columbus and St. Louis. Not surprising, because they'd been struggling since New Years but it left them all a little moody and of course he missed Ava like crazy, even though they FaceTimed regularly.

By the time the plane landed in the wee hours of the morning, he was exhausted, and he drove on autopilot to his parents' house in Winnetka, a nice suburb not too far from Evanston.

Ava had spent last night with Kara, but Jamie's mom had picked her up this morning and she was spending tonight with her grandparents.

Although Jamie's mom had always insisted Jamie was welcome to go straight home from the airport after a road trip, he hated the thought of being away from Ava any longer than he had to. He always crashed out in his parents' guest bedroom so he could see her first thing in the morning.

The house was dark and quiet when he pulled into the three-car garage and he let himself inside, creeping through so as not to disturb his parents.

As always, his throat felt a little tight when he thought about everything they'd done to help him and Ava. The only reason the judge had been so willing to give him shared custody with his erratic schedule was because he'd been able to prove his parents would be available to watch Ava any time he needed them.

The thought of not seeing his little girl killed him. Shared custody and the travel was difficult enough.

Jamie had thought about retiring. He wasn't getting any younger and missing out on time with Ava didn't sit well with him, but if he only had a few years left to play, he wanted to stick it out. After the messy way he'd left his previous team and his poor performance toward the end, he wanted his career to wrap up on a high note. He wanted a legacy Ava would be proud of when she was grown.

He felt a weird ache as he trudged down the hallway and slipped into his parents' guest room. He glanced at the wide empty bed and his heart sank.

Sometimes on nights like this, he really missed having someone to come home to.

Jamie tossed the bag on the bench at the end of the bed and rummaged through it for his glasses. He went into the en suite and flipped on the shower, stripping mechanically while the water heated for a moment.

It had been difficult when he and Kara were on the outs.

When he'd dreaded the thought of coming home to a cold shoulder and an even colder bed.

He'd tried. God, he'd tried so fucking hard to hold his marriage together. He'd have been willing to do nearly anything to make it work.

It bothered him he still didn't know why. Why she'd fucked his best friend. Why she'd abandoned their marriage. Why everything he gave her wasn't enough. They'd been young but not that young. They should have been able to make it work.

And yeah, Jamie knew the statistics, knew how many pro players' marriages fell apart. But he'd always chalked a lot of that up to guys being unfaithful.

He'd asked her once if she thought he'd ever cheated on her when he was on the road. She'd scoffed and told him he didn't have the balls.

Now, it was easy to look back and wonder why he'd ever married Kara. It was easy to wonder if he should have made different choices.

But if he had, he wouldn't have Ava now and she was the most important thing in the world to him.

With a sigh, Jamie turned off the water and toweled dry, then brushed his teeth and removed his contacts on autopilot. When he was done, he clicked out the light in the bathroom. The bedroom was dim and quiet as he tiredly dragged on sleep pants and a clean T-shirt, his heart aching at the thought of going to bed alone.

Jamie turned to the door, hesitating a moment before he slipped out and crept down the hall to Ava's room. His mom had decorated it nicely for her and she stayed here several nights a week during the season.

The door was cracked open a sliver and he peered in. Through the dim glow of the nightlight, he could see Ava was deep asleep, sprawled on her stomach like a starfish, tangled curls nearly obscuring her face.

She played hard and she slept hard. Just like him.

Jamie felt so much love for her his chest hurt. He stepped forward to brush those curls off her face, staring at her pink cheeks and turned-up little nose.

Jamie didn't want to wake her though, so he carefully crawled into the little bed beside her and closed his eyes, intending to rest for a few minutes.

He was out the second his eyes blinked closed, glasses askew where they pressed against the rainbow polka-dot pillow.

CHAPTER FIVE

The morning after the guys returned from their road trip, Taylor walked into the rink, surprised to see Jamie Walsh already there, lurking in the hallway like he'd been waiting for him.

"Uh, hey, Taylor." Jamie shifted his weight back on his heels, arms crossed, looking incredibly uncomfortable. Stupid hot in his Otters sweats but definitely uncomfortable. "Just the man I was looking for."

"Hey," Taylor managed, trying not to let his gaze drop below the waist. He had such a thing for dudes in gray sweatpants and Jamie was absolutely *deadly*. "What's up?"

"Do you have a minute?"

Unsure of where this was going, Taylor put on his media face. "Sure."

Jamie glanced around as if checking that they were alone. "I just wanted to make sure you were okay with, uh, the stuff between us. The family stuff, I mean. I know there's some bad blood there and—"

Taylor suppressed a grimace. "Well, yes, that's one way to put it," he said blandly.

Jamie winced. "Yeah. I uh, could have worded that better." Jamie reached out, his hand warm on Taylor's forearm. "I don't see any point in us continuing something that should have been dead and buried years ago."

"Easy for you to say."

"Fair enough." Jamie sighed, dropping his hand.

The miserable expression on Jamie's face made guilt rise and it hit Taylor how harsh he'd been. *Again.* God damn it. He needed to stop letting Jamie rile him up.

Carrying around this vendetta against Adam Walsh certainly hadn't made Taylor's father's life any better or happier and it wasn't doing anything positive for Taylor either. Jamie really did seem like a decent guy. His teammates had nothing but nice things to say about him, and he was an absolute sweetheart to his daughter and mom.

Sure, nice people could do shitty things, but it wasn't even Jamie Taylor was angry at. He didn't deserve to be punished for something he hadn't done.

Taylor took a deep breath and softened his tone a little. "Look, you're right. We're working together. We *should* focus on this media thing and leave the past where it belongs."

A smile lit up Jamie's face. "That would be great. I really hate the idea of this hanging over us, you know?"

"Yeah." Taylor softened a little further at the earnest look in Jamie's eyes. "I should probably apologize for the stuff I said at the Olympics too, huh? I was definitely an asshole to you."

Jamie's brow furrowed. "Why did you say it? Did you mean it?"

"At the time, yeah, I meant it," Taylor admitted. "Obviously, I'm pretty touchy about player safety."

"Sure, I get that." Jamie's expression grew troubled. "But I've always tried to be safe. I can't control everything on the ice. What happened with the Czech player was a fluke. It wasn't me being a dirty player."

Guilt rose at Jamie's earnest tone.

"No, I know," he admitted. "I mean, I know *now*. That night we met I had some other stuff going on in my personal life so when I realized who you were I, uh, overreacted."

Taylor was tempted to explain it all to Jamie but it was definitely oversharing to tell him about the struggles Charlie'd had for years with his eating disorder and Brayden, the skier Taylor'd had his heart broken by. It was, frankly, a miracle Taylor had even medaled that year, much less won multiple golds.

Taylor had been feeling pissed off and touchy when he'd realized who Jamie's dad was. His temper had flared and well, no one had ever accused Taylor of being the most chill guy out there.

"Anyway," he continued lamely. "This is my attempt to apologize. I shouldn't have taken my shitty mood out on you. When I saw what happened in that game against the Czech Republic, I overreacted and assumed the worst of you. When the media asked me about it, I told them what I was thinking but it was a mistake. I regret that I said otherwise."

Jamie's face relaxed and he leaned in a little. "Well, apology accepted. And yeah, if we can put everything behind us that would be great."

"It would," Taylor said, surprised to realize he felt lighter with everything out in the open. "Actually, that brings me to the other thing I want to talk to you about."

Jamie raised an eyebrow. "Sure. What's up?"

"How would you feel about one-on-one lessons?"

"Ouch." Jamie pressed a hand to his chest, chuckling a little. "Was I really that bad the other day?"

A surprised laugh burst out of Taylor before he could stop it, the tension from earlier fading. "No, not at all. It was just this idea Samantha had."

"Just you and me or …?"

"No, the whole team."

Jamie frowned. "Wow, that's a lot of work for you. I mean, you're already doing the lessons with the team, plus teaching the kids' classes. And the shows you're in … damn, do you ever sleep?"

Taylor chuckled, surprised Jamie even knew about his performances. "It *is* a lot but I don't have any shows right now. We wrapped up *The Nutcracker* and I could have been in *Swan Lake* but I took a break from it to do this stuff."

"Ava and I watched you in *The Nutcracker* before Christmas actually," Jamie said, rubbing the back of his neck. "You *do* know my daughter's in your class, right?"

"Yeah, I put the pieces together the other day," Taylor said vaguely. He wasn't about to admit to Jamie he'd witnessed their father-daughter bonding time. Or that he'd drooled shamelessly over it.

"Good. I was a little afraid you might not want to work with her anymore if you knew she was my kid."

"Oh no!" Taylor protested. "She loves skating. I'll admit I can be a vindictive little bitch at times but I would never take my feelings about a parent out on one of my students. I would never take skating away from someone who loved it."

Jamie smiled. "Well, I appreciate that, she really does love it."

"She's wonderful, by the way," Taylor said with a smile. Ava was a bundle of energy. Terrible skater, but the cutest thing he'd ever seen.

Jamie raised an eyebrow in disbelief. "Skills-wise? 'Cause I've seen the little videos my mom sends and … I mean, I love her to death but …"

"Uhh." Taylor grimaced. "I mean, Ava's making *progress*. It started out a little rocky but she'll get better with time and practice."

Jamie smiled, just a little twitch of his lips. "You're so tactful."

Taylor laughed. "Well, I'm not going to insult your *kid*. She's not someone who immediately took to the ice despite her enthusiasm for it." He shrugged. It happened. Some children weren't as naturally coordinated but they could always improve.

"Guess it wasn't any help having a dad who's a hockey player." Jamie gave him a rueful smile, the corner of his eyes crinkling warmly.

"Guess not." Taylor shrugged. "What about her mom?"

Jamie grimaced. "No. Kara was never a skater. And we're, uh, divorced now if you didn't know already."

His mouth flattened into a hard little line and Taylor saw the throb of his pulse along the side of his neck.

"Ahh." Well, Taylor could see that was a sore subject. He wasn't going to ask for details. "I know you mentioned it in your interview they recorded the other day."

"Surprised you didn't hear in the press."

Taylor raised an eyebrow at him and shrugged. "I don't follow hockey gossip closely."

"It was pretty much everywhere." Jamie's grimace deepened.

Taylor shrugged. "I missed it somehow. When was this?"

"Last season."

"Ahh, I was dealing with some … personal stuff then. I was lucky it didn't make the news."

"Relationship stuff?"

"No." He cleared his throat. "Someone I care about going through some health issues. I was wrapped up in getting him well."

"Boyfriend?" Jamie's cheeks went a little pink. "Never mind, I shouldn't have asked. It's none of my business."

"It's fine." He waved it off, amused Jamie appeared to be fishing for information about Taylor's personal life. "He's my best friend. Not a boyfriend. I'm single."

"Same." Jamie shoved his hands into his hoodie pockets. "Anyway, uh … I think we were talking about something but I forgot what it was."

Taylor mentally replayed the conversation. "We were talking about doing one-on-one lessons. And yes, my schedule is busy but it's flexible enough I could add those in."

And the pay was way, *way* too tempting to ignore. Samantha had sent him an email with a number that made his neatly plucked eyebrows climb to his hairline. He couldn't turn that down.

Taylor continued. "I mostly wanted to run it by you to make sure you were okay with the idea of working individually with me."

Jamie licked his lips. "Yeah, sure. That's no problem. I feel a lot better now that we cleared the air."

"Great. Me too." Taylor let out a relieved sigh. "I'll tell Samantha yes then."

"I look forward to it." Jamie backed up, smiling at him. "Should be fun having you telling me what to do."

With a little wink, he turned around and Taylor stared after him a moment, blinking stupidly, a perplexed smile on his face.

What the hell?

Was Jamie flirting with him now?

Taylor was starting to think maybe Charlie was on to something about Jamie being bi, or at the very least, bi-curious.

Jamie skated out onto the ice for warmups, grinning when he spotted his parents and Ava in the crowd. They hadn't been sure if they could make it to the game, but it was a matinee and Ava loved to watch him play whenever she could. He skated to the boards and waved at her through the glass. Her eyes lit up when Jamie's dad lifted her to stand on the edge of the boards.

"Hey, Ava-Bear!" he shouted, grinning at her.

She wore a small jersey with his number—thirty-four—on it and *Daddy* across the back. Plus giant earmuffs of course, because the games were much too loud for little ears like hers.

She waved wildly and pressed her hand against the glass, letting out a happy yell when he waved back. He gave the glass a tap with his glove and mouthed that he loved her. He smiled big at his parents too, thanking them for taking her to the game, then waved at some of the other team kids.

Tremblay's three children were there with his wife and so was Cooper's wife and baby. Hajek's wife was pregnant with their second kid and the families of a couple of the rookies and recent AHL call-ups were there as well.

The kids were all so cute Jamie could hardly stand it but eventually, he tore himself away to warm up, skating a few laps before he whacked some pucks into the net that Benny Dixon, their backup goalie, lazily blocked. He'd recently been given the nickname of Dicks, which he seemed unreasonably proud of.

Jamie laughed and joked with his team, and he was in a great mood by the time they skated off the ice. Having his family there always gave him an extra boost and by the time the puck dropped he was eager to play.

He watched intently from the bench as Lindholm deftly knocked the puck away from Nashville's center, passing it to Hartinger.

Jamie was raring to go by the time his first shift began, and he was over the boards, the ice smooth and perfect under his skates. His muscles were loose and ready, and his speed and control were dialed in.

It was one of those games where everything flowed. The team and the crowd's energy were high, and their lines and pairs worked seamlessly. Six minutes into the first period, Jamie got a goal with an assist from Cooper and Malone and at the end of the second period, Jamie got an assist on the third goal, putting them up for four goals to none.

"You are *killing* it, man," O'Shea shouted when Jamie slid onto the bench beside him at the beginning of the third period. He knocked shoulders with Jamie, who grinned. He was feeling pretty damn good.

Nashville tried to rally. They managed two goals in the third period but they were no match against Evanston. Jamie got another assist in the third period when he snuck a perfect pass to Theriault between the Nashville defenseman's skates and Theriault slammed the puck into the net to clinch the game at a blowout 7-2 win the team desperately needed.

As Murphy tore across the ice to celebrate, he lost his edge and landed on his stomach, sliding a few feet before he was up again, laughing.

Hartinger cackled as he slammed into his boyfriend. "Nice moves there, grace. I think you need more of those lessons with Taylor."

Jamie smiled at their interactions. He didn't miss the warm look between Theriault and Coach Tate when they met in the dressing room either. All Tate did was squeeze Gabriel's shoulder as he passed, but the connection was so intense it made Jamie's celebratory mood dim and his heart ache because damn, he missed it.

As Jamie stripped off his jersey and removed some of the padding, he admitted how lonely he was. His marriage had been shit but he ached to have someone to celebrate his accomplishments with.

Those thoughts were quickly swept away by the reminder from Samantha that he had media duties tonight.

"They're really pushing me to be allowed to ask some questions about you and Taylor," she said quietly. "Is that okay?"

Jamie thought of the conversation they'd had the other day and Taylor's apology. He'd felt a connection then, something beyond attraction to Taylor's body and his skill on the ice. He'd felt a magnetic little spark that widened his smile and made his heart beat a little faster.

"Yeah," Jamie said easily. "You know what? It's fine. I'll be happy to answer a few questions about the current media campaign. Anything about our families or the past is off-limits."

Samantha nodded. "Of course. I think that's wise."

The press was allowed in a few minutes later and Jamie sat in his stall, answering their questions.

"To what do you attribute your recent successes?" one of the reporters asked.

"Well, I think it's a combination of things. Certainly, this team is a great fit for me. I owe a lot to my teammates. There's a great culture here of working together and bringing out the best in each other. It's such a deep team and we all work hard to be the best we can be."

"Do you think Taylor Hollis deserves any credit for it?"

"Certainly," Jamie said with an easy smile. "He's taught the whole team a lot and I know I've personally benefited from that already. I'm stronger on my edges and being pushed out of my comfort zone has allowed me to explore some things I never would have tried before."

They asked Jamie a few more questions but no one pressed him about their family's histories and Jamie let out a quiet sigh of relief when they went on to Theriault.

Jamie managed a few minutes to talk to his family. He hugged and kissed Ava before his parents took her to Kara's for the night, and then it was onto his post-game recovery and showering.

As he dressed after, the mood in the locker room was still loose and celebratory.

"What do you think, boys?" Hartinger called out. "After a win like that, should we celebrate?"

The room filled with hooting and hollering, and Jamie grinned at the enthusiasm.

Evanston was a slightly older team than Chicago had been. More focused. More serious. There were the guys who partied hard—like Malone and O'Shea—but the team's core of Murphy, Hartinger, Lindholm, Tremblay—and now Theriault—were a little older. More dialed into their training regimes and their single-minded goal of winning the Cup.

They often went to team dinners on the road but rarely went out to the bar. They certainly weren't the ones to suggest a night of drinking. Jamie always turned down invitations when they were home and he had Ava, but when they were on the road or Ava was with his ex, he liked hanging out with the boys.

It took the edge off the lonely feeling that dogged him when he was moping in his big empty house in the North Shore.

"You coming out tonight, Theriault?" Jamie asked a few minutes later as he shrugged on his wool coat and buttoned it.

"*Non*. Lance and I will stay in."

"He could come too," Jamie offered.

Theriault gave him a little shrug, smoothing product through his shoulder-length dark hair. "It's always a little weird. The guys feel strange having their coach socializing with them, I think."

Jamie nodded. It didn't bother him but he rarely got drunk. He was there for the camaraderie more than anything but he could see why the rookies probably felt weird about it. "Fair enough."

Theriault grinned at him. "Besides, we've been so busy lately with media stuff we haven't had much alone time."

Jamie grinned and held out a fist to bump. Was it a little weird thinking about his teammate and their assistant coach screwing? Sure. But they were clearly happy which was all that mattered. "Enjoy your evening then, man."

With a small smile, Gabriel wished him the same, and Jamie wound a scarf around his neck as he went in search of the guys who were going out.

Jamie left his Range Rover at the arena and approached one of the two SUVs someone had hired for the evening. It turned out to be Murphy, and Jamie wasn't surprised. Their captain was always looking out for their safety. Especially the young guys.

Malone slid into the third row. "It's like you don't trust the kids to take care of themselves or something, Murph."

Murphy rolled his eyes as he settled in beside him, Hartinger following, three big bodies in too small of a space. "We've had enough press this season. I don't want to hear about one of our rookies booked on a drunk driving charge."

"Shit, we can't afford to have anyone out this time of year either," Hartinger said, swinging an arm over Murphy's shoulder. "I'm not willing to risk anything right now."

Lindholm nodded his agreement, then gestured for O'Shea to precede him so he could sit in the center seat. Jamie followed and Tremblay took the front passenger seat.

"Where to?" the driver asked when they were all situated.

Murphy rattled off the name of an upscale club nearby and the SUV pulled into traffic.

"What made you decide to do this?" Jamie asked curiously, turning to face Murphy and Hartinger.

Murphy shrugged. "It's been a while since we've gone out and it's a good time to do it. We're far enough from the end of the regular season and we've got two days off from games. I figure it's the perfect time for the guys to unwind. I'm trying to set a good example that it's possible to still have fun but be at least moderately responsible."

Jamie laughed when O'Shea slunk lower in his seat, and he remembered how cripplingly drunk Kelly had gotten last fall on their trip to Pittsburgh.

Lindy patted O'Shea, his arm stretched around his shoulders. "It's okay, Kelly, you learned your lesson. You'll do better tonight, yeah?"

Malone snorted. "Hey, no poaching my drinking buddies, Lindy. I already lost Coop when he knocked his wife up."

Lindholm made a scoffing noise, but he didn't reply and Jamie quickly changed the subject because there was nothing more annoying than when Malone got riled up about the team not being exciting enough for him.

"Hey, Shaysey, you want to play video games sometime soon?" Jamie asked. "It's been a while."

"Sure." O'Shea shot him a relieved glance. "That would be fun."

"Cool. We'll figure out a time soon."

O'Shea twisted in his seat. "Hey, did you hear Underhill will be back soon?"

"Yeah." Hartinger brightened. "He texted Murph about it the other day."

Kelly O'Shea and Trevor Underhill roomed together in a place in Evanston and Jamie had met Underhill numerous times throughout the season, but they'd never played together because he'd been out with a tricky ankle injury.

"It's great. He said he's going to start visiting the locker room, working out on site, and doing some practices with Horton and working on his conditioning," O'Shea added happily.

"Thank fuck," Malone said. "Feels like he's been out forever."

Underhill had been injured last season during the playoffs. It was before Jamie joined the Otters but everyone had seen the clips of him skating off the ice with the help of his teammates, his face white with pain.

After that, the conversation devolved into general trash talking and chirping each other and they were all laughing by the time they exited the SUV in front of the club.

Malone whistled lowly behind Jamie as they stepped inside, Murphy making a beeline for the hostess. "Swanky. Murph really splashed out tonight."

Hartinger shrugged. "I know you have a beef with him about his vision for the team but all he wants to do is look out for his boys."

"Dude, I get that," Malone said, sounding irritated. "I don't get why we can't have fun along the way though."

"Gentlemen, let's not argue," Tremblay said, draping his arms over both their shoulders. "We killed it out there tonight and I don't know about you but I'm ready to celebrate."

"What are you doing out anyway?" Malone asked. "You usually run home to the wife and kids."

"Yes, well, she suggested I have a night out," Tremblay said with a smile.

Malone made a whip-cracking noise that made Jamie roll his eyes. What an asshole.

Murphy appeared at Jamie's elbow. "All right. You can check in your coats down here, but we're all set otherwise. We're in the VIP lounge."

After their coats were taken care of, they followed the hostess up the stairs. They were ushered into the lounge and directed to several plush, curved banquettes.

"You really did splash out, huh?" Jamie asked after a waitress took their drink orders.

Murphy shrugged at him. "I figured we could all use a night to unwind."

"Sure we're not celebrating something special?" Tremblay asked, glancing between Murphy and Hartinger with a pointed look.

Hartinger laughed. "What, do you think I proposed or something?"

Murphy shot his boyfriend a look. "Who said you'd be the one proposing?"

"Guess we'll have to see who gets there first." Hartinger grinned.

"Oh Christ, you two are going to turn this into a competition, aren't you?" O'Shea asked with a laugh.

They grinned at each other and said, "Probably," in unison.

"I weep for your future children," Tremblay said with a shake of his head. "They're going to be the most competitive motherfuckers ever."

Hartinger nodded. "Definitely," he said with a laugh. "But they'll be cute as shit and killer hockey players."

Jamie chuckled and let their banter wash over him.

When he was with Chicago, he couldn't have imagined the team taking so easily to the idea of players getting married and having kids together someday. He'd been used to a locker room full of homophobic slurs and inappropriate comments. Not to mention the racist jokes said to guys like Tremblay, just for the color of his skin, and tons of casual sexism sprinkled through for good measure.

But Murphy didn't allow that kind of talk in his locker room. Jamie had tried to rein guys in when he was with Chicago but when their captain allowed it, there was only so much he could do.

Then again, what hadn't been toxic about Chicago's locker room?

The conversation turned to other things but Jamie, staring at the casual way Hartinger rested his hand on Murphy's thigh as he talked to Lindholm, imagined a life where he could do the same thing.

Where he could date a guy, and nobody would bat an eyelash.

Of course, the only guy he'd ever had his eye on was Taylor.

That was weird, wasn't it?

The fact that he'd never looked twice at anyone else was strange.

No other guy made his heart beat fast or his palms sweat. It wasn't hard to spot a handsome man, Jamie was surrounded by them at the moment, but none of his teammates made him feel that shaky sort of breathless anticipation he felt being around Taylor.

Knowing Taylor hadn't lessened that feeling.

If anything, it had grown. Jamie liked that Taylor wasn't afraid to stand up to him. He liked that Taylor had apologized and explained why he'd reacted the way he did at the Olympics.

Jamie wasn't the type to hold a grudge anyway, but he found it impossible to look into Taylor's big eyes and stay mad at him.

So maybe Jamie was a pushover for more than Ava.

Maybe he was a big old pushover in general.

But if Jamie wasn't totally imagining things, Taylor had looked *pleased* when Jamie flirted with him.

The thought made Jamie's skin go hot and he yanked at his tie. He balled it up and stuffed it in his suit jacket before he stripped that off too, unbuttoning the top button of his shirt and rolling up the cuffs.

He caught a glimpse of a woman across the bar staring at him. She crossed her long legs and licked her lips as she smiled coyly at him. She was an absolute rocket. The kind of woman that ten years ago, he'd have bought a drink for.

But his mind kept drifting back to Taylor's laugh and the look in his eyes. It was stupid and crazy to ever think Taylor would seriously look twice at him, but thoughts of Taylor made Jamie hotter than any woman he'd run across recently.

"You seeing anyone?" Murphy asked, as his gaze followed Jamie's to the rocket across the bar.

Jamie shook his head and lifted his drink to his lips. "Not at the moment. There's someone I'm interested in, but I think it's a long shot."

Not to mention stupid and risky.

"Yeah?" Murphy gave him a quizzical glance. "You want to talk about it?"

Jamie shook his head. He could. Obviously, Murphy wouldn't have any qualms about Jamie being attracted to a man, but the situation was too messy to explain aloud. Too confusing to explain to anyone else.

Jamie had a giant, inconvenient crush on their figure skating instructor and it wasn't going away.

The question was: if Taylor was interested too, should Jamie do something about it?

Or was he setting himself up for another messy, drama-filled situation destined to end in heartbreak?

CHAPTER SIX

Taylor had never been at the rink when it was so quiet and empty but Jamie's schedule and custody arrangement meant an evening one-on-one lesson was the best fit for him. Taylor didn't mind but the rink felt strange at this time of day without the usual bustle of equipment people and support staff.

It felt huge and echoey, yet somehow private, even if there were media people roaming around with cameras and microphones, calling out instructions, their voices reverberating in the open practice space.

"How are the skates feeling?" Taylor asked as they glided out onto the ice.

"Still weird." Jamie made a face. "But I'll survive."

"Good. I don't think your team would be very happy with me if they had to replace one of their third line forwards," he teased.

"Uh, second." Jamie rubbed the back of his neck. "They moved me up to the second line recently. My numbers have been really good lately and they've shifted Keegan Truro to our second line center so I'll be playing on his wing."

Taylor suppressed a smile. Jamie only made that gesture whenever he got nervous or felt embarrassed. He was being *bashful.* How cute.

"It must be my great lessons."

Jamie laughed, his nose wrinkling a little. "I don't know about that but I *do* feel like I've incorporated some new techniques into my play. I definitely feel like my balance is getting better."

To Jamie's credit, it had never been *bad.* Even the worst pro player was an elite athlete and Jamie was far, far from the worst. But the guys who worked their asses off to constantly improve their skills were the ones who rose to the top and continued to be relevant players with long careers.

And Taylor had definitely noticed the way Jamie seemed more sure-footed and deft as he wove around Calgary's defense to score.

Charlie had shot Taylor a *look* when he'd said he wanted to watch the game the other night but Taylor had protested that he was merely following up on the work he was putting in. Charlie had pursed his lips like he didn't believe it, but he hadn't argued.

And ten minutes into the first period, he'd been screaming at the guys on their TV screen about getting the puck in deep.

Then again, that might have just been Charlie thirsting over the sweaty hockey players they kept showing on the bench.

So far, Taylor had only done a few group lessons with the team and a handful of individual ones. He'd worked with Zane Murphy, Ryan Hartinger, and Brett Cooper this past week but this was his first individual lesson with Jamie tonight and for some damn reason Taylor was *nervous*.

Which was the stupidest thing ever but his brain was an asshole.

Taylor had been getting these odd fluttery feelings every time he thought about Jamie and he'd done a little surreptitious social media stalking. He'd nearly died seeing the cute exchange between Jamie and Ava that had been posted on the team's social media account from the game last weekend.

Unfortunately, all of Jamie's accounts were locked down to private and Taylor didn't quite have the balls to send a request.

Which was also stupid, but again, asshole brain.

But online snooping led to Taylor knowing more than he wanted about Jamie's divorce—what a traitorous bitch to betray a guy by sleeping with his teammate, his *linemate*, Taylor thought venomously—and he silently prayed Kara would never drop Ava off at lessons again or he might not be responsible for his actions.

Taylor had watched all the public interviews of Jamie too and damn it, it was almost becoming an obsession, but Jamie Walsh interviewed *very* well.

"We ready to start now?" Jamie asked and Taylor snapped back to attention.

"Yes. Let's begin."

Taylor could run anyone through skating drills with only half his brain engaged so it wasn't hard to give the lesson while trying not to notice the way Jamie's workout gear clung to his body, the sound of his laugh, or the way he lit up with a smile when Taylor praised him.

The disconcerting thing was that he'd seen that exact same desire to do well and the pleasure at having mastered something in Ava. And Taylor's stupid little heart melted every time he imagined Jamie and Ava skating together.

Taylor tried to ignore his traitorous thoughts about Jamie's body when he pressed a hand to Jamie's back as he guided him into the correct posture, gently touching his stomach to coax him to engage his abs.

But how could Taylor not notice his hard muscles under his clothing, his broad shoulders, and his bright and easy smile while they bantered in front of the camera.

Jamie Walsh was the absolute last person Taylor should be thinking of this way but he couldn't stop to save his life.

"Okay, I think that's it," Taylor said with a little sigh of relief after he'd run through everything he had planned for the lesson. He turned to face the crew. "Unless you need something in particular."

"No, I think we're good," the camera guy said. "We got some great footage tonight. Thanks, guys."

"Thank *you*. Great work, everyone," Taylor said with a sunny smile as the crew began to pack up their gear.

They said their goodbyes and disappeared until it was just Jamie and Taylor out on the ice. It really *was* empty now and Taylor felt a little crackle of electricity when Jamie shot him a smile.

Jamie moved like he was going to go after them, but Taylor called out, "Hey, do you have anything you want to work on without a camera crew around?"

It was a valid question but Taylor was definitely looking for an excuse to spend more time together.

"No, I don't think so," Jamie said with a thoughtful frown, slowly skating toward Taylor. "I feel like I'm getting the hang of things."

"You are." Taylor shot him a little smile. "You're doing *very* well, actually."

"Think you'll make a figure skater out of me yet?"

"Well, I wouldn't go *that* far."

"Ouch." Jamie pressed a hand to his chest. "Brutal. I hope you're nicer to the kids."

"I'm very nice!" Taylor protested, laughing. "I'm sweet as can be."

"So you save the brutality for the adults?"

"Brutality?" Taylor sputtered. "If you think that's brutality, babe, you wouldn't last twenty minutes with a figure skating coach. I went *easy* on you."

Jamie smirked. "Suuure you did."

Taylor skated a little closer. "You want me to go hard?"

Something flared hot in Jamie's eyes. "I'm not sure I should answer that."

"No?" Taylor looked up at him through his lashes. "Why is that?"

"Uhh." Jamie riffled a hand through his hair. "Can I plead the fifth?"

"We're in an ice rink. Not a courtroom." Taylor gave him a slow smile.

Jamie licked his lips. "Then, uh, because I might say something I'd regret."

"What kind of something?" Taylor teased, gliding a little closer until there was less than a skate-length between them.

"Something about me not minding the idea of you going hard."

Well, fuck. That was another point in the *Jamie Walsh is bi-curious* column. But Taylor couldn't possibly be imagining this flirty energy between them.

Maybe Jamie had more experience with men than Taylor knew but there was something oddly bashful about the way he flirted. It didn't feel like he was simply afraid of someone finding out about him. No, Taylor couldn't quite put his finger on it but it sure seemed like Jamie was testing the waters of something he'd never explored before.

And damn it, that intrigued Taylor even more.

"Now that's interesting." Taylor smirked. "You definitely have my curiosity piqued."

Jamie smirked back. "I'm starting to think I made a mistake saying anything."

"Does it have to be a mistake?" Taylor countered.

"You don't think it would be?"

Taylor was pretty certain they were no longer talking about what they originally began with, but he wasn't entirely sure what Jamie was saying. He wasn't sure *Jamie* knew what he was saying.

But God, Taylor *loved* this. He loved the sly smile and the heat in Jamie's eyes. He liked the way he stood on his skates, arms crossed, a little cocky but a little shy too.

Taylor liked the way this felt even if he was scared shitless he'd gotten his signals wrong.

Flirting with Jamie Walsh was a stupid choice.

But damn, it was fun.

"Taylor?" Jamie's voice seemed lower than usual. Sensations raced across Taylor's skin, making it difficult to catch his breath.

"Right, so there's one thing I want to show you before I let you go," Taylor said, turning away before they did something stupid. Like kiss. "Ever heard of twizzles?"

He skated away from Jamie in an arc and caught a glimpse of his expression falling.

Huh. Jamie was *disappointed* by Taylor getting back to work. Another check in that damn column.

"Twizzles?" Jamie gave Taylor a skeptical glance.

"Yeah." It was the first thing that had popped into Taylor's head.

"Sounds like candy or something."

Silly name or not, the move was deceptively complicated. Twizzles were a rapid forward and backward turn up and down the ice. To make it fluid and effortless looking required a great deal of coordination and balance.

Jamie had his three turns down solidly—something that would really help him with his abrupt direction changes during games—and they were the basis for twizzles. Taylor was pretty sure Jamie could handle the challenge.

Taylor demonstrated the moves and talked Jamie through the various steps. Jamie's brow furrowed as he tried his best but he nearly bit it.

"Shoulders rotate in," Taylor called out. "In the direction of your twizzle."

Jamie flailed, trying to correct his posture, and went down, landing with a solid whomp on his back. He burst into laughter.

"Nope, didn't quite get it," Taylor joked as he skated toward him. "Close though."

Jamie sat up, still laughing, wiping at his eyes.

Taylor reached out a hand to him, intending to haul him up but Jamie was so much heavier that it jerked Taylor forward and only succeeded in getting their skates tangled. Taylor flailed, knowing he was heading toward the ice, his only thought of not landing on top of Jamie and kneeing him in the groin.

But Jamie wrapped his arms around Taylor, taking the brunt of the blow as he landed on his back on the ice again.

They both gasped and Taylor caught a glimpse of Jamie's grimace before it morphed into a look of amusement.

And then Jamie burst out laughing again.

It was infectious and Taylor laughed too.

"Well, that didn't go quite the way I planned," Taylor gasped against Jamie's neck.

Jamie snorted. "Me neither."

Taylor braced himself on the ice to get up but he went still when he realized he lay draped over Jamie's body, his hips cradled between Jamie's thighs. The movement rocked their lower bodies together and heat flared when their gazes met. The laughter faded, replaced by simmering tension.

Taylor licked his lips.

Jamie licked his too.

That earlier electricity was back, crackling between them, the tiny hairs on Taylor's arms standing on end when Jamie wrapped his hand around the back of Taylor's neck and pulled him in with a rough noise of need.

His lips were soft and a little damp, hungry as he tilted his head to deepen the kiss. Taylor let out a quiet moan when Jamie teased his tongue between the seam of his lips and let him in, winding his hand through Jamie's thick hair.

Jamie splayed a hand on Taylor's back and hauled him closer, his kiss turning hungry. Taylor grabbed a fistful of Jamie's fleece, taking control of the kiss and drawing a low moan from Jamie.

The sounds of a door clanging shut somewhere in the distance registered and when Jamie let go, Taylor scrambled away quickly, falling onto his butt when he lost his balance.

Taylor pressed his fingers to his lips and stared.

Jamie was wide-eyed too, his gaze shocked, his lips still shiny from their kiss.

"I didn't mean—"

"I shouldn't have—"

Their words overlapped but they both abruptly stopped. Taylor scrambled to his feet but Jamie got up a little slower.

"Are you okay?" Taylor asked, concerned when he grimaced.

"Yeah. Just not used to getting taken out by another skater when I'm not wearing pads." His grin was rueful.

"Shit, is your tailbone okay?" Taylor would be in so much trouble with the team if he broke one of their players.

Jamie chuckled, looking more relaxed as he dusted a bit of shaved ice from the back of his pants. It fell to the smooth surface below their feet like falling snow. "Yeah, I'll be fine. It just surprised me."

"You surprised me with the kiss," Taylor said, a little breathless thinking about it.

Jamie turned pink. "Um, yeah. I think I surprised myself there too. I hope you, uh, were okay with that."

"Yeah. Yeah. It was, uh, really good," Taylor admitted. "I didn't know you were …" He flailed for a moment, unsure of how to finish the sentence. Did Jamie even *know* what he was?

Jamie cleared his throat. "That would be a first, actually."

"A first …"

"Um." Jamie cleared his throat again. "Kiss with a guy."

"*Oh.*" Well damn. There was something charming about a guy who kissed like *that* and then got shy after.

Jamie stuffed his hands in his pockets. "I wouldn't mind doing it again though." He licked his lips, looking through his lashes at Taylor.

Taylor blinked at him. "Is that a good idea, given our history?"

"Probably not." Jamie's smile was crooked and dirty and sweet all at once and it made Taylor want to kiss it off his face. "I, um, I guess I've had a lot of questions and thoughts that I've never been able to answer and I thought maybe you'd uh—"

"Be up for answering them?" Taylor finished.

Jamie nodded.

"Well—"

"Are you guys done with the rink?" a voice called out and they both jumped before turning to face the Zamboni guy who waited in the tunnel across the ice, expression bored.

Shit. They'd been caught.

Jamie's cheeks were hot as he skated off the ice and clomped his way to the dressing room. He unlaced his boots with quick, jerky movements, wondering how much Martin, the Zamboni guy, had seen.

It wasn't until Jamie heard the sound of someone clearing their throat that he glanced up.

Taylor stood nearby, his skates dangling from one hand, an uncomfortable expression on his face. "I don't think that guy saw or heard anything," he said quietly.

Jamie swallowed hard. "Yeah. Probably not."

"How much are you freaking out?"

"About being caught kissing a guy?" He dragged a hand through his hair. "Some. Not so terrified I'm going to call my agent in a panic or anything, but it's not really something I ever thought I'd have to worry about."

Taylor chewed at his lip. "Do you need to talk?"

Jamie raised an eyebrow as he worked the figure skates off his feet. "About?"

"I mean, on a scale of one to ten, how freaked out about your sexuality are you right now?"

Jamie shrugged. His stomach still tumbled like a dryer on a spin cycle but that had more to do with having no idea how to act around Taylor than anything. "Well, it isn't like this is a brand-new thing. It's been fou—a *few* years since I realized I might be into a guy, so I've had some time to think about it."

Taylor gave him a slightly puzzled look. "I'm not saying you *should* be freaking out right now. It would be understandable if you were feeling a little bit unsettled though. I can imagine it's a big shift to have grown up considering yourself straight and having to change that idea."

"Yeah, it's definitely something that takes some mental adjustment," Jamie agreed.

"If you need someone to talk to, I'd be happy to listen."

Taylor stepped closer and Jamie resisted the urge to drag him onto his lap and kiss him again.

"One kiss and we're friends?" Jamie asked. He rose to his feet, tucking his hands in his hoodie pockets to keep himself from reaching out like he wanted.

Taylor shrugged. "Look, you have guys on your team you can talk to about it. Hell, maybe you've *already* talked to them. But if you want to talk to me, I'm offering. That's all."

"True." Jamie considered the idea. He imagined there were plenty of guys in the league who would kill to have a captain, coach, and two teammates that they could go to about this sort of thing. "I guess there's an advantage to being on this team, isn't there?"

"Absolutely," Taylor said.

"I … I appreciate the offer though, that's nice of you." Jamie cleared his throat. "It's not so much the 'am I attracted to guys' thing that's the weird part for me though."

"Oh." Taylor offered him a tight little smile. "Just that it's *me*, huh?"

"What?" Jamie looked at him, baffled.

"Well, our families …"

"Oh. Right. Um, no, not that exactly." Jamie's face warmed. "It's just kind of … having other people know about it that's a little strange, I guess? There's nothing wrong with me kissing a guy, obviously. Or even kissing you. I wasn't really prepared to have anyone find out about it, you know?"

Taylor's expression tightened but he nodded. "Yeah, I get that."

"So how about this? I'll buy you a coffee sometime and we can get to know each other better," Jamie offered.

Taylor arched an eyebrow and Jamie realized how much it sounded like he'd asked him on a date. Which, he wasn't totally opposed to but there were a lot of things he really wasn't clear on at the moment. "I mean, to talk, like you offered. If you're not too busy."

"Sure," Taylor said slowly. "I'm free tonight actually, if you are."

"Ava's at her mom's, so yeah, I'm free," Jamie said, his heart speeding up a little.

"Considering our families' history, it might be better if we weren't seen out in public together."

"Everyone knows we're working together for the team," Jamie pointed out.

"If you want to spill your guts about your sexuality in public and risk pictures of us ending up on the *JockGossip* site, you're more than welcome to," Taylor said drily. "But I suspect that's something you'd like to avoid."

Jamie nodded. "Right. Good point. Where did you have in mind?"

"My place?" Taylor offered and Jamie took a deep breath, hit by the memory of the way Taylor's lips had felt against his, sweet and soft. God, he wanted that again.

"Um, sure." Jamie licked his lips. "Your place is fine. I'm gonna grab a shower first, okay? I did my workout before the lesson and I feel gross."

"Sure. My stuff's in the public shower room so I'll use that. See you in the lounge in twenty?"

"Sure."

For a few minutes after Taylor left, Jamie sat staring after him, his heart beating too fast as he wondered what the hell he was doing going to Taylor's place tonight.

And if they were going to kiss again.

CHAPTER SEVEN

Jamie Walsh was awkward as fuck.

He was hot. He was one of the hottest men Taylor had laid eyes on. But wow, did he look uncomfortable sitting at Taylor's kitchen table.

Of course, he was about half a foot too tall for the chairs and cramped space of the little nook the table was tucked in, so that didn't help.

Though that probably wasn't why he'd been rambling about Ava for the past twenty minutes.

"Would you like to move to the couch?" Taylor asked, interrupting something about Play-Doh.

Jamie froze, eyes wide. "Uhh, sure?"

"You look uncomfortable." Taylor rose from his chair with a little smile. "You're not quite built for the scale of my tiny apartment."

"It's fine." Jamie let out a relieved groan as he stood. "Okay, maybe not. I'm too old to crunch up like that the day after a really physical game."

"It was a good game," Taylor threw over his shoulder as he led Jamie to the living room and the much more comfortable sectional there. "Nice goal there in overtime against Calgary, by the way."

"Thanks. I, uh, didn't know you watched hockey."

Taylor caught a glimpse of his pink cheeks as he took a seat. Taylor chuckled. "I grew up with the game, how could I not?"

"Ahh, true." Jamie gave him a searching look. "How pissed is your dad about you doing this media stuff with me?"

"Honestly, pretty pissed," Taylor admitted. "But I'm a grown man. I can make my own choices."

Jamie nodded.

"I have a confession to make though," Taylor said over the rim of his mug.

Jamie went still, a furrow appearing on his forehead. "About what?"

"I'm not usually rooting for Evanston. I'm a Detroit fan."

"Oof."

"Well, it's who my dad played for when I was little," he pointed out. "So that's the team I've *always* rooted for. I spent quite a bit of time at that arena."

"I bet you were cute."

Taylor's face heated. "The guys called me their good luck charm when they were on a hot streak."

"Adorable." Jamie's gaze was soft as he looked Taylor over and he was pretty sure he wasn't talking about Taylor's childhood.

"You were with Chicago before this, right?" Taylor asked. He was trying to slowly nudge Jamie back into talking about their kiss and how he felt about his sexuality but Jamie seemed determined to talk around it.

"Yeah." Jamie chewed at his lower lip. It was a little chapped like most skaters'. The dry, cold air was irritating and Taylor had the strongest urge to press his mouth to Jamie's and soothe the ragged spot. "Like I said, last season, things were rough with my team. I desperately wanted out of there and Chicago wanted me gone. Evanston picked me up for a song and it was perfect because I didn't have to leave Ava. I didn't care about the pay cut if I could stay in the area for her."

"It seems like Evanston is good at taking in guys who've been struggling and making them shine. You and Theriault are both doing so much better than you were in previous years."

Jamie gave him an admiring look. "Detroit fan or not, I'm impressed. I wouldn't have expected you to follow hockey so closely."

"Why, because I look like this?" Taylor said teasingly. He swept a hand up and down his body to indicate his fabulous fashion sense and makeup. He'd touched up his makeup after his shower at the arena. Charlie was better, but Taylor had halfway decent skills.

To Taylor's surprise, Jamie turned pink again. "No! There's nothing wrong with the way you dress."

Taylor smirked at him. "I never said there was."

"Oh. True. Uh, I mean …" Jamie scrubbed his fingertips through his hair, his face twisted up in an awkward little frown. "I should probably stop before I dig myself in any further."

Taylor chuckled.

"It's fine. I know I'm not exactly the sort of guy who looks like he fits with a bunch of hockey players," he said lightly.

"You do look good though."

They stared at each other for a few heartbeats. Taylor set his mug on the coffee table. Jamie did the same with a quiet little rattle like his hand was trembling.

"Yeah? You like the way I look, huh?" Taylor said teasingly, testing the waters a little by leaning in and letting his tongue drag across his lower lip.

Jamie nodded, his gaze glued to Taylor's mouth.

"Do you just think I'm nice to look at or does it go further than that?" He settled a hand on Jamie's thigh, enjoying the flex of hard muscle under his palm.

"Uh, further." His voice had gone a little hoarse and that encouraged Taylor to slide closer, his hand venturing higher on Jamie's leg. "I mean, *obviously*. I kissed you earlier."

"I had noticed that." Taylor reached out and tugged the front of Jamie's hoodie, pulling him close. Jamie straightened, leaning in until their mouths were inches apart. Taylor smoothed his hand across Jamie's chest, skimming over the Otters logo.

Jamie's blue eyes were wide, and his heart pounded under Taylor's palm. When Taylor wrapped his hand around the back of Jamie's neck, he let out a shuddering little breath that gusted against Taylor's lips.

"Do you want this?" Taylor whispered against his mouth.

Jamie's breathing went shallow, and he licked his lips. "Yes."

"Because you seem pretty nervous right now."

"I am." Jamie dragged in air. "I didn't really think about it earlier, I just went for it but …"

Taylor could imagine the tangle of thoughts in Jamie's head right now but he sounded quite sure, so Taylor gently tugged him in for a kiss.

There was a split second where Jamie's teeth nicked Taylor's lip and they couldn't quite find the right angle and rhythm, but Jamie quickly settled into the kiss, his mouth warm and soft as their lips feathered together.

And then Jamie's tongue teased at the seam of Taylor's lips, delving in with a skillful flick that made him gasp and press their bodies more tightly together.

Taylor slipped a hand into Jamie's hair as he walked forward on his knees and straddled Jamie's lap.

Jamie groaned and wrapped his hands around Taylor's hips, the kiss deepening, his mouth urgent and hungry before he pulled back, eyes glittering with need.

"Oh shit," Jamie whispered, his tone oddly reverent. "I didn't know …"

"Didn't know what?" Taylor asked, dropping his head to kiss the hinge of Jamie's jaw, his short beard a pleasantly soft abrasion against Taylor's lips.

"That it was going to be like *this*." Jamie let out a shaky laugh.

"Good?" Taylor moved lower, pressing light, soft kisses to Jamie's neck.

"So fucking good." Jamie lowered onto his back, pulling Taylor down until he was sprawled over Jamie's big body, reminiscent of their accidental embrace on the ice earlier.

Taylor propped himself on one elbow and looked down at the shocked but needy expression in Jamie's eyes. Jamie slid a hand up Taylor's back, his warm palm leaving shivers in its wake that erupted into heat when Jamie shifted to stretch out his legs fully and Taylor fell between them.

Like someone had touched a match to dry kindling, the fire flared between them again, and Jamie let out a rough groan and pulled Taylor in for another kiss. It was deep and wet, and Taylor's head swam.

His face tingled from the soft rub of Jamie's short beard. He tried to keep his hips still, but it was impossible when Jamie slid his big hands from Taylor's back to cup his ass and urge him to move.

"Yeah, like that," Jamie rasped. His head fell back, exposing his throat again. Taylor kissed along his Adam's apple, interspersing little pecks with teasing licks, and the rumble of pleasure that went through Jamie's chest shot through Taylor's body.

"Fuck. Taylor."

Hearing his name fall from Jamie's lips on a ragged moan encouraged Taylor and he reached for the neck of the hoodie, tugging it lower so he could get his mouth on Jamie's collarbone, licking and nipping a little until Jamie shuddered under him.

"Fuck," Jamie muttered again. "Want me to take it off?"

"Yeah." They sat up long enough for Jamie to strip off the sweat-shirt. He tossed it away and lay back, pulling Taylor down onto his chest again. The thin T-shirt he wore was warm from his skin and allowed Taylor to really explore, kissing along the neckline and dipping his tongue into the hollow at Jamie's throat.

Jamie shivered, hips bucking up, Taylor went a little light-headed at the feel of Jamie's hardness against his thigh, torn between the urge to greedily beg for more or check in and make sure Jamie was doing okay.

"You like that?" Taylor whispered.

"Yes. God. Don't stop," Jamie begged. His hands were hot and possessive as he gripped Taylor's hips, coaxing him into a rocking motion.

Taylor was hit with a sudden desperate image of what it would look like if they were both naked, Jamie using his strength to lift Taylor up and down to ride his cock.

Taylor moaned, his breath going ragged. He slid his hand down, working it up under Jamie's T-shirt to touch his warm skin.

Jamie hissed when Taylor reached his nipple and he toyed with it a minute, flicking his thumb across it until it hardened into a tight little peak. He wanted his mouth on it and he dipped his head, trying to slither backward to get up under the fabric, but Jamie must not have understood, because he let out a little whine.

"Where are you going?"

"Want this shirt off too."

"Oh." Jamie's laugh was a little breathless. He let Taylor ruck the fabric up under his armpits but before he could get it off, Taylor got distracted by the sight of all that gorgeous skin over hard muscle. Damn. He brushed his lips across Jamie's abs, feeling the pleasant tickle of the golden hairs sprinkled in a line down his belly.

His skin smelled good, like warm, spicy citrus that tickled Taylor's nostrils and made him want to drag his mouth lower. Instead, he dipped his tongue into one of the grooves along Jamie's obliques, licking his way up to his ribs.

Jamie shivered, his breath going ragged. "Fuck, Taylor."

"Tell me what you want," he whispered.

"*Everything*," Jamie said with a gasp. "Anything. Fuck, I need you."

It sent a powerful shudder through Taylor's body to hear how strung out and desperate Jamie was already and although there was a dim part of Taylor's brain that knew they should probably have a conversation about this first, all he wanted was Jamie naked in his bed.

"C'mon," he said, scrambling up off the couch. "Let's move this to the bedroom."

Jamie's gaze flared hot and needy as he stood. There was no mistaking the hard jut of his erection in his sweats.

Taylor licked his lips. "I want to suck you off so bad."

"Shit." Jamie swiped his hoodie off the floor and took Taylor's hand. "Show me where the bedroom is or I'm going to beg you to get your mouth on me right here."

CHAPTER EIGHT

A jittery feeling filled Jamie's chest when they stepped into Taylor's bedroom.

Taylor flicked on the light switch, turning on a lamp on the nearby dresser. Jamie glanced around to see a mirrored closet door behind him, a desk and chair by the windows, and on the far wall, the bed and two nightstands flanking it.

It was the bed his gaze kept returning to though and the thought of what they might do there made his heart race.

The door softly clicked shut behind them and Jamie jerked in surprise, his heart rabbiting even faster.

He tossed his hoodie on the dresser, then turned to look at Taylor. "Can I be honest?" he rasped.

Taylor stepped closer and reached up to trace his fingers across Jamie's cheek. "I'd rather you were that than anything else."

"I—I like you, Taylor. I …" He forced himself to look him in the eye and not down at the floor. "I've kind of had a thing for you for a while and I thought you should know before we went any further."

Taylor's lips turned up at one corner. "A thing, huh?"

Jamie swallowed. "Yeah. A thing."

Taylor gently pushed Jamie's shoulder, coaxing him to walk backward until he bumped into the mattress. He fell back on the bed, breathing going shallow as Taylor looked him over.

Jamie shifted until his feet were actually on the bed, groaning when Taylor crawled up over him, and straddled his thighs. Jamie reached out, grasping Taylor's narrow hips, his sweater soft under Jamie's palms.

"What kind of thing?"

"An 'I find you really hot thing'?" Jamie offered. "How about that?"

"Oh, *that* kind of thing." Taylor grinned.

"Yeah. So that's my cards on the table." He stared up at Taylor, loving the flush in his pale cheeks and the brightness of his eyes.

"Well, I definitely find you really hot too."

"Yeah?" Jamie squeezed Taylor's hips, way, way too happy to hear that. After the making out on the couch, obviously he'd figured out Taylor was into him, but it was nice to hear.

"Yeah." Taylor dragged a finger down Jamie's chest and Jamie shuddered. "But we have some *complications*."

"Like the fact that our families *hate* each other."

"Yeah, that's a huge one."

"It is." It felt pretty dim in comparison to Taylor's toned thighs straddling him though.

"But …" Taylor slid a hand under Jamie's shirt and he shuddered at the feel of his warm hand. "Maybe we can … keep it quiet. I mean, I don't really advertise who I'm hooking up with anyway."

"I don't either." Not that Jamie had hooked up a ton since his divorce but he hadn't been a total monk.

Taylor planted his hands on the mattress beside Jamie's ears and smiled down at him. "So …"

"So, I'm on board with that."

"And it's casual, right?" A flicker of something crossed Taylor's face. "I mean, it would be silly to try to make it *more*, right?"

"Right. And I have Ava to think about."

"Of course."

"But I really do want you. I remember the first time I saw you skate at the Olympics and you … wow." Jamie realized his grip had tightened and he gentled his touch, rubbing his thumbs in a circular motion. Taylor's sweater slid up and they both gasped when he touched Taylor's bare skin. "You're really incredible."

"So, you've had a thing for me since then?"

"Pretty much." Jamie's face went hot.

"You *were* flirting with me that night."

"I … I don't know," Jamie admitted. "Maybe. I was pretty mixed up and I was married at the time—not happily but my vows really did mean something to me—so I don't know what I was doing that night. But I do know I thought about you a lot after that. And I watched all your performances on video. And your interviews. And, um, I might have fantasized about what it would have been like if I'd been single and we'd flirted, and what that could have led to."

"What did you imagine?" Taylor whispered. "What kind of things did you picture doing to me?"

"Oh God." Jamie let out a shaky little laugh. "I imagined you naked in bed with me. Your mouth on my cock. I pictured you showing me how you liked to be sucked off too."

"Mmm. That's hot." Taylor moved his hips, beginning a slow, rocking motion. "What else?"

"I pictured you riding me. *A lot.* Still do, in fact."

Taylor's eyes gleamed. "Mmm. You want to fuck me, huh?"

Jamie's whole body went hot at the idea. "I definitely do but …"

"But you're not ready for that." There was no judgment in Taylor's voice.

Jamie shook his head. "I am." He was growing hard and if Taylor shifted his hips back a little more, he'd feel exactly how ready for it Jamie was. "Just um, a little bit nervous about the whole thing if I'm being honest here."

"Oh." Taylor stared down at Jamie a moment. "Well, we don't have to go any faster than you want, I promise."

"No, it's not that. I want you." Jamie rasped. "I'm worried that I won't make it good for you."

"Oh, Jamie." Taylor's expression turned soft and warm. "You're going to make it so good. And if I need you to do something different, I'll tell you. I hope you'll tell me if there's anything you want, too."

"I can do that," Jamie said, his hands trembling a little as he skimmed them up Taylor's lean midsection. "Right now I want you to kiss me again."

Jamie pulled Taylor down on top of him, the abrupt movement forcing the air out of Taylor's lungs and making all thoughts flee from his head. He parted his lips as Jamie brought their mouths together.

Jamie kissed him deeply, roaming his hands across Taylor's body as they rolled onto their sides. "Just because I'm nervous doesn't mean I don't want this," Jamie whispered. "I want you. If *you* want to go slow, we absolutely can but …"

He slid his hands under the stretchy waistband of Taylor's leggings, squeezing his ass cheek, the touch soothing but arousing all at once.

"But?"

Jamie slipped his hand out of Taylor's pants to grasp Taylor's wrist. He gently guided it to where he was thick and long beneath his sweats. "But I'm really hard for you."

They both let out a gasp.

Jamie's eyes fluttered closed.

Damn, he felt amazing. Taylor stroked, watching Jamie's face tighten like he was in pain. But there was a warm flush to his cheeks, and the way his hips flexed up into Taylor's hand made Taylor very sure pain wasn't the cause.

"Mmm, you *are* hard for me," Taylor said with a little noise of appreciation. He knocked Jamie's hand away and took over, exploring him through the soft fabric. Jamie hissed when Taylor teased at the waistband, gently tugging it away from Jamie's abs.

"Please," Jamie begged. His pupils were blown wide, and he shivered when Taylor skimmed his hand beneath the sweats and his underwear.

"Please what?" Taylor whispered.

"Touch me. I want to feel your hand on my cock."

When Taylor finally reached his destination, Jamie let out a groan.

"Like that?" Taylor asked, caressing the hot, hard length while he leaned in for another kiss.

"Yesss." The word dragged out into a hiss when Taylor teased his thumb over the sticky crown. Soft hair brushed against his knuckles as he stroked gently.

"Fuck, fuck," Jamie chanted. He grasped Taylor's hand and stilled his movements, gently tugging his hand away. He kissed Taylor's palm like it was an apology. "That might be too good."

Taylor tried not to smile that Jamie had gotten that worked up, not wanting him to think he was laughing at him. "How about touching me?"

Heat flared in Jamie's eyes. "Yes."

He pushed Taylor down onto the bed and reached for his shirt. "Can this come off?"

"It can all come off if you want."

Jamie stripped Taylor. It was more efficient than sexy but that didn't dim Taylor's enjoyment at the way Jamie's gaze roamed over his naked body.

"Fuck, look at you." Jamie kissed his hip. "You have no idea how many times I imagined this."

Taylor laughed, sliding his hands through Jamie's thick hair as he kissed his way up Taylor's abs. He lapped at Taylor's nipples, sucking on them until Taylor arched into the sensation, his cock aching with the need to be touched.

Jamie slowed, dragging his warm palm down the center of Taylor's body, hesitating a moment before he wrapped his palm around Taylor's cock.

"Mmm," Taylor said, his eyes closing at the pleasure of a big rough hand working his dick. "Perfect."

"Yeah?" Jamie whispered in his ear, nipping at the lobe with his teeth. "Have anything to make it nice and slick?"

"Sure." Taylor wet his lips and gestured vaguely to the right. "In the nightstand there."

When the touch of Jamie's hand disappeared, Taylor missed it but it wasn't all bad having Jamie stretched out over him. He was much too dressed though.

"Want to lose some of your clothes too?" he asked as Jamie rummaged around.

"Sure." Jamie sat back, tossing a few things on the bed. Something bounced gently against Taylor's ribs. He was too distracted by the sight of Jamie stripping off his shirt to bare his upper body to care.

Shirtless Jamie occupied all his focus.

Biceps. Shoulders. Pecs. Abs.

Jesus.

If Taylor wasn't careful, he was going to slide right out of bed thanks to the drool he needed to mop up.

Jamie kept the sweatpants on, crawling back on the bed to kneel by Taylor's legs. Probably just as well for Taylor's sanity and ability to control himself.

"So, what did you find in there?" Taylor teased. He twisted to the side to grab the stuff Jamie had pulled from the drawer, laughing when Jamie palmed his ass and let out a desperate little groan.

Taylor would swear Jamie's hand covered one whole cheek.

He definitely, definitely didn't mind.

Taylor grabbed the supplies on the bed beside him and wasn't surprised to find a bottle of lube and a condom, but he raised his eyebrow at the slim vibrator.

"Oh yeah?" He settled on his back again, waving the toy.

Jamie gave him a crooked little grin, shy and pleased with himself all at once. "It looked fun."

Taylor laughed. "It's *very* fun. It just depends on how you want to use it. Ever tried anything like that?"

"Uh, well," Jamie hesitated, and Taylor remembered he'd been with plenty of women. Had been married.

"On yourself," he clarified.

"Oh. Nope."

"Okay. Well, this is fun as hell on the outside. But never, ever use it inside." He waggled the toy. "Not unless you want to risk losing it in you and having to make a very awkward trip to the ER."

Jamie winced. "Nope, don't want that."

"Me either." Taylor rolled onto his stomach again and stretched out to reach the drawer of toys. "This will be better."

He held up a toy with a flared base.

"Yeah?" Jamie sounded distracted though and Taylor looked over his shoulder to see Jamie's gaze locked on his butt.

He wiggled a little and Jamie let out a huffing laugh, his sheepish gaze meeting Taylor's. "Sorry, you have a great ass."

"Oh, you don't have to be sorry about that," Taylor said. He twisted to flip on his back again. "Just say, 'Taylor, you have a spectacular ass. Best I've ever seen.'"

"Taylor, you have a spectacular ass." Jamie bit his lip. "Best though, that might be stretching it."

"Hey!" Taylor protested, surprised but laughing as he shoved at Jamie's chest. "Rude."

"C'mon." Jamie grinned down at him. "Have you ever seen Matty Carlson's?"

"Sadly, no. Not in real life, anyway."

Jamie's grin widened. "Well, I have. Naked."

Taylor cocked his head. "When did you play with Matt Carlson?"

"We were in the AHL together for a little while. Just a few months but it was enough to be sure he's got a hell of a butt."

Matt Carlson was a defenseman for the Toronto Fisher Cats, and he was one of the biggest active players in the NHL. He was very well known for his powerful quads and glutes.

"Well, let me be clear," Taylor said teasingly. "I am incredibly jealous that you got to see the gloriousness of Matty Carlson's legendary butt live and in person. And I will concede that it might be more spectacular than mine."

Jamie laughed.

"But my ass is the one you've apparently been lusting after, so I think it's about time you get your hands on it."

"Lusting after?" Jamie sputtered but he slid his hands under Taylor's backside and gripped his cheeks, squeezing a little and Taylor let his legs fall open to either side, draped over Jamie's thighs.

Jamie's gaze strayed lower, and he licked his lips.

"Mmm, yeah, definitely not lusting," Taylor said drily.

"Shut up," Jamie muttered. He stretched out over Taylor to kiss him, growing a little more serious. "Now what?"

"Now, we do whatever you feel good about doing. Do you want to fuck me?"

"Absolutely." Jamie's voice was a little rough but there wasn't even a second of hesitation.

"Ever fucked anyone's ass?"

"Yes." Jamie licked his lips, his hair falling into his eyes as he remained propped up over Taylor. "I know how to get you ready. Lube. Fingers. Maybe that toy if you're into that idea."

"I'm into it." Taylor felt a little breathless as he brushed Jamie's hair away.

"Okay. Then that's what we'll do." Jamie gave him a quick, hard kiss, then sat back, a determined expression on his face like Taylor was a puzzle to be solved. Something to be *won*.

It was surprisingly arousing, and Taylor wrapped a hand around his half-hard cock, stroking slowly while he watched Jamie slick his fingers.

He gasped a little at the cool touch against his opening but he rocked his hips, nudging Jamie to continue when he paused.

Jamie teased a finger around Taylor's rim for a moment before he gently pressed forward. He sank in easily and the feel of his thick finger made Taylor whimper.

"Good?" Jamie whispered.

"Yeah, really good," Taylor said as Jamie began slow, even strokes. "Another finger would be even better."

Jamie grinned at him. "Eager?"

"*Very*."

Taylor idly stroked his cock while Jamie got a little more slick on his fingers. He let out a gasp when Jamie slid them in. "Mmm, yeah that's it."

"Fuck," Jamie said. He looked up through his lashes at Taylor's face. "It's so fucking hot to watch you take my fingers like that."

"Feels pretty good too."

"Pretty good?" Jamie got this determined little look on his face, his gaze sharpening as he sped up. "Just *pretty good*?"

"Ahh." Taylor threw his head back when Jamie grazed his prostate. "Yeah, it's …"

Jamie curled his fingers and Taylor let out a strangled little gasp, his grip tightening on his cock.

"You were saying?" Jamie said smugly.

"Your fingers feel fucking *amazing*."

"Thought so." Jamie loomed over him, bracing his arm on the bed next to Taylor's head, continuing to finger-fuck Taylor with slow, even thrusts as he stared down at his face. "I might not have any previous experience with fingering a guy, but trust me, I've done my research."

"Shit." Taylor let out a groan, picturing that. "That's kind of hot."

"Yeah?"

Jamie had a little smirk on his face that Taylor wanted to kiss away.

So he did.

"Taylor," Jamie whispered almost reverently before he pressed their lips together again.

They made out for a while, Jamie's tongue gently mimicking the thrusts he made with his fingers until Taylor was writhing on the bed under him.

"I need something more," Taylor whispered against his mouth. "Toy, your cock … whatever you want."

"Okay." Jamie sat up, gently sliding his fingers out.

Taylor missed them, but it was so hot to watch Jamie cover the vibrator in lube and bite his lip as he focused on carefully pushing it into Taylor's body.

Taylor let out a gasp when it snugged tight, the base holding it in position. "*Mmm.*"

Jamie teased him with it for a few minutes, gently pushing it in and out while Taylor squirmed.

And then Jamie pressed the button at the base. Taylor knew it was coming but he still let out a strangled gasp at the hum, hips rising as he clenched around the intrusion, hot waves of pleasure working through him. "Fuck, Jamie."

"Yeah? Good?"

"So fucking good," Taylor rasped. "God."

Taylor reached for his dick but Jamie batted his hand away. "I want to make you come this way."

Taylor was ready to protest that he wasn't sure if he *could* come from only the vibrator inside him but Jamie wrapped a slick palm around his cock and began to stroke.

"Shit, shit," Taylor whined, his body going tight as he struggled to not come that very second. Together it was a lot. Enough to make his head spin and his breath come in gasping pants.

Jamie stroked him, grip slick and firm while he toyed with the vibrator buzzing inside Taylor.

"Fuck, fuck …"

"Please, Taylor," Jamie said, his voice husky. "I want to see you come. Tell me what you need."

"Keep doing *that*," he begged.

He felt a tug on the base of the toy and then Jamie was fucking it in and out of him, the pace perfectly matching the steady strokes of his hand. Everything went tight, Taylor's muscles clenching, ass clamping around the vibrator, tension coiling in his belly.

When Jamie twisted his wrist on the upstroke right as he angled the toy, Taylor came apart.

He grabbed for the sheets below him, twisting them in his hands and closing his eyes tightly. Pleasure washed over him in huge, rolling waves. Jamie stroked him through it until it was too much, and Taylor let out a garbled noise slapping at the sheets in a desperate attempt to get him to stop.

It took a moment of fumbling but the vibration stopped and Jamie softened his grip.

"Fuck, fuck," Taylor chanted, panting as his entire body trembled. "Oh shit."

Jamie brushed his lips against Taylor's cheek. "Good?"

"Fuck yes," he slurred.

Jamie chuckled softly. "Good. I'm glad."

Taylor's eyes flew open. "Shit, you haven't come."

"Not yet." But there was no urgency in Jamie's eyes, just a smug sort of pleasure that made Taylor want to smack him and kiss him all at once.

"How do you want it?" Taylor bit his lip. "I could suck you."

"I'm not sure I'd last long enough to really enjoy it. Can I jerk off on you instead?"

"God yes."

Jamie hooked his thumb in the waistband of his sweats, leaving a wet smear from the lube as he pushed the fabric below his ass until it circled his thighs. His cock was flushed red, hard and shiny at the tip, and Taylor traced his tongue across his lips when he glimpsed the damp spot on the front of the material.

"Where do you want it?" Jamie said, knee walking toward him until he knelt beside Taylor's hip.

"Chest and abs."

"Okay." Jamie stroked, slowly at first, his face tightening with concentration as he moved his slick hand along the shaft, using Taylor's cum as lube.

That sent a little thrill through Taylor, and he reached up to caress Jamie's hip, smoothing over the swell of his ass to cup one cheek. Jamie must have thought he was going further because he widened his stance, the speed of his strokes increasing.

Taylor certainly wasn't going to pass up that opportunity when it was willingly offered, so he teased his middle finger into the cleft of Jamie's ass, searching for his hole. Taylor had barely brushed over the sensitive ring before Jamie's cheeks clenched tight around Taylor's finger and he shot onto Taylor's chest. The first covered his nipples, the second hit his navel, the third spurting onto his lower abs.

Taylor tapped his hole twice and Jamie let out a strangled groan, the last few shots of his orgasm sliding down Taylor's hip before Jamie shuddered and slowed his hand.

"Fuck. Fuck. Holy shit." Jamie trembled over him. "*Taylor*."

Jamie sat back on his heels, staring at Taylor with wide eyes. His gaze traced down from Taylor's face, heated and hungry as he passed over the mess they'd both left on Taylor's body. "Wow."

"Yeah?" Taylor felt a little smug.

"Jesus, that was hot." Jamie licked his lips and reached out, trailing his fingers through the puddles of cum cooling on Taylor's skin. It wasn't the most comfortable feeling but it was unbearably arousing to watch him drag his slick fingertips across Taylor's nipples, sending a little shiver through him.

Jamie moved lower, skirting around his navel and teasing over his hip before he stopped, smiling down at Taylor.

"It was," Taylor agreed, reaching out to touch Jamie's thigh. His cock lay softening in his lap, draped over the top of the waistband of his sweats. "How are you feeling?"

"Sticky." Jamie looked up at him, gaze heavy lidded. "Sticky but fucking incredible."

Taylor laughed and sat up, leaning in to kiss him despite the awkward position. "Me too."

"Taylor-babe!" The words and the rattle of the doorknob were the only warning they got before the bedroom door opened.

"Whoopsies," an amused voice trilled. "Did I come at a bad time?"

Damn it, Charlie, Taylor thought before Jamie bolted off the bed, nearly dumping Taylor to the floor in his haste to get away.

Fuck.

CHAPTER NINE

"Shit," Jamie blurted as he tumbled out of bed. "This isn't what it looks like." He tripped over his feet as he yanked his sweats up to cover his junk, adrenaline flooding his body.

"Oh, really?" A pretty blond guy about Taylor's age stood on the other side of the room, staring at them with a curious expression. "Because it looks like you're freaking out about being caught in bed with my roommate, dude."

Jamie ducked away from his intent gaze, searching for his shirt on the floor. He yanked it on, his heart slamming against his ribs, his tacky, shaking hands refusing to cooperate.

Jamie turned, intent on getting the fuck out of there when he caught a glimpse of Taylor's expression. He looked betrayed, his blue eyes filled with hurt so piercing Jamie froze.

"Shit. I'm sorry, Taylor," he rasped.

Jamie automatically reached for him but when Taylor jerked away, it was like a bucket of ice water to the face, shocking him back into reality.

Jamie curled his hand into a fist and dropped it to his side, knowing he was an absolute asshole.

Now that the panic had begun to recede, guilt replaced it. Oh God, he must have made Taylor feel so shitty when he reacted like that. Said that. But how could he make this right?

"You okay, Taylor?" the guy asked, a frown furrowing his brow.

"Yeah. Just peachy." Taylor climbed out of bed naked, his back straight, his chin lifted as he reached for the peacock blue robe that hung from a hook on the wall nearby. He yanked the belt tight and ran his hands through his hair. If not for his reddened lips and the pink irritation around his mouth from Jamie's beard, he would have looked as neat and perfect as he did at the rink.

That was almost worse. If Jamie walked out now, it would be like this never happened. Like he'd had no impact on Taylor whatsoever. Like he hadn't just had Taylor in his arms coming apart with desperate, needy little noises.

Like he hadn't finally had sex with the guy he'd been dreaming about for years.

"What exactly is going on here, honey?" the guy in the doorway asked in a soft, concerned voice.

"Nothing, Charlie." Taylor's tone was clipped and tight as he stepped forward. "Just … forget you saw anything. And keep your fucking mouth shut about this, you hear me? You were mistaken. You didn't see anyone you might have recognized."

The sharp rebuke made Jamie and the other guy—Charlie, apparently—freeze.

Charlie lifted his hands. "Forget I said anything. I came home to an empty apartment."

"Good." Taylor turned to Jamie with a brittle smile. "There, your secret is safe with us. You can leave now."

Jamie stood there a moment, struggling to pull in air and knew in that second, he had a choice to make.

He could bolt out the door and pretend like this never happened, or he could apologize to Taylor for his reaction and try to fix it.

It wasn't an easy decision, but there was only one choice he could live with.

Heart in his throat, breaking out in a cold sweat, Jamie turned, stepped forward, and held out his hand to Charlie. At the last moment, he realized it was still rather sticky, so he dropped it to his side. "Hi. Nice to meet you. I'm Jamie Walsh. Forward with the Evanston River Otters. I'd shake your hand but, uh …"

He grabbed some tissues from the box on the nearby dresser.

Charlie blinked at him, then grimaced. "Uhh, hi. Charlie Monaghan. Taylor's best friend and roommate."

"Great. Sorry we had to meet this way."

"Uh, Taylor?" Charlie's gaze darted between the two of them. "What the *hell* is going on here exactly?"

Taylor shrugged. "Honestly, I have no fucking idea."

Jamie turned to look at him. "Can we talk?"

"I thought that's what we originally came here to do in the first place," Taylor said, his lips pursed, his tone a little tart.

"Well, we, uh, got a little bit distracted, I guess." Jamie wasn't going to point out that *he'd* been the one to initiate the kiss this time.

"That much is clear." Charlie's voice was silky but when Taylor shot him a look, he threw up his hands. "I'm going, I'm going. Just … lock the door if you plan to have more sex and please try to keep it down. It's already late and I'm going to need to eat dinner at some point. I don't need to hear Taylor moaning or anything while I enjoy my stir fry."

Jamie's whole body went hot with embarrassment. "I, uh, don't think …"

Charlie snickered.

"Don't be a dick, Charles," Taylor snapped. He stepped forward and poked Charlie in the chest.

"I'm not!" Charlie widened his eyes innocently. "I pinkie swear I'll be a good boy and keep my mouth shut about this … development in your sex life."

Taylor stuck up his middle finger. "Swear on this."

"Bite me," Charlie retorted. He gave Jamie a big smile and waggled his fingers at them. "Toodles, babies."

When the door was shut firmly behind him and Taylor had locked it, Jamie forced air in and out of his lungs a few times before he stepped forward to look Taylor in the eye.

"I'm so sorry. What I said to Charlie earlier … That didn't come out the way I meant it."

"No?" Taylor arched an accusatory eyebrow at him, arms crossed over his chest.

Jamie sighed. "It wasn't my best look. I panicked."

"Yeah, that part I'd worked out."

The painfully dry note in Taylor's voice made Jamie wince.

"I've … I've never talked to *anyone* about being—being bi before. Until tonight not a single, solitary human on the planet knew. I don't even … I have no idea what I'm doing. Or what we're doing or what I want to be doing. I just—" He swallowed hard. "Look, I like you, okay? And I didn't mean to do anything to hurt you."

Taylor remained silent, his eyes still filled with pain.

"Can we talk about this?" Jamie pleaded. "I don't want to walk away without at least clearing the air. Even if you don't want to keep, uh, doing anything else. I want to make this right. You didn't deserve to be treated that way."

Taylor's expression softened. "Yeah, we can talk. C'mon."

He held out a hand and Jamie took it, relieved by the soft press of Taylor's warm palm.

"Interesting relationship you have with your roommate," Jamie said.

Taylor tugged him onto the bed, his expression softening further as he stretched out on his side, the rigid fragility melting away. "I love the fuck out of that man but some days I would cheerfully strangle him."

"So kinda like siblings?" Jamie lay on his side too, facing Taylor and trying to avoid the wet spot.

"Basically. Charlie is definitely my brother from another mother. Sometimes I wish I could wrap him up in packing tape and mark him return to sender though."

Jamie laughed, relieved that the tension was beginning to fade. "That's definitely how I feel about my brother."

Taylor cleared his throat. "So, uh, sorry about Charlie walking in on us. We generally have an open-door policy around here and we give each other a heads-up and lock our bedrooms if we have, um, company over. But I forgot to do either."

"Hopefully I didn't scar him for life."

Taylor cackled. "Charlie? God no. I'd bet you a lot of money—that I really don't have—that he'll jerk off thinking about you tonight. He's not the one who's going to end up scarred by this, trust me."

"Oh God." Jamie laughed a little helplessly. "Well, okay then. As long as he's not going to sell the info to the highest bidder ..."

"God no. He's dirty minded and incurably nosy but harmless. You can trust him not to blab about what he saw. He's a strong believer that everyone gets to come out whenever they're ready."

"That's a relief." Jamie toyed with the sheet below him. "I mean ... maybe that's dickish of me but I'm not quite ready to have more of my personal life splashed around in the news."

"I can understand that," Taylor said softly.

"But I still fucked up earlier, didn't I?"

Taylor's expression closed off. "Fucked up by kissing me or ..."

"No!" Jamie glanced at the door and softened his voice. "God no. I meant I fucked up when I reacted like that about being caught. I'm sorry. It was a shock. I didn't expect for someone to bust in on us in bed."

Taylor sighed. "You know, I understood you getting kinda freaked out at the rink. That's your work, you're not out, you were startled. But it really looked like after Charlie walked in on us, you were about to bolt out of my apartment without so much as a goodbye, and trust me, honey, I've done the hooking up with closeted athletes way too many times to count. I'm not doing it again."

Taylor rolled onto his back and Jamie's throat tightened at the expression on his face. He looked miserable.

"Do you want to talk about it?"

Taylor cleared his throat, still staring at the ceiling. "I really don't but I suppose I was the one who brought it up."

Jamie shrugged. "Still doesn't mean you *have* to talk about it."

"It's … whatever." Taylor sighed. "So, I'm into guys who are, well, like *you*."

Jamie's throat felt very dry. "Closeted?"

"Sure, but that's not the appeal. I know guys who get off on the 'turning the straight guy' vibe and that's not it for me at all. I … I like athletes, okay? I like muscles and athletic competence and … well, *you* know what pro sports are like. Being out has not exactly been encouraged." Taylor sighed noisily. "So I've been involved with a lot of guys who are in the closet because they feel they have to be."

Jamie nodded.

"I want to be clear; I don't want to force anyone out before they're ready. That's shitty. There are a thousand and one reasons why someone would need to hide and I respect that. I really do."

Taylor dragged in a deep breath. "But I had a series of flings and relationships with people who made me feel like crap about being this secret, hidden thing in their life. I could live with the secrecy for the right person but it was the being lied to and strung along and disrespected that I won't tolerate."

Jamie winced but kept silent.

"The worst was this skier I was involved with. I won't say his name because he's still not out, but he's an Olympic athlete. And he—he treated me like shit."

Jamie's heart ached. Taylor was still protecting the privacy of someone who had clearly hurt him. "Like shit how?"

"I was the person he wanted to be with in private but he sure as fuck wasn't going to parade me around to the media and his family. Hell, he wouldn't even acknowledge me as a *friend* in public." There was a bitter edge to Taylor's voice that made Jamie want to pull him close but he wasn't sure if that was allowed, so he stayed still.

"He lived out in Colorado and his family had a shit ton of money, so he'd fly me out to visit. Lots of lavish private dinners and swanky hotel rooms and it took me a long time to realize that he was trying to buy my silence. Buy my tolerance for being a secret. He assured me he'd come out. That the gorgeous girl in the pictures was a family friend and it was good press for *us*, because then we didn't have to worry about people coming after us. That it was romantic to sneak around for now and when the time was right, we'd announce our relationship."

"Taylor …"

"Yeah, I was dumb." Taylor turned his head and looked at him.

"I would never say that." Jamie reached out, tentatively resting his hand on Taylor's hip. "It just makes me sad for you."

Taylor gave him a lopsided, hurt-filled smile. "I was seventeen when we met. What did I know?"

Jamie frowned. "How old was he?"

"Nineteen. It wasn't super sketchy or anything."

"He was still a dick."

Though was Jamie any better? He was ten years older than Taylor and he wasn't rushing to come out of the closet. Then again, he'd never promised Taylor he would. And Taylor was in his mid-twenties now.

Or maybe Jamie was trying to rationalize that he was less of an asshole than the skier who had broken Taylor's heart.

"He was a dick for sure," Taylor agreed. "And when I finally broke it off with him for good at the Olympics, he threw a shit fit. He couldn't understand why I was tired of putting up with being treated like garbage."

"I get why my earlier freakout upset you," Jamie said with a sigh. "And I get why getting involved with me is probably, um, a bad idea. 'Cause I'm not so much better, am I?"

Taylor's gaze turned soft. "You've already been far more honest than he was the whole time we were together."

That wasn't necessarily saying much.

Jamie frowned. "Can we talk about what we're doing here?"

"Sure."

"Do you want to hook up again?"

"Do *you* want to?"

"At the moment, I'm not exactly sure what I want," Jamie admitted. "I just know tonight was incredible. Everything I imagined it would be and more. Well, minus the roommate."

Taylor smiled. "That's fair."

"It, um, answered a lot of questions for me," Jamie said, scratching his jaw.

"About your sexuality?"

"Yeah." Jamie gave him a lopsided smile. "Now I know."

"Know what?"

Jamie chewed at his lip a moment. He knew that Taylor made him achingly hard. That kissing Taylor was perfect and watching him come was somehow even better than that. But that seemed like way too much so all he said was, "What it's like to be with a guy, I guess."

"So is that it then?" Taylor's voice was carefully neutral but Jamie could see a little flash of something in his eyes like Jamie had somehow hurt Taylor again and damn it, he definitely didn't want that. "You got all your questions answered."

"I got my questions answered, yeah," Jamie said. He slid a hand along Taylor's waist and pulled him a little closer. "I *hope* that's not all though."

Taylor's gaze slid away from his. "I guess it depends on what you're looking for. Because let's be honest. I don't think either of us are in a position where we want the public to find out what we're doing. The public *or* our families."

"Agreed." Though it made Jamie feel a little guilty admitting that aloud but realistically, this thing with Taylor wasn't going anywhere long-term. Jamie wasn't going to settle down and make a life with Taylor or anything.

Their family stuff was bad enough but Taylor was still young. Not the kind of guy who'd want to tie himself to a closeted single dad who was a decade older.

Probably not the kind of guy who was looking for a ready-made family.

Even if Jamie was ready to come out and have that in the open, when it came to Ava, he had to be honest about who he was. If he didn't have a kid, maybe he could have lived with being in a secret relationship. But even if that was something that Taylor wanted, and clearly he didn't, that wasn't fair to Ava.

Jamie couldn't expect her to keep his secrets and she definitely wasn't old enough to understand why she'd need to.

"Argh." Taylor flopped onto his back. "Why are we making this so difficult?"

"No idea," Jamie said with a little laugh.

"Do you want to fuck again or not?" There was an annoyed edge to Taylor's voice.

"Yes."

"And we don't want anyone to know."

"Correct." Jamie reached out to touch Taylor's stomach, fingertips skimming over the bare soft spot where the robe had parted. "But I don't want to hurt you either. The stuff with your ex, I get how that can get in your head and screw with it. I don't want to be someone who makes you feel shitty."

"I know you don't. It's … it's a different situation, right?" Taylor finally met his gaze again.

"It is," Jamie said slowly. "But before we go any further, I want you to know how sincerely sorry I am about the way I acted earlier. I fucked up and I'll make it up to you if you'll let me."

Taylor looked at Jamie a minute, sorting through the confusing tumble of emotions churning in him.

It had hurt like a kick to the chest when Jamie had rocketed out of bed and denied that he was doing anything with Taylor.

Taylor knew Jamie hadn't been thinking rationally. He'd been operating on pure panic. He'd bolted out of fear.

Even if there hadn't been lube, condoms, and a sex toy scattered across the sheets, Taylor had been naked and Jamie'd had his cock out.

How the fuck had Jamie thought he was going to explain *that* away?

Taylor had spent years of his life bouncing from one shitty guy to another. Casual or serious, they'd all been the same. More concerned with their reputation than how their actions hurt Taylor.

The pressure of competing to secure a position in men's singles skating had been crushing. Charlie and Taylor had both struggled with it. Charlie had used food as a weapon against himself, an attempt to control something in a life where the pressure grew with every competition, where it was an unrelenting grind where he was never good enough. He'd sabotaged his own success because it was killing him to continue.

Taylor had pretty much done the same with shitty men. Maybe not as drastically, but he'd let himself be used and treated like crap because it was something *outside* of his career. Because it had made him feel powerful to have successful athletes in his bed, lavishing him with gifts and praise. He'd chosen to ignore the ways it was destroying him from the inside out in the same way Charlie had ignored that he was starving himself, shrinking day by day in front of Taylor's eyes.

Taylor's hurt had been harder to see on the outside, but no less emotionally dangerous.

After the last time, Taylor had sworn to himself that he wouldn't do it again.

He'd gone into this knowing Jamie was closeted but Taylor had thought—he'd *hoped*—that Jamie was different. In some ways, he was like every other guy in the past. He'd panicked when faced with the idea that someone might discover that he was bi.

But he'd also stayed. He'd realized his mistake. He'd *listened.*

He'd made a choice to introduce himself to Charlie and make himself vulnerable.

That thought made something in Taylor's chest flutter dangerously. He'd never had that before.

As Taylor looked into Jamie's eyes and considered his sincere apology, he decided to trust him.

Besides, this was never going to be more than a fling. As long as he didn't get emotionally invested, it would be fine.

"You're forgiven," Taylor said softly as he scooted toward Jamie.

Jamie blinked. "Just like that?"

Taylor shrugged, a little confused by his reaction. "Sure? I mean if you want to beg for it, we can talk about that but it's not really my kink."

Jamie laughed, clearly too surprised to do anything else. "I guess I expected—"

Taylor sobered. "Expected what, Jamie?"

"I don't know exactly." His teeth grazed over his lower lip as he seemed to consider Taylor's words. "I guess I expected you to be madder about my reaction."

"Why? You apologized. As long as you don't keep doing stuff like that, I see no reason not to put it behind us." He gently touched Jamie's short beard.

"I mean, if we're not telling anyone about us, is it going to really come up again?"

"Well, probably not. I don't like feeling like someone is ashamed of me though. So, if we're hanging out in the living room some time and Charlie walks by, I'd like it if you didn't leap away from me like someone zapped you with electricity," Taylor said lightly.

"Of course." Jamie dragged him tightly against his body. "I'll do better."

"Then we're good. You don't need to keep apologizing or anything. It's over and done with."

Jamie sucked in a deep breath. "That's, uh, not something I'm used to."

"Forgiveness?" Taylor sounded a little incredulous.

"Without a lot of work, yeah. My ex. She, um, well let's just say she was the kind of person who really, really liked to make me work for her affection."

Taylor grimaced. "Gross."

Jamie shrugged. "I didn't mind some of it, but it didn't feel great to grovel over every little thing."

"Well, no groveling required here," Taylor said with a dismissive flap of his hand. "I'm not the type who is looking for that. And we're not dating anyway so …"

"Right."

"It doesn't have to be complicated. Our schedules are both crazy. You have a kid and travel all the time. We'll hook up when we can and be discreet about it."

"Yeah, okay. That sounds pretty good to me."

"Good." Taylor grinned at him. "Now tell me how soon you need to be home."

Jamie shrugged and glanced at the clock on the nightstand. "Technically I don't need to be anywhere until practice tomorrow morning."

"Well, I don't share my bed with hookups," Taylor said with a little smirk. "So I'm going to send you home at some point."

"Rude," Jamie teased but he didn't actually look offended.

"What do you think? Can you miss a few hours of sleep? I wouldn't mind you hanging around for a little longer."

"I could do that," Jamie agreed, rolling over until he lay half on top of Taylor.

He leaned in and brushed their lips together. Taylor was already half-hard against his thigh and Jamie reached down, cupping Taylor's dick and slowly stroking.

"Think we should take care of this?"

"Definitely," Taylor said, a little breathless as he curled a hand around the back of Jamie's neck. But when Jamie flipped back his robe, Taylor yelped as it separated from where it had been stuck to his skin by their earlier messy orgasms.

"*Oww*. On second thought, let's move this to the shower. I think you just ripped off some leg hair."

CHAPTER TEN

"Okay, *spill*," Charlie said.

Taylor pressed a hand to his sternum, realizing he'd been staring blankly at the door Jamie had walked through a few minutes ago. "Jesus, are you practicing to be a ninja or something?"

"I think the real question is, are you really fucking the son of your family's sworn enemy?" Charlie sounded both scandalized and impressed.

Taylor flushed and tightened his bathrobe. He didn't know *why*. Charlie had seen him naked or half-naked a million times over the years but he felt strangely shy about the whole thing.

"I am," he admitted, feeling an odd guilty thrill run through him.

"Okay, so I'm gonna need you to elaborate on that." Charlie grabbed his elbow and tugged him toward the couch that was still rather askew from Taylor and Jamie's earlier make-out session.

Taylor touched his face and winced. Christ, he was going to have beard burn like whoa.

"It's two a.m!" he protested. "I have an early class to teach in the morning."

"Well, then talk fast." Charlie gently shoved him onto the couch. "'Cause I have questions."

"Fuuuuck." Taylor flopped back against an armrest. "Why do I live with you again?"

"Because you love me more than life itself."

"Do I?"

"Start talking." Charlie jabbed at his chest. "How did you get *Mr. Bi-Curious* into bed?"

"Oh, for fuck's sake." Knowing he was merely delaying the inevitable by stalling, Taylor dragged a throw blanket up over his lower half so he didn't accidentally flash his junk at Charlie. He had underwear on but *still.* "We had a one-on-one lesson tonight."

Charlie smirked, taking a seat next to Taylor. "Don't I know it. Honey, I saw the aftermath."

"Would you quit it?" Taylor kicked his thigh. "Stop being a menace."

"Too late. It's a permanent condition."

"Ugh, tell me about it."

"Anywhoodles … your one-on-one lessons." Charlie waggled his eyebrows.

"At the *rink.* We recorded a skating lesson and after the crew went home we, uh, flirted a little, and we kissed."

Taylor went through what had happened, the kiss and the invitation to come back here to talk. Which, if Taylor had to be honest, had been a rather flimsy excuse to get Jamie's lips on him again. And then he moved on to the sex and the talk after Charlie had walked in on them.

"Are you sure it's a good idea to make this an ongoing thing?" Charlie asked gently when he was done.

"No, I'm not," Taylor admitted.

"But you're going to do it anyway."

"I'm going to see how it goes."

"What happened to your promise that you'd never put yourself in a position to get hurt again?"

Heat crawled up Taylor's cheeks. "I mean, isn't getting involved with *anyone* risky?"

Charlie gave him a look. "Yes, but that's avoiding the point. You have a history of bad relationships with guys like this."

"It's not a relationship!" Taylor protested. "We're hooking up! As you pointed out, our families—especially mine—would be apoplectic about us being involved. Besides, Jamie's a single dad. He has his daughter to think about."

Charlie snorted. "Oh yes, because a hot DILF is really going to be a turn-off to you. You want a husband and babies. That's going to make it worse."

Taylor squirmed the way he always did when Charlie called him out on something. That was the problem with having people in your life who knew you down to the very depths of your soul. Taylor hated that Charlie was probably right but he couldn't deny it either.

"For me, yeah. But it also means he's going to be careful to, you know, keep a separation there," he argued. "It's not like I'm going to be hanging out with his kid on the reg."

"She's one of your students!"

"But that's different," Taylor said weakly. He threw an arm up over his eyes so he didn't have to look at Charlie's know-it-all face.

"Is it?"

"Jamie doesn't bring Ava to classes. I'll never see them at the same time or anything," he mumbled.

"Except the other day when grandma brought the kid to see her daddy?"

"Shut the fuck up," Taylor whined, too tired and sex drunk to come up with a better retort. "Jamie's a good guy."

"He's a hot jock with a big dick. At least be honest about it."

Jamie was definitely both of those things, but Taylor would swear he was a good guy too. God, Taylor *hoped* Jamie was a good guy. If he wasn't, well, Taylor might give up and admit he should never be allowed to get involved with anyone ever again.

He dropped his arm to look at Charlie. "Should I break it off?"

Charlie sighed. "I can't answer that for you, honey. I just want you to be careful. I'm looking out for you the same way you look out for me."

"I know." Taylor dragged Charlie toward him until he lay draped over Taylor's body, his face mashed into the side of Taylor's neck. "I appreciate you, you know that, right?"

"Yes." Charlie's voice was slightly muffled until he squirmed away. "But you reek of sex. Let me up. It's gross."

"Only 'cause you're jealous I got good dick and you didn't," he taunted.

Charlie gave him a withering look. "You're damn right I am."

Sometimes, Jamie really hated hockey.

He loved the game, but the team leaving on a three-day road trip right after his hookup with Taylor was annoying as hell.

Jamie didn't even have Taylor's phone number. He *did* have his email from Ava's classes, but it felt weirdly formal to email him after they'd gotten naked together. He debated sliding into Taylor's DMs on social media but that also felt weird and desperate, so he moped anxiously about Taylor's interest cooling before Jamie got back home.

At least Taylor knew where Jamie was and what he was doing.

Which was mainly losing games.

The Otters slunk out of New Jersey after a 5-8 defeat, then lost 3-4 to New York, which put the whole team in a funk. Malone had a wrist injury which would keep him out of the game for a while too, so they were down a D-man for the foreseeable future.

The flight home from New York was subdued and Jamie had driven halfway to his parents' place before he remembered Ava was at Kara's that night, which put him in a worse mood when he got home to his empty house.

By the time Jamie showered and staggered into bed, he was exhausted, grumpy, and annoyed. He burrowed under the covers and grabbed his phone from the nightstand.

Tomorrow was a day off, but he was so tired his head ached, his shoulder was bugging him *again*, despite the trainer's best efforts, and his thigh hurt where he'd taken a puck shot.

Nothing was better than sleep, but he was also horny, antsy, and too wound up to rest. He gave in to his baser instincts and pulled up Taylor's Instagram profile. He typed out a message, his finger hovering over the Send button for a minute before he took the plunge.

Sorry I was MIA for a few days.

A few moments later the message showed as read but Jamie was half-drifting off before a reply actually came through.

Who IS this?

Jamie mentally facepalmed. He'd forgotten this was his private, unverified account with a generic icon and name that he'd previously used to check out Taylor's posts without outing himself as a total stalker.

The guy who went home with you the other night. You teach my daughter skating lessons. I realized I don't have your phone number.

OH. Hi. How was the, er, work trip?

Long. Terrible. We didn't do well.

I noticed that. Is that why you're sliding into my DMs for a late-night hookup?

Jamie grimaced at the words and the time on his phone before he typed out a response. ***That wasn't really my goal. I wanted to let you know I was thinking about you. I hope me going silent didn't make you wonder if I'd changed my mind or something.***

It was a little weird to not hear from you but I knew you were on the road. When I realized we hadn't exchanged numbers I understood.

How've you been?

Busy with lessons. Went to a concert with Charlie the other night.

Fun, who'd you see?

Taylor answered and they bantered for a while before the conversation turned flirty.

What are you up to now? Jamie asked.

Relaxing on the couch. Thinking about heading to bed soon.

Want some company? I've gotta admit, ever since you mentioned a late-night hookup that's all I've been able to think about.

Sure. My place or yours?

Jamie blinked at the response. ***Well, I'm naked in bed. I can put on clothes and drive over but if you're offering to come to my place I wouldn't turn it down.***

Address? Oh, and don't bother to get dressed.

And that was how Jamie found himself answering the door half an hour later, wearing nothing but a blanket. He shivered as the frigid January air followed Taylor inside the house.

"Hey," Jamie said, freezing and a little awkward as he closed the door behind Taylor. He definitely wasn't tired anymore though. "Thanks for coming over."

Taylor's gaze swept over him, head to toe, then back up again. "Pleasure's all mine." He kicked off his shoes and hung his outerwear on the hook by the door.

"I haven't been able to stop thinking about the other night."

"Yeah?" Taylor shot him a little grin. "That so?"

"Yep. It was good company on a lonely road trip."

"It's not like we're dating. You can hook up on the road—or here for that matter, you know?"

"Yeah, I know," Jamie admitted. Most of his hookups in the past year had been on the road so he wasn't opposed to the idea in general. "I dunno. I wasn't feeling it this trip. It was more fun thinking about you."

Taylor bit his lip and stepped forward. His clothing was cool against Jamie's body and the tip of his nose was icy against Jamie's face when he dragged him down for a kiss. "I thought about you too," he whispered.

Jamie groaned and pressed Taylor up against his front door, sweeping his tongue into Taylor's mouth for a brief, heated kiss. "What did you think about?"

"Mmm, lots of things. How hot it was to watch you jerk off on me," Taylor said against his mouth. "How it was even hotter when you got me off in the shower."

Jamie groaned. God, that was the best shower he'd ever taken. Feeling Taylor's naked, slippery body against his, hearing him moan as Jamie pressed him against the shower wall and wrapped a hand around his cock had been the perfect spank bank fodder the past few days.

"So hot," he agreed. He reluctantly tore himself away and took Taylor's hand. "C'mon, bedroom's this way."

"Not gonna pin me to the door and fuck me?" Taylor's voice was teasing but the mental image nearly made Jamie drop the blanket he had wrapped around his waist and he tripped over the trailing ends.

"Jesus," he muttered hoarsely. He turned to look at Taylor, absently gathering the blanket into a makeshift toga again. "Well, I didn't know that was an option."

Taylor chuckled and bit his lip. "It would be pretty hot."

"It would," Jamie said, a little lightheaded at the idea. "Damn. Uhh, *wow*."

For a moment he seriously considered it and then he remembered his various aches and pains.

"Might need a raincheck on that though. My left shoulder's hurting tonight."

"Oh." Taylor leaned forward and pressed his lips to Jamie's skin, right where the joint ached. "That's okay. I understand."

"Did you … did you just kiss it better?"

Taylor squirmed and looked away. "Um, no?"

"You totally did! God, and *I'm* the dad." Laughing, Jamie tugged on Taylor's hand, dragging him up the stairs.

"Charlie called you a DILF the other night."

Jamie sputtered and tried not to walk into the doorframe instead of through the bedroom door. "What?"

"Well, you are."

"You think I'm a DILF, huh?" Jamie teased. He let go of the blanket, allowing it to drop to the wood floor.

Taylor's gaze swept up and down his body. "Well, you're a dad and I'd definitely like to fuck you."

Jamie coughed. Well, that was honest. "I've never … uh …"

"It's a general statement." Taylor ripped off his sweater and tossed it on a nearby chair. "Doesn't mean I need to have my dick in you to do it."

"Right. True," Jamie said faintly. "Um. Well, then I guess I better let you have your way with me."

Taylor grinned, shimmying out of his snug leggings. "Don't have to ask me twice."

When they were both naked, Jamie pulled Taylor in for another kiss. His heart beat fast as they pressed together from head to toe and he palmed Taylor's ass cheeks. "What do you want?" he asked breathlessly.

"I was thinking I'd suck your cock," Taylor said, remarkably calm about the whole thing. "Get you hard. Then ride you until we both come."

Jamie choked on air. No one from his past had been quite so blunt about what they wanted. He liked the boldness, rather than the coy flirting where he had to guess if someone actually wanted something or, in fact, wanted him to guess they wanted the complete opposite.

"Please?" was all Jamie managed but Taylor took that at face value and nodded.

"You have supplies?"

"Yeah." Jamie nodded at the nightstand. When Taylor said he was on his way, Jamie had pulled out the brand-new bottle of lube and condoms.

"Perfect." Taylor dropped to his knees at Jamie's feet and placed his palms on Jamie's thighs. "Now, let's get started."

For a moment, all Jamie did was breathe as Taylor grasped his cock and swallowed him down. He'd been half-hard when he'd answered the door and was now achingly aroused after seeing Taylor naked and hearing what he wanted.

Jamie let out a shaky little sigh when Taylor began to bob his head, taking him deeper than expected.

Taylor's fingertips were cool as he explored Jamie's balls but his mouth was burning hot, slick and eager while he gave Jamie the cocksucking of his life. Jamie tentatively lifted his hands to Taylor's head, unsure if he'd like that, but he just hummed a pleased noise, so Jamie played with his hair while Taylor bobbed over him.

"Fuck, fuck that's so good," Jamie said with a groan, realizing he'd been way too quiet.

Taylor slid off with a swirl of his tongue. "Tell me if you get too close. I'd love to have you come in my mouth sometime, but tonight I need your dick in my ass."

"Yeah, okay," Jamie said breathlessly. He made the mistake of looking down and moaned at the sight of Taylor's big blue-gray eyes peering up at him, his lips stretched around Jamie's cock. "Fuck, you look hot like that."

Taylor's eyes smiled, though he merely kept working Jamie over, the slick sounds only ramping up the pleasure.

When Jamie's stomach went tight and his balls drew up, he gently tugged Taylor away. "Gotta stop."

Taylor slid off with a wet pop and rose gracefully to his feet. "Okay."

"Where do you want me?"

"Middle of the bed on your back."

When Jamie was sprawled out, he intently watched Taylor kneel on the mattress and work two fingers into his own ass. "Damn, I love watching you do that."

Taylor grinned. "Thought you would."

In way less time than Jamie would have expected, Taylor had opened himself up and covered Jamie's dick with a condom. He swiped some lube over Jamie, then straddled his thighs. "You ready for this?"

"Fuck yes."

Taylor chuckled. "Love the enthusiasm. Very hot."

Jamie's face went warm but he could hardly complain when Taylor wriggled into position. Jamie held his dick in place, watching Taylor's toned thighs and abs flex as he slowly sank down.

Jamie couldn't look without losing his mind, so he slammed his eyes shut. The hot clutch of Taylor's body was more than enough to make him go lightheaded. A strangled moan left his mouth when Taylor's ass finally met his thighs.

"Fuck," he spat, clutching Taylor's hips. "Gimme a minute."

"Okay."

Jamie opened his eyes to see Taylor on top of him, lips parted as he settled his hands on Jamie's abs, stroking the defined ridges and leaving trails of heat in his wake.

"God you're gorgeous," Taylor whispered.

"So are you." Jamie let his gaze roam over Taylor's body and brought his hands up to brush his thumbs across his tight pink nipples.

Taylor hissed, clenching around him, and Jamie groaned and thrust up. And then they were moving, Taylor rising and falling over him in sweet, steady strokes.

For a moment all Jamie could do was grit his teeth and allow him to take the lead but when Taylor shifted and let out a shaky little moan, Jamie reached for his ass, cupping it. Taylor was light enough that Jamie could easily lift him without straining his shoulder, and it wasn't long before sweat slicked both of their bodies.

Taylor planted a hand on Jamie's chest, right between his pecs, his eyes closing as he let out a gorgeous breathy sound. "Fuck, fuck, right there."

Jamie shoved up with his hips, bouncing Taylor over top of him and fighting off the urgent need that licked at his spine.

"Harder," Taylor said with a desperate little whimper.

"I don't want to hurt you."

"I can take it." Taylor's head dropped, his chest flushing pink. "Please, Jamie."

There was no way Jamie could resist that, so he dug his feet into the mattress for leverage and fucked up into Taylor with everything he had, grip tight to keep his hands from sliding on his sweat-slicked body.

"Fuck. Fuck," Taylor whined. A tremor shuddered through his body. "Almost there."

Jamie grabbed his shoulder in one hand and spat into the other, gripping Taylor's cock. Taylor let out a strangled moan and a few jerks later, he came apart, mouth opening when he threw his head back. He tightened around Jamie and shuddered, soft little panting moans leaving his lips with every spurt of his cock until he slumped down on Jamie, his words slurred. "Gimme a sec and I'll—"

But Jamie was coming too, his vision going white and fuzzy around the edges as he held Taylor tightly against his body, pumping into the snug heat of his ass with a few desperate thrusts, filling the condom.

"Fuck, fuck, fuck," Jamie muttered nonsensically against Taylor's hair while the white-hot pleasure finally receded. He rubbed his hands up and down Taylor's back, his hands slipping on the cooling sweat that dotted his skin.

"Un-huh," Taylor muttered against his chest. "Swear I'll get up in a minute. When I can move again."

"S'okay." Jamie clumsily patted his hip, eyelids too heavy to lift.

They lay there panting for a while until Taylor began to shiver.

Jamie wrapped his arms around Taylor and rolled him onto his back. Taylor whined when Jamie sat up, but he was beginning to soften, so he grasped the base of the condom and eased out.

Taylor let out a little noise of discontent, but when Jamie looked up, there was a sleepy half-smile on his face.

"You okay?" Jamie tied off the condom, then disposed of it in the nearby trash.

Taylor's lazy thumbs-up made Jamie snort quietly.

Jamie cleaned up in the bathroom, bringing a warm cloth to Taylor, who was sprawled exactly where Jamie had left him, although he'd yanked up the sheet to cover his body.

"Here you go."

Taylor cracked an eye open. "Thanks." He sat up with a groan. "I think I can feel my limbs now."

"I made you lose feeling in your extremities?" Jamie teased. "I'll take that as a compliment."

Taylor clambered off the bed and took the cloth from Jamie's hand. "You don't need your ego fed. You know you have a big dick and how to handle it."

"It's still nice to hear," Jamie said with a shrug. In the end, it wasn't so different having sex with a man, but that didn't mean Jamie wasn't concerned about pleasing the person he was with. Whoever they were.

"Good game, bud." Taylor patted his shoulder as he passed by on his way to the bathroom, apparently preferring to clean up in private. "You got the puck in deep."

Laughing, Jamie sprawled on the bed while he waited for Taylor to return, unsure if he was going to head out immediately or stick around.

Taylor approached the bed hesitantly, head cocked like he was weighing his options.

Jamie held out an arm. "You can leave if you want. I won't be offended. But if you want to stick around for a bit, I'm up for some cuddling."

Taylor rolled his eyes, but he climbed under the covers, sidling up to Jamie.

"What can I say, I'm a snuggler," Jamie said with a shrug, unashamed. It was the one thing he missed more than anything about being married. Though the sweet, easy affection of their relationship had worn off long before the end.

"It is nice." Taylor rested his head on Jamie's shoulder, splaying his hand on Jamie's stomach. "Charlie's too wriggly."

They lay there in silence, the high of the orgasm slowly melting away, leaving Jamie with a drowsy contentment. Eventually, Taylor stirred and sat up. The sheet and blanket tumbled down, leaving his upper body bare.

Jamie rubbed his hand along Taylor's slim but toned arm. "Heading out?"

"I should." He yawned. "Still gotta drive home."

Jamie looked at the clock and winced. Skating itself was optional tomorrow but he'd at least get in a workout. He never missed it unless he was sick or the trainers told him he needed a day to rest. He was going to be dead on his feet but he couldn't find it in himself to regret inviting Taylor over.

"Thanks for coming over."

"Thanks for having me." Taylor's lips twitched like he wanted to make a joke. "I know I teased you earlier, but it really was amazing."

"Good. Let me know when you'd like to do it again."

Jamie pulled Taylor in for a slow, easy kiss before he let him go. Taylor hopped off the bed to dress, but when Jamie reached for the covers, Taylor shook his head. "You look comfy. I can let myself out."

Jamie was comfortable, so he didn't argue. "Okay."

"Want me to lock up behind me?"

"Please."

When Taylor was dressed, he stood beside the bed, staring at Jamie a moment before he shook his head. He'd almost reached the door before Jamie remembered he didn't have Taylor's phone number.

"Wait!" he called out.

Taylor turned to him with a quizzical smile. "Missing me already?"

"Wanted to get your number." He reached for his phone on the nightstand.

"Oh, right." Taylor leaned against the doorway as he fished his cell out of his pocket, rattling off the digits. Jamie punched it in, then sent a quick text, watching Taylor while he saved the contact.

He appeared relaxed, his skin still flushed pink, his dark, short hair a little disheveled. He looked soft and happy and it pleased Jamie that he'd done that for Taylor.

"Night, Jamie. Text soon." Taylor turned to go.

"Night, Taylor," Jamie murmured back, resisting the urge to get up to steal one last kiss.

A few minutes later he heard the quiet sound of the front door opening and closing, and he stretched, reaching to turn off the lamp until he remembered he still needed to take his contacts out.

Damn it. If he had to get up anyway, he should have snuck in a final kiss from Taylor.

When Jamie caught a glimpse of himself in the mirror, he was still smiling. He was relaxed, the weight of the bad games distant, the ache of loneliness gone. His shoulder still hurt, but the contentment of a great orgasm pushed it to a mild hum in the background.

Jamie took off his glasses and crawled in bed. It felt soft and cozy, the scent of Taylor's cologne lingering as he settled against the pillow. Jamie thought of the Olympics four years ago and smiled.

If someone had told him then that he'd find himself in bed with the gorgeous figure skater he'd been drooling over, he'd never have believed it. But whatever that spark had been as he watched Taylor skate, it hadn't faded. He didn't know *why* Taylor was the man who'd ignited it, but he had, and all those questions that had worried the edges of Jamie's thoughts since then finally made sense.

CHAPTER ELEVEN

"Hey, sweetheart." Lindsey Hollis kissed Taylor's cheek as he stepped inside the brick two-story home his parents had purchased after they moved from Detroit to Chicago.

"Hey, Mom."

"Glad you could make it tonight," she said with a bright smile.

Jamie was kid-less this weekend and was leaving for a road trip tomorrow so Taylor would much rather have gone to Jamie's place and sucked his dick until his ears rang, but it had been a few weeks since he'd seen his parents and he couldn't avoid them forever.

Plus, he didn't want to hurt their feelings.

"And Charlie!" His mom threw her arms around him. "Oh, it's so good to see you."

Taylor sniffed. "She's more excited to see my roommate than me. Rude!"

His mom whacked his arm. "We love you too, but Charlie hasn't been over in ages."

"Nah. It's 'cause they love me better," Charlie said smugly as he sauntered past Taylor, kicking off his shoes and hanging up his coat with practiced ease.

"I can leave," Taylor threatened, but he was laughing too hard for anyone to take him too seriously.

"Ignore him." Charlie slipped an arm through Lindsey's and shot a look over his shoulder at Taylor. "He's looking for an excuse to spend more time with his boyfriend."

"You're seeing someone?" Her face lit up. "Oh, that's wonderful."

Taylor contemplated strangling Charlie but then he remembered how terrible he looked in prison orange.

"I don't have a boyfriend," he said with a sigh. "There's a guy I've hooked up with a few times. That's all. Ignore Charlie."

"Oh, well, you never know," his mom said. "Maybe it'll turn into something."

Taylor imagined bringing Jamie over to meet his parents and snorted. "Yeah, no. Not going to happen. Nice try though."

"I'm not trying to add any pressure," she said as they reached the kitchen. "I just want you to be happy, sweetie."

"I know." Taylor pasted a smile on his face. "Something serious will happen when it's meant to. I'm not rushing anything."

"That's good. Now, what about you, Charlie? Any handsome men vying for your attention?"

"Oh, one or two," Charlie said with a coy smile. "No one as hot as Taylor's guy."

"You boys and your hookups," she said with a shake of her head. "I will never understand it but as long as you're being safe."

"We are, Mom," Taylor promised before she went any further with *that* topic of conversation.

He took a seat at the island and Charlie plopped down beside him. It had been remodeled recently, with creamy sage-colored shaker-style cabinets and handmade tiles that glistened in the light. His mom was an interior designer, so she was constantly testing out new looks in their house.

"Can I get either of you anything to drink?" she asked. "I opened a bottle of white."

"Water's fine," Taylor said. He had a low-grade headache from the weather system moving in and wine didn't seem like a good choice.

"Charlie?"

"Wine, please."

"Hey there!" Rick Hollis strolled into the kitchen with a smile, clapping his hands on Taylor's and Charlie's shoulders. "There are my boys."

Taylor smiled. He loved the way his parents had folded Charlie into the family that way. Charlie's parents were … well, assholes, to put it mildly. They'd always been more concerned with their own lives than their son's and after Charlie had learned that his parents had lied to him about being adopted, their relationship had never really recovered.

Taylor had always privately wondered if Charlie's eating disorder had played into that. If it had been a cry to them to pay attention.

Unfortunately, it hadn't worked. But the Hollises had always treated Charlie like one of their own.

Taylor got a warm hug from his dad, who turned to Charlie with his arms open.

"Hi, Rick," Charlie said softly as he cuddled close. "It's good to see you guys. How's work?"

After his retirement, Rick had gone on to become an investment broker, which was a topic he was always happy to talk about.

Rick and Charlie caught up for a while as Taylor helped his mom assemble a mixed greens salad. A short while later they sat down to eat that along with roast chicken and potatoes.

Taylor didn't miss the way his mom's eyes glistened when Charlie took a good helping of everything and appeared to eat with real enjoyment. Her expression was soft and pleased as she looked at him, though she didn't say anything out loud, knowing it would make Charlie uncomfortable that people had noticed.

"So, how's the skating going?" his dad asked.

Tension settled along Taylor's spine. "It's been good. I love the classes I teach."

"And your work with the Otters?"

"It's good too," he said blandly. "The PR campaign is going well, and the skaters are seeing results. It's been positive all around."

"And that Walsh boy?"

"Boy?" His mom laughed. "Hardly. He's, what, ten years older than Taylor, I think?"

"Around there," Taylor agreed. "But it's been fine working with him. He's been very polite. Willing to learn."

Charlie snickered and Taylor kicked him under the table.

Charlie shot him a wounded look. "Rude," he mouthed when Taylor's parents were looking at each other.

"He doesn't have a problem with gay skaters, does he?" Rick's tone was combative as he speared a potato.

"No, Dad," Taylor said with a sigh. "He's been very nice. And remember, several of his teammates are out now."

"Doesn't mean the whole team is okay with it."

"I know that." Taylor poked at his chicken. "But he seems like a good guy, okay? I know you don't like his father but—"

"Don't like?" Rick scowled across the table. "He's a dangerous asshole who should have been drummed out of the league years before he retired."

"Which you've mentioned in every interview you've ever done."

"Honey," Lindsey said, patting Rick's hand. "Please, leave it. You're making Charlie uncomfortable."

Charlie looked more entertained than uncomfortable but he was happy to play along, so he gave them a sweet little smile. "Did I tell you about the promotion I got?"

Lindsey perked up. "Oh no, you didn't."

"Well, they offered me an entry-level designer position now that my internship is wrapping up."

"That's wonderful," Lindsey said. "Isn't that great, Rick?"

"It is." He thawed enough to give Charlie a warm smile. "We're very proud of you, kiddo."

"Thanks! I couldn't have done it if you hadn't hooked me up with your friend's firm, Lindsey."

"You deserve it. You're very talented."

Charlie bubbled over with enthusiasm at the praise and Taylor was doubly glad he'd invited him to dinner tonight. Charlie was always welcome, so it was more of an open invitation, but he hadn't hesitated when Taylor had pled for company tonight to avoid an argument with his dad.

Charlie could be a little shit when he wanted, but Taylor was still grateful to have him in his life.

This road trip is never going to end. Jamie sent the text to Taylor, knowing that he might not respond immediately.

It was the Otters' last night on the road actually, but it had felt endless. Washington, New York, and then Boston.

They'd won against Washington and New York so far, although Boston could be a rough team to go up against.

Jamie's phone remained silent, so he got comfy on the bed and reached for the remote. He had about an hour before he needed to lie down for his pre-game nap. He found a movie he could fall asleep to but moments after he tossed his phone aside, his phone buzzed.

Aren't you home tonight?

Jamie smiled. ***I might have been exaggerating a little about it never ending. It just feels endless.***

Ha. Looking forward to playing Boston?

Ehh. They're good but one of their players has a hard-on for pummeling Theriault. We'll see how it goes.

Gabriel had toned down his fighting but Crawford could get under anyone's skin, and Gabriel had admitted that Crawford hadn't forgotten their fight last season. They were all going to need to have his back tonight.

Be safe, Taylor said.

I promise, I'll be on my best behavior.

What fun is that?

Jamie smiled and typed out a response. ***Just on the ice, I promise.***

Oh, well I suppose that's okay.

I could stop by tonight and show you how fun I can be off the ice.

Mmm. I bet you could. I have an early class tomorrow though.

****sighs* fine.***

So needy!

Jamie winced. That was something Kara had called him. He threw the phone aside again, a little knot forming in his stomach. He wasn't great at playing it cool. Had he texted too much lately?

They'd had fun sexting the other night and Jamie had sent Taylor a few shirtless hotel mirror selfies and dick pics but they were supposed to be keeping this casual and maybe Jamie was being too pushy.

Tayler had seemed into the flirty messages he'd sent in the past few days but maybe Jamie had misjudged it.

Jamie's phone buzzed again. He picked it up, feeling guilty when he saw the message from Taylor. ***Did I say something wrong?***

It's fine. I'm getting ready for a nap.

Because I really was kidding. I've enjoyed the messages you've sent lately.

The sick feeling in the pit of Jamie's stomach dissipated. ***Good.***

So, a nap, huh? Does that mean you're in bed?

Rather than answer, Jamie took a quick pic, double checked that it looked okay, and sent it.

Hot. Did I ever tell you about my fondness for gray sweatpants?

Nope. But that's good to know.

Honestly, he was pretty lazy when it came to dressing. He had his nice game day suits but unlike some of the guys on the team, he was perfectly happy in sweats and a hoodie the rest of the time. Kara had always bitched at him about it, and he'd dutifully dressed up more for her but he was happiest in team gear.

His phone buzzed again with a message from Taylor. ***So, if you did come over tonight, what would you want to do?***

Suck your cock.

Well, someone's feeling bold.

You complaining? Jamie asked.

Nope.

Jamie had been thinking about it for so long. Wondering what it would feel like to have a dick slide across his tongue, wondering if the velvety-soft skin would feel good brushing across his lips. If the scent and taste of Taylor's body would make Jamie hard.

He sent that to Taylor and grinned when he got a response back.

You can't stay stuff like that when I'm here—in my car at the rink!—and you're there. Allll the way in Boston.

You started this.

Damn, guess I did.

What are you doing in your car, anyway? Jamie asked.

Killing time before lessons. I've got about ten minutes before I have to go in, so we better not get too worked up.

Speak for yourself. I'm in a hotel room bed and a quick and dirty orgasm before a nap would make me sleep really well.

You're dangerous.

I think you like it.

Maybe I do.

Jamie smiled at his phone, his hand drifting to the front of his sweats to tease the hardness there. He rarely jerked off before games but today it felt more urgent than usual.

Mind if I think about you while I do it? He asked.

Feel free. Did you save the photos I sent you?

Yeah. That okay?

Of course. That's why I sent them. Happy to provide some inspiration. ;)

Jamie thumbed through his photos and groaned. God, that one Taylor had sent was deadly. He was just out of the shower, standing in front of his bathroom mirror, hand casually resting on his hard cock. He had a little smirk on his face like he knew how good he looked.

It did nothing to make Jamie want to suck him off any less. He could picture laying Taylor out on his bed and sliding between his legs, licking and kissing his way up the shaft. Would he be salty or sweet when Jamie sucked on the head?

Jamie loved the sounds Taylor made when he was getting fucked but he wondered if they'd be different when Jamie was tonguing his smooth balls and working his way up his length. Maybe he'd like a finger or two inside him at the same time.

Jamie wanted to take his time and learn every little twitch and moan Taylor let out, learn what made him arch his hips and pant and beg for more. Jamie wanted him strung out and begging, bossy as he gasped out how much he needed to come.

Jamie stretched out to fumble for his nearby bag and pull out the bottle of lube he traveled with. He shoved the sweats halfway down his thighs, then slicked himself while he stared at the pictures from Taylor. Slow strokes quickly turned into quick, hard jerks that wound Jamie tightly until he let out a strangled shout and came everywhere, panting through the final stomach-clenching spurts.

After, when his head stopped spinning, he glanced down the length of his body and laughed at the mess he'd made.

He took a shot of his softening dick, the white jizz beginning to darken the light fabric of his sweats. He sent the image to Taylor, knowing he was playing dirty but too pleased to care.

Fuck that's hot! Message me when your flight lands tonight. If it's not too late, I want you to come over.

"Why are you pouting?" Charlie asked when Taylor flopped onto the couch with a huff.

"Jamie's stuck in Boston tonight. Snowstorm has the plane grounded."

"Aww, do you miss him?"

"I miss his dick."

Charlie flicked his nose. "Be honest."

"I *do* miss his dick!"

God, Taylor couldn't stop thinking about that picture Jamie had sent him. He'd wanted to *strangle* him because he'd been in the rink's public locker room at the time. Thankfully there had been no one around to see his hard-on but he'd had to sit on the bench and think of gross, awful things before it was safe to go out on the ice to teach his class.

"What else do you miss?" Charlie asked. "And I don't mean his fingers and tongue."

Taylor rolled his eyes. "I dunno. He's kind of growing on me but it doesn't—"

"I knew it!"

"Not like that," Taylor protested. "It's … he's easy to talk to and the flirting has been fun. That's all."

"Mm-hmm." Charlie's look was skeptical.

"What about you?" Taylor nudged him. "I noticed you got home late last night."

"I was at work."

"Until two in the morning?" His tone was dubious.

Charlie giggled. "Well, I worked late, then swung by a guy's house for a nightcap."

"Oh, is that what you call it?"

"Would you rather I call it a good dicking down?"

"Was it?"

"Ehh, not bad. I've had better."

"Aww, poor Charlie."

"It's okay." Charlie patted his leg. "I've got another one lined up for tonight. He should be here in like ten minutes."

"Jesus, do you ever sleep?"

"Oh, like you didn't come in late the other night after *your* dicking down from Jamie?"

"That was days ago!" he protested.

"Don't slut-shame me." Charlie flicked his nose again and Taylor swatted his hand away. "A boy has needs and it's not my fault I haven't found a fat-cocked hockey player to keep me satisfied." He brightened. "Hey, we should go to one of the games sometime."

Taylor groaned. "Are you kidding me? You'd be a *menace*."

"I know. It would be fun." He bounced a little in his seat. "Maybe your player can get us tickets."

"He's not mine," Taylor protested. "He's a dude I'm fucking. That's all."

"Sure, honey. You keep telling yourself that." Charlie patted his cheek. "Besides, you can still get us tickets either way."

"I am *trying* to do this differently. No spendy gifts that make me forget when guys treat me like crap."

Charlie shrugged. "Dudes are going to treat you like crap whether or not they give you gifts. You might as well get us something nice out of it."

"Ouch. Why me in particular?"

"I didn't mean *that*. It was a general you." He waved vaguely. "Not a Taylor-specific one."

Taylor sighed. "Not the point."

"What is your point?"

"That I'm not going to ask Jamie for tickets to the game because it would be a very bad idea."

"Okay, okay. Get your dick and forget the shiny things he can buy you." Charlie's phone buzzed on the coffee table and his face brightened. "Ooh, speaking of dick, tonight's gentleman is downstairs. Gotta go let him in."

"Aaand that's my cue to hide in my bedroom," Taylor said with a laugh. "Have fun. Be safe."

"Always." Charlie gave Taylor a peck on the cheek.

Taylor turned off the TV, then disappeared into his bedroom. A few minutes later he heard quiet laughter and male voices pass by his door and he quickly popped into the bathroom to brush his teeth and get ready for bed.

They were already getting started by the time Taylor was done and he popped earbuds in and queued up some white noise to drown out the sounds while he read.

But later, as Taylor lay in bed trying to ignore the rhythmic banging across the hall and sleep, he let out a noisy sigh.

Stupid snowstorms.

He'd really been looking forward to seeing Jamie again.

"Thanks for the eggs, Mom." Jamie wiped at Ava's messy hands and face. How had she ended up with yolk on her *neck*?

"Of course. I enjoy cooking for everyone. You know that."

"Can I go play now?" Ava wriggled to get free of his gentle clutch.

"Sure, Bear." He smiled and patted her back before she ran off to the living room to find her toys.

He stood and cleared the table, loading the dishwasher while his mom sipped her second cup of coffee.

By the time they'd finally made it out of Boston, it was nearly morning and the sun had been beginning to rise when they landed at O'Hare. Worst of all, the flight had been too turbulent for him to nap.

As they'd staggered off the plane, bleary-eyed, Coach Daniels had told them all to go home and rest up for the game tomorrow. Not a single guy had argued with him canceling morning skate. Not even their captain.

"I think you should take the day off today, Mom," Jamie said firmly. She'd managed to wrangle Ava this morning long enough so he could sleep for a couple of hours, and it was the least he could do to thank her for that and the big breakfast she'd whipped up. "I don't have practice today, so I'll take Ava to her lesson this afternoon."

She looked confused. "I always take her. You know I don't mind."

"I know but you deserve some time off."

"So do you. You are allowed to have a personal life, you know. It doesn't have to be all hockey and Ava. For goodness' sake, I don't know how you're ever going to date like this."

Jamie shrugged and ignored the dating comment. "I've been missing Ava. It'll be good to spend some time with her."

"Hey, far be it from me to keep you from spending time with your daughter," she said with a laugh. "I thought you might not want to spend more time with that cute little skater, though I find him delightful."

"What cute little skater?" Adam Walsh stepped into the kitchen, carrying the newspaper.

"Oh, Taylor Hollis. The one who teaches Ava's classes."

"Ahh. Yeah, I know who he is."

"Seems like our families keep bumping up against each other." Jamie slipped another plate into the dishwasher rack.

His dad grunted. "I suppose. I just wish Rick wasn't such a hard-headed asshole. How many times does a man need to apologize?"

"Oh sweetheart, I shouldn't have brought it up. I know how much it bothers you that no one talks about your career without mentioning that game."

Adam slapped the paper onto the counter. "No one ever brings up the stats. It's all about what I did to Hollis. And they never show the full clip where Tucker slams into me and shoves me into Hollis. The media gets the worst possible angle where I look like the asshole. Jesus Christ, I spent weeks feeling sick to my stomach until Rick Hollis recovered. And the league cleared me! But until Hollis lays it to rest, I'm the one the media blames."

He lowered his voice, scowling. "I know Ava likes that Taylor kid and I'd never badmouth him around her, but the son is just as bad. Dragging this feud on forever."

"Hey, he's not that bad," Jamie protested. "He apologized to me."

His mother gave him a perplexed frown. "For *what*?"

"For what he said about me at the Olympics."

"Four years too late," Adam muttered.

Jodi threw up her hands. "I think you *all* need to move past these grudges. It isn't good for anyone. Do you want Ava picking fights on the playground if she ends up in the same class as Taylor's kid someday?"

"Taylor is gay, Mom," Jamie pointed out.

"That doesn't mean he can't have kids."

"I know that. But he's single and he doesn't have any kids now, so it's pretty unlikely Ava and Taylor's hypothetical future kid would end up in school together."

"You know what I mean. And how do you know so much about him anyway?"

"Well, we're constantly being thrown together because of the skating stuff," he mumbled. "I mean, it's not like I can *avoid* him."

"You're the one who wanted to take Ava to her lessons today."

"I …" Jamie sighed. He couldn't argue that. "Look, I actually like Taylor, okay? He seems like a great guy. Ava loves him and he's doing a great job teaching the team—"

"Your edgework *has* looked really good lately," Adam said, his tone a little grudging.

"So, yeah, Mom, I agree. I think this feud needs to be put to rest. Forget the next generation. Taylor and I are getting along well, and I don't see any reason to hold any more grudges."

Getting along well was putting it mildly when they talked every day and were getting naked and sweaty together as often as they could manage, but Jamie couldn't exactly tell his parents that.

He didn't think they would care that he was attracted to a guy. When La Bouche had come out as bi two years ago his father had nodded and said, "Well, it's about time someone in the league was brave enough to do it."

His parents' neighbors were a gay married couple, and his mom was always talking about gardening with one of the guys. He and his husband came over regularly for dinner and stuff too.

But Jamie couldn't imagine his parents being cool with him hooking up with Taylor.

His *mom* might understand, but his dad … no, there was no way.

"Adam?" Jodi prompted.

"You're right, you're right," he grumbled. "It's a stupid feud. I just hate the way he ruined my reputation in the process. How long do I have to feel bad about something that wasn't my fault?"

Jodi sighed noisily because this was an ongoing argument that never went anywhere.

Jamie was equally tired of it, so he closed the dishwasher and turned to face his parents. "I'm going to go grab a shower. Ava and I will head home, and I'll take her to her lessons this afternoon."

"Okay," his mom said. "Whatever you want."

"I want you to get some time off," he said. "You take care of everyone. How about you spend a day taking care of yourself?"

She glanced down at her hands with a rueful little smile. "I *am* overdue for a mani/pedi."

"There you go," he said, kissing the top of her head. "Go have a spa day while I wrangle my kid."

The part he didn't add was that it was the perfect opportunity for him to see Taylor again.

CHAPTER TWELVE

Jamie ignored the flutter of nervous anticipation that swept through him as he stepped into the rink that afternoon.

He hadn't lied about wanting to spend more time with Ava, but the thought of seeing Taylor had definitely sweetened the deal.

Taylor was already on the ice, and Ava was impatient, so it took some wrangling for Jamie to get her skates on and her striped hat in place before he sent her off. When he turned to the bleachers, he was surprised to see Naomi Tremblay there.

Jamie took a seat beside her. "Hey, what are you doing here?"

"Andre is in the class." She pointed to her middle child, a six-year-old boy who was skating circles around the rest of the kids. "I could ask you the same thing, you know?"

"Just giving my mom a break," he said with a shrug. "I thought you were always off doing important bakery things."

She smiled and stretched out her long legs encased in snug leggings. "Sometimes those business things can wait. They're only this age for a little while."

Many of the wives and girlfriends of players were full-time moms—which had been Kara's role—or focused on charity work, but some like Naomi had demanding jobs along with parenting and trying to keep up with the grueling NHL schedule.

Naomi owned a bakery that made award-winning wedding cakes and other gourmet treats. Her bakery had provided cupcakes for various team events throughout the season and Jamie could testify that they deserved every single award out there.

He'd asked her once what she'd do if her husband ever got traded and she shrugged. "Open a second location, I guess," and he'd smiled, liking how fearless she was.

He liked both Naomi and Dean, and he'd been over to their house a handful of times for dinner, so he and Naomi fell into easy conversation while they watched the lesson, and Jamie tried not to get lost in thoughts of Taylor's long legs and the way they would look over his shoulders.

"He's great with the kids, isn't he?" Naomi said, and Jamie snapped back to attention, watching Taylor crouch down to talk to the kids one on one, laughing and joking with them, coaxing them to try something new, gently correcting them when they faltered.

"He really is," Jamie said, trying to keep the fond sigh out of his voice.

"You seem to be doing okay with his lessons."

Jamie groaned. "I am not cut out to be a figure skater, but yeah, it's been good."

"Dean comes home grumbling about it, but the videos are a huge hit."

"You've been watching, I take it?"

She chuckled, her brown skin crinkling at the corners of her dark eyes. "Hell yes. You better believe I will find any opportunity to chirp that man I can get."

Jamie laughed. "True love, huh?"

"Definitely," she said with a soft smile. "What about you? Are you dating?"

"Nah. Still a little gun-shy over the divorce, you know?"

She nodded sympathetically, familiar with the history.

"Well, when the time is right, you'll know it." She nodded toward Ava, who was working on a shaky spin under Taylor's watchful guidance. "Besides, it's more complicated with kids, I'd imagine."

"It is," Jamie agreed. "I went on a few dates last summer and spent most of the time thinking that I'd really like to find someone who loves my little girl."

Naomi's gaze softened. "Who wouldn't love her?"

"Well." Jamie laughed. "I have no idea. I think she's pretty great."

"She is."

"And obviously I'm pretty protective of who I bring around her. A lot of the women I've met … they're …"

"Not mom material?" Naomi said lightly.

He shrugged and propped his feet up on the bench in front of him, wrapping his arms around his knees, the stretch in his back and shoulders feeling good. "I'm sure they're perfectly lovely people when you get to know them, but I'm realistic that a lot of them have one thing in mind when they meet me."

"Sex?" Naomi's mouth quirked up in a little smile.

He chuckled. "Well, sure. But probably it's a status thing too. They're the women who want a certain lifestyle. Want to snag the pro player so they can brag about how much money and status he has and live the WAG lifestyle, you know?"

She let out a little snort. "Yeah, I know the type."

"I'm sure."

It was something they'd talked about before, the way Naomi felt like she didn't quite fit with the other wives and girlfriends. Most of them were younger and a whole lot whiter.

"Don't get me wrong," she said. "Some of them are amazing but others …"

He was silent, letting her continue at her own pace.

"Well, some of them are spoiled little brats who are in it for the lifestyle and won't stick it out through the hard times," she finished.

"Yeah." Jamie cleared his throat. "Well, my ex was one of the second kind."

She patted his arm, her smile sympathetic. "You're a great guy, Jamie. Dean and I are glad to have you for a friend. I hope you meet someone who deserves what you and Ava have to offer."

Without meaning to, his glance drifted up to Taylor who was lying on the ice while giggling kids clambered all over him. "I hope so too."

Taylor wasn't going to be that person, of course, no matter how much Jamie'd begun to wish it could be different. But he *did* hope he'd find someone like that. Someone kind and funny and down-to-earth. Someone who was great with kids. Someone who looked at Ava and saw what Jamie did—that she was priceless and deserved all the love in the world.

Jamie and Naomi sat in companionable silence for the rest of the lesson, watching Taylor guide the kids through a few more drills—something using cones that reminded Jamie a lot of hockey lessons—and Jamie felt the first stirrings of hope that maybe he would meet someone again.

What he had with Taylor was great in the meantime. But someday he wanted *more.*

When class was over, Ava skated over to him, cheeks flushed and eyes sparkling, her hat askew and her curls tangled.

He helped her out of her skates and got her boots on, then took off her hat. "Bear, your hair is a little wild. You want me to put it in a braid?"

"Okay," she said happily, turning her back to him. "Did you see me skate?"

"Of course I did! You're doing great."

"Some of the other kids are better than me." She sounded a little sad and he pressed a kiss to the top of her head, gently finger combing through the worst of the tangles.

"Well, some of the skaters on my team are better than me." He fished a bright pink elastic out of his coat pocket. He'd learned to carry them everywhere he went, and they sometimes came in handy for wrangling electronics cords. The guys liked to tease him about it, but he'd noticed a couple of the other dads on the team doing the same thing. "But it doesn't mean I'm not good at it. Or that I'm not an important part of the team."

"Oh. That's true."

"It's okay to want to get better," he said, carefully separating her hair into three sections. He wasn't great at braiding but he'd watched a bunch of YouTube tutorials recently. "But you shouldn't feel bad if you aren't there yet. We all get places in our own time."

"I'll keep trying," she promised, and Jamie smiled, weaving the strands of hair across each other before securing the end. A little clumsy still, but there were fewer bumps than there used to be.

"That's all I can ask."

When he was done, Ava turned to face him. "I think we should get ice cream after this. I tried really hard today."

Jamie laughed and swooped Ava up into his arms. "Oh yeah? 'Cause I thought it was January. That's too cold for ice cream!"

Ava giggled. "It's *never* too cold for ice cream, Daddy!"

"Hmm." He narrowed his eyes at her playfully. "Are you sure?"

"That's what Grandpa says."

Jamie laughed. That *was* what his dad said. "Well, if that's what Grandpa says, I guess we can't argue with it."

"Oh my God, they're cute," Naomi Tremblay muttered, staring at Jamie Walsh and his daughter. "If I weren't a happily married woman …"

Taylor chuckled, still swooning a little at the hair-braiding and the sweet encouragement he'd been shamelessly eavesdropping on. "I hear you. Not that I'm married but … you know."

"Ahh, well." She grinned at him and winked. "At least we can watch, even if we can't touch."

Oh, but she had no idea Taylor *could* touch. Which he really shouldn't think about too much when he wore leggings this snug.

Ava ran over to talk to Naomi's son Andre. Jamie ambled over a little more slowly. Naomi's phone rang and she turned away, lifting her phone to her ear, speaking in a businesslike tone.

"Jamie. Hi," Taylor said, more breathlessly than he'd intended.

"Hey." Jamie gave him a slow smile. "How are you?"

"Surprised to see you here. It's usually Jodi or your—uhm, Ava's mom here."

"We didn't have practice today since we got in so late, and I thought my mom could use the day off."

"Aww, that's nice of you."

Taylor's skin buzzed with a jittery awareness of Jamie standing close enough he could smell his cologne. He looked a little tired—not a surprise since he probably hadn't gotten much sleep—but so good.

He wore gray sweatpants—the bastard, he had to know what that made Taylor think of—and a hoodie under a warm winter coat. An Otters stocking cap hung half out of his pocket and his hair was a little disheveled.

It made Taylor want to run his fingers through it, settling the thick golden waves into place. He thought Jamie would like being touched like that. It was easy to picture him tipping his head back as Taylor gently rubbed his dull fingernails into his scalp.

Jamie always looked so big and warm, and Taylor could picture him turning soft and lazy if Taylor pampered him that way. His face would go slack and content, his lips parting, his eyes closing as he pushed up against the touch.

They stared at each other for a moment, the hum of the few remaining parents and kids dropping to a low buzz in the background.

Taylor hesitated. "I should—"

"Andre, we need to go, sweetie. Thanks for the lesson, Taylor."

Taylor and Naomi spoke at the same time and Taylor shook himself out of his stupor, saying goodbye to her and praising Andre, who beamed at him. Now *that* was a kid with natural talent.

Taylor gave Jamie and Ava a distracted wave and mumbled something about needing to grab his bag and coat while he fled to the public locker room.

The whole time, his head spun at the thought of kissing Jamie again, of feeling his big hands sliding up and down his back and holding him close. God. Why had Jamie come today?

It was too distracting to have him around. It made Taylor forget how he was supposed to behave.

On the way out of the rink, he sputtered out a goodbye to another girl in his class and her mom, then walked through the doors, jamming his warm wooly hat with the pom-pom on over his ears because whatever Ava said about it never being too cold for ice cream, it was freezing right now. The temps had dropped significantly overnight, and he'd had to scrape heavy frost off his car this morning and leave it running for fifteen minutes before he could go anywhere.

One of these days, when Taylor had more money, he'd get a new car with heated seats and remote start and all of those little luxuries he kept having to delay so he could get the bills paid.

He was halfway across the parking lot when something slammed into his side. He looked down to see Ava hugging his legs.

"Taylor! You should come for ice cream with us!"

"Ava Grace Walsh, don't you ever run away from me like that in the parking lot again!" Jamie hollered, jogging toward Taylor and Ava.

She ducked and pressed her face against Taylor's hip like she was hiding.

Taylor glanced around to be sure there weren't any cars barreling down on them before he gently disentangled Ava. When he saw her big tear-filled eyes, he crouched down and gently patted her back.

"Hey. You're okay. Your dad just got worried about you getting hurt," he said gently.

Jamie reached them and dropped into a crouch too. "Hey, what's going on, Bear?" His voice had gone soft and concerned.

"You're mad at me." Her lip quivered.

"Ava, no," Jamie said gently. "Taylor was right, I was scared something bad would happen to you. Why did you take off like that?"

"I was asking Taylor if he wanted to have ice cream with us."

Jamie sucked in a deep breath and closed his eyes for a moment, but Taylor didn't think it had anything to do with the invitation. He was trying to keep his composure after a fright. When he was calm, he looked her in the eye. "Well, I need you to listen to me now, okay? I'm not mad. But I was very, very scared and I need you to understand why."

She nodded.

"There are a lot of cars around here. People drive fast and they might not see you until it's too late. You know we've talked about this before."

"I know."

"And you have to be even more careful in the winter. People can't always stop their car as fast. Do you understand?"

"I think so."

"What are you going to do differently next time?"

She frowned. "Um, not run away?"

"Yes. What else?"

"I don't know." She scuffed the dirty snow under her boot.

"Okay. You're going to ask me first. I would have been happy to walk back with you to talk to Taylor. Do you understand?"

"Yep. I've gotta ask first," she repeated, and Jamie nodded, letting out a relieved sigh.

"Okay, Bear." He gently tugged her hat down to cover her ears. "Remember, I'm not mad. I just want to keep you safe."

"Can I have a hug?"

"Always."

She wrapped her arms around Jamie and clung to him for a moment and dear God, if Taylor could die from cuteness this would definitely do it.

Damn it, Charlie was right. DILF-y guys being great dads were absolutely Taylor's weakness.

Jamie pressed a kiss to Ava's hair for a brief second before he met Taylor's gaze. The weary eye roll he shot Taylor conveyed so much.

"Okay, Bear, how about we try this again?" he said after he drew back. "Do you have something you want to ask Taylor?"

"Oh!" She perked up immediately, turning in Jamie's arms and Taylor realized they were both still crouched down. "Wanna go get ice cream with us, Taylor?"

He straightened and Jamie did too. Taylor raised an eyebrow at him, asking if he was okay with the invitation. Jamie gave him a brief nod.

"I don't know," Taylor joked to Ava. "It is pretty cold out!"

Ava tugged at his jacket, pulling on him until he bent down to her level again. "That's why you ask for hot fudge and a hot chocolate," she whispered—not very quietly—and Taylor stifled a laugh. "That's what I do."

"Oh, yeah?" he said, smiling down at her. "That sounds like a great plan."

"If you're busy, you don't have to come. Ava will understand," Jamie said, with a look and tone that told him that it was a message to Ava more than him.

"I actually don't have anywhere I *have* to be," Taylor admitted. "No more lessons today and Charlie works late, so I was just planning a quiet evening in."

"Well, Scoops has pretty great ice cream. Seems worth it."

"Hmm. I'm not sure that's enough." Taylor crossed his arms. "Can I get hot fudge and hot chocolate for me and my friend here?"

Ava giggled. "Please, Daddy!"

Jamie smirked at Taylor and shook his head. "I think you're a bad influence, Taylor."

"Me?" Taylor sputtered. "She was the one who suggested it."

"You're both bad influences," Jamie said with a laugh. "Fine. Hot fudge and chocolate for both of you."

"Yay!" Ava jumped up and down, and Taylor offered her a high five.

"C'mon," Jamie said with a laugh. "Let's go."

"Do you want me to meet you there or …?"

"Nah." Jamie shrugged. "We'll just take my vehicle. It's the Range Rover over there."

Taylor hesitated, not sure if they should really be seen together like that, but what were people going to think if they saw them together? It was no secret that Taylor was working with the team and the media people had even done a little feature on Taylor's beginners lessons for kids.

It wasn't like Jamie was the kind of guy who had rumors going around about his sexuality. No one would read anything into it.

Taylor must have paused too long though, because Jamie hesitated. "You can drive separately if you want. Are you familiar with Scoops? It's a few blocks over and—"

"I've been there before but yeah, it's fine," Taylor said with a smile. "I can ride with you if you'll give me a ride back here."

Jamie laughed and nudged his shoulder. "No, I'll make you walk all that way in twenty-degree weather."

"Rude," Taylor teased as they approached the vehicle and Jamie unlocked it with a beep. It was already running, probably warm and toasty inside.

Jamie opened the door for Ava, and she quickly scrambled into the back seat of the black SUV. "Need help getting buckled up?" he asked.

She shook her head. "Nope. I've got it!"

"Good job," Jamie said after she was done.

He shut the door and turned to Taylor.

"I hope you don't feel pressured into this," he said with a little frown. "If you had other plans or …"

"Nope. Not at all. I'm looking forward to that sundae absolutely drenched in hot fudge and the nice big mug of hot chocolate that you promised me though."

Jamie laughed. "You really are a bad influence. You're gonna have to help me get her to bed if she's bouncing off the walls hyped up on sugar tonight."

Taylor grinned and leaned in. "Sure. But only if you promise to put *me* to bed if I'm all hyped up on sugar too."

He batted his lashes and turned to reach for the door handle, but not before he heard Jamie's low, muttered, "definitely a bad influence."

Jamie stretched his legs, trying not to stare at the sight of Taylor daintily eating his hot fudge sundae. He hadn't actually gotten a hot chocolate but Ava had offered him a couple of sips of hers.

She'd been chatty and giggly since they made it to Scoops, dancing around both of them well before she got any sugar in her, so Jamie was pretty sure she was just hyped up about having both of them there with her.

She wore at least half of the hot fudge from her sundae all over her face and hands and was talking at top speed about something Jamie should probably be paying more attention to. But all he could see was Taylor's pink tongue as he dragged it across his spoon.

Jamie was hyper-aware of the way their feet kept bumping under the table and the sound of Taylor's laugh while he listened intently to Ava's chatter.

She collapsed into a fit of giggles, leaning against Taylor's arm, and Taylor glanced up and smiled at Jamie, his expression bright and happy before he turned back to Ava, not missing a beat.

Jamie's scoop of black raspberry chocolate chunk and Taylor's two scoops of dark chocolate sea salt caramel with hot fudge were long gone by the time Ava finally admitted defeat on her birthday cake ice cream topped with hot fudge and whipped cream.

She hadn't quite finished but Taylor smiled at her as she pushed her bowl away. "That's okay. It's important to listen to our tummies when they tell us we're hungry or full. I'm sure your dad will take you here again."

"Of course." Jamie reached for a napkin to wipe Ava's face but Taylor was already there, wetting the corner of it in the glass of water he'd ordered.

"Hands, please," he said, and Ava held them out dutifully, letting him wipe them clean. "May I get your face?"

She squirmed a little as Taylor gently dabbed at her face, like she did with Jamie, but Jamie was struck by how Taylor was with Ava. Taylor liked kids and he was a great teacher, but this one-on-one stuff was often harder.

Taylor had been so good with her when she'd darted across the parking lot, talking calmly to her, backing up Jamie when he'd freaked out. Taylor was great at listening to Ava, giving her his full attention.

He was patient and sweet and someday he was going to make a fantastic parent. Not with Jamie, unfortunately. Even if Taylor wanted it at this age, their families would never accept it, but damn did Jamie feel another traitorous flutter of how it *could* be if the situation was different.

"Okay," Jamie said, clearing his throat when the word came out a little rougher than planned. "Shall we head out?"

Taylor nodded and stood, but Ava was drooping as she got out of her chair and struggled into her outerwear.

"Can you carry me?" she whined. "I'm tired."

Jamie groaned, because his shoulder was killing him after a nasty check from Boston's defense last night, but Taylor finished wrapping his scarf around his neck, and held out his arms. "How about a ride from me?"

"Yay!" she said, going easily into his arms.

Jamie held the door for them, and he resisted the sudden urge to place his hand on Taylor's back and lean in for a soft, quick kiss. It was something he'd done a thousand times with Kara, but he'd never wanted that with a man before.

And yet, with Ava bundled in Taylor's arms, snug and sleepy as she laid her head on his shoulder, Jamie allowed himself to *want* that public closeness.

He wasn't dating Taylor—he couldn't—but damn, in that moment, he was genuinely disappointed.

This quick glimpse of what it could be like kept growing more tempting.

They were all quiet as they walked toward the parking lot and Taylor's elbow brushed Jamie's arm every so often. It was impossible to feel much through the layers they wore but when a group of older kids walked by, Jamie used the excuse to gently crowd closer to him.

Taylor shot him a little smile and despite the icy wind, his look was warm and filled with something Jamie couldn't identify.

"This was fun," Taylor said softly as they approached the vehicle. "Thank you for letting me tag along."

"I'm glad you came." Jamie meant every word of it, surprised but pleased what a nice afternoon it had been. It had been so long since he'd hung out with anyone but his parents or the team, and even then it had been his brother and his family, visiting from California.

Ava let out a tired little sigh and with a guilty start, Jamie remembered she was still there, tucked in Taylor's careful grip. For a moment, Jamie had forgotten it wasn't just him and Taylor out together.

Once Ava was secured in the Range Rover, Jamie shut the door. "So, tonight I've got Ava. Are you free tomorrow? I've got a game, but if you'd be up for some company after that …"

"Yes," Taylor said without hesitating. "I'd like that."

Jamie gave him a slow smile, relieved. "That's great to hear. Sorry this week's been so crazy."

Taylor shrugged. "I knew what I was getting into."

"I know." Jamie stuffed his hands in his pockets. "We're coming up on the bye week pretty soon though. Murphy and Theriault are heading to All-Star Weekend and the Olympics, but the rest of us will have a nice chunk of time off during that."

"Not going anywhere?" Taylor asked with a tilt of his head. "I know some guys jet off to somewhere warm."

"Nah, I haven't done that in years." Not since Ava was born. Once she was a little older, he might take her to Disney World or something. Although next year she'd be in kindergarten, and he'd have to figure out a way to get his schedule and her school calendar to work. "I was thinking we could maybe, uh, hang out a little bit more then."

Taylor looked surprised, but he nodded. "Sure, I'll take a look at when I have lessons scheduled."

The wind came up, whipping around the car and Taylor shivered.

"Shit, you're cold. Let's get you in where it's warm." Jamie held the passenger-side door for Taylor, who shot him a surprised but pleased smile.

Jamie carefully closed the door, then jogged around to get in the driver's seat. "Brr, it's cold out there."

"You're so silly, Daddy," Ava sleepily said.

Jamie chuckled and caught a glimpse of Taylor's sweet smile.

Yeah, Jamie really was.

Silly for feeling soft over a guy who could never be anything but casual.

"Okay, let's get you back to your car," Jamie said, cranking up the heat and making sure the seat warmers were on.

"Getting me *out* of this vehicle is going to take some work." Taylor made a contented little sound, snuggling into the warmth. "God, I would *kill* for seat warmers and a remote start."

"I bet. I am pretty spoiled."

They rode the rest of the way back to the rink in silence, Ava's quiet little snores in the backseat a comforting soundtrack. Taylor quietly pointed out his car and Jamie pulled up beside it.

"Thanks for the ride!" Taylor whispered. "And for the ice cream."

"It was my pleasure."

"See you tomorrow night?"

"Yeah. Definitely." Jamie glanced at Taylor's car, which was covered in a thin layer of snow. The sun had gone behind the clouds and the wind was up, making the person on the nearby sidewalk hunch into their coat. "Hey, give me your keys."

"What?" Taylor froze mid-reach, fingers inches from the bag he'd stashed at his feet.

"I'll warm your car up for you. You stay here."

Taylor's eyes got big, and he blinked at Jamie a moment before rummaging around in the bag. He held out a set of keys but when Jamie closed a hand around them, he held on.

"You don't have to—"

"I know." Jamie gently tugged until Taylor finally let go. "But I want to."

Jamie got out of the SUV before Taylor could argue again.

It didn't take long to start the car or scrape the snow from the windows, but his fingers were pretty icy by the time he slipped back in the driver's seat of his vehicle. Taylor was looking at him like he'd done something truly bizarre, like strip all his clothes off and roll around in the snow.

"Thank you," he said faintly, a little furrow between his brows.

Jamie shrugged and rubbed his hands together, holding them near the heater blasting out hot air. "It's no big deal. We can hang out here for a bit while your car has time to heat up."

"You really didn't have to—"

"I *know*. But you made Ava's day. This is the least I can do."

Taylor held his gaze for a few heartbeats before he nodded. "Thank you," he whispered. "That was really sweet."

CHAPTER THIRTEEN

"Hey, can I talk to you for a sec?" Coach Tate said as Jamie walked down the hall after morning practice the following day.

"Sure, Coach."

A little concerned but not overly worried, Jamie followed him into his office and closed the door most of the way. "This okay?"

"Yep. And you're not in any trouble." Tate smiled as Jamie took a seat. "I just wanted to touch base with you. I know that we're playing Chicago tonight and that might be … a little difficult for you."

Jamie nodded. Obviously, everyone in the organization knew about the messy final season he'd had with the Windstorm and Jamie had even discussed his feelings about his ex-wife and his former linemate when he joined the team. But he'd been avoiding thinking too much about playing against Boyd tonight.

"You're in the lineup, but if you want to sit this game out, we'll understand."

"If I'm a healthy scratch, people are going to figure it out."

"Your shoulder has been bugging you, right? We'll say it was a last-minute decision to rest you and—"

"No. I appreciate that, but unless you don't think I should play, I'm going to do it." He'd look like more of a coward if he refused to face Boyd on the ice tonight.

"I don't want you out there with your head a mess if we can avoid it."

"Look, I'm no fighter. The few tussles I've gotten into on the ice over the years can't even be called fights."

"No. You're not Gabriel," Tate said, his lips twitching at the corners a little.

"Hey, he did great the other night against Boston. He didn't let Crawford get under his skin at all."

"He handled it perfectly." Tate's smile was soft. "He knows no one—not even a piece of shit like Luke Crawford—is worth risking what he has here."

"With you?"

"With the team." Tate cleared his throat. "But yes, also with me."

"This team is important to me too. I'm doing well and—"

"Hey, no one is disputing that," Tate said gently, leaning back in his chair, lacing his fingers together behind his head. "You're a valuable member of our lineup and you've contributed a lot already this season. But we—Daniels and I—get that what happened between you and your linemate was very personal. It violates every bond players create and no one would think less of you if you felt like it'll impact your performance tonight."

"I want to play." Jamie lifted his chin. "I'll handle it."

"If you're sure."

"I'm sure."

Jamie *had* been sure when he left the rink, but as the bus approached Chicago's arena that evening, he felt like he might throw up the chicken and pasta he'd eaten for his pre-game meal.

He hadn't napped that afternoon—just stared at the ceiling of his bedroom— and now there was a jittery feeling in his body he couldn't shake.

It was surreal being in the building where he'd made his NHL debut. With the team he'd hoped to spend his entire career with.

"Hey, where are you going?" Hartinger said, nudging him to the right when he tried to turn left. "Visitors' locker room is this way, dude."

"Right." Jamie laughed awkwardly. "I knew that."

"Easy to get turned around. I swear, all of these places look alike," Hartinger said with a smile, though something in his gaze told Jamie he knew it was more than a simple mix-up.

"Yeah."

But Jamie knew every inch of this building. He knew the way the door handle stuck on the equipment room and recognized the squeak of a laundry cart someone pushed past them.

Jamie's chest tightened at the smell—ice and sweat mostly, but that faint hint of something else that was unique to Chicago's arena—nostalgia and pain mingling within him.

The visitors' locker room here looked nothing like the players' dressing room, but it still brought up memories of Jamie's final day with the team for locker clean-out and exit interviews with the media.

The team hadn't made it to the playoffs. No big surprise when they were fractured right down the middle.

Jamie swallowed hard, remembering the bland answers he'd given the press about their season, knowing every one of them had heard the rumors about his ex-wife and his linemate.

He had never officially confirmed or denied anything, but persistent fans put together the pieces after he and Kara had separated and some nosy fan had snapped pictures of her out on a date with Boyd, their arms around each other, the embrace too heated to be anything but sexual.

Jerkily, he walked over to his stall and took a seat, assaulted with memories.

That day, the mood had been unnaturally quiet and filled with nervous tension. Jamie had haphazardly thrown things in his bag, the silence thick and oppressive. His teammates had tried to approach him, but he'd shut everyone down.

Had they known? Had Boyd confessed that he was falling for Kara to anyone? Had one of Jamie's teammates known that two of the most important people in his life had betrayed him and kept silent?

Fearing *that* made his throat thick with grief and anger.

Had word spread throughout the team?

Maybe not to all of them, not the call-ups, but enough. The core guys. The ones who should have had his back. Had they known something was up between Boyd and Kara?

His best friend had betrayed him. His wife had betrayed him. How could he trust anyone else?

Tonight, Jamie went through his routine on autopilot, laughing on the outside when Hartinger nearly took out one of their social media people with a stray soccer ball during two-touch. Inside, raw and flayed open from never-healed wounds.

Later, settling his pads into place like armor, as if that would somehow keep the hurt from leaking out.

Warmups were hell.

Jamie could feel the suffocating pressure of the crowd, the weight of their judgment and expectations. It was worse seeing the people in the crowd holding up signs with his name or number. Wearing his jersey.

The loyalty and support were a double-edged sword, appreciated but too much when he only wanted to hide.

It would be better if they'd forgotten him. He'd tried to forget how it had felt to leave his former team, head down, shame burning inside him.

Jamie pointedly ignored his former teammates as they skated on the other side of the blue line. A few hovered near the edges, hoping for a chance to talk, but Jamie hugged the boards near the Otters' net, flipping pucks over the glass to kids, their joy the only thing keeping him from skating off the ice and leaving the arena.

"You sure you want to do this?" Murphy asked later as they waited in the tunnel, ready to go out on the ice for the national anthem.

"I'm sure," Jamie insisted, though he didn't believe it anymore.

He played whenever his line was up, muscle memory enough to keep him going. He didn't play well, but he contributed enough that no one called him out on it.

Jamie was dimly aware of the curious, concerned looks from his teammates on the bench, but he couldn't even feel Truro's thigh pressed against him on one side or Cooper's elbow digging into his ribs on the other.

"I'm fine, I'm fine," Jamie told Daniels after the first period, and he'd given him a sharp, searching glance, then nodded.

"I miss you, Jamers," one of his former D-men said as they passed by each other on the ice, and Jamie looked past him and focused on the puck, because if he let himself think about it, if he let himself wish things had gone down differently at the end, he'd lose it.

He got an assist on a goal that put the Otters ahead at the end of the second period. He joined in the celly, his new teammates enthusiastically hugging him and Keegan Truro in celebration, but his heart wasn't in it.

Jamie was raw and numb at once, gaze lowered in the locker room while he scarfed a power bar that tasted like dust in his mouth, downing the too-sweet electrolyte drink to wash away the lump in his throat.

He kept reminding himself the game was almost over, and he wasn't at all prepared for the moment Boyd chased after him and crowded him up against the boards.

"I'm sorry, man," he said lowly as they battled for the puck, Tremblay and another Chicago player he didn't recognize pressing in close.

The pressure built as Jamie was physically and mentally crowded in, unable to escape.

Jamie couldn't look up and see the brown eyes of his former best friend, so he fought harder, getting a good jab with his elbow into Boyd's ribs.

"Don't." His voice was strangled, his emotions bleeding onto the ice like he'd been sliced by a skate. "Just … don't. I don't want your apologies. Least of all *here*."

"You won't answer my calls." Boyd sounded a little breathless, his stick smacking against Jamie's as he tried to dig the puck away. "You've been avoiding me for a fucking year, man."

"Damn right." Jamie glared down at the ice, carved up and scuffed by their blades. "You're still with her, so what the fuck are you doing saying you're sorry? It doesn't mean shit."

Something pressed at his tongue, but he couldn't say if it was grief or anger or both.

"C'mon, break it up, guys." Tremblay was there, wedging a shoulder between them, a glove pressed to Boyd's chest. "This isn't the place for it."

Jamie got the puck and shot away from the boards, smacking it toward the net, heedless of if there was a clear lane for shooting. The rubber pinged off the pipe, ricocheting before being swept away by one of Chicago's new forwards.

My replacement, Jamie thought dully, skating toward the bench for the line change.

He heard the crowd chanting something, but he had no idea what they were saying. He had no idea what the score was or how many minutes were left in the period.

There was only Boyd's voice repeating, 'I'm sorry.'

When they left the ice—a win in their pocket, no thanks to him—Jamie calmly walked down the tunnel. It wasn't until he was well away from view of the cameras that he crashed his stick against the cinderblock wall, smashing and smashing until it splintered into a thousand little pieces.

His legs went out from under him, and he dropped down, head bowed.

Someone sat beside him, and it wasn't until he heard the murmur of French that he knew it was Theriault.

Jamie leaned against him a moment, shoulders shaking with dry-eyed grief and anger.

Leaving the arena. Your place or mine?

Taylor blinked at the short-and-to-the-point message from Jamie. He'd never been so abrupt before, but maybe he was using voice to text or something.

Yours, unless you want to risk Charlie walking in on us.

My place is fine. See you in forty?

Taylor glanced at the clock. ***Yeah, I can do that.***

There was no response.

Unease prickled the back of Taylor's neck as he drove to Jamie's house. Was that from the sweet gesture yesterday or tonight's brusqueness? He wasn't sure.

Jamie's smile was tight when he opened the door. "Hey." He pressed a dry kiss to Taylor's cheek, then took his coat.

"How was the game?" Taylor asked, wondering if maybe they'd lost.

"We won." He didn't sound very happy about that. "Did you watch?"

"No. I had dinner with friends. I got home a few minutes before you texted me."

"Good." Jamie leaned in and pressed a hard kiss to his lips. His mouth was needy and demanding and he immediately slid his hands under Taylor's sweater, his grip tight and desperate.

Something was off but it was difficult to think when Jamie crowded Taylor back against the door and mouthed at his neck.

When Jamie bit roughly, Taylor let out a gasp. He shivered, little sparks racing through his blood at the sting and the pressure of Jamie's knee between his legs, nudging at his cock. All he wanted to do was ride his thigh until he shot messily in his pants.

"Bedroom?" Taylor finally gasped. Jamie let out a grunt but stepped back. His shoulders were tight as Taylor followed him to the room, but before Taylor could ask to slow down, Jamie pulled off his shirt.

Taylor's mouth went dry at the sight of all that beautiful lean muscle. Jamie stared him in the eye as he hooked his thumbs into the elastic of his sweats, dragging them down to show that he was bare beneath, hard for him.

"Fuck, Jamie."

Taylor's head spun as Jamie went after Taylor's clothes, boxing him against the bed when they were both naked.

Jamie roamed his hands across Taylor's body, his dick hard against Taylor's hip while they kissed messily, Taylor rising a little on his toes to reach his lips. Jamie reached down to grasp Taylor's ass, kneading the muscles before skimming between. The dry brush of his finger across Taylor's hole a shivery sort of pleasure that made Taylor buck against him, the tip of his cock over-sensitive when it dragged across the sparse hair on Jamie's thigh.

"Can I fuck you?" Jamie panted against his neck, teeth scraping against the skin, sending a shudder down Taylor's spine that lit up his nerves until he felt equally frantic.

"Yeah, yeah." Taylor gripped his biceps. "I want it, Jamie."

Taylor's feet left the floor and he out a startled squawk when the world tilted. He flew through the air to land on the mattress, bouncing once, panting as he stared up at Jamie.

Jamie hesitated; expression conflicted as he stared down at Taylor. There was something heated and hungry in his eyes though and Taylor swallowed hard. He didn't know what Jamie needed or why he seemed so off, but if he was desperate to get away from whatever was going on in his head, Taylor could give it to him.

"Fuck me, Jamie," he coaxed, parting his legs.

The noise Jamie let out was rough and needy. He fumbled for something on the bed beside him. Taylor's heart hammered at the slick pressure against his entrance. Jamie worked fast, maybe a little too fast, but the feel of his thick fingers spreading him open was too good to protest.

Jamie stared down at him, gaze unusually serious, hair hanging in his eyes as he loomed over Taylor. Taylor ran his hand up and down Jamie's braced arm, encouraging him with the roll of his hips and not even attempting to hide the desperate little groans that welled up in his throat.

"C'mon, Jamie," Taylor begged, and Jamie straightened, immediately snatching a condom from the nightstand. His gaze never left Taylor's while he ripped the wrapper open with his teeth, then spat it away. His movements were rough and jerky as he rolled the latex on.

Jamie let out a low growl and dragged him to the edge of the mattress. Taylor's breath caught when Jamie roughly pushed one leg up over his shoulders, nudging against him with his cock.

"You ready?" Jamie asked, voice ragged, and Taylor nodded, even though Jamie hadn't added any more lube.

It burned a little as Jamie worked his way inside, but that was good, too and Taylor threw his head back when Jamie was all the way in.

He only paused a moment before he pulled out partway, then snapped his hips forward, driving into Taylor with a thrust that pulled a harsh, punched-out gasp from Taylor's lungs. Jamie's gaze drilled into Taylor's, checking to make sure he was okay, so Taylor nodded and tilted his hips, encouraging him.

Jamie thrust into him again, moving with a quick, steady pace that stole the breath from Taylor's body and left him unable to do anything but hang on to the sheets. Jamie's hands bit into his thighs, one hand low and hooked around Taylor's hip, the other pressing his knee against his midsection.

Words seemed unnecessary, panted breaths and desperate groans enough as Jamie fucked him like a man possessed. His abs flexed, sweat slicking wherever their bodies touched and dampening his golden hair into darker waves.

Jamie's ragged breath and the slap of their bodies colliding filled the air. Taylor let out a desperate moan when Jamie spat in his palm, then wrapped his hand around Taylor's cock to stroke him.

"Are you close?" he growled.

"Harder," Taylor begged.

Jamie let go of Taylor's cock to press both of his legs back until his knees were up near his ears, his hamstrings protesting a little as Jamie bent him in half.

Taylor would be sore tomorrow but what did it matter when Jamie was drilling into him, the angle hitting him perfectly and making heat flare. It burned through Taylor like wildfire, and he panted Jamie's name, pleading for more, urging him on, need roiling in his belly until his whole body seized tight.

Taylor shouted his release, eyes closing as the pleasure took over, Jamie's hard thrusts just this side of painful before he came too. His groan was low and almost agonized, wrung from his lips like something reluctantly given.

Jamie slumped over Taylor for a moment before Taylor gently slapped at his shoulder, his weight too heavy for that position, compressing his lungs.

Jamie's touch was gentle as he lowered Taylor's legs, his expression almost ashamed as he rubbed Taylor's thighs in what felt like apology. He didn't speak as he eased out. He stripped off the condom, tossed it in the trash, then turned and disappeared into the bathroom.

Taylor lay there panting, his release cooling on his belly while he waited for Jamie to come back. Instead, the shower turned on.

"Well, okay," Taylor muttered with a frown. Ordinarily, he would have joined Jamie but it seemed like tonight he needed the space. Taylor sat up and reached for the tissues on the nightstand. He mopped up the mess they'd made, tossed the ruined condom wrapper, and put away the lube.

But then he stilled, unsure of what he was supposed to do now.

Jamie was clearly going through something. Something to do with his ex, maybe, but Taylor had no idea what would have triggered it.

Taylor didn't mind the rough sex. It had been hot, but the aftermath left him feeling off-kilter and worried that he'd done something wrong. He hesitated, torn between putting his clothes on and leaving or staying to find out what was going on.

Because something clearly was. This wasn't the Jamie who'd sweetly smiled at him over Ava's head yesterday as they walked to his Range Rover. This wasn't the guy who'd scraped the snow off his windshield, his blue eyes soft.

And then Taylor heard the sobs. There were just a few rough bitten-off noises under the rush of the water, but they were enough to make Taylor's heart ache. He wanted nothing more than to go in and soothe Jamie, but he didn't think it would be welcome.

He waited, shivering a little in the cool bedroom until Jamie stepped through the bathroom door with a towel wrapped around his hips, unable to hide the surprise on his face when he saw Taylor was still there.

Which … *ouch*.

"Uh, hey," Jamie said, raking a hand through his hair. "You can shower now, if you want."

"I'm okay," Taylor said, swallowing hard, unsure of what came next.

Jamie walked over to the dresser and pulled out a long-sleeve tee and a pair of shorts, dressing quickly. He tossed the towel in the hamper in the corner of the room, then turned to face the bed.

Taylor rose to his knees, then crawled over to the edge of the mattress, as close as he thought Jamie could handle. "Are you okay?"

Jamie's shoulders slumped, his expression crumpling. "No."

Taylor sat back on his heels, naked and cold, but worried. Earlier, he'd noticed Jamie's shoulder was wrapped in Kinesio tape from the trainers and it was still in place. "Are you in pain from the game or …"

"No, it's not that." Jamie sat heavily on the bed beside Taylor, head hung low. "The game did fuck with my head tonight though."

Taylor risked reaching out to run a hand across Jamie's back. He shuddered but he didn't shrug Taylor off.

"What happened?"

Jamie glanced over at him. "Are you sure you want to hear it?"

"If you want to share. I'm a pretty good listener."

Jamie studied his face for a long time before he nodded. "Okay."

Taylor shivered, too obvious to hide, and a worried frown crossed Jamie's drawn expression.

"Shit. You're cold."

Taylor shifted, intending to reach for his clothes but Jamie beat him to it, holding out Taylor's underwear and a shirt.

Not any shirt, Taylor realized as he dragged it on. *Jamie's.*

It was hugely baggy on him and smelled of Jamie's cologne and unfamiliar soap but it had *Walsh* across the back and the Otters' logo on the front.

Taylor wasn't sure what *that* meant, especially after Jamie's hot and cold behavior, but he settled on the bed against the headboard, waiting expectantly for Jamie's story.

Whatever it was Jamie was working through right now, Taylor knew it wasn't good.

CHAPTER FOURTEEN

Jamie stretched out on the bed on his right side, at an angle to Taylor. He felt cleaned out after the tears he'd let loose in the shower, tired but more settled.

He liked how small and soft Taylor appeared inside his shirt. Jamie hadn't meant to grab it, but it looked good on him.

He'd almost canceled on Taylor tonight, but he'd felt this frantic, clawing sensation inside him and caved into the urge to feel Taylor's skin against his.

The sex had unsettled him though, made him wonder what kind of man he was now that he could see the red marks on Taylor's thighs from his tight grip. He gently skimmed his fingers across the marks in apology but frowned when it made goosebumps pop up on Taylor's skin and a shiver wrack his body.

Jamie tugged a blanket up, draping it over Taylor's bare legs.

If Jamie had been at Taylor's place tonight, he might have left after they fucked. He'd half expected Taylor to leave on his own, but he hadn't and now Jamie wasn't sure if he was relieved he was still here or not.

Jamie had shoved down every single scrap of pain last year and now it bubbled out, forced loose by being on the ice with Boyd again, skating against his former team in the arena where he'd won a Cup with them. He dreaded the thought of dredging all of this up again, especially when he was still so raw from earlier.

Taylor deserved his honesty though, so Jamie dragged in a breath, starting at the beginning.

"After I left college and the NHL seemed uninterested in me, I played for a few seasons in Minnesota on a one-way AHL contract. I eventually got some interest from a Swedish team, and I signed a two-year deal with them."

Taylor nodded; his brows drawn together in a perplexed frown.

"I don't know if I was a late developer or finally got the right coach, but my game got substantially better. The Chicago Windstorm were interested in me. They were who my dad had played for, so when they reached out, I was thrilled. Their roster was full, so I was skating with their AHL affiliate. I was only there for a few months when the Windstorm hit a rough patch. They lost a lot of guys all at once, a couple of players waived, some weird fluke injuries … so I ended up playing with them for a while. And I did well."

Jamie cleared his throat. "I fucking loved that team. The guys were great, and we were winning a lot. My linemate was this dude named Boyd Marsh. He was … it was like … instant friendship. Brotherhood, I thought. We clicked immediately. On the ice we were great, and we were pretty into the going out and drinking thing after, and it was fun. I was in my mid-twenties with a solid initial 1.5 mil a year contract, and for a few years I thought the world was my fucking oyster, you know? I could have anything I wanted. We both could.

"The two of us were out one night and we met this group of women. Kara, uh, actually approached Boyd first, but he had an eye on her friend and I ended up talking to her instead. She was a few years younger but gorgeous and fun and we dated a bit. It really seemed like she was the perfect woman for me. She wanted kids and she seemed to understand what that kind of life required."

"It's not easy," Taylor said, his tone laced with sympathy. "I mean, I saw that with my mom for sure. Always knowing you might have to move at a moment's notice, not really being able to focus on your own career because your husband's schedule is so demanding, having so much to take care of at home with the kids. It's a lot."

"It is," Jamie agreed. "And for a while we were doing really well together. But after we'd been dating for about a year, she seemed to get really antsy. Constantly talking about wanting to get married. And I did too, but I kept stalling."

He swallowed hard and Taylor reached out and offered his hand, long-fingered and slender, delicate but strong.

Jamie hesitated before he clasped it, weaving their fingers together.

"Was it because …" Taylor lifted their joined hands.

"Because I'm into guys?"

Taylor nodded.

"No. Honestly, the thought never crossed my mind then. At that point I'd never had feelings for another guy. There was someone when I was in Sweden who was bi or whatever and he offered once. I was flattered, but I said no, and he nodded and slapped me on the shoulder and that was it. I never seriously thought about it then. Not with him or anyone else until …" He cleared his throat. "Anyway, we had lots of problems but it wasn't that."

"So, you and Kara …?"

"We dated for a while and maybe things between us weren't perfect but hey, it's always tough during the season, right?" Jamie cleared his throat again. "And then uh, she got pregnant."

He looked up at Taylor. "I thought it was a sign. Most of the guys my age were already married, had kids … and I wanted that too. I wanted someone to come home to. I wanted children really badly, so I was excited about the pregnancy, and I ignored what wasn't going so well between us."

"I don't think that's unusual."

"No, I'm sure it isn't. I just feel really stupid now. I thought once we were married and had the baby, everything would get better between us."

"Oh, Jamie."

"Yeah. Pretty fucking naïve, huh?" His voice became strained. "So, I bought her the huge-ass ring, and we did the giant overblown wedding, and we had Ava, and it was good for a little while."

"Until it wasn't?"

"Yeah. Until it wasn't. Things kinda tapered off with our sex life, and I was trying to be a good husband and not push, you know? She was home with the baby, and I was on the road, and it was hard on her. My mom helped a lot, but it was still tough, and maybe I thought our marriage shouldn't always be such a struggle, but I loved her, and I wanted it to work."

Taylor nodded.

Jamie's voice grew rougher as he continued. "Boyd and I were still super close and after he broke things off with his long-term girlfriend, Kara and I invited him over a lot. He seemed lonely, and he was my friend. It … it felt natural to include him in our family. Ava loved him, and he was like her uncle, so it wasn't unusual for him to pop in with a gift for her or to show up unannounced for dinner or whatever."

Jamie dragged in a deep breath, his grip tightening on Taylor's.

"He'd had some nagging wrist issues so last season he decided to get surgery. He was on the IR list for about a month after. He had rehab and stuff for a while, and he wasn't traveling with the team. He was single, and I thought it was nice when Kara dropped off meals for him sometimes or they hung out on their own. He was Ava's godfather too, and I knew he was bummed that he was stuck at home, so I encouraged Kara to bring Ava over there when I was on the road, and I thought it would be nice if they kept him company."

The look of horrified understanding settled over Taylor's face, and Jamie nodded stiffly.

"We had an issue at the practice rink one morning. They were having trouble with the ice. The cooling system wasn't working properly, so they sent us home after tape review and gym time and said not to worry about skating. I decided to swing by Boyd's place and figured I'd bring him lunch to cheer him up. I wasn't even surprised when I got there and saw Kara's car."

Taylor squeezed his hand harder. It hurt, but in a good way. The pain was sharp and real, keeping him grounded.

"We both knew the code on his gate and his house and he knew ours, so I never thought twice about walking in. That was the kind of friends we were, you know? The sounds didn't even register at first. I must have heard them, but I walked into the living room, and there they were." His chest was beginning to feel tight, and he dragged in a shaky breath.

"She was on top of him on the couch. Riding him. She had her head turned away, her face kind of buried in his neck and for like two seconds, I thought I'd been the one to fuck up. That it wasn't Kara's car, it was one that was really similar, and he had some other hot blonde over. I thought we'd chirp each other about me walking in on him and for him being too much of a horndog to use a bed, and then I saw the ring. The ring I fucking bought her, and it was all tangled up in his hair, and I ..."

Jamie couldn't really remember what happened after. It was all hazy for a while, but that one single moment was buried in his head and would never go away.

Kara's ring glinting in Boyd's dark hair. Boyd's big hands wrapped around her ass. His deep groans mingling with her soft panting breaths.

Jamie had to take a few deep breaths before he could continue. "I dropped the food and smashed a lamp. It shattered, and I cut myself. I didn't even know I was bleeding, but I must have looked fucking deranged when I stormed into the head office. I totally lost my shit. Told them I'd never play with Boyd again. I needed out."

"What did they say?"

"They pleaded with me to stay at least through the end of the season. Said they'd help Boyd and me to work it out. But *fuck*," he spat. "How could I trust him ever again?

"How could I trust *any* of them?" he ground out. "If push came to shove, Boyd was the higher scorer. The one the franchise really needed. I was more expendable and I … I couldn't keep playing like that. I begged for them to let me go."

Taylor rubbed his thumb across the back of Jamie's hand.

"Our stats tanked after that anyway." He laughed hollowly. "I mean, they switched up the lines, so I wasn't playing on Boyd's wing anymore, but it wasn't like my head was in the game. You need a good bond with your teammates, and we were a fucking mess. The head office finally agreed to let me go. By the end of the season, I was in the middle of a messy divorce and off the team."

"God, Jamie, I am so sorry." The pain in Taylor's voice nearly ripped Jamie open and he had to bend his head to look at their joined hands because he couldn't look him in the eye anymore.

"Thanks. It was … it was fucking bad. But I had to be there for Ava. So, I … I did my best to explain that sometimes people fall out of love and fall in love with other people even when I wanted to say nasty things about Kara. But she's … she was a shitty wife but a good mom otherwise, so I had to do what was best for Ava. She had a bit of a rough time for a while though. It was almost easier to focus on her because I didn't have to think about myself anymore. I stuffed down all of my feelings and threw myself into being the best dad for Ava I could possibly be."

"You're an amazing dad." Taylor wriggled his fingers until Jamie let go of his hand and reached up to brush Jamie's hair off his forehead.

Jamie wrapped an arm around him, pulling Taylor close until they were stretched out together. Jamie got his hand up under Taylor's shirt—*his* shirt—and stroked his narrow back with the tips of his fingers, the touch of his skin making some of the hurt fade.

They lay there in silence for a few minutes before Taylor pulled away to look him in the eye. "Why tonight? What brought this all up?"

"Our game was in Chicago," he rasped. "It's the first time we've played against them this season."

Taylor's sharp indrawn breath was gratifying. "Oh shit."

"Yeah. I thought I could handle it. I sunk into this weird head-space where I tried to forget who we were playing against but at one point Boyd got all up in my face and started apologizing and I couldn't—" His voice cracked. "I kept it together until I got off the ice and then I fucking lost it. Smashed my stick in the hallway and scared the shit out of everyone on the team, I think."

He grimaced. "Theriault sat down and talked to me a bit and I appreciated what he was trying to do, but I couldn't talk to him about it. Not tonight anyway."

He tightened his grip on Taylor.

"I want to apologize for earlier though. I—I don't think I was very good to you tonight. I hope I didn't scare you."

Taylor let out a thoughtful hum. "Scare me? No. Worry me, yes."

"I hurt you." Jamie pushed back the blanket to expose Taylor's thighs and skimmed his fingers across the marks there. He thought they might bruise, and he hated that.

"A few marks after some great sex is no big deal," Taylor said dismissively. "Were you *trying* to hurt me?"

"God no." Jamie had just needed to lose himself in something pure and sweet, something untainted by the stain of last year, by the hurt and betrayal.

Taylor looked at him for a long moment, expression serious as he smoothed Jamie's hair off his forehead.

"I'm sorry that happened to you," Taylor said softly. "I'm sorry your ex and your best friend hurt you that way."

"Thanks," he said roughly.

"I think …" Taylor's words came out slow and measured. "I think it's pretty clear you're not in a good place about it. I think maybe you have some things you need to deal with."

"I know I do. I … I realized that tonight. I stuffed a lot of it down for a very long time, but I can't keep ignoring it anymore, I guess."

Taylor nodded. "You said your—your former linemate apologized tonight. Is that the first time he's tried?"

"No. He left me a bunch of voicemails last summer before I blocked his number. I didn't want to hear it."

"I understand." Taylor scooted even closer, looking at Jamie very seriously. "Do you think maybe you need to clear the air with him though?"

"He's still with her," Jamie said bitterly. "It's not like he fucked up once and then promised to never do it again."

Taylor's brows drew together. "Do you think he loves her?"

"I have no idea. I think maybe when it happened, he was lonely and grateful for the help. She was fucking beautiful, so I understand why he wanted her."

"I think that's infatuation, not love."

"Maybe he loved her or maybe he just convinced himself he did. I …" He sucked in a breath. "I can't understand why he thought it was worth fucking up our friendship and the way we worked on the team unless he really believed he loved her."

"People have sex and get in relationships for all kinds of reasons. Some of them healthy, some of them not."

"Yeah."

"I'm not saying you need to forgive him, because what he did is pretty damn unforgivable if you ask me. But maybe you should talk to him. For your sake, not his."

Jamie's immediate reaction was no, but he hesitated. "I … I'll think about it, okay?"

"Okay." Taylor's smile was a little tentative. "I mean, it's not my place to tell you what to do. We're just …"

"Just what?" Jamie prompted.

"Well, we're just fucking, right? It isn't like we're dating." He chewed at his lip.

"This doesn't really feel like just fucking to me anymore," Jamie said slowly. "Does it to you?"

Taylor stared at Jamie for a long moment, his heart beating much too fast.

"No," he croaked. "But I … Jamie, I'm not sure this is a good time to talk about this changing."

"Because you aren't ready to or because you think I'm not?"

"Both, probably. I think—I think maybe we need some time to decide what we want. Tonight's been a lot. For both of us."

Jamie nodded. "True. Plus, I'm in the closet and we work together and there's our family stuff and … I've got a kid."

Taylor winced. "Right. There's all that. And I—I like you, Jamie. I do. There are many reasons I want to date you but everything else we have going on scares the hell out of me."

"I get that."

Taylor drew in a sharp breath. "I'm not sure you do."

"What do you mean?"

"I mean, my ex fucked me up pretty good too. So, I—I need some time to think before I make any decisions."

"Right. Okay. Whatever you need."

"Thanks."

"Of course." Jamie smoothed his hand up and down Taylor's thigh. "Do you want to keep hooking up? Or do you want space?"

Taylor chewed at his lip for a moment. "Let's keep seeing each other."

"Can I make a suggestion?"

"Sure."

"Well, next week is our bye week, so I've got some free time. What if we spent it together? You, me, and some time with Ava too. See how we all click. See how it feels to be together before we talk about if we're going to try to work around all of the obstacles."

Taylor searched Jamie's face for several long moments before he nodded. "Okay. Yeah, let's try that."

Jamie's soft little squeeze made Taylor's heart flutter.

He left shortly after, needing some time alone to process everything that had happened. After he was dressed, Jamie walked him to the door and kissed him goodbye.

He cupped Taylor's face in his hands, staring into Taylor's eyes, his brow furrowed. "Thank you for being sweet to me tonight. I feel like I was selfish. I really hope I didn't hurt you."

Taylor sighed, looping his arms around Jamie's neck and nestling close. "You *worried* me. You didn't hurt me, but thank you for being concerned. In the future, I'd rather you tell me you need to get out of your head though."

"I can do that."

"Thanks." Taylor gave him a peck on the lips. "And think about talking to someone about the stuff with your ex, okay?"

"Okay." Jamie brushed his thumb against the corner of Taylor's eye, and he wondered if his mascara was smeared there.

"Thanks for trusting me with what happened."

"Thanks for caring."

Oh, but caring wasn't the problem. Taylor couldn't help but care. It was protecting himself from caring too much that he was bad at.

With one final kiss, Taylor left Jamie's big-ass house in the fancy North Shore neighborhood and drove south to Evanston.

His apartment felt small and dingy when he let himself in, and he was surprised to see an unfamiliar pair of shoes in the entryway.

Hmm. Charlie must have a visitor.

But the apartment was quiet and still as Taylor walked to his bedroom. He swiped his robe from the hook by the bed, then went into the bathroom. He flipped on the shower to warm up the water, leaning a hip against the sink while he waited.

Tonight had been weird. Intense and good and worrisome all wrapped up together. Taylor had meant what he said. He had no problem with the frantic, passionate sex. He brushed a finger across the bruise on his thigh and heat rose in him at the memory of Jamie fucking him like a man possessed.

But Taylor's heart felt tender after hearing Jamie's story.

What a fucking *bitch* Kara was. Who in their right mind would cheat on a guy like Jamie? And with his best friend? Did neither of them have a soul?

The thought enraged Taylor. He could understand falling in love with a person you couldn't or shouldn't be with. Sometimes life was messy, and hearts didn't always do what they were supposed to. But to sneak behind her husband's back and betray his trust that way …

Taylor let out a low growl and once again hoped Kara wouldn't show up to any of Ava's lessons. Because he really didn't trust himself to behave now that he knew the whole truth.

He'd love to let loose on her and give her a piece of his mind.

And Boyd! What an asshole.

Singles skating was a bit different—more competitive and cutthroat—but Taylor knew exactly how close a hockey team could be. His father's lineys and teammates had been staunch supporters of him after his accident, and Adam Walsh had seen plenty of their retaliatory rage on the ice because of their anger at what he'd done to their friend.

The reminder of *that* messy situation made Taylor sigh and he belatedly realized the room was filling with steam.

In the shower, Taylor groaned with pleasure at the hot water raining down, loosening his tight muscles. Jamie really had left his mark and it had been a long time since Taylor had been fucked hard enough he'd feel it the next day. He liked it, but he hated that Jamie had been in such a bad place tonight.

And were they completely *insane* for even considering dating?

With a little groan, Taylor dumped face wash in his hands and scrubbed the makeup away.

How the fuck could they date?

Even if they figured out their family situation, Taylor couldn't do another relationship with a guy who wanted to keep him a secret, and Jamie wasn't going to announce he was dating a makeup-wearing figure skater who would never fit in with the world he lived in.

What was Taylor going to do? Become one of the team's WAGs?

This whole thing was impossible.

When Taylor was scrubbed clean, he cranked the handle to shut off the water, then stepped out of the shower, patting his skin dry with a scratchy purple towel he really needed to replace.

Sure, when Taylor was in Jamie's bed, it felt like it might be possible for them to be a couple, but once they were out in the real world, it would all fall apart. It had to.

They were too different, and Taylor had learned the hard way that when push came to shove, a guy's career was always going to come first.

Taylor was melancholy by the time he settled into bed, his hair still damp. He was vaguely surprised he hadn't heard a peep from Charlie's room yet. Were he and the dick du jour really sleeping?

Charlie had the same rule Taylor did; no hookups were allowed to spend the night.

Odd.

Maybe the guy had snuck out while Taylor was showering or something.

Taylor clicked off the light, then reached for his phone to plug it in. He frowned at the notifications waiting for him.

They were three texts from Jamie. ***Hope you made it home safe.***

A few minutes had passed between that and the next one. ***Let me know when you want to get together again. Tomorrow's pretty busy, I have some meetings and stuff but maybe the day after?***

And a final one. ***Sweet dreams.***

Taylor's stupid little heart tripped madly at the sight of the kiss emoji, and he replied, trying to convince himself it was only because he didn't want Jamie to worry that he'd gotten in a car wreck.

Home safe. I was in the shower. Tomorrow I'll let you know what my schedule looks like. G'night. He hesitated, then sent an answering kissy face.

Taylor's phone buzzed in his hand as he plugged it in. He silenced it, then brought up the message.

Glad you're safe. I'd hate it if something bad happened to you.

"Argh." Taylor let out a disgruntled noise, turned the phone face-down on the nightstand, and flopped onto his back. "What are you doing to me, Jamie Walsh?"

CHAPTER FIFTEEN

Everyone treated Jamie like spun glass the following morning at practice, their final one before bye week began. He couldn't blame them. He'd definitely made a spectacle of himself after the Chicago game.

"You doing okay?" Theriault asked as they walked down the hall toward the exit. "Last night seemed rough."

"That's putting it mildly." Jamie glanced over at Gabriel, taking in his worried frown.

Could Jamie trust him? He wanted to. He'd never found it difficult to make friends and he could talk about Ava and hockey until he was blue in the face to anyone, but he hadn't let any of his teammates here get close enough to talk about the fucking mess in his life last year.

Jamie winced. Guess he knew why now. A part of him *wanted* to trust all these guys but it felt fucking impossible after what he'd been through. But he couldn't forget that last night they'd all tried to be there for him. Especially Gabriel.

Gabriel had sat with Jamie while he sucked in deep breaths and tried to calm the trembling in his hands after destroying his stick.

He'd pulled Jamie to his feet and guided him into the locker room and to the showers, his dark eyes filled with understanding. Dealing with a father suffering from CTE was totally different from being cheated on but Gabriel definitely knew what it was like to play with pain twisting him up inside.

He understood what it was like to carry secrets.

So maybe Jamie needed to try to share some of those secrets.

Along with Hartinger and Murphy, Jamie and Gabriel had a meeting with Prescott Helmets this afternoon to discuss a campaign about traumatic head injury. They were headed there now, and Jamie hesitated before he got in his Range Rover, parked next to Gabriel's much more modest compact car.

"Can I talk to you about something?" Jamie asked.

Gabriel turned to him, his door open. "*Oui.* Of course. What is it?"

Jamie glanced around. "I was wondering if maybe we could drive together to the meeting? What I want to discuss, it's … it's private."

Gabriel nodded. "Your vehicle or mine?"

His instant response was a relief.

"Mine, if that's fine with you," Jamie offered.

"*Absolument.*" Gabriel shut his door and hit the remote lock before climbing into Jamie's passenger seat.

Jamie punched the Prescott Helmet office location into his GPS, and it wasn't until they were on the road that he spoke. "When did you realize you were bi?"

Out of the corner of Jamie's eye, he saw Gabriel arch one eyebrow. "I was twelve, I think? Yes. Twelve."

Wow. Jamie felt way behind now.

"And did you just have a crush or …?"

"I kissed my teammate after practice."

"You weren't worried you'd get punched in the face?" Jamie stopped at a light and glanced over, surprised.

Gabriel's teeth gleamed as he shot Jamie a smile. "*Non*. I knew I was a better fighter. Besides, I'd seen the way he looked at me."

"Makes sense."

"Why do you ask?"

Jamie tensed. "I, uh, there's this guy … we've been spending a lot of time together and …" He cleared his throat.

"Oh." Gabriel's smile turned a little wicked and smug. "Well, it's understandable. I'm very attractive. And I am flattered. But I'm sorry, I'm in love with Coach."

It took a second to process but once it did, Jamie snorted and reached out to smack his arm. "Not *you*, asshole." The teasing broke the ice though and Jamie felt better. Lighter.

"I know." Gabriel's tone grew serious. "So, there's a guy?"

"Yes. We, uh, we've had sex a few times."

"And you're not sure if you're bi?" Gabriel asked, his tone a little quizzical.

"Well." Jamie licked his lips. "I mean, I'm definitely good with the sex part. It's the rest I'm questioning, maybe?"

"Sure," Gabriel said. "It's one thing to do something physical, it's quite another to fall in love."

"I'm a long way from love," Jamie said cautiously. "We're just getting to know each other. But I do care for him. And he was there for me last night. I talked to him about—about what happened last year with my linemate and my ex and—" His throat closed up tight.

"That's good you have someone to talk to." Gabriel's tone was soft and sympathetic.

Jamie's grip tightened on the wheel. "I've got some stuff to deal with there. I, uh, locked it down pretty hard and it sort of … came out last night."

"I know something about that."

"I thought you might." Jamie drummed his fingers on the steering wheel. "But I … I think maybe, if I let myself, I *could* fall for this guy. It's complicated though."

"Why?"

"There's Ava of course. She always comes first."

"Of course."

Jamie didn't know how to explain the next part. "But uh, there's some other stuff."

"Like having to come out?"

Jamie winced. "That's definitely part of it. And, um, there's some stuff in our families that will make this tough. We're not the kind of guys who should be together, you know? Other people won't like it."

"I also know something about that." Gabriel's tone was dry.

Jamie laughed, surprised. "Yeah, I guess you really do."

"I think sometimes we meet people who aren't who we're 'supposed' to be with but they're too important to let go of. No matter the cost."

"Maybe." Jamie thought of Kara and Boyd and wondered if it had felt like that for them.

God, he'd have been angry if they came to him and told him they had feelings for each other. It would have ripped his heart out. But it would have hurt less than finding out the way he had, seeing them together in that moment of raw intimacy, his life shattering into little pieces around him with no warning.

In the end, they'd had a choice. Maybe there had been no *good* choices but they'd certainly made the wrong one.

Had Kara thought about what breaking up their marriage would do to Ava? That was what upset him the most.

"Do you think I should go for it?" Jamie asked.

"I don't think that's for me to say," Gabriel said slowly. "I think you have to listen to your own heart. But I do think if you want to be with someone bad enough, it's worth a risk."

"You have no regrets about being with Lance." That was more of a statement than a question but Gabriel answered anyway.

"Not a one."

Jamie nodded thoughtfully. "That's good to know."

"I do have one piece of advice though. Don't wait to tell the team. My relationship with Lance put us in a precarious position. Don't blindside the guys or management. Be upfront about it. Even if you aren't ready to tell the public, make sure you get the team on board. Because I don't know how much more drama we can withstand. I do feel a lot of guilt for the way everything happened with Lance. We should have come clean sooner."

"True." And Jamie knew better than anyone what secrets and betrayal could do to a team. Mistrust could create fractures too wide to heal. "Thank you," he said softly. "I appreciate you listening."

"Of course. I'm here if you need me."

"No, you're going to All-Star Weekend and the fucking Olympics," Jamie said teasingly. "Shit, man, that's awesome."

"I … I did not see that coming," Gabriel said, sounding uncharacteristically modest but he didn't protest the change in subject. "I mean, I knew my game had really improved this year but I never expected to be a part of either event."

"I think it's amazing."

"It is. I'm honored to take part."

"Is Coach, uh, Lance going with you?"

"*Non*, he has work here to deal with. Besides, I feel better having him home to keep an eye on things with my father when I'm going to be out of the country."

"That makes sense. Murphy is going too, though, right?"

"*Oui.* It'll be great to have him there."

The conversation turned strictly to hockey but Jamie felt better having told one person he was bi.

It was a very small step, but it was *something*.

“Thanks for letting me take part in this,” Jamie said to Gabriel as they walked into Prescott Helmet’s headquarters a short while later.

Gabriel shrugged. “Player safety is important. I don’t want to see guys’ lives wrecked because they love a game. The more of us who speak up about it, the better.”

“It’s just … with my dad’s history with, um, Taylor’s dad, I wondered if I was the ideal choice.”

Gabriel gave an eloquent shrug. “Maybe that’s a good reason to have you part of the conversation.”

“Maybe.”

They were immediately ushered to a conference room where their contact, Brent Cameron, waited.

He was an attractive guy a few years younger than Jamie with thick sun-streaked light brown hair. He was dressed well in a sharply tailored blue suit and Jamie wondered if he should have dressed up more. He looked down ruefully at his sweats.

Brent had heavy brows and he looked stern but his expression lightened the moment he saw them.

“Hey, guys. Good seeing you.” He held out a hand. “Thanks for squeezing this meeting in before you fly out, Theriault.”

Gabriel nodded as they shook. “Glad we could make it.”

Brent grinned at him. “And you must be Jamie Walsh.”

“I am. Nice to meet you, Mr. Cameron.”

“Brent, please.” His grip was firm. “Would you like some water or coffee?”

“Water please,” Jamie said, and Gabriel asked for the same.

Zane and Ryan joined them a few minutes later and when they'd all helped themselves to the lunch buffet set up on the far side of the room, he invited them to take seats at the conference table. A man walked in to take notes, and Brent took his own seat and smiled at them.

"This is an informal getting-to-know-you meeting, guys. I've talked to Gabriel quite a bit and I met you briefly at the New Year's Eve fundraiser, Zane and Ryan, but I want to discuss plans for this campaign."

He cleared his throat. "When I was playing hockey for Western Michigan my freshman year, I saw a guy take a head hit that fucked him up permanently. Post-concussion syndrome benched him for the rest of the season, and he never really fully recovered. He had to leave school and the last I heard, he was still struggling with depression.

"I was a halfway-decent defenseman at the time but I always knew I wasn't going to have what it took to make it in the NHL. I decided to turn my focus to protecting the guys who *could*. It was always my dream to work with a helmet company and design a better product." He gave them a half-smile. "Admittedly, I got a lucky break when I started dating the son and heir of the owner of Prescott Helmets."

They all laughed before he continued. "But let me assure you, I've now spent nearly a decade working my ass off to improve our helmets. I had a leg up here, no question, but I've always been committed to player safety, and I know you guys are too. What I want to do is get current and former players talking about what we can do to keep hockey the fast, exciting, aggressive game it is without you becoming collateral damage."

Gabriel wore an impassive expression but a muscle in his cheek twitched as he fiddled with the silver ring he wore, food abandoned, untouched. Undoubtedly thinking of his father's degenerative brain disease caused by his long and brutal hockey career.

Jamie tapped Gabriel's foot with his and Gabriel flashed dark eyes at him, his gaze appreciative, like he knew Jamie was offering support. He was the kind of guy who had remained on the periphery of the team at first, unwilling to let anyone in.

Oddly enough, his relationship with their assistant coach had brought him closer to some of them.

For all of Jamie's attempts to get to know his teammates, he'd hidden things too. Kept guys out of his personal life. He'd pretended like everything was fine inside—even to himself—but Taylor was right, he wasn't.

And he needed to fix that.

They ate while Brent outlined some of the plans already in place, which included getting league-wide support from players, media campaigns, panel discussions with current and former players, and aggressive fundraising for further head trauma research.

"We're folding as much of our profits here into research as our shareholders will allow and we're partnered with the Chicago Center for Traumatic Brain Injury now, so I'm hopeful we can do better in the coming years." Brent clasped his hands together on the table. He'd stripped off his jacket, loosened his tie, and rolled up his sleeves, clearly intent on getting down to business. "Now, I want to know what ideas you have."

"Education is huge," Gabriel said. "Not just players but fans. They've got to see what the consequences are. We want to keep playing. All of us. But the majority of us don't want to see guys suffering and dying early because of the game. I think most fans will feel the same."

Brent nodded seriously. "I think so too."

"And really, isn't it about changing the overall culture?" Zane asked, leaning forward. "Trying to strip away the idea that it's more manly to suffer through depression and anxiety after concussions and ignore symptoms until it's too late? I mean, I really think mental health is a huge part of this."

A head popped in the door. "Did someone say mental health?"

To Jamie's surprise, Brent's face lit up. "Lowell, babe, what are you doing here?"

"Sorry to interrupt." The guy—Lowell—stepped into the room with a smile. He was about Jamie's age too, dressed in a slim cut black suit with a gray turtleneck sweater underneath, a gray, black, and tan plaid overcoat draped over his arm.

Jamie knew fuck all about fashion but even he could tell the guy was stylishly dressed. Something about him reminded Jamie of Taylor. They were both lean and strong, with pale skin and dark hair, but that wasn't all of it.

Maybe it was the touch of gracefulness in their walk or the soft way they spoke.

"No interruption." Brent's expression turned fond. "This is a nice surprise. Seriously though, what are you doing here? Did we have a lunch date I forgot about?"

Lowell laughed quietly. "No, Dad and I grabbed a late lunch together. You weren't invited."

Brent gave him a wry little smile. "Tell the truth. I know you wanted to hang out with the hockey players."

Lowell laughed and bit his lip. "*Maaaybe.*"

"C'mon, let me introduce you." Brent took Lowell's hand and all four of them rose to their feet.

"No introductions needed." Lowell sauntered forward and held out a hand to Zane Murphy. "Lowell Prescott. Good to see you again, Zane."

Zane grinned. "You too."

He turned to Ryan and held out his hand. "And Ryan."

"Aww, I'm really more of a hugger," he said with a bright grin.

"Well, if you insist." With a flutter of lashes, Lowell wrapped his arms around Ryan.

Beside him, Brent let out a little grumble but his expression was fond as he looked at Lowell. Based on the rings they wore on their left hands, Jamie assumed they were married.

Lowell's eyes sparkled as he looked Gabriel up and down. "And *you* are Gabriel Theriault."

"Guilty," he said with a smile. He bowed his head over Lowell's hand and kissed it. "Very nice to meet you."

Lowell glanced over his shoulder. "Brent, honey, I might need to leave you for this handsome French-Canadian. Sorry, dearest, he's just so charming."

"We're married. You can't leave me. You even said, 'til death do us part'." Brent crossed his arms over his chest.

"Sweetie." Lowell stepped back to tuck his arm through Brent's. "Have you looked at this man? Do you see that hair? Hear that accent? Exceptions can be made."

"Not by me." Brent pressed a kiss to Lowell's temple. "You're mine. I'm yours. That's the agreement."

"Ugh, fine. You ruin all my fun. It's a good thing I love you."

"It is indeed," Brent said with what sounded like a long-suffering sigh. "Lucky, lucky me."

Lowell turned to Jamie and pointed a finger at him. "And you are Jamie Walsh."

"Guilty as charged."

"We were season ticket holders for the Windstorm for years. We switched teams once the two of them switched teams." Lowell gave Zane and Ryan a little wink at his play on words and Brent groaned.

Ryan looked delighted. "Nice pun, man." He held out a fist and Lowell bumped it; expression amused.

Lowell glanced at his phone. "I really should be heading out though. I have patients to see."

"Are you a doctor?" Jamie asked.

"Ha! Only technically. I have a doctorate but not in medicine. My mother would have loved it if I'd followed in her footsteps but instead, I run a therapy practice. We primarily focus on LGBTQ teens but really anyone who needs mental health assistance is welcome."

"Wow. Sounds like quite a job."

Lowell gave him a small smile. "Well, it's not as exciting as playing pro hockey but I quite like it."

"Is there a big need for mental health care for LGBTQ teens?" Zane asked, his expression curious.

Brent groaned. "Oh no. Now you've done it. He'll *never* shut up now."

Lowell elbowed his husband in the ribs. "Yes. The need is huge. Eighty-six percent of LGBTQ youth report being harassed or assaulted at school, which is of course very detrimental at such a formative stage in one's life. Suicide rates are nearly three times that of heterosexual teens, and trans children are particularly vulnerable. Really though, it's often the same for adults. The stress of navigating a world that still isn't exactly friendly to guys like us can have a massive impact on mental health."

"Ehh, not quite all of us." Ryan jerked his thumb in Jamie's direction. "He's our token straight guy here today."

Jamie hid a wince. No, he wasn't. But he wasn't ready to blurt that out to the whole room, even if they were all guys who would understand.

"Well, I suppose that's allowed." Lowell's eyes twinkled as he winked at Jamie. "I'd tell you if you ever changed your mind to give me a call, but my husband might stroke out."

Jamie laughed. "I'm flattered."

"I'm glad to hear you at least have good taste." Lowell turned to look at the other three guys. "But I do want to say how incredible I think all of you are. Coming out the way you did has been such a big thing for the kids I see in my practice. They need role models like you, and you have no idea how much good you do just by being out players."

"Stanley-Cup-winning out players," Ryan said with a grin.

Lowell grinned. "Hey, the better your team does, the harder it is for people to say coming out has impacted the game negatively."

Zane nodded. "It definitely has added to the pressure of wanting to do well."

Lowell winced. "Oh dear. No, I don't want to do that. I want you guys to win, and I love that you're doing well this season but please don't sacrifice yourselves to be role models."

"Oh, no, I don't think that," Zane said hastily. "It's a privilege to play for a team that allows us to be open and honest about who we are. And that helps fuel me to win. I think it's the same for Ryan and Gabriel."

They nodded.

"For sure," Ryan said. "We're lucky as hell. We all know that."

"Why do you think we haven't seen many guys on other teams coming out?" Lowell asked with a puzzled tilt of his head.

Zane shrugged. "Not every franchise is ready for it. There are still issues with management in a lot of places. Different fan bases have different reactions. Toronto, Evanston … they're a lot more welcoming to players like us than say, Nashville, you know?"

Lowell shuddered delicately. "I can only imagine."

"Babe," Brent said quietly. "You said you needed to head out …"

"Oh, yes." Lowell looked startled. "Listen to me gabbing away like I don't have places to be and patients to see."

There was a flurry of goodbyes and hugs from Lowell, and then a quick kiss for Brent and a promise to bring home takeout for dinner before he left.

Jamie, who had been debating if this was a sign he shouldn't ignore, hesitated a second before he jogged into the hall after him. "Hey, Lowell?"

He turned with a smile. "Yes? Did you change your mind? Are you going to beg me to leave my husband?"

Jamie laughed, put at ease by his smile and joke.

"Ahh, no," he said quietly. "But I, um, would like to talk to someone about—about some past relationship stuff that came up recently and um, maybe some questions I have about my sexuality. Is that something you could help me with?"

Lowell's face went soft. "Oh, sweetheart, of course I'd be happy to help with that." He pulled a slim silver case out of his jacket pocket, then handed over a business card. "You just email me or call that number to set up an appointment and I'd be happy to talk to you about *anything* you'd like to discuss."

"Great," Jamie said, surprised by the lump in his throat. "I—I really appreciate that."

"Of course." Lowell squeezed his forearm. "Actually, it might be better if you met with one of my colleagues. Since you and my husband will be working together, and I've been a shameless flirt today, I want to avoid any conflict of interest. Would you be okay with that?"

"Oh, sure. I mean, whatever you think is best."

"I know the perfect person for you to chat with. You email me, and we'll work it all out, I promise."

"Thank you," Jamie said, his throat still thicker than he'd like. "That sounds really great."

"Happy to help." Lowell beamed, and he reminded Jamie so much of Taylor that he blinked. "I look forward to hearing from you."

After Lowell was gone, Jamie stood in the hall, wondering what he would say to the other guys about why he'd run off. In the end, he decided to settle for the truth.

"Hey, sorry," he said when he stepped into the conference room again, rubbing the back of his neck. "I thought maybe I should talk to someone about the relationship baggage I have. I, uh, thought Lowell might know someone I could meet with."

"That's great," Zane said, looking him in the eye. "Whatever you need to talk about, I'm glad you're getting help. And we're all here for you if you need us."

"Thanks, man," Jamie said, dragging him into a one-armed hug that turned into hugs from all three of the guys and a firm pat on the arm from Brent Cameron.

Jamie's throat was still suspiciously tight as they took a seat at the table and got back to business.

CHAPTER SIXTEEN

"How are the lessons going?" Samantha gave him a serious look.

Taylor blinked at her. "Um, fine. Why? Are there concerns?"

"No. I'm just doing a check-in."

"Overall, great."

"But?"

Taylor glanced toward Samantha's open office door, then got up to shut it.

She raised an eyebrow when he returned to his seat.

"So, I had a one-on-one with Jack Malone today."

She sighed and brushed her strawberry blonde hair behind her ears. "Didn't go well, I take it?"

"Not so much." Taylor grimaced.

"I wish I could say I was surprised. He's a misogynistic asshole." The venom in her voice was startling and Taylor blinked.

"I feel like I should be asking you what happened."

She shrugged. "Nothing concrete. He's … made his interest in me known and I shut it down, obviously."

"Did you talk to HR?"

"Yes. But it was subtle enough that it's tricky." She gave Taylor a tight little smile. "And let's be realistic, their role is to protect the franchise overall. I have my doubts that they'd back me over Malone."

Taylor leaned forward. "Have you talked to Zane Murphy? I mean, as captain …"

"Yeah, I did. And he's been great. He promised he'd have a word with Malone. The coaches have been informed too. But we all know the higher ups don't seem inclined to do much."

"True."

She glanced at Taylor. "What were *you* saying about him?"

"Oh, he's just … clearly not into this whole figure-skating thing." Taylor waved it off. "Lots of shitty little comments. I get the impression he's even less into a gay man teaching it but who knows? I don't like him. Way less serious than what you're talking about though."

"This is just between the two of us, okay?" Samantha said. "But apparently he really had issues with all of the guys coming out."

"Great. So, a misogynist and a homophobe. Fun!"

Samantha sniffed. "They so often go hand-in-hand."

"True."

"Did *you* say something to HR?"

"No. I mean, it's nothing I can really prove or even an obvious statement he made. He's never said anything that's outright hostile. He gets this attitude like he's too good for the lessons, you know?"

Samantha nodded. "He's one of those guys who's gotten everything he's ever wanted, and he doesn't do well with being told no."

"Exactly." Taylor sighed. "But I've wasted enough of my time talking about that asshole. Let's move on."

They discussed the team and how the media campaign was going before Taylor glanced at the time and realized he needed to wrap it up.

"Okay, one more lesson today." Taylor stood with a sigh. "Thankfully, it's Hajek. He may not speak a ton of English, but he's super nice and he's a great skater."

Samantha smiled. "Well, that's something."

"Actually, most of the guys are great."

"They are. They're a good group."

"Minus Jack Malone."

"Minus Jack Malone," she agreed. "Ahh well, I guess they can't all be winners."

Taylor thought of Jamie and had to suppress a smile as he walked toward the door.

"Hey, how are things going with Walsh?"

He turned back, eyes wide. "Good, why?"

She shrugged. "Just wanted to make sure there weren't any issues with your family situation."

"Ahh, no. It's been okay."

"Oh! I keep forgetting to ask you this. Do you think you'd be up for a mini lesson with Walsh and his daughter?"

"Uh, sure. If he's good with it."

"Yeah, of course. I just think that would be an adorable addition. I'm picturing some really cute father-daughter pairs skating. How old is she?"

Taylor blinked. "Uh, Ava is five."

"Ava. Good name," Samantha said in a thoughtful tone.

"It might be a little complicated though," Taylor said slowly. "He'd probably have to run it by his ex-wife, and I imagine that could be … complicated."

She grimaced. "Yes, I do remember hearing about their ugly divorce."

"Talk about a PR nightmare," he muttered.

"That's an understatement if I ever heard one." She let out an inelegant little snort. "Well, if you're willing, I'll see what I can do to get Jamie Walsh on board."

"Just let me know. I'm always up for anything involving skating and adorable children."

"And hot men?" she teased.

"Well, they don't hurt."

And really, they didn't get much hotter than Jamie.

As Taylor got ready for his next lesson, he thought again about the conversation he'd had with Jamie the night before.

It seemed surreal that they were even considering dating but Taylor couldn't deny there was a real pull there.

He grabbed his phone, intending to send Jamie a quick message but the arrival of the camera crew stopped him and when Hajek arrived a few minutes later, Taylor had to focus on work.

Sadly, daydreaming about Jamie didn't pay the bills.

As Jamie pulled up at Kelly O'Shea and Trevor Underhill's apartment building later that night, he regretted agreeing to hang out.

Their place wasn't far from his and he normally enjoyed playing video games with them but he would rather have seen Taylor.

Taylor, who hadn't texted him once today.

Jamie hoped it was because he was busy and had skating stuff to focus on but Jamie was beginning to worry it was because of the conversation they'd had last night.

Jamie got out of his Range Rover with a sigh and snagged the beer he'd bought on the way over.

A few minutes later, O'Shea opened the door wide and stepped back to let him in. "Hey, man. Glad you could come over."

"Yeah, it's been a while, huh?" Jamie held up the two six-packs. "I brought refreshments."

"Thanks. Those look great." A smile lit up O'Shea's face. "C'mon in."

He turned and led him down the hall to the kitchen, kicking a few stray pairs of shoes out of the way.

It was a nice place, or at least had been when they moved in, but they were definitely slobs.

O'Shea had to clear a place on the spacious counter to set the beer, pushing aside mail and empty pizza boxes. "Sorry. We need to clean," he muttered.

It had pretty much looked like that the last time Jamie was over so he didn't figure that was going to be any time soon, but he'd been that guy at their age too, so it didn't bother him much.

"Whatever. So." Jamie drummed his hands on the counter. "What are we playing tonight?"

O'Shea smirked at him. "Impatient much? You looking to get out of here so you can go hook up after or what?"

Jamie laughed. "No, no plans tonight. I'm looking forward to this. It's been too long."

"True." O'Shea twisted the bottle cap off. "But Trev's almost back with the pizza. We'll decide then."

"Okay."

"*Are* you seeing someone? You never really talk about your personal life other than your daughter."

Jamie shrugged. "There's someone but I dunno what's going on. We're trying to figure it out. At least I'll have some time at home for the next couple of weeks. That should help."

"Good."

"What about you?"

"I'm heading to Boston tomorrow to see the fam."

"Cool. I meant dating though. You seeing anyone?"

"Nah. Enjoying the single life, you know?"

There was a weird little twist to his mouth that made Jamie wonder though.

Jamie tried to remember if he'd ever seen Kelly with anyone. He *had* seen him with his arm around a girl at a bar a few times, and he'd occasionally gone home with those girls after a night out. But to Jamie's knowledge, he never dated any women seriously or even hooked up with the same person twice.

He opened his mouth to ask but the sound of the door opening interrupted. "Boys, I come bearing pizza!"

Trevor appeared in the doorway and dumped a couple of pizza boxes on top of several—hopefully empty—ones already there.

"Hey, Walsh," Underhill said with a nod of his square, stubbly jaw.

Trevor Underhill was neither the tallest nor the shortest guy on the team, but he had a wiry body he could never seem to keep enough calories on. He shrugged out of his jacket and tossed it on the stool by the counter, revealing heavily tattooed forearms.

"Hey, good to see you, man," Jamie said. "How's the ankle?"

"Better." Underhill shot him a smile. "I'm dying to get back to playing."

"Soon, right?"

"Yeah, the St. Louis game after bye week is my first one back unless I have a setback or something. It's feeling solid though."

"Awesome. I'm excited for you." Jamie held out a fist to bump and Underhill grinned at him. "So, I brought beer."

"Hell yes." Underhill rubbed his palms together. "Pizza, beer, and video games. Does life get better than that?"

"Nope," O'Shea said, flipping back the lid and snagging a piece, biting into the molten cheese and sausage. "Fuck that's hot," he muttered around the food before swallowing.

He reached for his beer and guzzled it down.

Jamie snorted. "I've heard it helps to let it cool."

"Shut up, Dad," O'Shea dropped the remainder of the piece on a paper plate. "Don't go using your logic and shit on me."

Jamie laughed. "Sorry. Won't make that mistake again."

They migrated to the living room, plates loaded with pizza and clutching beer in their free hands.

Underhill and O'Shea were probably young enough they'd never notice it if they deviated from the recommended diet plan the team nutritionist made for them. Jamie, on the other hand, would have to work all this off so he didn't kill his momentum on the ice.

But for now, he was going to enjoy this.

When the pizza was polished off and they were set up with fresh bottles of beer, O'Shea glanced at them.

"Mario Kart?"

"Mario Kart," Jamie said with a nod.

"Hell yes," Underhill said. "I'm gonna kick both your asses."

"That's what you said last time, dude," O'Shea teased. "And we both beat you."

"Don't remind me."

As they always did, Jamie chose Bowser, O'Shea Yoshi, and Underhill went for Waluigi.

They trash talked their way through the first race, with Jamie mostly focused on picking up coins and Underhill repeatedly crashing into them in the anti-gravity sections.

"Would you fucking quit it, you asshole?" Jamie yelled when Underhill smashed into him again.

He cackled. "You should watch where you're going."

"You're gonna have to watch out for him on the ice too," O'Shea said, shoulder bumping Jamie's as he drifted around the turn. He was one of those very physical players who moved like he was actually in the game.

"Fuck off," Underhill grumbled. "I don't take out my own teammates, O'Shea."

"Last season you took out—"

"Shut your damn pie hole," Underhill snarked. "That was an accident. *Goddamn it! Fuck*!"

The last part was because O'Shea had drifted long enough to trigger a speed boost and shot ahead of the two of them.

The chirping continued through the rest of the race and O'Shea swore violently when Jamie and Underhill came out ahead of him.

"Yes!" Jamie crowed. "Suck it, Shaysey."

"You wish," O'Shea shot back.

"Nah, you're not my type." Jamie tossed down his controller.

He brought out his phone and snuck a peek at it, brightening when he saw there was a message from Taylor. ***How was your day?***

Not bad, he replied, grinning. ***Playing some Mario Kart with O'Shea and Underhill.***

Fun! I'm always Princess Peach and Charlie kicks my ass when we play. Hey, ask Underhill if he's going to do lessons with me, btw.

"Hey, Underhill," Jamie said. "Taylor wants to know if you're going to do lessons with him."

Underhill finished his beer and squinted at him. "Taylor?"

"Hollis."

"Oh, right. Why the fuck are you texting the figure skater?"

Jamie froze, unsure of how to answer but O'Shea chimed in. "Taylor gives lessons to kids too. Jamie's daughter's in his class, right?"

"Yeah," Jamie said a little hoarsely. He took a hefty swallow of beer to give himself time to think.

Another message popped up and Jamie glanced at it.

Samantha would like to get some footage of you, me, and Ava sometime too if you're interested. I know that might be complicated with Kara though, so let me know.

He repeated that to Underhill who nodded, seemingly satisfied.

"Makes sense. I know they're trying to make us all look family-friendly and shit." Underhill stood. "Hey, I'm gonna go smoke. Let the skater know I'll do his lessons. I'm not going anywhere for bye week, so he can text me whenever. You can give him my number if he doesn't have it."

Underhill disappeared through the sliding door onto the balcony and Jamie relayed all that to Taylor.

Thanks. I'll text him.

Do you have any plans tomorrow? It's supposed to snow overnight, and I thought it might be fun to go sledding with Ava.

Sure, sounds fun. What time?

Ten AM? She's at Kara's tonight but that would give us a couple of hours alone before she's back.

I like the thought of that.

"You sure that's Taylor you're texting?" O'Shea said with a grin. "You're smiling at your phone a lot, dude."

"Mmm," Jamie made a noncommittal noise. "Making plans for tomorrow with the person I've been seeing."

He wondered if O'Shea would call him out on the use of "person" rather than woman, but he nodded. "Nice."

"Is Underhill cool with the guys being out?"

O'Shea raised an eyebrow. "Huh?"

"Oh, I was just thinking about his comment about the PR stuff being family friendly and all that. It made me wonder if Trevor was cool with Murphy and Hartinger and Coach and Gabriel and all that."

O'Shea shrugged. "I think so. He's not like Malone."

"Yeah well, thank God for that. One of him is more than enough. Look, I know you're friends with Malone, but doesn't it bug you that he's so blatant about the cheating?" Jamie asked, his tone more bitter than he'd intended.

"It's shitty." O'Shea tipped his beer back. "But what are we supposed to do about it?"

"Tell him?"

"I *have*." O'Shea snorted. "Most of us on the team have. Do you think he really cares?"

"No, I guess not. I just …"

"Is this about your ex?" Jamie drew in a sharp breath and O'Shea winced. "Sorry, man. I shouldn't have—"

"No, you're right. It's … it brings up some shit, you know?"

"Yeah, I imagine it would." O'Shea's smile was sympathetic. "Look, Coop, Underhill, and I have all tried to tell Malone he's a dick to his wife. He calls us pussies."

Jamie rolled his eyes. "I guess I don't get what you guys see in him. Like, he's a good player. I'm not denying that. And I understand the front office thinks he draws in fans. He just seems too fucking toxic to handle."

O'Shea picked at the bottle label. "I dunno. I guess he was one of my first friends on the team. Murphy and Hartinger were always totally wrapped up in each other and he was my D-partner my rookie year and we wound up spending a lot of time together, you know?"

"Sure, I get that." Jamie got up to snag a water from the refrigerator. "But the shit he tried to pull with Theriault and Coach was ugly."

"It was. And I'm not excusing his behavior. I guess I'm kinda lonely though, you know? Everyone else has their buddies and I always feel like I'm left out. It's really sucked this season with Trev out too."

"You're close to Lindy too, right?"

O'Shea's face turned a little pink. "Yeah, I mean, we're friends but he's pretty much a homebody. He doesn't go out much. Besides, he's friends with my brothers and he's always acting like he's another fucking *brother*, you know? Not what I'm going for."

Jamie chuckled. "Yeah, my older brother could be pretty overbearing when we were growing up. I can't imagine having two of them."

"Three," O'Shea said gloomily. "Three brothers who play hockey. Well, one of them is retired now but Lindy seems determined to fill in there so …"

Jamie nodded. It made a little more sense now. "Well, I'm always up for hanging out. I mean when I don't have the kid, obviously, but I'm up for having some fun without going totally off the rails."

O'Shea brightened. "Thanks, man. That would be great. And seriously, Underhill's a good guy. He has a bit of an attitude about some things but he's decent. He really does care about the team, and I don't think he'd ever do anything that would hurt someone deliberately."

"Good to know. Other than our gaming nights, I really don't know him at all."

"It'll be good now that he's back. We can play video games on the plane too 'cause he always brings his Switch."

"Nice." Jamie grinned. "Though the closer to the playoffs we get, the more I'll probably just crash."

"Yeah, 'cause you're an old man."

"Oh, fuck off. I'm young compared to Lindholm. I can't believe he's still playing. Christ. How does he not hurt all the goddamn time?"

O'Shea shrugged. "He doesn't do this stuff." He nudged the pizza box with his beer bottle. "And he meditates and shit."

Jamie laughed. He probably should be stricter about his diet and training but at the end of the day, he wasn't one of the top players like Lindholm and he never would be. He was good. He was getting better, thanks to great coaching and the right line-mates. But he'd never be a point scorer like Lindy or be able to read the game the way Murphy and Hartinger did.

"Hey, clearly it's working for him," Jamie said.

"It is."

"What's working?" Underhill asked as he stepped inside, bringing a cold draft with him.

"Lindholm's obsession with healthy food and training."

"Oh, fuck that." Underhill plopped down in the seat next to Jamie, bringing a whiff of tobacco—and weed, if Jamie wasn't mistaken—with him. He reached for a beer. "Look, I want to play in this league as much as the next guy but I'm going to enjoy myself while I do it, man."

"I hear you." O'Shea held out his bottle and clinked it with Trevor's.

Jamie raised his in agreement. He could appreciate the players with the dedication to eke every last bit of skill and longevity from their bodies but for him, it wasn't worth it.

He wanted a good career in hockey but at the end of the day, he wanted more than that.

He glanced at his phone and saw an unread message from Taylor. ***Should I bring anything tomorrow?***

Nah, Jamie replied. ***Just your cute self. And some winter gear for playing in the snow.***

Just for saying that, you get an extra big kiss tomorrow.

Hey, only speaking the truth, Jamie replied. ***But I won't turn that down.***

"You are so gone," O'Shea said. "Damn. Look, Walshy's all sappy looking over some girl, Underhill."

Jamie typed out a response to Taylor one-handed while he flipped his teammates off with the other.

"Better him than me," Underhill said with a snort. "Now, c'mon. I want to get a few more games in before I go out tonight."

"He's abandoning us to go to the bar," O'Shea grumbled.

"Hey, you can come with if you want." Underhill laughed as he picked up his controller. "But it looks like Walshy already has someone he's into and you whine when I ditch you for a hookup."

"I don't whine," O'Shea protested, bringing up the game again. "Fuck you."

"I keep telling you. Not my thing," Underhill insisted. "Now, are we playing, or what?"

Jamie smiled at their banter and the thought of Taylor, who yeah, he was definitely into.

But would O'Shea and Underhill be quite as chill about it if he told them who that person was?

CHAPTER SEVENTEEN

Taylor *shouldn't* have been nervous about going to Jamie's house —he'd been there twice before—but as he parked in the driveway, his stomach filled with butterflies at the idea of spending the day with Jamie and Ava.

Taylor had never been to their house in the daytime, and the bright sunlight sparkling off the fresh snow revealed how nice Jamie's place was. He lived in the North Shore—a collection of exclusive neighborhoods north of Evanston that ran along Lake Michigan—so of course it was a pricey place.

But it really hit home when Taylor got out of his car and glanced around, taking in the sprawling houses, and wide lots. Even the few vehicles parked in driveways were luxury automobiles. Taylor's car stuck out like a sore thumb.

But oh, how Taylor loved Jamie's house. The shape reminded him of a Tudor, with a steep-pitched roof and thick trim around the windows, but it was a modern take on it, without the heavy timber framing and with cream-colored painted brick and all the windows and trim done in a deep charcoal color.

Taylor knocked on the door and a few moments later, Jamie opened it with a smile. He looked so warm and cozy, Taylor wanted to walk straight into his arms for a hug.

"Hey there." Jamie let Taylor inside and the moment the door closed, he opened his arms to pull Taylor close.

Taylor's shaky nerves disappeared the moment he was in Jamie's arms but when he leaned in to press their lips together, Jamie deftly avoided his kiss, turning his head so Taylor's lips barely grazed his cheek.

Taylor frowned, opening his mouth to ask if something was wrong, when an excited giggle explained everything.

"Taylor! You're here! Daddy said you were coming but I didn't think it was *real*."

Taylor stepped back and smiled down at Ava, surprised to see her. Jamie had said she wouldn't be home from her mom's house for a few hours. "I don't think your dad is the type who would make things up."

Ava's forehead wrinkled before she nodded. "So, we really are gonna go sledding?"

"Of course." Jamie smiled. "Did you clean up what we were playing with earlier?"

"Nooo."

"Well, the sooner you get that done, the sooner we can go out and play in the snow."

"Okay!" Ava scampered off and Jamie smiled at Taylor, his gaze warm enough to melt all the snow outside.

"Sorry about that. I thought we'd have a little while just the two of us but Kara left on vacation a little earlier than expected and

..."

Taylor shrugged. "That's okay. I understand."

Jamie rubbed the back of his neck. "I don't want you to feel like I'm forcing things or—"

"Hey, I promise it's okay. I'm happy to spend time with both of you," he said honestly.

"You are really great, you know that?"

Taylor preened. "Well, I like to think so but it's always nice to hear."

Jamie wrapped his hands around Taylor's waist and looked into his eyes. "Well, Taylor Hollis, you are great. And I'm going to make sure you hear that as often as you deserve."

"Oh, my," Taylor said, feeling a little fluttery at all of that attention focused on him. "I look forward to it."

Jamie's smile was slow and pleased and he dipped his head to gently brush his lips across Taylor's. It was brief and rather chaste but it made Taylor's heart beat a little faster.

"Want to take off your coat and shoes? It might be a little while before we go out again."

"Sure." Taylor reluctantly stepped back and from the way Jamie's hand lingered on his waist, he wasn't in any hurry to let go either.

"You look good." Taylor stripped off his jacket, then stepped out of his winter boots. "Happier than you did the other night."

"I feel better."

"Yeah? Why's that?"

"A couple of things but I, uh, talked to Gabriel a little. About being bi."

Taylor gaped at him. "Wow. Really?"

"Yeah. It seemed like he'd understand, and it was kind of nice to get that out there, you know?"

"Of course. I think that's fantastic. What—"

"Daddy, Daddy, I'm done! Can we go sledding now? *Pleaaase.*" Ava came skidding into the entryway. Her eyes were very big and very round and Taylor thought it was a miracle that anyone ever said no to her. About *anything.*

Jamie grinned at her. "Well, I think we better check to make sure you got everything put away."

"I kinda had trouble with a couple of things but I *tried.*"

"Trying is what's important." Jamie patted her back and glanced at Taylor. "We'll be back in a few."

Ava piped up. "Can we give Taylor a tour of the house? I want him to see my bedroom!"

"Sure. If he doesn't mind."

Taylor grinned at Ava. "I'd love that."

Ava held out her hand and Taylor took it, noticing Jamie's soft smile as he was tugged past.

The interior of the house was as impressive as the exterior. Taylor loved the gorgeous hardwood floors and white-painted board and batten trim he encountered as Ava marched him through the first floor, bypassing a split staircase.

"Bedrooms are up there," Jamie said, pointing to the one that led upstairs, then the one that went down. "Rec area and workout room are downstairs."

He also showed off a massive kitchen with light wood cabinets and beautifully veined white marble countertops that Taylor's mom and Charlie would drool over.

There was also a breakfast nook, formal dining room, and sprawling living room that he pointed out before he turned back and led them to the upstairs which held four bedrooms and at least that many bathrooms.

Taylor's parents' home was oversized too but this seemed ridiculously enormous for two people.

"Planning a big family when you bought this?" Taylor asked, amused.

The flicker of hurt that crossed Jamie's face made Taylor instantly regret his question.

"I had originally wanted a couple of kids. Two or three, maybe. I was in the middle of the divorce when I bought this place but I … yeah, I guess I've always hoped I'd meet someone and have that."

"Oh God, Jamie, I'm sorry." Taylor laid a hand on Jamie's upper arm, hating that he'd touched a sore spot.

Jamie gave Taylor a lopsided smile that didn't quite reach his eyes. "It's okay. I understand why you asked."

Ava tugged a little harder. "C'mon. My room's this way."

"I'm coming, I'm coming," Taylor said with a laugh, relieved she'd broken the heavy mood. Ava's bedroom was surprisingly clean, with a hastily made bed and a few toys that hadn't quite made it into the toy box or shelves lined with bins.

Taylor glanced around, liking the bright, colorful room, but his gaze skidded to a stop when he saw an image of himself on the wall.

"You have a poster of me." Taylor blinked.

"Isn't it *pretty*? I think you're the prettiest skater ever, Taylor," Ava said with a sigh, leaning her head against Taylor's arm and looking up at him.

Taylor smiled at her. "That's very sweet. I think my friend Charlie is pretty too, though."

"Charlie Mona—mona—" Her face screwed up. "I can't say his name right."

"Monaghan," Taylor supplied.

"Yeah, him!"

"Oh shit," Jamie said under his breath. "I know he introduced himself the other night but I never put the two together. He was a competitive skater too. He retired from the sport at the same time you did, right?"

"He did. You know your men's figure skaters," Taylor said with an amused smile.

Jamie rubbed the back of his neck. "Uh, well I kinda got into it after the Olympics."

Taylor gently poked his chest. "I think I'm going to need to hear more about that in the future."

"Maybe later."

"It won't fit." Ava was trying to jam a plastic dollhouse into a purple toy box. "Help, Daddy."

"A please would be appreciated." Jamie knelt beside her on the rug. "And how about we take out a couple of things that are getting in the way first?"

"Please, Daddy? I need your help."

Taylor watched them work together, feeling another dangerous flutter of his heart at the sight of them, Ava's blonde curls a few shades lighter than Jamie's darker gold waves, their determined expressions so alike.

"Okay, I think that's acceptable." Jamie closed the lid, then rose to his feet. "Now, let's get dressed and go outside!"

It took a while, but they eventually got Ava and themselves bundled up in winter gear and Jamie led them out into the back yard.

"When you mentioned a sledding hill, I thought it might be a little taller than this," Taylor said with a chuckle. The gentle slope in the backyard was maybe eight or ten feet at most. Not quite the skiing hill he'd pictured.

"Ehh, it's good for now," Jamie said with a shrug. "We may have to go elsewhere when she gets a bit bigger but for now she's happy and it saves me from having a heart attack about her crashing into a tree and breaking an arm or something."

Taylor laughed. "Fair enough."

Sledding mostly consisted of Jamie gently pushing Ava's pink sled down the slope, accompanied by her delighted giggles, before he had to haul the sled back up to the top with her still on it. Taylor noticed he favored one arm, and worried that his shoulder was bothering him. His strength was impressive though.

"I see what this is," Taylor joked. "You're secretly working out."

Jamie laughed. "No, the secret is that with kids around, *everything* is a workout."

Taylor took a few turns hauling Ava around too, and at the end, she convinced him to sit on the sled with her. "C'mon. It's fun. We go *so* fast."

They did go faster than Taylor expected, and he enjoyed Ava's delighted giggles the whole way down. He tried not to notice that Jamie was recording them with his phone. When they reached the bottom of the 'hill', Taylor fell back, smiling up at the sky.

"C'mon." Jamie walked over. "Don't tell me you're tired yet. Which one of us is an old man?"

"You're thirty-four," Taylor protested. "You're not old."

"Ten years older than you," Jamie countered but Taylor gave him the raspberries. He wasn't *that* much older.

"Age is just a number," he said breezily. "Now, help me up."

Ava had run off, apparently done with sledding, so Jamie held out a hand and pulled Taylor to his feet.

They helped Ava make a rather haphazard snowman before she got distracted by pelting Jamie with snowballs. Of course, Taylor teamed up with her and added a few of his own.

"Rude!" Jamie laughed, his smile gleaming like the remnants of snow that dusted his deep blue jacket.

He scooped up a handful of snow and went after Taylor and Ava. They dodged and weaved until Ava finally darted around Taylor, hiding behind him. Taylor wound up with a faceful of snow, sputtering as he wiped it off.

"*I'm* rude?" Taylor protested, laughing.

Jamie walked closer and gently dusted off Taylor's face with his soft fleecy gloves, his eyes so warm and happy that Taylor let out an audible sigh. He turned away and blindly scooped up snow, pelting Jamie with it before he did something stupid like kiss him in front of Ava.

By the time they finally declared the battle a draw, Taylor was winded. "I think I might need to do some more conditioning. I've been slacking on my cardio," he gasped. "Sooo not in shape anymore."

Ava giggled but Jamie gave him another one of those fond looks when Ava tugged at his hand. "Could've fooled me."

Jamie let out an '*oof*' when Ava pulled him down and he toppled into the snow.

"We should make snow angels, Daddy!"

Taylor stared down at them both for a moment.

God, Jamie looked good like this. His cheeks were flushed and his eyes sparkled. Snow clung to the little tufts of hair that peeked out from under his cap, making the ends of it curl.

Unable to look a moment longer, Taylor flopped onto the snow beside him, staring at the cloud-speckled blue sky instead. This was painfully close to what he wanted for a future; a husband and kids and sledding and building snowmen.

He knew raising children wasn't *only* moments like that. There were tantrums and puking. Difficult and painful challenges that would test even the most experienced and level-headed parent.

But Taylor still wanted it. Still felt that tug in his gut that told him this was the life he was meant for.

He turned his head to look at Jamie, who was already staring at him. His face was so soft, eyes warm, lips curved up at the corners, fondness radiating from every inch of him.

And then he reached out, bumping Taylor's mitten with his glove until he could hold Taylor's hand.

Taylor let out a ridiculous little squeaking sound. He was done for.

Absolutely done for.

Watching Taylor fit right into his and Ava's shenanigans was enough to make Jamie want to pin Taylor to a snowbank and kiss him senseless but since Ava was there and he and Taylor weren't sure what they were doing, Jamie reluctantly got to his feet and held out two hands instead.

"Okay, I think I'm about done out here. What do you say we go inside and get warmed up?"

Taylor and Ava let him pull them to their feet and Jamie noticed their cheeks were flushed the same shade of pink. He wanted to grab them both, pull them into a hug, and never let go.

They trooped inside, stomping the snow off their boots as they tromped through the garage and into the mudroom.

Jamie'd hired a renovation company to redo the house before he moved in, and he was still pleased with how the mudroom had turned out. It was lined with white board and batten that matched the rest of the house and built-in cabinets the same dark gray shade they'd used on the exterior.

It looked nice, but mostly he loved the cubbies for shoes and hooks everywhere, and the floors made of slate tiles. It was easy for Ava to keep her belongings put away and easy for Jamie to clean.

He had a cleaning service that came in once a week to scrub the toilets and mop the floors, but he tried to keep the house from turning into a total wreck otherwise. Today, he might have done some extra tidying before Taylor came over, however, wanting to make a good impression.

Ava quickly stripped out of her outerwear but Jamie hesitated. "Hey, why don't we park your car in the garage, Taylor? We're supposed to get some more snow this afternoon."

Taylor seemed surprised. "That's sweet but I can head out now."

Ava gave Taylor a mournful look, poised in the middle of wrestling her second boot off. "But we're gonna have *hot chocolate*. You can't go before that!"

"Well, if there's hot chocolate …"

Ava grinned and stuffed her boots into the cubby to drip dry onto a mat. "Gotta pee!" she yelled, running full speed to the bathroom.

Chuckling, Jamie bumped Taylor's elbow. "If you're really good, I'll make my famous grilled cheese and tomato soup for lunch."

"That does sound tempting." Taylor lowered his voice, smirking up at Jamie. "What do I get if I'm bad?"

Jamie licked his lips, imagining what it would feel like to get his mouth on Taylor's cock. "You *know* what you get."

"Do I? I might need you to refresh my memory." Taylor batted his lashes.

Jamie let out a little noise, somewhere between a growl of frustration and a scoff. "I doubt that."

"Humor me," Taylor said.

Jamie couldn't resist pressing another quick kiss to his lips.

"Later," he promised, and Taylor let out a grumbly sigh that made Jamie smile.

Taylor fished his keys out of his zippered coat pocket, then dropped them into Jamie's hand. "Okay, I'll stay a while."

Jamie went into the garage and pulled Taylor's car into the empty spot beside his Range Rover.

After, he followed the sound of quiet laughter into the kitchen.

His heart did something funny as he watched Taylor gently run a brush through Ava's tangled hair, Taylor intently listening while she chattered on about her favorite cartoon.

They were *good* together.

Taylor was good with him and Ava. And Jamie knew this was the very beginning but it was too easy to see what it could be like if they became a family.

If only he knew if Taylor wanted this life.

What if he wanted to date around? What if he didn't want serious commitment?

"Who's ready for some hot chocolate?" Jamie asked, forcing the fear away and injecting some cheer into his voice. He pulled open one of the floor-to-ceiling pantry cabinet doors and grabbed the mix and some marshmallows.

"Me!" Ava and Taylor both chorused.

It didn't take long to make the cocoa, and Jamie liked the sight of Ava and Taylor both sipping their warm drink across the wide marble island.

He cradled his own mug in his hands. "Now, how about some lunch to go along with all of that chocolate?"

"I believe I was promised grilled cheese and tomato soup," Taylor said, and Ava let out a little cheer.

"*Yummm*, Daddy makes the best grilled cheese."

"Does he now?" Taylor gave Jamie a challenging look.

"I do."

"Well, I'm looking forward to that."

Twenty minutes later, Jamie set out plates and bowls in front of Taylor.

Taylor inspected his sandwich dubiously. "Mayo instead of butter on the bread, huh? I don't know how I feel about that."

"It's my mom's trick. Try it. It makes the bread nice and crispy."

"It's the *best*," Ava gushed.

Taylor took a cautious bite, his expression surprised as he chewed and swallowed. "Okay, that *is* pretty good."

Jamie grinned and went to fix himself one.

"Don't forget to eat some vegetables," he called over his shoulder as he slapped the sandwich into the pan.

"Me too?" Taylor said and Jamie looked over his shoulder to see him with a cheeky grin on his face.

Jamie brandished a spatula at him. "Yes, you too."

Taylor grinned as he crunched into one of the baby carrots Jamie had put out and warmth settled into Jamie's chest. He'd been missing moments like this for so damn long and all he could do was hope that this was something he could hold on to.

"We should watch a movie, Daddy!" Ava begged as she finished helping Jamie load the dishwasher.

Jamie glanced at Taylor. "Would you be up for that?"

"Yeah." Taylor smiled. "That sounds nice."

He'd totally fallen under the Walsh family's spell, enjoying the warm, cozy vibes of the day too much to tear himself away although he knew he should.

"Yay! I'm gonna pick out a movie!" Ava shouted, running from the kitchen.

"Taylor gets veto rights!" Jamie called after her.

"Are you sure you don't need any help?" Taylor asked.

Jamie gave the counter a final wipe down. "Nah, we've got a pretty good routine going. Thanks though."

"Thanks for lunch." Taylor slipped down from the brown leather stool. "It was delicious."

"Any time." Jamie dried his hands on a dish towel. "Now, do you think we might have a minute alone?"

"You tell me," Taylor said with a laugh. "How patient is she?"

"Not very." Jamie made a face and reached out, tugging Taylor close. "Gets that from me."

Taylor rested his palms on Jamie's chest, smiling up at him. "At least you're both charming."

"We try." Jamie slipped a hand around Taylor's neck, pulling him in for a kiss.

Taylor settled against him with a sigh, winding his arms around Jamie's neck and kissing him back.

His mouth tasted a bit like lunch but Taylor had no complaints as they made out, Jamie shifting to pin Taylor against the counter.

"God, I need you," he whispered, tugging down Taylor's gray cowl neck sweater to drag kisses up his neck.

"Jamie," Taylor whispered, clutching his biceps.

"You have no idea how badly I want to lift you up onto this counter and work you open with my fingers," Jamie rasped in his ear. "Then slide my cock into you until you come all over both of us."

Taylor shuddered in his arms. He opened his mouth to beg for that when Ava bellowed, "Are you coming?" from the other room.

"Sadly, no," Jamie grumbled, burying his head against Taylor's shoulder.

"Aww, poor baby," Taylor crooned. He slid his fingers through Jamie's hair for a moment before disentangling their bodies. He stepped away, grimacing when he realized he was half-hard from a few kisses and heated words.

"We'll be there in a minute," Taylor called to Ava, walking toward the living room.

He glanced back at Jamie who was adjusting his own erection in his sweats. He gave Taylor a shrug. "I'm gonna need a few."

Taylor grinned all the way to the living room.

Ava was sprawled on the big sectional, a fuzzy blanket pulled over her, looking very cozy.

Taylor took a seat on the couch.

Ava gestured to the movie she had cued up. "My *favorite*."

Jamie joined them and groaned. "We've watched this at least eighty-two times, Bear."

"But Taylor hasn't seen it, right?"

Taylor shook his head.

"Then we gotta watch."

Jamie gave Taylor a long-suffering look as he dropped onto the couch between them. "I guess I can't argue with that."

The movie was cute but Taylor had a difficult time focusing when Ava nestled close to Jamie on one side and Jamie draped an arm over the back of the couch, behind Taylor's shoulders. It was perfectly platonic, and Taylor didn't snuggle in, but he didn't pull away from the occasional brush of Jamie's fingers against his upper arm either.

Jamie's comfortable sprawl meant his thigh was pressed right to Taylor's.

It was distracting, and Taylor was hyperaware of his proximity and how badly he wanted to curl up and tuck himself close.

"Look at that," Jamie said quietly, about twenty minutes into the movie. "I guess all of that fresh air and exercise wore her out."

Taylor glanced over to see Ava with her head against Jamie's thigh, mouth slightly parted, lashes long against her cheeks.

"Aww." Taylor smiled.

Jamie's arm tightened around Taylor's shoulder for a moment, and he nuzzled into his cheek with his nose. "If I thought we could sneak upstairs without waking her up, I'd try," Jamie whispered in his ear.

"Shh," Taylor chastised. "I'm trying to watch the movie."

Jamie laughed softly and kissed his cheek. "Bet I could distract you."

"I bet you could too." Taylor rested a hand on Jamie's thigh and squeezed. He left it there, enjoying the heat from Jamie's firm muscles radiating through the soft fabric of his sweats.

He shifted to press his cheek against Jamie's shoulder and returned to watching the movie, smiling when he felt the press of lips against his hair.

It was a silly kids' adventure movie but much better than he'd expected and even Jamie—who had apparently seen it numerous times—chuckled frequently.

But after a little while, he grew quiet and still too, slumping heavily against Taylor.

Taylor yawned and shifted, drawing his legs up to the side. The weight of Jamie's arm around him and the cozy warmth of being held close made his eyes drift shut.

With a soft sigh, Taylor slept too.

CHAPTER EIGHTEEN

"I'm so excited." Ava hopped from one foot to the other as they walked toward the rink. "I get to skate with you and Taylor. This is the best day ever!"

Jamie chuckled, then gripped her hand when her pink boots slipped on a patch of slushy snow. "It'll be fun," he agreed.

"I liked when Taylor came over yesterday."

"I did too, Bear. It was fun to go sledding and watch a movie with him. Even if we fell asleep on him."

Ava giggled. "He fell asleep too."

"He did," Jamie said with a soft smile, remembering the slight weight of Taylor curled against his side, warm and tucked close.

He'd been adorably sleepy after and Jamie had wanted nothing more than to wrap him up in his arms and refuse to let him go.

Unfortunately, he'd excused himself soon after to go home. Jamie *and* Ava had both been disappointed that he hadn't at least stayed for dinner. Jamie had been even more disappointed he hadn't managed to sneak away with Taylor for a quick hand job in the laundry room or even a few minutes of making out.

Later that night, he'd texted Taylor to make sure he was okay. He'd assured Jamie he was, only worried that Ava had seen them cuddling. But Jamie wasn't concerned. If he didn't treat it like it was a big deal, Ava wouldn't think it was a big deal.

And since Kara was out of town and Ava couldn't accidentally slip and tell her about it, Jamie figured they were fine. Hopefully, by the time she returned, Jamie would know what was going on with Taylor.

God, Jamie hadn't thought about that. Not only would they have to tell their families and the team, Jamie would have to tell his ex. He wasn't looking forward to *that* conversation.

But that was a problem for another day.

Once they were inside the building, Ava took off, running full tilt toward the ice.

"Taylor! Taylor!" she shouted. Jamie smiled when Ava ran straight for him, throwing her arms around his waist.

She was getting so tall, and Jamie made a mental note to check that she wasn't outgrowing her skates. At that age, he'd gone through pairs constantly.

Taylor wrapped Ava in a big hug. "Hi! You made it today. And look how cute your braids are. Did your dad do that?"

"Sure did," Jamie bragged. "Because I am the coolest dad ever."

Taylor grinned. "Well, hello there, Mr. Modest."

"Hi." Jamie wanted to lean in and kiss Taylor but he settled for a hug and a barely noticeable brush of his lips against Taylor's cheek.

When he drew back, Taylor's expression was warm and soft, lips parted, his head tilted back like he was dying for a kiss on the lips too.

Later, Jamie silently promised himself. Even if he had to drag Taylor into the locker room or something. Ava would be fine in the player lounge area, right? The place was pretty much deserted except for a few support staff people.

Taylor clapped his hands. "Okay, who's ready to skate!"

Jamie looked around. "I thought we had a crew with us today."

"Nope. It's just the three of us. A few members of the media team are at All-Star Weekend and the rest are not filming any new content here until the team returns to play. Mostly just keeping up with social media and stuff."

"I probably should have paid more attention to the emails I got about the schedule."

Taylor chuckled. "Probably. But it sounds like Ava's mom is okay with these lessons getting filmed, right?"

"Yeah, when I emailed about it, she said that she signed the waiver, so we're all set."

"Great."

Ava tugged at Jamie's sleeve. "Can we skate now, Daddy?"

Taylor laughed. "She's as eager to get on the ice as I am."

"Yes," Jamie said. "Let me grab some equipment and then we can get our skates on and do this!"

When they were on the ice, they did a few lazy warmup circles. They had no real agenda today and since they weren't being filmed, Jamie chose his hockey skates, which were still so much more comfortable than the figure skates.

He handed a mini stick to Ava who immediately took off with it, then handed Taylor an old stick of his he'd cut down, sized for Taylor's shorter height. "How does that feel?" he asked.

"Fine." Taylor shrugged. "It's been a while but it's not like this is the first stick I've handled."

He said it without a trace of guile, wide-eyed and earnest, and Jamie skated toward him and gently checked him with his hip. "I bet it's not. I'm looking forward to having you handle *my* stick again."

"Five minutes for bad jokes!"

Jamie squawked. "Five minutes! That's excessive. I'm going to need that penalty reviewed, ref."

Taylor giggled. He looked so fucking cute dressed in his snug blue leggings and cream and blue oversized sweater. He even had a matching hat and gloves, and his eyes were dusted with something sparkly and blue. Jamie fucking loved it and all he wanted to do was kiss the sticky pink gloss off his lips.

He cleared his throat and turned away. "Okay, let's shoot some pucks!"

They spent a little while playfully competing to see who could get the most pucks in. With no one to mind the net, it wasn't difficult and, unsurprisingly, Jamie excelled at it.

Taylor held his own though and he was remarkably accurate.

"Wow, I'm impressed," Jamie said when they stopped to take a break.

Taylor scoffed. "You think my dad wasn't hoping for a son who played hockey? Trust me. I grew up doing this shi—stuff."

Jamie smirked at his correction. "Did he mind that you didn't follow in his footsteps?"

"A little bit at first, I think," Taylor said thoughtfully. He skated past, bending down to pick up pucks and place them in the bucket. "But he quickly saw how much I loved figure skating and when it came time to get serious about one or the other, he was gracious about it. Told me that my happiness was what mattered most."

"Why *did* you quit?" Jamie asked. It hadn't really occurred to him until now that he had no idea why both Taylor and Charlie had retired from competitive skating. Neither of them had spoken about it with the press other than some vague statements.

Taylor glanced at Ava who was doing some twirls. "That's a story for another day, I'm afraid."

"Okay." Jamie skated closer. "I want to know more about you though, okay?"

Taylor brushed his fingers against Jamie's as they passed. "Yeah, I promise I'll tell you more soon."

"Sounds good."

Jamie approached Ava. "How's it going, Bear? Did you have fun hitting some pucks?"

"Yes!" She giggled. "So much fun. I wanna do some twirls now though."

"You can twirl to your heart's content," he promised.

They fooled around with figure skating tricks for a while, Taylor mainly working with Ava since Jamie had his hockey skates on and without a toe pick, he couldn't do most of them.

After a while, Ava took Jamie's hands and tugged. "I want you to spin me, Daddy."

Jamie laughed. "Just a few. My shoulder is hurting."

It was actually feeling a bit better than it had last week. A couple of days of rest helped and Jamie thought by their next game, he'd be almost back to normal. Which was good, because he was a little afraid of how much it would ache by the time they hit the playoffs.

It was one of those slow, nagging injuries. There was a good chance they'd have to shoot him up with steroids to get him through the playoffs and he'd probably have to have an arthroscopic procedure done at the end of the season to clean up some of the fraying to his tendons.

Ugh. He wasn't looking forward to *that*.

But again, that was a problem for another day.

Still, Jamie was careful when he picked Ava up, engaging his core to lift her as he spun in a circle. She giggled the whole time as she flew through the air and Jamie grinned at her unapologetic joy.

"Nice moves there, Walsh!" Taylor called. "Are you sure you don't want a career in pairs skating?"

Jamie cracked up as he slowed and gently lowered Ava to the ice. "Not unless they start letting five-year-olds compete in the Olympics. I don't think I should lift much more weight than that."

Taylor let out a little shudder. "There's enough pressure on teenage skaters. I don't want to think about what that would do to little ones."

Jamie's laughter faded as he wondered if Taylor's retirement had anything to do with that pressure.

"Well, Ava doesn't get any pressure from me," Jamie said lightly. "If she wants to do figure skating, I'll support that. Or she can be a hockey player. Or whatever else she wants to be on or off the ice."

"I'm gonna be a mermaid astronaut!" Ava shouted, her voice echoing in the otherwise empty rink.

Taylor laughed. "I love it!"

"I'm still trying to figure out how they're going to make a space-suit that'll work with the tail but I'm confident by the time she's old enough, someone will have worked out the technology," Jamie said with a shrug.

Taylor grinned at Ava. "I think you'll be wonderful."

"Daddy says I can be anything I want!" She took off toward the other end of the rink, skating as fast as she could, a little wobbly but more solid on her skates than she had been when she started lessons.

"Except a jerk!" Jamie called out. "I won't have that, Bear."

"Why do you call her Bear?" Taylor asked.

Jamie smiled. "We brought her home from the hospital in a tiny bear onesie. It was made from brown fleece and had these little ears on the hood."

"Oh God, that sounds adorable." Taylor sighed. "I can totally imagine it."

"It was. So yeah, I started calling her Ava-Bear, which is mostly just Bear now."

"That's so cute." Taylor tucked his arm through Jamie's so they were skating together, their strides easily falling into rhythm.

"I'll show you the photos sometime," Jamie promised. He paused and blurted out the question he'd been wondering for a while. "Do you think you'd ever want kids?"

Taylor blinked at him. "Of course I want kids. I've wanted that for a long time."

"What about being with someone who already had a kid?" He held his breath.

"I'd love that kid too," Taylor said firmly. He let his shoulder rest against Jamie's arm, squeezing his forearm gently.

"That's … that's really good to hear." Jamie swallowed against the emotion rising in his throat. "I'm glad."

"Look at me, Daddy! Taylor!" Ava called and they turned to give her their full attention.

"All right, my mermaid astronaut," Jamie said a while later, when Ava was beginning to look tired. He swooped in to catch her and spin her one last time before pulling her close again. "What do you think about calling it a day?"

She stuck out her lower lip as he swept her up into his arms. "But I'm having *fun*."

"We can do it again," Taylor said. He glanced over at Jamie to confirm it. "I mean, I'd like to do it again, if that works for your dad."

"Of course," Jamie said easily. "We'll definitely come back."

Taylor patted her shoulder. "Maybe sometime I'll invite my friend Charlie too. I bet he'd have fun hanging out with us."

"Really?" Ava went wide-eyed. "Oh, that would be *so cool*."

"That's 'cause Taylor's a very cool guy," Jamie said.

Taylor looked at Ava. "Your dad, however, is a really big dork."

"I am not!" Jamie protested but he was laughing. "I'm very cool."

"Mm-hmm. You keep telling yourself that."

Ava giggled.

They were all laughing as they skated toward the exit and the bench where they'd left their belongings.

Jamie put Ava down when they reached the rubber and she waddled over to take off her skates. Jamie looped an arm around Taylor's shoulder, brushing his nose against Taylor's cheek. "Thank you for this," he whispered. "This has been so great today."

"You're welcome. I had a great time too." Taylor turned his head, and their mouths were inches apart. The look in his eyes was so filled with need that Jamie could hardly draw in a breath.

"God, Taylor," he whispered. "I—"

"Hi, Mr. Coach!" Ava's words made both Jamie and Taylor freeze.

Taylor tried to pull away but Jamie remembered the moment when Charlie had walked in on them and forced himself to hold still. He squeezed Taylor once, pressing a soft kiss to his cheek before he pulled back, arm still around his shoulders.

When Jamie looked over at Ava, he saw Lance Tate standing nearby. His expression was filled with surprise and confusion but he glanced down at Ava with a sincere smile. "Hi, it's nice to see you again, Ava. Did you have fun skating today?"

“I did! I had so much fun with Daddy and Taylor. We did jumps and shot pucks. It was the best day ever!”

“That does sound like a great day.” Lance’s smile was kind. He looked away from Ava to meet Jamie’s eyes. “Sorry to interrupt your skating time. I heard people having fun and I wanted to see who was out on the ice. I hope you don’t mind.”

His gaze flicked between the two of them but Jamie didn’t drop his arm from around Taylor’s shoulders.

“No problem,” Jamie said. Taylor’s body was still rigid beside him, and Jamie rubbed his upper arm.

Trust me, Taylor, he thought.

“Hey, do you have a minute to talk, Coach?” Jamie asked, finally letting go of Taylor with one last squeeze. He sat down to unlace his skates.

“Sure.”

“Do you mind?” He glanced over at Taylor as he unlaced.

“I’m pretty sure Ava and I can entertain ourselves for a few minutes,” Taylor said with a smile, but his face was filled with soft concern.

It’s okay, Jamie tried to convey with his gaze. *I’m fine.*

“I’ll be back in a bit, Ava,” Jamie said after his winter boots were on. “Listen to Taylor, please.”

She looked up and nodded, so Jamie followed Tate down the hall and to his office.

“I don’t want to assume anything,” Coach said slowly when they were behind closed doors. “But if I drew a conclusion from what I saw earlier, I want to promise you I won’t repeat it to anyone if that’s what you prefer.”

Jamie smiled. "So, I guess that answers the question if Gabriel said anything to you."

Lance looked startled. "No, he didn't breathe a word about you and Taylor."

"Well, I didn't tell him that the other day," Jamie admitted. "Just mentioned I was, uh, questioning my sexuality."

"Ahh." Lance's nod was understanding.

"This is complicated though, right?" Jamie said. "I mean with the team and all?"

Lance grimaced. "Yes. Although that's more Gabriel and my fault than yours and Taylor's. Unfortunately, management is pretty touchy now and HR read us the riot act after we were caught. Taylor may not be on the team or part of our official support staff but he is working closely with the organization, so I strongly suggest you come clean about it quickly."

Jamie sighed. "I know. Taylor and I have some things we need to figure out first but if we *do* choose to give this relationship a shot, we'll disclose to management immediately, Coach."

"Lance, please. And it looks to me like you've both chosen already," Lance said softly. "And that little girl of yours clearly adores Taylor."

"She does. That's not the problem," Jamie admitted. "It's, uh, our families."

Lance winced. "Oh, I hadn't even thought about the history there. I certainly understand the concern. That's a lot to overcome."

"The worst part is, I have some shit I'm dealing with too. Like from my ex." Jamie slumped back in his chair with a sigh.

"That can't have been an easy situation." Lance's tone was diplomatic but Jamie thought he might understand. He was also divorced and someone who hadn't realized he was bi until later.

"No, not easy at all. But I—I don't want to lose Taylor, you know? I am seeing a therapist now so I don't screw it all up this time. I have my first appointment the day after tomorrow actually."

"Good." Lance's smile was encouraging. "I think that's very healthy."

Jamie sighed. "Maybe Taylor and I can drag our families in for a huge group session too or something."

Lance chuckled. "Might be worth a try. You never know."

Jamie rubbed at his forehead. "I *do* know it's going to get ugly. More for Taylor than me but I still don't want his relationship with me to come between him and his family, you know?"

"I understand that. I think you have to be careful not to let what they want overrule what you want though."

Jamie considered that idea. "True. I guess I have done that in the past."

Not so much with his parents or anything but with Kara. He'd felt so guilty about being gone so much that he'd caved to everything she'd wanted and ignored his own needs. He'd let her call the shots even when he knew it would make him miserable.

That was … hmm, probably something he needed to think more about actually.

"Thanks for understanding and giving Taylor and me time to figure out how we want to go about this."

Jamie held out a hand to his coach who took it and gave him a firm handshake although with a sincere smile.

"Of course. And you're welcome to reach out to Gabriel or me any time, okay? If you ever need to talk."

"I appreciate that. It means a lot."

"We'll have your back if it comes to that," Lance added. "I can promise that."

"Thank you." Jamie nodded at him gratefully and left his office, his body buzzing with the weight of what had happened. His coach knew he and Taylor were involved. That was pretty huge.

Now Jamie just had to hope that Taylor was okay with how he'd handled it.

———

"You're doing *what* today?" Charlie blinked at Taylor across the breakfast table.

"Watching Ava," Taylor mumbled around the rim of his mug.

Charlie raised an eyebrow. "Dude. I know he's got a big dick but are you seriously letting your booty call turn you into a babysitter?"

Taylor reeled back at the venom in Charlie's voice. "He's not turning me into a *babysitter*. He asked me if I'd watch her for a few hours while he's going to his first therapy appointment. His ex is out of town and his parents are taking some time off to visit his brother who lives out of state. Jesus."

"Oh." Charlie looked a little sheepish.

"And for what it's worth," Taylor continued. "I *volunteered* when the neighbor girl who fills in sometimes couldn't do it."

"Okay, okay!" Charlie held up his hands. "Color me corrected. I leapt to conclusions there."

"Also, we're talking about dating *and* he told his coach about us yesterday."

Charlie froze, staring at Taylor wide-eyed, his spoon lifted halfway to his lips. "What now?"

Taylor repeated the story and Charlie blinked at him.

"I dunno, Tay," he said, this time sounding a little reluctant. "Did he tell his coach or did the guy see something he couldn't explain away?"

"Coach Tate saw us but Jamie was great about it. He acted like he was proud of being with me *and* asked the coach to talk. He told him that once we made a decision about what we're doing, he'll disclose our relationship to management."

"Okay, that's something." The skeptical look remained on Charlie's face. "But I still worry. You need to be realistic. Your dad is going to flip his fucking lid when he finds out."

"I know." Taylor exhaled. "I know he will and it's going to be fucking awful and ugh, I hate that. But this is a feud that should have been dead and buried a decade ago."

"Yeah well, it hasn't so …" Charlie spread his hands wide. "I don't think that's magically going to go away, no matter how much you want it to."

"I watched the videos of my dad's injury last night."

Charlie looked startled. "Whoa. You've never wanted to before."

"I didn't. And it was fucking horrible." Taylor's voice shook a little, remembering. God, the sound of the board-rattling hit. The image of his father lying motionless on the ice. The sight of him being strapped onto a backboard and taken out of the rink by paramedics … they were seared into Taylor's brain now and he'd never get them out.

But it was important for him to finally see it for what it really was. An *accident*. A horrible, tragic accident.

And yes, maybe it could have been avoided. But Jamie's father hadn't been a dirty player. Or at least that hit certainly hadn't been. Most of the videos floating around made it look bad. It *did* look like Adam Walsh had accelerated to hit Rick Hollis but he hadn't. Taylor had dug up a longer clip that showed the whole sequence from start to finish and what he'd seen in that had been exactly what Jamie had described before.

Tucker—one of Adam Walsh's teammates on the Chicago Windstorm—had slammed into him after a hit from one of Rick Hollis's own teammates from Detroit. In the end, it was like a line of toppling dominoes or a Rube Goldberg machine. One action had led to another and, unfortunately, Rick Hollis had ended up having to pay the consequences.

It was a career-ending injury. It could have paralyzed him or even killed him. But it hadn't. He was alive and healthy and he worked happily as an investment broker now. The accident had changed Rick's future but it hadn't destroyed it. And it seemed grossly unfair to punish a man who hadn't really been at fault.

"Tay?" Charlie said and Taylor shook his head before looking him in the eye.

"Yeah, it was hard to watch," he repeated. "But I discovered the truth. My dad was wrong about how it all went down. I'm just going to have to convince him of that."

"That does not sound like an easy job."

Taylor snorted. "Oh God no. It'll be awful. But hopefully, I can get my mom on board. We'll have to work up to it. And we'll wait to tell him until he's softened up a little to the idea first."

"Good luck with that." Charlie raised his mug in a cheers gesture. "Let me know if there's anything I can do to help."

"Well, it would be nice if you weren't questioning Jamie's motives in the meantime," Taylor pointed out. "I know this is complicated, but I really like him, Charlie."

"I'm a little confused by the abrupt change," Charlie said, his forehead wrinkling. "One minute you wanted nothing to do with him. Then you were fuck buddies. And now you're talking about blowing up your family to be with him."

"It's been a big change," Taylor admitted. "And yeah, it's been fast. But I think if you give him a chance, you'll really like him."

"I'll try to keep an open mind."

"Thanks." Taylor stood, intending to clear away both of their bowls but he saw that Charlie's was still nearly full. "Hey, babe, you haven't eaten much. Not feeling hungry this morning?"

"Oh, just got distracted listening to you yammer," Charlie said breezily. "You know how it is."

A flicker of worry went through Taylor because that was exactly the kind of shit that Charlie had pulled in the past when he was struggling with his eating disorder. But he lifted his spoon to his lips, his expression guileless as he took another bite, so Taylor cleared his own dishes without commenting.

He turned to take a seat again but there was a quiet rap on the door.

"Oh, they're here already!" Taylor said with a glance at the clock. *Whoops*. He'd totally lost track of time.

"Hi, Taylor!" Ava said when he opened the door. She walked in like she owned the place, already wriggling out of her winter coat. "Daddy said we're hanging out today."

"We are!" Taylor said with a smile. "And I have a surprise for you. We're hanging out with another friend of mine you know."

"I believe that's my cue!" Charlie appeared in the doorway, posing dramatically.

Ava's eyes got big, and she whispered, "That's *Charlie*."

"Yep, he's my roommate," Taylor said. "Ava, meet Charlie Monaghan. Charlie, this is Ava Walsh."

"Hi," Ava breathed. "Wow, you're as pretty as Taylor."

Charlie beamed. For all he claimed to find children a nuisance, he was really good with them. Taylor could respect that he didn't want any of his own but Taylor was honestly looking forward to Charlie being an uncle to his future kids.

And then it hit him that if things went really well with Jamie and they figured all their shit out, someday Taylor would be Ava's *stepdad*. That was enough to make him feel a little lightheaded. It wasn't a bad thing. Far from it, actually, but it was the first time he'd really truly considered the idea.

"So, it looks like you're going to be in really good hands for the morning," Jamie said with a smile. "Now, remember what we talked about on the drive here, Ava?"

"Yep. I'm gonna listen to what Taylor says. And I hafta pick up after my messes and use my words when I need something," she parroted.

"Exactly. I know you can do it." Jamie bent down and kissed the top of her head. He gave Taylor a hug and kissed his cheek.

"And you have my number if you need anything. I'm not worried but just in case …"

"Oh, don't you fret," Charlie said with a smile. "We can handle this."

Jamie grinned. "I have no doubt of it. Nice to see you again, Charlie."

Ava craned her neck. "You know Charlie too, Daddy?"

Jamie's lips twitched like he was trying not to laugh. "Yeah, we met once."

Charlie smothered a snort, probably remembering the sight of a mostly naked Jamie tumbling out of Taylor's bed.

"Cool! Can I see your house, Taylor?" Ava asked.

"Sure," he said. "One sec."

"I'll show her the kitchen," Charlie said, gently guiding Ava away with a knowing wink.

"I like Charlie," Jamie said when they were gone. He pulled Taylor close, and he settled against him with a happy sigh. "And we need to figure out a way to get some alone time. Because I really miss kissing you."

Jamie slipped his hand around the back of Taylor's neck and pulled him in for a heated kiss. Taylor closed his eyes and tried not to moan loudly. God, it felt so good to be close to Jamie like this.

They made out for a few minutes until Jamie finally drew back. His gaze was molten, and his lips were slick and shiny. "I really have to go. Don't wanna be late for my first appointment. Miss you though."

"Miss you too," Taylor said with a little smile as Jamie reached for the doorknob.

Taylor watched Jamie walk down the hallway, a little flutter of warmth blossoming in his heart as he pressed his fingers to his lips, still flushed from the kiss.

And then he shook his head and went in search of Ava and Charlie.

"This place is so small," Ava said when they'd finished giving her a tour. She looked around Charlie's room. "My bedroom at home is bigger."

"Well," Taylor said diplomatically. "Your dad picked out a very nice house for the two of you. We needed something a little simpler."

"Because you don't have kids?" Ava asked.

"That's part of it," Taylor said, wondering how exactly he was going to explain the idea of being too broke to afford anything else to her.

But thankfully, she got distracted by Charlie's vanity table. "Oooh, do you have *makeup*, Charlie?"

"I do!"

"Could we play with it?" She tugged at his hand. "Please, please, please. I'll be really careful. Mommy lets me play with hers sometimes."

Charlie smiled. "Yeah, definitely."

"There's one thing I want to do first," Taylor said quickly. "What do you think about making homemade pizza today, Ava?"

Her face lit up. "We can *do* that?"

"Sure!" Taylor grinned. He'd already checked with Jamie to make sure he was okay staying for lunch after. "We'll mix everything up for the crust this morning, and then let it sit for a few hours. After your dad gets back, we can all cook it together."

"Awesome! That sounds *so* fun."

Taylor helped Ava tie her hair back and put on a too-big apron before they got to work. "So, first you have to get out flour and mix it with yeast and salt."

Ava wrinkled her nose, holding onto the back of the chair she stood on to peer into the bowl as Taylor measured and poured the ingredients in. "What's yeast? It smells kinda funny."

"It's what makes bread get all puffy and delicious."

"Okay."

Taylor carefully measured the water and poured it in before he handed Ava a wooden spoon. "Now you stir. You have to go slow, or the flour goes flying everywhere and makes a big mess."

Ava giggled. "I like messes."

Taylor grinned. "Me too. But if you make it, you have to help me clean it up!"

Her laugh was even louder. "You sound like Daddy."

Ava was careful as she stirred, her lip caught between her teeth. Some of the flour did go flying out of the bowl but she was trying to be careful, so Taylor just showed her how to use a spatula to scrape the flour down from the edges of the bowl.

"Okay, that looks good," Taylor said when it was mostly together. "Now, I'm going to put my hands in and squish it all together and make it into a ball."

Ava watched intently while he did it, then held out her hands, wiggling her fingers. "I wanna help."

"Okay." Taylor supervised while Ava squished the dough with more enthusiasm than skill.

"Now, I'm going to finish it, and then we put it in the oven." Taylor shaped the dough into a ball.

"That's silly. It doesn't look like a pizza yet!" Ava giggled again.

Taylor laughed too. "It doesn't. But we're not baking it now. I warmed the oven up earlier and turned it off. So it's only a little bit warm. We're going to cover the bowl with a towel and stick it in the warm oven. It helps the yeast grow big and strong. It's going to puff up and turn into a huge round ball while it's in there."

"Coooool." Ava's eyes got even bigger, and she brushed her hair off her forehead with her arm, leaving a streak of flour on her skin. "I'm excited."

"I think it's fun," Taylor said. He covered the bowl, washed his hands, then helped Ava wash hers. After, they carefully tucked the bowl into the warm oven. "Now, we just let it do its thing."

"Makeup now?" she said hopefully.

"Soon. I want to clean off the counter first and wash the dishes."

She looked around. "I load the dishwasher at home!"

"I don't have one," Taylor admitted as he ran water into the sink and squirted in some soap.

"Yay, bubbles!" Ava said, easily distracted.

Taylor chuckled and put the few dishes into the soapy water to soak for a minute while he cleaned off the counter.

He lifted the lid of the trashcan to throw away an empty flour bag and grumbled when he realized the trash was full. He dropped the garbage in and grabbed the edges of the bag, but he froze when the contents shifted and revealed a little mound of oatmeal and blueberries.

Was that Charlie's uneaten breakfast? Was he fucking doing this again?

God, Taylor had been so sure he was doing better.

"What's wrong, Taylor?" Ava piped up.

Taylor realized he'd been standing there staring down into a trash bag for a while, his stomach knotted with tension.

"Nothing, sweetie. I just need to run the trash out. You go find Charlie, okay?" he said numbly as he cinched the top and tied it off. "I'll be there in a few minutes."

CHAPTER NINETEEN

"Oh, hey, Charlie," Jamie said when he answered the apartment door.

"Hey," Charlie said, letting him inside with a bright smile. "You're probably wondering where your boyfriend and daughter are."

Jamie raised an eyebrow. The thought had vaguely crossed his mind but now he was *really* wondering that. Also pleased to hear Charlie call him Taylor's boyfriend. That was a good sign, right?

"Should I be concerned?" Jamie asked warily, looking around as he stripped off his coat and took off his shoes.

"No. Just brace yourself for some monumental cuteness."

"Cuter than the makeup videos and pics Taylor sent earlier?"

"Cuter than that. Though I did a nice job on her makeup, if I do say so myself."

Jamie chuckled. "You did."

He'd watched them in his vehicle after his first therapy appointment. It had gone well. It was mostly getting the guy caught up on who he was and what was going on in his life, but he was easy to talk to and very laid back about Jamie's sexuality.

Which Jamie had pretty much expected since he was someone Lowell Prescott had suggested but *still.*

Jamie had felt a little raw after spewing out a bunch of crap from his marriage though, and the messages Taylor had sent had been nice. Watching Taylor, Charlie, and Ava clown around on camera had made that tender, bruised feeling in his chest go away.

"C'mon," Charlie coaxed.

He led Jamie to Taylor's bedroom. The door was open, and Jamie paused in the doorway, heart beating fast at the sight in front of him. Taylor was stretched out on the bed, asleep, a book clutched in his hand. His lips were parted as he gently snored and Ava was tucked up beside him, a tangle of blonde curls fanned out over his shoulder.

It was the most achingly sweet scene Jamie had ever seen.

"Oh God," he whispered.

"Right?" Charlie said. "They're grossly adorable."

Jamie chuckled. "I'm tempted to climb in there with them."

Charlie laughed softly. "Why not?"

"I … okay, good point."

Charlie nudged his shoulder. "Go on then."

Jamie shot him a smile, then carefully crawled onto the bed beside Taylor. The door clicked softly shut behind him but as he stretched out, Taylor woke.

"Sorry," Jamie whispered. "You can go back to sleep."

Taylor rubbed his eyes. "I must have been more worn out than I thought."

"Ava will do that to you."

Taylor's smile turned soft and sweet. "I don't mind."

"How about we all snooze for a while longer?"

"Okay." Taylor snuggled close, burying his head against Jamie's chest and he let out a low, relieved sigh.

God, this felt right.

This future they were tentatively exploring wouldn't be easy to create but the past few days had shown Jamie how much he wanted it.

He wanted a shot at a life with Taylor and Ava and if Taylor wanted that too, Jamie would fight for it.

He stroked Taylor's back as he closed his eyes, Taylor's breathing already slow and steady, and soon, Jamie was out too.

"You should kiss Taylor, Daddy."

Jamie blinked, swimming out of a deep sleep at the sound of his daughter's voice.

"Huh? What?" he whispered hoarsely.

Ava had apparently clambered over both of them because she now lay on Jamie's other side. She giggled quietly and rested her head on Jamie's arm. Taylor's head was on Jamie's chest.

"Taylor looks like a sleeping princess. You should kiss him awake like they do in the movies," she said, eyes shining as she stared up at him.

Jamie rubbed his face, trying to process the words.

Taylor did look beautiful. His lashes were thick and dark against his pink cheeks and his lips were even redder against his pale, clear skin. A little lock of black hair curled on his forehead and Jamie could easily picture him as Snow White.

Jamie smiled at him. "He'd be a prince though."

"You *said* princes can kiss other princes," she said stubbornly.

"They can," Jamie agreed.

"So, kiss him!" Ava hissed as she poked his ribs. "You like him, I can tell. 'Cause he makes you laugh a lot."

"I do like Taylor but we don't kiss people who are asleep," Jamie rasped. "They've gotta be awake to say it's okay."

"I'm awake," Taylor said quietly, without opening his eyes. "It's okay."

Jamie smiled and leaned in, brushing his lips across Taylor's in a soft kiss.

Taylor let out a happy little sigh and Jamie lingered, tasting him softly.

It was only Ava's delighted giggle that made Jamie draw back. "See. I told you, Daddy!"

"Good thing you're so smart, Bear," Jamie said, wrapping an arm around her to pull her even closer.

"Now me!"

He gave her a kiss on the forehead and smoothed her wild curls down. He guessed that answered the question if Ava was on board with the idea of them together.

Taylor let out a contented little noise and Jamie and Ava both turned to look at him. His eyes were bright and happy, and he threw his leg over Jamie's thigh, snuggling in closer.

"Hi there," Jamie said. "How did you sleep?"

"Like the dead, apparently." Taylor yawned. "What time is it?"

Jamie fished in his pocket for his phone. "Wow, way later than I realized."

"Do you have anywhere you needed to be?" Taylor sat up, sounding concerned.

"Nope."

"I'm hungry though," Ava said. "We were s'posed to have pizza for lunch."

"It can still be lunch," Taylor said. "Just … late lunch. It won't take us too long to make, I promise."

"Okay." She scrambled off the bed and yanked the door open. "I'm gonna go find Charlie and tell him!"

When she was gone, Jamie took a moment to look at Taylor. He had a crease on his cheek from Jamie's shirt and his hair stuck up on one side and he looked so perfect Jamie had to touch him. He rubbed his hand up and down Taylor's back, under his sweater, enjoying the warmth of his body and the softness of his skin.

"Thanks for watching Ava today."

"It was my pleasure," Taylor said. "She's wonderful. We had a great time."

"It's not always so easy," Jamie warned him. "She can be a challenge when things don't go well."

"I know. But we can all be like that if we have a bad day. I'm prepared."

"Good. Because I want this."

Taylor reached out and threaded their fingers together. "Me too. I wasn't sure at first but … yeah. I care about you and Ava a lot. I want to figure it out. See if we can make this work."

"It's not going to be easy," Jamie admitted. "But I think it could be worth it."

"Me too." Taylor leaned in to kiss Jamie but before their lips could touch, there was a lot of noise in the hallway.

"It's pizza time!" Ava yelled. "Charlie said he'd help me make it and if you don't come help, we're gonna eat it all."

Taylor laughed. "We're coming, we're coming."

But all Jamie could do was lie there and watch Taylor walk toward the door. He turned back, smiling, and Jamie's heart felt very full.

By the time he got up, smoothed down the covers of Taylor's bed, and used the bathroom, the pizza-making was already well under way.

Jamie stood in the doorway to the little kitchen, smiling as he watched Taylor, Charlie, and Ava work.

"There seems to be a lot of flour around here," he commented.

"We *might* have had a little accident," Taylor admitted, blowing out a breath that sent flour soaring into the air. "The good news is, we're cleaning it up."

"I see that." Jamie smiled softly at them. "Need any help?"

"Nope, I think we've got it," Taylor said. "What about you, Ava?"

"We've got this, Daddy!"

"Then I'll watch if that's okay." There was barely room for two slim guys and a five-year-old. Jamie would never fit in the tiny kitchen.

"Sure!" Ava said.

"Okay, watch this, Ava." Taylor plopped a big round ball of dough onto the floury counter.

"Do you roll it out like cookies?" Ava asked.

"Nope. You use your fingers to stretch it." Taylor demonstrated and Ava nodded, frowning very seriously as she tried to copy his movements.

They all did their part and when it was ready, Charlie held out a pan. "Now, we put it on here."

"Then, we add a little sauce on it." Taylor produced a bowl and a spoon. "We just spread it around a bit. We don't want to put it on very thick."

Taylor glanced over his shoulder. "I prepped all of the ingredients earlier, so it'll be quick to assemble. What do you want on your pizza? We've got enough for two pies."

Jamie shrugged. "I'm pretty much good with anything."

"Even pineapple?" Charlie asked with a disdainful curl of his lip.

"Ava likes it," Jamie said. "I can go either way."

Charlie waggled his eyebrows shamelessly at him over Ava's head and Jamie stifled a laugh.

"A little birdie told me you like olives on your pizza, Ava," Taylor said, clearly choosing to ignore them both.

Charlie wrinkled his nose. "Olives? Eww. You're a weird kid."

Ava giggled. "*You're* weird."

"True." Charlie seemed to consider the idea. "But at least I don't like nasty old olives."

That turned into a fit of giggling and Jamie wanted to walk over and hug all three of them.

He thought again of his relationship with Kara and couldn't believe the difference between their life together and this.

Kara had wanted the perfect Instagrammable existence where she could show the world how pretty and shiny everything was.

But Jamie had wanted *this*.

A big family. Lots of laughter. Lots of messes.

He'd wanted two or three kids and to have his extended family around. He wanted to make memories instead of stage them.

And maybe someday, if Jamie and Taylor got to that point and Taylor wanted it, they could talk about another kid or two. Jamie had the money to adopt or pay a surrogate or whatever they decided on. But he could easily imagine friends like Charlie in their life as well.

Jamie pictured some of the guys on the team hanging out making homemade pizza or grilling and he wanted that too. People like Naomi and Dean Tremblay. Ryan Hartinger and Zane Murphy. O'Shea cracking jokes in his Boston accent and Theriault snarking back with his Quebecois lilt.

Jamie wanted a family and team all blended into one.

A few years ago, he'd thought he'd had that, but he'd been wrong.

This time though, he knew he was on the right path.

Being with Taylor felt true and real and this time Jamie was sure he could have everything he'd ever dreamed of if he worked hard at it.

There was just one really big thing he had to do: figure out how to come out and mend the rift between their families.

Fuck.

"Jamie?" Taylor's voice was soft, and he looked up to see Taylor staring at him with a quizzical expression. "You okay?"

"I'm okay," Jamie said, his voice a little thick. "Great, in fact."

Forty minutes later, they all squeezed onto the couch, plates filled with homemade pizza and salad. It was some of the best pizza Jamie had ever had and Ava was over the moon about it.

"How'd you two start doing this pizza thing?" Jamie asked.

Charlie and Taylor looked at each other and Charlie hesitated before he spoke. "I, uh, had some issues with food. Like … eating disorder stuff. And it helped to make it at home. Getting involved in the cooking made it easier for me to want to eat. It was a big part of my recovery."

"You're doing better though?" Jamie asked, concerned.

Charlie nodded. "It's a process but yeah. I'm really trying."

"Good."

Thankfully Ava was paying no attention to them. Her gaze was firmly on the movie they'd put on. Just as well because Jamie didn't particularly want to explain what an eating disorder was.

It was something they'd have to talk about but it didn't have to be today.

After they'd polished off two pizzas between the four of them, Jamie volunteered to do the dishes.

"I can help," Taylor protested. "You'll have to do them all by hand."

Jamie shrugged. "I don't mind. You did all of the hard work watching Ava and making pizza."

Taylor smiled. "Trust me, it wasn't difficult."

"Well, I still appreciate it. Let me do this for you."

"Okay. Can I keep you company while you wash?" Taylor asked. Ava and Charlie appeared totally engrossed in the movie they were watching.

"Of course."

Taylor helped Jamie carry plates into the tiny kitchen and showed Jamie where everything was. But when Taylor walked toward the small table, Jamie gently grabbed his hand.

"Wait, Taylor."

Taylor gave him a quizzical glance and he bent his head and captured Taylor's mouth in a heated kiss.

When he drew back Taylor's eyes were wide, hand pressed against Jamie's chest.

"What was that for?"

Tongue-tied, Jamie shrugged. "The past few days have been ..."

Taylor squeezed his side. "They have."

"And God, watching you two curled up asleep and cooking together…" Jamie's voice was raw. It did something to him, seeing Taylor and Ava interact that way.

"Yeah? You liked that?" Taylor smiled up at him.

"I loved seeing you both like that." Jamie pulled Taylor close, brushing his lips against Taylor's forehead. "I know we still have a lot to talk about but I have a lot of hope for the future."

Taylor smiled softly. "Me too, Jamie. Me too."

Taylor was busy with kids' group lessons and fitting in private lessons with a few of the hockey players who had stayed in the area.

He kept missing Charlie, who was working on a big project for a new client. Taylor wanted to check in but they were never home at the same time long enough for Taylor to bring his concerns up.

Food kept steadily disappearing from the refrigerator and cupboards though and Taylor didn't find any uneaten in the trash again, so he chalked the oatmeal incident up to a fluke. Maybe Charlie just hadn't had time to finish before Jamie and Ava had arrived. Taylor had watched with his own eyes as Charlie enjoyed the pizza they'd baked so he had to trust that Charlie was managing.

Besides, Taylor had a life of his own to worry about. He couldn't spend all his time monitoring what Charlie did.

Taylor also fretted over the state of his bank balance and the looming bills but there was little he could do about that either. So he did some conditioning work for his skating and it felt good to push himself again. He'd been a little lax lately and he had a new ice show that would begin soon.

Jamie was busy too. He had another appointment with the therapist and did some volunteering at the Evanston Youth Center Sports League where the team donated both time and money.

He also invited Taylor over to spend time with him and Ava as often as possible.

The three of them went to the movies and played board games and cooked together and Taylor was the happiest he'd been in years. Jamie hadn't said much but every time Taylor caught him looking at him, he thought it might be the same for Jamie.

Unfortunately, the one thing they couldn't seem to find was *alone* time. Whenever Jamie tried to drag Taylor into the mudroom to make out against the washer and dryer, Ava popped up with a question or something she needed.

"I love her, I swear," Jamie muttered against Taylor's shoulder one evening when they'd distracted her with a movie and snuck off to the kitchen to make out for a few minutes. Taylor stifled a laugh at the frustration in Jamie's voice. "But I am dying for her to go off to school in the fall."

Taylor chuckled. "Your mom will be back from California soon, right?"

"Yes. Thank God." Jamie dove in for another kiss. "Fuck. I would kill for a couple of hours to drag you up to my bedroom."

"Soon." Taylor dipped his fingertip into the waistband of Jamie's sweats, toying with the string and biting his lip as he thought about getting his mouth around Jamie's dick again.

"Or even twenty minutes," Jamie muttered, dropping his head to kiss along Taylor's neck, making him shiver with pleasure. "Although we probably need to talk."

"We do," Taylor agreed. He let his head fall back and Jamie nuzzled in closer, nipping at the skin there and making Taylor let out a desperate little whine he couldn't quite stifle.

"But I'm not going to be able to think straight until I can touch you." Jamie splayed his hands on Taylor's ass, pulling him in close until he straddled Jamie's thigh. "I need to suck your cock, baby."

Taylor shivered in his arms. "I need that too."

"Daddy!" Ava hollered and they jerked apart.

Taylor fluttered his hands to smooth down his hair and tug at the neckline of his shirt while Jamie pulled his hoodie lower to cover his hard-on. Taylor was grateful Ava was yelling from the living room and hadn't come in the kitchen yet.

Jamie cleared his throat. "What is it, Bear?"

"Can I have ice cream? I ate all my veggies at dinner."

"Yes," Jamie called back. "Give me a minute."

"Okay!"

Jamie turned to Taylor with a rueful glance. "I wouldn't blame you if you wanted to bail on this thing."

Taylor frowned. "Bail on what?"

"This." Jamie waved between them. "Dating me or whatever we're doing. I know it's a lot when there's a kid around 24/7."

"Well, she's not always around 24/7," Taylor said lightly. "This week is a little unusual for you, right?"

Jamie nodded. "When I made plans to have Ava while Kara and my parents were both out of town, the last thing I expected was that I'd be wanting some alone time with you."

"It's okay. Besides." Taylor settled into his arms again, tipping his head up to smile at Jamie. "It's been great."

"You really think so?" Jamie asked, his expression a little doubtful. "I haven't had a chance to take you out on a date or anything."

Taylor shook his head. "Remember that whole issue I had with guys trying to splash out a lot of money without giving me anything of substance emotionally?"

Jamie nodded.

"Well, this has been the complete opposite. So, I love it. Quiet nights in with Ava are perfect. It shows me that you actually want me to be a part of your life."

"I do," Jamie said, sounding like he had a little lump in his throat. "I mean, I know it's moving fast but …"

"It is," Taylor agreed. "But sometimes when it's right, it's right."

"I want to be right for you," Jamie said fervently.

"You are," Taylor reassured him. "I definitely believe that."

"Daddy!" Ava bellowed again. "You're missing the best part of the movie!"

Jamie dropped his forehead against Taylor's and let out a sigh. "The glamorous life of a dad."

Taylor giggled and gave him a peck on the lips. "You're still the DILF I have my heart set on."

"Well, at least I've got that going for me," Jamie said with a lopsided smile as he slipped away and reached for the handle of the freezer. "If we can ever get two seconds alone," he muttered.

Five minutes later, they joined Ava in the living room, bowls of ice cream clutched in their hands.

And while it wasn't an orgasm, Taylor had no complaints as he ate his strawberry cheesecake ice cream and watched Ava and Jamie enjoying theirs.

There was only a twinge of the nagging worry that if they didn't talk soon, they'd end up so deep in this that it would break his heart to let it go if they couldn't find a path to move forward.

CHAPTER TWENTY

As bye week break neared its end, Jamie was ready to lose his mind.

His parents' flight home from California had been delayed and Kara wouldn't be home until the following week, because she'd stayed in Miami to visit friends.

Jamie was sure he'd lose the last threads of his fraying control if he didn't get his hand or his mouth or *some* part of his body on Taylor immediately.

Today, the three of them had spent the day at the Museum of Science and Industry, then picked up takeout on the way home. Thankfully, Ava was so exhausted that she conked out halfway through Jamie reading her a bedtime story.

After Ava was deeply asleep, Jamie pulled Taylor into the rec room in the basement. There was a big, wide couch and they were taking full advantage of it.

After twenty minutes of making out, Jamie was about to burst.

"God, I want to suck your cock," Jamie panted, palming Taylor's erection through his snug leggings while they traded deep, needy kisses.

"What if Ava comes looking for us?" Taylor gasped. "There's no door and it's a straight view from the stairs."

Jamie grumbled. "Damn it."

They'd already ruled out Jamie's bedroom because the lock kept refusing to stay latched and Ava knew how to jiggle it open.

"You have like eighty-two spare bedrooms," Taylor whined, rubbing up against Jamie's hand. "Can't we use one of those?"

Jamie groaned and buried his head against Taylor's neck. "No beds. I never got around to decorating them. No mattresses. Floor sex sounds hot but I'm old and I'd be asking to fuck up my knees on the hardwood."

His mom had been prodding him to pick out the paint colors and finish decorating and apparently this was his punishment for putting it off.

"I don't care where," Taylor gasped, clutching at Jamie's shoulders. "Bend me over the dryer. Fuck me in your garage. God, I *need* you, Jamie."

He'd clearly reached the end of his rope too.

Stupid open-floor plan designs. There was no door to the mudroom where the washer and dryer were and the garage was insulated but not heated so it would still be fucking freezing.

Inspiration struck.

"The Range Rover." Jamie levered himself into a plank position. "We'll be a little warmer and even if Ava comes in the garage, we'll have a few minutes to re-dress and make ourselves presentable."

"Sure, great, let's do that," Taylor said breathlessly. He slithered out from under Jamie and hopped to his feet, eyes bright, hair mussed, cock stretching the fabric of his thin pants. "Race you there."

Jamie moved a little slower than Taylor but it wasn't for lack of wanting to get to Taylor's body. All the blood was in Jamie's lower half and his brain wasn't quite operating at full speed, which apparently impacted his ability to use his limbs.

They tore up the stairs, laughing quietly. Jamie's socks skidded on the wood floors as Taylor threw the garage door open. Jamie yelped when he walked across the cold concrete, then threw himself in the back seat of the Range Rover

Taylor pushed Jamie into a seated position, then dropped to his knees, wedging himself between the front and middle rows before he slammed the vehicle door shut behind him.

Jamie's hands were shaking as he stared at Taylor in the dim glow that filtered in from the garage's overhead light.

Taylor licked his lips and tugged at Jamie's sweats. Jamie lifted his hips enough to push the fabric down to mid-thigh and then Taylor's mouth was on him, wet and warm, pulling deep groans from his lips.

"Taylor," Jamie said, the name escaping on a helpless breath of air. He'd desperately wanted to suck Taylor off but this was too good to argue with.

Jamie was already strung so tight with need that he could feel his pulse in the rigid shaft of his dick and his thighs trembled every time Taylor swirled his tongue around the leaking head.

"Fuck, baby, so good," Jamie babbled. "God, your mouth feels amazing."

He dragged his hands through Taylor's hair and groaned low and long when the tip of his cock bumped the back of Taylor's throat.

Taylor lifted off, licking his lips, eyes glittering even in the dim light. "You can fuck my face if you want."

"Oh God," Jamie breathed, helplessly overcome by the idea. It wasn't like Taylor was the first person to offer that but he never wanted to assume and—

He let out a choked sound as Taylor bathed his cock with spit before sinking deep again. For a few moments, he just closed his eyes and hung on. Taylor bobbed over him with long, wet strokes, the sounds obscene in the quiet of the vehicle.

And then Jamie began to guide Taylor, gently at first, testing how deep he could go. Jamie tentatively pushed past the tightness of Taylor's throat but when he let out a choked gurgle, Jamie tried to draw back.

Taylor squeezed his thighs, refusing to let him pull out.

Hands shaking, Jamie kept going, rocking in and out of Taylor's throat until his abs clenched and the urgent need in his balls was too much to deny.

"Gonna come soon," he gasped.

Taylor lifted his head, Jamie's cock gripped firmly in his fist as he looked up at him through his lashes.

"Come on my tongue, Jamie. Wanna taste you."

Jamie guided Taylor back down and it only took a few more bobs of Taylor's head before Jamie was helplessly coming, thighs shaking as he emptied his balls down Taylor's throat, whispering his name like a prayer.

After Jamie's brain began to function again, he yanked Taylor up to straddle him. He nearly hit his head on the ceiling of the SUV and Jamie whispered an apology before he plunged his tongue into Taylor's mouth, tasting his own bitter release.

Desperate to make Taylor feel good, Jamie shoved a hand beneath his leggings, palming his ass. Jamie's cock was softening but God, he wanted to fuck him so bad.

"You don't have any lube, do you?" he rasped.

"What? No," Taylor choked out, laughing against his mouth. "I don't carry it everywhere with me, Jamie."

"Damn." Jamie held two fingers in front of Taylor's mouth, and he opened, sucking them, soaking them in spit.

Jamie worked his fingers between Taylor's cheeks, brushing over his hole. Taylor let out a whine and Jamie circled the rim, sinking one finger inside.

Taylor felt so damn hot and tight Jamie wished he'd dragged Taylor up to his bedroom and moved a dresser in front of the door or something. The need to get his cock inside him was nearly unbearable.

Taylor rocked against his stomach, grinding down over his softening dick. It hurt a little but Jamie wanted him to come too bad to change position.

"I need to fuck you again," he rasped. "Wanna feel you come all around me. Wanna make you cry out my name."

"Jamie," Taylor said breathlessly, the word a broken, needy little moan as he trembled in Jamie's arms.

"Yeah, just like that baby. Wanna hear how good I make you feel."

"I don't know if I can come this way," he whimpered. "So close but ..."

"Tell me what you need," Jamie begged.

"Your mouth. Please, would you suck me, Jamie?"

"Yes. Fuck, yes."

Jamie *did* hit his head on the ceiling when he shifted positions. He cursed and moved a little more slowly. Depositing Taylor into the seat, he tried to squeeze himself into the space between the front and middle seats and realized there was no way in hell he'd fit.

He grumbled and yanked his sweats up before he threw the door open, praying Ava wouldn't appear in the garage. He yanked Taylor toward him, then tugged at his leggings until they were halfway down his thighs.

He was too eager to be nervous about sucking cock for the first time and faced with Taylor's hard shaft and slick, leaking head, Jamie dove in, licking at the tip.

"Jamie!" Taylor gasped and that made him feel good, so he wrapped his fist around the base and began to suck.

He knew he wasn't going to be able to deepthroat on his first try, so he didn't attempt anything fancy. The angle was awkward and the edge of the SUV bit into his shins whenever he moved so he bobbed over the top half of Taylor's cock, making it slick and using his hand on the lower half.

He was gratified by Taylor's needy little whimpers. His hands were soft as he combed them through Jamie's hair, whispering encouragement.

"Close," Taylor whispered. "So close. Please, Jamie."

That please made him renew his efforts and he sucked harder, the salty flavor bursting over his tongue as Taylor came with a strangled shout. Jamie choked for a moment, surprised by the amount, but he swallowed it down until Taylor gently urged him to lift his head.

Jamie licked his lips and looked up to see Taylor staring at him with glazed eyes and parted lips, panting lightly.

"Was that okay?" He pressed a kiss to Taylor's inner thigh, below the soft skin of his balls.

"Mm-hmm." Taylor seemed dazed and Jamie sat back with a smug smile.

Taylor shivered, probably freezing with his damp cock out.

"Sorry." Jamie helped Taylor re-dress before he pulled him close, Taylor's body sliding against his when he dropped to stand between Jamie's feet.

They kissed for a few minutes, Jamie cupping Taylor's cheek as they came down from their respective highs with soft pecks. After a moment, Taylor buried his head against Jamie's shoulder and clung to him.

Jamie wrapped him up tight and breathed him in, the tension that had been building in him for the past two weeks finally settling into a calm hum.

"My feet are freezing," Taylor eventually whispered, and Jamie chuckled.

"Mine too. Let's go inside."

Jamie took a moment to make sure they hadn't left a mess in the Range Rover, then shut the door and tugged Taylor into the living room.

He flicked on the gas fireplace and coaxed Taylor onto the couch before he covered him with a blanket. "I'm going to check on Ava a minute. I'll be right back."

"Okay." Taylor smiled sleepily at him. "I'll be here trying to get feeling back in my feet."

Jamie chuckled and kissed him before he straightened and headed for the stairs.

Ava was fast asleep when Jamie peeked in on her and he realized he'd probably worried unnecessarily about where he and Taylor fooled around. She was as dead to the world as always.

As Jamie slowly jogged down the stairs, he realized they needed to make some decisions about what they were doing. He wanted Taylor to be able to spend the night and until he was sure that they were on the same page about their future and how they were going to make it happen, he needed to hold off on the sleepovers.

Taylor looked so sweet and drowsy as he stared into the flames that Jamie almost chickened out. But he took a seat and gently patted Taylor's legs to get his attention.

"Hey, do you think we should have a conversation about what we're doing now?"

Taylor's eyes widened, the sleepy relaxation he'd been sinking into abruptly ripped away.

"Um, yeah, probably should." Taylor shifted to rest against the pillows propped against the sofa arm, then straightened his legs, draping them over Jamie's thighs.

"So, I guess we need to start with the basics, huh?" Jamie asked. He dragged a hand through his hair. "You do want to date me, yeah?"

Taylor swallowed hard. "Yeah, I do."

"Okay." Jamie squeezed his shin. "And you know I'm looking for, well, something serious right?"

"I kinda assumed that it would be," Taylor said softly. "I mean, with Ava …"

"Yeah." Jamie looked back toward the fire. "We're a package deal and the last thing I want is to bring people in and out of her life who aren't interested in sticking around. So, if you aren't ready for this kind of relationship, I need you to let me know now."

"I want it," Taylor said confidently. "I've wanted it for a long time. I just hadn't met anyone I could have that with."

Jamie let out a relieved-sounding sigh. "Okay, well, that's—that's a good start, right?"

"I think so."

Jamie swallowed. "So, we need to tell the team and our families. Which do you want to tackle first?"

"Are you ready for that step?" Taylor asked. "I don't want to rush you."

"I have to be, don't I?" Jamie said. "Because I don't want to be that guy who …"

When he fell silent, Taylor gently prompted him. "Which guy is that?"

"You know. The closeted athlete who treats his boyfriend like dirt because he isn't ready to come out. You've had enough of that in your life."

"I have," Taylor agreed. "But there's a difference between never and not yet."

"I know." Jamie looked down. "But it's true, right? You want a future with someone who can do that."

"Yeah. I do." It was hard to admit. But if they wanted a relationship, a real relationship, they had to be willing to be honest with each other.

"So, you need me to do this." Jamie squared his shoulders.

"I need you to be sure you're *ready* to do this," Taylor gently corrected. "Because it's not going to be one little thing, Jamie. It's telling the team and our families, and your ex—"

Jamie flinched.

"You'll need to, right?" Taylor asked. "Because otherwise, she's going to find out from Ava."

"Yeah." Jamie's voice had turned gravelly.

"So, it'll mean telling your whole family."

"And the media."

"Realistically, yeah. The more we're out in public together, the quicker someone will notice."

"I know." Jamie rubbed his thumb against the bony part of Taylor's ankle.

"And it's not a one-time thing. It's your whole lifetime. If we're thinking about a long-term future together, that means coming out over and over. It'll come up at parent-teacher conferences and every professional thing you do for the rest of your life. Once hockey is over, you'll be looking for a new career and it'll come up then. It's … it's no small thing, Jamie. If you aren't ready, I get it."

"But if I'm not, I'll lose you."

There was real sadness in Jamie's eyes and Taylor shifted to tuck himself under Jamie's arm. Not because he didn't want to look him in the face but because he needed the reassurance of his touch.

"It doesn't have to be an either-or." He played with Jamie's fingers, tracing along the little calluses that came from years of hockey and weightlifting.

"What do you mean?"

"I don't expect you to hold a press conference tomorrow. If you want to start slow and work your way up, I'd be okay with that."

"Like, tell the team and management next week and then figure out a plan for telling our families and go from there?"

"Exactly." Taylor hesitated, staring into the fire. "It just can't be an indefinite thing. I want to give you time but I also don't want to be strung along."

Jamie smoothed a hand across his hair before settling his palm against the back of Taylor's neck. "And the last thing I want is to string you along," he said firmly.

Taylor truly believed that. But he knew how easy it could be to put off the things that were hard. In the past, he'd put off talking to Charlie, even when he saw he was wasting away. He'd put off breakups because he didn't want to be alone. But there was so much more at stake now. He wanted to do this right. And with Ava in the mix, they couldn't screw it up.

"What if … what if we made a timeline?" he suggested.

"Hmm." Jamie rubbed his thumb against the skin behind Taylor's ear and he shivered. "Like due dates?"

Taylor made a face and flipped onto his back, resting his head against Jamie's thigh so he could look up into his face. His beard looked dark in the light, darker than the golden streaks through his hair.

"I don't know if I like the word due dates," Taylor said. "It reminds me too much of assignments and I don't want you to feel like I'm giving you tasks you have to check off to be with me. But maybe … target dates? We can figure out when it feels right to *both* of us to take the various steps together."

"I …" Jamie seemed to consider the idea. "I like that actually."

"Yeah?" Taylor smiled up at him and Jamie reached out, rubbing his thumb against Taylor's lower lip. When he kissed it, Jamie gave him a soft look.

"Yeah," Jamie said. "So, I guess I need to decide what comes first. Definitely the team. I think that'll be the easiest. Although I should make talking to Kara a priority so you can spend the night when Ava's over. Actually, considering the way she encouraged us to kiss the other day, it really should go at the top of the list I guess."

"Are you okay with that?"

Jamie's expression had turned grave but he nodded. "I am. I … I'll be honest, I'm dreading it but I think it'll be for the best to get it over and done with. Shit. Gonna have to tell my parents

ASAP too. Or they'll find out from Ava. She is not subtle, and she talks about you *a lot*."

Taylor smiled at the idea of that, reaching up to tug on the string from Jamie's hoodie. "That's a lot at once. Do you feel okay about that?"

Jamie nodded again. "I do. I … I think maybe it'll get easier as we go?"

"I hope so. Do you expect a lot of problems with your family?"

"My mom will be fine," Jamie said confidently. "I don't really foresee any issues with me being bi from either of them. My dad finding out whose son you are …" He shrugged. "That I don't know."

"That's fair. My dad will blow his top."

"I know." Jamie grimaced. "We can tell him together if you want."

"That's very sweet," Taylor said, "but no, I think it needs to be one-on-one. I'm tempted to drag Charlie in to soften him up but that's probably not fair either."

"So, we kind of have a plan? I'll talk to my parents and Kara when they're back. I'll meet with my agent and management to get the ball rolling there. And then … we tackle the rest."

"Yeah, sounds good to me. I'll start strategizing my plan to get through to my dad."

Jamie dragged a hand through his hair. "Jesus, I've had games that I've stressed about less."

Taylor opened his mouth to say they didn't have to rush if Jamie wasn't ready but Jamie shook his head.

"No, it's okay. I don't like secrets so I think getting some of that out of the way will actually help."

"Okay."

"And obviously I'll talk to my therapist about all this."

"Is it helping?"

Jamie shrugged. "It's good to have someone to talk to. I mean, there are already some things that have come up that have been useful. Stuff that went really wrong in my marriage that I want to do better at now."

"That's good." Taylor squeezed his hand. "I saw someone for a while too, after I quit competitive skating."

Jamie's heavy brows drew together. "Why did you quit? You said it was a conversation for another day but …"

But it was another day and if Jamie was willing to take this big leap for him, the least Taylor could do was talk about his past.

He let out a gusty sigh.

"So, it was a combination of things. One of the big ones was Charlie. He mentioned his eating disorder the other day and he made it sound like it wasn't a big deal but—" Taylor swallowed hard. "He could have died. He's in recovery from anorexia but last year he was hospitalized. He was dangerously underweight, and it put a lot of strain on his heart."

"That's awful."

Taylor nodded.

"It was. But that's part of the culture of competitive skating. In our field, small and light has its advantages. It's substantially worse for women—especially pairs skaters—but we're all encouraged from a very young age to pay careful attention to our weight and monitor every last calorie that goes in or out. For people who have a predisposition or other triggering factors, it can get really ugly. It varies depending on who you talk to, but estimates are that round a third of guys in sports with a heavy emphasis on weight class or aesthetics develop eating disorders. I was, quite frankly, lucky. My mom is fine-boned and I inherited her build and metabolism. I could easily eat double what Charlie did and we'd be around the same weight and body mass."

Jamie nodded but didn't speak.

"It nearly broke me seeing Charlie in the hospital. I … his family is fucking awful. They should have helped but they only made it worse. Charlie cut them out of his life but then he couldn't afford to go to rehab. I figured out a way to make it happen for him but between the hospital bills and the rehab facility … I'm in pretty bad debt."

That was not an easy thing for him to admit to a man who made several million dollars a year.

A concerned expression crossed Jamie's face. "Is that something you'd be willing to let me help with?"

"Ooof." Taylor sucked in a breath. "I … I'm glad you worded it that way. Honestly, no. It's way too soon and with the history I have with guys I've dated in the past, it would be a really bad idea."

"I get that."

"Why do I feel like there's a 'but' lurking around."

Jamie shrugged. "But I'm the guy who likes to be there for the people I care about. Knowing I can help you but not being able to is hard."

"I understand," Taylor said. "And … maybe that's something we could talk about someday down the road. But for now, I can't. I'm afraid if I accepted money from you, I'd feel like I'd have to hold back on things I said or squash down what I needed or agree to things that I really shouldn't, because I'd be beholden to you. Does that make sense?"

"Yeah, it does." Jamie threaded their fingers together and squeezed. "I respect that."

A weight slipped from Taylor's shoulders. "Thank you."

"Was that why you quit then? The stuff going on with Charlie and the expense of training?"

"Training is expensive but what I made in endorsements could have offset it. I just … I got really disillusioned with the sport and the way it's run. God, I love figure skating. I love the classes I teach now and the ice shows but the competition got so ugly," Taylor said with a frown. "There's a lot of toxicity in the way kids and young adults are treated and I couldn't stand it anymore. Watching Charlie nearly kill himself to win took all the luster out of it for me. And, honestly, I was harming myself too. It wasn't by trying to lose weight but I was accepting less than I deserved. Making myself smaller for the men I was too much for."

"I don't ever want you to make yourself smaller for me," Jamie said hoarsely, his voice thick with emotion. "I know I have to figure out how to come out but I swear to you, I will prove to you that it's never because I'm ashamed of being with you. You are … you're exactly the kind of person I want to be with."

Taylor closed his eyes at the hot well of tears those words brought on but all Jamie did was gently rub his thumb against the salty liquid that trickled down Taylor's cheeks, then bend in for a soft kiss.

CHAPTER TWENTY-ONE

Although it was great to drink coffee in his parents' sun-filled kitchen, catching up on the past two weeks, Jamie's knee had been jogging up and down for the past twenty minutes.

"Goodness, you're full of energy today," his mom said.

"Maybe lay off that coffee for a bit, son," his dad added with a chuckle.

Jamie laughed but he did set down his mug. He kept his fingers wrapped tightly around the smooth ceramic surface though, needing that warm anchor.

The conversation had fallen into a lull after his parents brought him up to speed about how his brother and his family were doing. Which Jamie really should be better about keeping up on himself but he kinda sucked at it and that probably wasn't going to change any time soon.

His brother was equally terrible and Jamie always went out to visit him and his family in the off-season at least once, so it was *fine*.

He cleared his throat, knowing he was internally spinning his wheels because he was nervous about the conversation he needed to have. "Can I, uh, talk to you guys about something?"

"Sure. Of course. What is it, honey?" his mom said with a warm smile.

His dad gave him a quizzical smile and nod.

"What would you say if I told you I was dating someone? A, uh, man."

They both blinked at him but his mom recovered first. "Well, this is certainly a *surprise*. Is there a reason you didn't tell us before now?"

"I, uh, it's new? We just started spending time together this winter and it grew from there."

"But surely you knew you were …" His mom frowned at him. "Is this why you and Kara—"

"What? No! Jesus, no. That was one hundred percent on her," he said bitterly. "She made a choice to cheat on me. It wasn't because I was gay and couldn't satisfy her in the bedroom or something."

His parents both winced.

"I'm sorry," his mom said. "I shouldn't have implied that. I'm just so surprised. But of course we're supportive if you're … bisexual? Is that right?"

Jamie nodded. "Yeah, that seems to be the right fit."

His dad reached out and patted his hand. "Well, of course we want you to be happy. I'm surprised you didn't say something when Boucher came out a few years ago."

"I was *married*," Jamie sputtered. "Maybe it wasn't going great but I was really working at it. I never thought I'd be dating anyone again."

"True." His dad cleared his throat. "I hope you weren't worried we'd have a problem with it."

"Well, no." Jamie scratched the back of his neck. "I never really thought that. Although this situation is, uh, a little more complicated than just dating any random guy."

"Who *is* he?" his mom asked. "Someone on the team? Keegan Truro is handsome."

"As far as I know, Keegan is straight and he and his girlfriend got engaged over bye week, so no."

She shrugged. "Well, he is your center, and you seem to be clicking well on the ice."

Jamie snorted. "I click pretty well with Tremblay too but I'm not about to date a happily married man."

"Spit it out," his dad said, a perplexed frown on his face. "What's the complication?"

Jamie sucked in a deep breath. "Well, the man I've been seeing is, uh, Taylor Hollis."

There was dead silence from both of his parents, the only sound in the room the tick of the large clock on the wall behind him.

"Well, I sure didn't see that coming," his dad eventually said, rubbing his stubbly cheek. "Really? The Hollis boy?"

"He's twenty-four," Jamie said a little defensively.

"I don't mean the age. You do know what a mess this is going to be, right?"

"Yeah, I do," Jamie said with a sigh. "But … I really care about him. He's … he's just this really kind person and he cares so much for Ava, and he makes me feel …"

Jamie didn't know how to put it into words. All he knew was that after the misery of his failed marriage and divorce, Taylor felt like a breath of fresh air. He made Jamie feel centered and hopeful again.

"He *is* great with Ava, Adam," Jodi said. "You should see it."

"I'm sure he's wonderful," Adam said gruffly. "Ava raves about him nonstop. I'm just concerned about Jamie's career and what impact this will have on it."

"Being bi or dating Taylor?"

"Well," his dad said slowly. "The Hollis boy specifically. I mean, he's quite …"

Jamie dragged in a deep breath. "What people expect a gay male figure skater to be like?"

"Yes." But before Jamie could open his mouth, his dad held up his hands. "I have no problem with it, but you know what reactions will be like. You took enough of a beating on social media after your divorce. You know the conclusions people will leap to."

"Yeah, I know."

"And then you pile on who he is. Who his *father* is … Jamie, I love you, son, but this has the potential to get ugly."

"Yeah, I know that," Jamie said through gritted teeth. "Taylor and I have *talked* about it."

"Does Rick Hollis know yet?"

"Not yet. We're … taking things slowly. We figured we'd see how this went and go from there."

His mom looked hurt. "You didn't really think we'd have a problem with it, did you?"

Jamie shrugged and glanced at his father. "Well …"

Adam sighed. "I can't say I like the way Rick handled any of our shit but if you say Taylor is the right—right *partner* for you then of course I support you. Your mother and I both do. We just want you and Ava to be happy."

They'd moved onto other topics after that but Jamie wasn't entirely sure how to take the conversation with his parents. He appreciated the support but clearly they were worried about how it would go over. And, well, that made *him* worry.

Over the next few days, tension filled Jamie as the rest of the team trickled back into town, but he was still happy to go to practice on Monday and see everyone.

They were sitting smack-dab in the middle of the rankings. They'd have to really work for a good playoff spot. January had been rough but if they buckled down through the rest of February and March, they had a shot at it. No one looked forward to the stress of hoping for a wildcard spot.

The next two days flew by in a blur of practices and then they hit the road for a three-game winning streak. They had a solid 7-3 win against Buffalo, squeaked in a 4-3 win in overtime against Minnesota, then went on to beat Edmonton 6-2 in regulation.

The mood was high when they landed back home in Illinois. Although Jamie missed Ava, he took advantage of his mom's suggestion that he spend the night at Taylor's place.

"Of course you should see your—your boyfriend," she'd said quietly when they spoke on the phone. Adam was off tucking Ava in and reading her a bedtime story. "I know you miss your daughter but she'll be asleep long before you get home. You can always stop by in the morning before practice if you want, but you should spend the night with Taylor."

"I do miss him."

"Well, then you should see him." His mom sounded like she was smiling. "I hope you know I'm happy for you. This is a surprise but all I've ever wanted is for you to find someone good enough for you and Ava."

She'd gotten along well enough with Kara when they were married but she'd made her feelings for her abundantly clear after the divorce. So Jamie had listened to his mom and asked Taylor if he was okay with him coming by that night.

They were both dead on their feet as Taylor opened the door. Jamie did little more than give Taylor a warm kiss, hop in the shower, then stumble into the bedroom where Taylor was already softly snoring.

Jamie curled around Taylor, his hair damp on the pillow, contentment settling in.

Taylor let out a soft, sleepy noise and Jamie kissed his shoulder and closed his eyes, passing out between one breath and the next.

In the morning, there was only time for quick hand jobs under the covers and a lot of kissing, but they squeezed into the snug shower together to clean up before Jamie cooked them breakfast.

"Where's Charlie?" he asked, looking around the quiet apartment as the eggs sizzled in the pan.

Taylor frowned. "I dunno. He's been out a lot lately. We never seem to be home at the same time anymore."

"I hope everything is okay with him."

Taylor sighed. "Yeah, me too. I worry about him."

But the toast popped up then and they talked about the plans for the upcoming week as Jamie inhaled three eggs, toast, and turkey sausage. Taylor ate a little more sedately.

"So, I've got a meeting with my agent today." Jamie dragged a bite of sausage through the runny yolk. "And then once I talk to him, I'll have to have a discussion with HR and management and all that."

Taylor bit his lip. "You ready for that?"

Jamie took a deep breath. "No, but I'm probably not going to get more ready."

"Do you want me to be there too?"

"I don't think so," Jamie said. "I mean, obviously, if you *want* to be, you can. But your contract is almost up. By the time anything actually gets rolling, you'll be done working with the team."

"Small mercies," Taylor said, reaching for his coffee cup with a little sigh. "Not that it hasn't been fun but I think the more distance I have from the organization, the more it will help our cause."

"Yeah, you're probably right." Jamie sat back, debating if he wanted to cook another egg. He reached for some blueberries instead. "I just want to make sure they have a plan in place in case things go sideways with Kara."

"Ugh. You really think it'll happen?"

"I mean, it fucking shouldn't," Jamie groused, popping a berry in his mouth. "Because it would be insanely hypocritical if she went on social media about *my* personal life but I've accepted that I don't understand her at all. I'm prepared for the worst."

"I'm sorry."

Jamie shrugged. "I'm the idiot who married her."

"I mean, she can't be all bad, right?" Taylor argued. "You said she's a good mom."

"She is." Jamie sighed. "And no, I don't think she's all bad. But we were fucking horrible together, apparently."

"But that's ancient history," Taylor said, coming around the table to drop a kiss on Jamie's lips. "Now you have me and I'm a delight."

Jamie laughed and dragged Taylor onto his lap. "You are a delight. But if you're going to be in my life the way I want, you're going to be dealing with Kara too."

Taylor cupped his cheek. "Well, I do want to be in your life and Ava's life, so we'll have to figure out how to navigate that. I'm in if you are."

"I'm in," Jamie promised.

"Good." Taylor wriggled free and reached for the plates. "But you have to see Ava and get to practice. And apparently, you'll have some meetings today too, huh?"

"Yeah," Jamie agreed. "The one, anyway. I have a late-afternoon appointment downtown with my agent."

Taylor rested his hand on Jamie's shoulder. "Hey, is it okay if I give Samantha a heads-up about us? We're friends and I'd feel bad if she was blindsided about my relationship with you in a meeting or something."

Jamie hesitated. "If you're sure she can be trusted to keep quiet until we're ready to make an announcement."

"Absolutely. And look at it this way, it gives her time to start thinking about how to spin it."

"That's true." Jamie chewed his lip. "Okay, well, whatever you think is best. I trust *you*."

"Oh, Jamie." Taylor's voice went soft. "That means a lot to me actually."

"Good. And don't forget we have a game tomorrow night."

"Busy, busy. And you have Ava tonight, don't you?"

"Yeah. You're coming for dinner, right?" Jamie stood, stretching, catching a glimpse of Taylor's heated gaze when his shirt rode up.

"I am. Looking forward to it."

"Good." Jamie leaned in and kissed Taylor, slowly and thoroughly. "Pack an overnight bag."

Taylor blinked. "Are you sure?"

"I'm sure." Jamie nodded decisively. "I'm ready to tell Ava about us."

Taylor's day flew by in a blur of lessons, personal conditioning, and skating practice. He managed to corral Samantha on her way out of the building though.

"Hey, could I snag you for some happy hour drinks now?" he asked. "I was thinking we could stop by that cute little place in Rogers Park we both liked so much last time."

She raised an eyebrow. "Should I be concerned you're trying to butter me up for something?"

"Probably."

She closed her eyes and took a deep breath. "Okay. But you're buying."

They drove separately. When they had drinks in front of them and were tucked in a quiet corner of the bar with no one close enough to overhear, Samantha leaned forward. "Talk to me. I have a bad feeling about this."

There was zero point in beating around the bush, so Taylor folded his hands together. "I'm dating Jamie Walsh."

"I was afraid of that." She reached for her dirty gin martini and downed half of it in one gulp. Taylor winced.

"Not even an 'I'm happy for you, Taylor?'" he asked.

"If I weren't working for this organization, I'd be delighted. He seems like a sweet guy and that daughter of his is adorable. However, I have a lot of concerns."

"I know." Taylor slumped back and took a much more moderate sip of his orange-pineapple vodka martini. "I know this isn't a great situation for the team."

"There's a lot of volatility here, Taylor," she said earnestly. "And not just the social media angle. They've been struggling since the last guy on the team came out."

"It's a different situation though, right?" Taylor played with the stem of his glass. "I mean, I'm not even a part of the organization. Not really. And we're doing wrap-up shooting next week, yeah?"

"It helps," she agreed. "But you have to understand, change like this is hard. And it usually happens slowly. The franchise has weathered the sudden onslaught of players coming out remarkably well, but what we thought was going to be a cute little feel-good series is now going to be used against the team."

He bristled. "How do you figure?"

"Come on, Taylor. Think about it. Jamie already got the shit beat out of him on social media for his wife stepping out on him. It shouldn't happen but it does. Surely, you've seen the names he was called online and in the stands. Saw the signs at that last game against Chicago."

Taylor winced. "Okay, yeah. I've seen them."

He'd also seen a lot of gorgeous pictures of Jamie's ex. Her social media accounts were private but there were still plenty of photos out there.

And while Taylor wasn't generally an insecure person, it was easy to let doubts creep in after looking at photos of a gorgeous, stacked blonde with mile-long legs, a heart-shaped face, and full pouty lips.

Taylor was attractive too, but when it came down to it, it was *much* easier for Jamie to date a beautiful woman than him.

Samantha sighed. "Look, I don't mean to be discouraging. I did a deep dive into his socials when I joined the team, and I can't find a legitimate complaint about him. He's not the *most* skilled player on the team but he's a solid winger and other than the bullshit with his ex, I can't find any dirt on him. He's always been a committed family man and great dad and you deserve a guy like that. From a personal perspective, I can see how this would be a wonderful relationship. Professionally, this is going to be hard on him. And that's without the potential landmine of your family history. I just want to be sure you've both thought this through."

"We have." Taylor's mouth felt dry though, and he took another sip of his cocktail.

"Okay." Samantha sat back in her seat and beckoned to the waitress on the other side of the room. "Buy me another drink and we'll start strategizing about how to tackle this."

"I'm going to have to pay for your cab home at this rate," Taylor said drily.

She shrugged. "Probably. Are you sure you guys can't wait until the off-season at least?"

Even if Taylor could stomach being a secret that long, there was no way they'd manage to keep it under wraps that long. "How many five-year-olds do you know who are good at keeping secrets?"

She winced. "Okay, fair point. So, we're doing this?"

"We're doing this," Taylor said with a decisive nod. Somehow or another, they'd muddle through.

By the time their strategy session wrapped up, neither of them were in any shape to drive. Samantha paid for her own cab but Taylor ended up having to call Jamie for a ride. Thankfully, he was on his way back from his appointment in The Loop, so it wasn't too far out of his way to swing by Rogers Park on the way to the North Shore.

"I might have had a *teensy* bit too much to drink," Taylor admitted on the ride to Jamie's house.

Jamie smirked and handed over a black and teal water bottle with the Otters' logo. "I can see that. Drink some water, maybe. Just to be safe. Why did you and Samantha decide to get shitfaced?"

"We were *strategizing*." Taylor took a long pull on the water bottle. "With martinis."

"How'd that go?"

"She's not enthusiastic about this relationship."

Jamie winced. "You aren't having second thoughts, are you?"

"Not really," Taylor said. "Maybe a few nerves though?"

Jamie held out a hand, twining their fingers together. "Why's that?"

"Fear you'll change your mind at the last minute, I guess? It wouldn't be the first time a guy promised to come out, then abruptly decided not to when he saw how difficult it would be."

"Oh fuck, baby. I'm sorry." Jamie squeezed his hand. "All I can do is keep pushing forward and show you that I mean it though."

"I know." Taylor stared out the window for a moment. "How did your meeting with your agent go?"

"Okay. He sounded surprised but perfectly willing to work with me."

"Who are you with?"

"Premier Talent. I've been with them for years."

"Oh, funny. I'm with them too. That's how I met Samantha, actually. She used to work there."

"Small world."

"It really is." Though they were the largest and most successful agency in North America. So maybe not *so* surprising.

"But yeah, Mathias—my agent—he suggested looping in one of the other guys in their office. Wade Cannon is who Murphy, Hartinger, and Theriault are with. He knows how to manage the LGBTQ angle." Jamie made a face. "It feels weird. I don't think of myself as part of that community."

Taylor nodded. "It takes time. And in general, I think a lot of bisexual people—particularly ones in straight relationships—don't always feel like they belong."

"Maybe it would be easier if I was ever attracted to another guy."

Taylor blinked at him. "Uh, hello." He gestured up and down his body.

"No. I mean other than you," Jamie said.

Taylor blinked at him. He didn't feel *that* drunk but something wasn't making sense. "Uhh, what?"

"Well, you're the only guy who's ever really made me feel this way. I'm not saying I can't look at another man and go, 'yeah, he's attractive' but I don't want to hook up with him or anything."

"Well, I would hope not," Taylor said. "Cause you're with me."

Jamie squeezed his hand. "I am. And I'm glad I'm with you. But you know what I mean."

"I guess?"

Jamie shrugged. "I don't know. Is that weird? I just … I saw you at the Olympics four years ago and you rocked my world off its axis. I'd never wanted to be with a guy before but I took one look at you skating and it hit me like a ton of bricks. And I haven't really been attracted to any other guys since."

"Huh," Taylor said, trying to process that. "So … you've never like … jerked off to thoughts of some random famous actor or something?"

"No." Jamie looked uncomfortable all of a sudden. "Should I?"

Taylor snorted. "You can if you want. Fantasies are healthy and all that. But … well, maybe it makes me a little bit nervous."

"Why?"

He sighed and leaned his head against the smooth leather. "I keep thinking about what Samantha said. That fans are going to say I turned you gay."

"I don't think that's how that works, right?" They were stopped at a light, so Jamie turned to him, eyebrows scrunched up in confusion. "That's what my therapist said, anyway."

"Of course not. I just feel a little weird about it."

"Do you want to do this?" Jamie asked. "I mean, I'm starting to get worried here, Taylor."

"I want to do this," Taylor said firmly. "It's just scary. The thought of you blowing up your life and your career to be with me."

"I'm scared about you blowing up your family to be with me," Jamie said with a sigh. "But we're either in this together or we're not."

Taylor squeezed his hand. "Then we're in this together."

CHAPTER TWENTY-TWO

Jamie was still feeling apprehensive when they picked up Ava at Jamie's parents' house, but thankfully his mom was the only one home. Taylor had met her dozens of times at Ava's lessons, and they chatted easily enough while Jamie got Ava ready to go.

"Sorry I'm uh, a little tipsy." Taylor's cheeks flushed very pink. "I had drinks with a friend, and um, I might have misjudged how quickly the orange-pineapple vodka martinis went down."

Jodi laughed. "Oh, you're fine. And that sounds delicious. Maybe you'll have to introduce me to them sometime."

Taylor smiled. "I'd like that, Jodi."

"And maybe sometime Adam and I can have you three over for dinner," she said with a sincere smile. "When you're all ready for that."

"I'd *love* that, Mom," Jamie said, kissing her cheek. "Thanks for watching Ava."

"You never need to thank me. I enjoy every minute of it."

"And I appreciate it," Jamie countered. "See you tomorrow?"

"Yes. Just drop her off in the morning on your way to practice."

"Will do." He swept Ava up. "Ready to go, Bear?"

"Ready!"

Jodi and Taylor hugged goodbye and Jamie felt a little flutter in his chest that his mom was so accepting.

The short drive to his place was filled with Ava's chatter about her day with Grandma. She still hadn't run out of words by the time they got her inside, and Jamie only interrupted long enough to coax her to wash her hands in the powder room so she could help them with dinner.

"I thought we'd make spinach and artichoke stuffed chicken tonight," he said to Taylor. "Ava really likes it and it's one of my favorites."

Jamie was always pleased with what an adventurous eater Ava was although at the moment she inexplicably hated anything involving potatoes.

"Sounds great." Taylor beamed, and Jamie was relieved. He'd wanted to cook something impressive for Taylor and the dish was easier than it sounded because he cheated and used the already prepared dip from the nearby high-end market to stuff the chicken.

Taylor was still a little pink-cheeked and bright eyed from the earlier drinks, and Jamie dug in the cupboard for another team-branded water bottle because he had approximately eighty-two of them rattling around his house and vehicle. He filled one and held it out to Taylor.

"Here, this can be yours. I try to keep the number of dishes down by assigning one to everyone in the house. My mom even has one."

Taylor laughed as he took it, leaning a hip against the counter. "Got it."

"I like the sound of that, by the way," Jamie said huskily. He grabbed the front of Taylor's purple sweater and tugged him close. The water was still running in the bathroom and Ava was singing to herself and undoubtedly splashing everywhere, so they had at least sixty seconds before she'd tear herself away.

Taylor looked up at him coyly. "The sound of what?"

"You being around here a lot more." He dropped a kiss on Taylor's lips, quick and dirty, silently promising him more tonight.

"I like the thought of that too," Taylor said with a smile, tucking his head against Jamie's shoulder. "I'll work on the nerves, okay?"

Jamie squeezed him tighter. "We'll take it one step at a time. Tonight, we'll have a nice night with Ava. Watch a movie together, maybe. And then let her know that you'll be around here more because we're dating. I'll tell Kara when she's back from Miami."

"Sounds good." Taylor kissed his neck, sending a little shiver down Jamie's spine.

The water shut off in the bathroom, so Jamie gave Taylor one last squeeze and reluctantly stepped back.

Dinner prep was easy. Taylor threw together a salad while Jamie worked with Ava on the chicken and started rice.

They set the table while the food cooked, and Ava gave him a funny look as she carried the napkins over. "Why are we eating here? We usually eat in the kitchen."

It was true. Jamie very rarely bothered with the formal dining room but tonight it had felt like the right choice. "Well, tonight's a special occasion."

Taylor's gaze flicked up to meet his.

"Ooh, is it your birthday, Taylor?" Ava asked. "Mine is at the end of Feb'ry and Daddy's is in April."

Taylor shook his head. "No, mine isn't until September."

"It's a special occasion because Taylor is going to be around here a lot more in the future," Jamie said, his tone calm but his heart beating very fast. "In fact, he's going to have a sleepover tonight."

Ava cheered. "*Ohhh.* Yay! That's going to be so much fun. You can sleep in my room. My bed's kinda small but if we squeeze, we can both fit. Or I have sleeping bags. I can sleep on the floor if you want my bed. I've got two pillows and you can have one, promise."

"That's very sweet, Ava," Taylor said with a smile.

"It is sweet," Jamie agreed. "But Taylor isn't going to sleep in your room. He's going to sleep in mine."

"Oooh." Ava's eyes got big. "Can I stay in there too?"

"Ahh, no," Jamie said. "Taylor and I are dating. We're … we're boyfriends now."

"Oh, yay!" Ava's eyes shone as she clapped her palms together.

"You know what that means, right?" Jamie asked.

"Yeah, you'll kiss a lot and stuff. Like Mommy and Uncle Boyd."

Jamie hid a wince. "Yeah, kinda like that."

The timer beeped then, and Jamie wasn't sure if he was sorry or relieved.

Still, by the time they had food on their plates and Jamie was cutting up Ava's chicken so she could blow on it until it was cool enough to eat, he felt a little better. That was one hurdle down. Ava seemed nonchalant about the idea of Jamie and Taylor dating, and that was the most important thing.

After dinner, they cleaned up, then watched a movie. By the time the credits rolled, it was a little later than Jamie usually got Ava to bed.

"I want Taylor to read to me," she shouted, stamping her bare foot. She'd been in bed, but she'd quickly slithered out to better throw a more effective tantrum.

"Ava," Jamie warned, trying to remain calm. "It's late. I told you if we watched the movie, there would only be one story and I already read it to you."

His head throbbed a little and he wondered if this tantrum was actually a reaction to the news he was dating someone. He thought Ava would be okay with it, but maybe not.

"Hey," Taylor said, kneeling beside Ava, his expression serious. "I have an idea for a compromise. How about I read you a story in the morning instead?"

Ava's lip quivered for a moment but she eventually nodded and rubbed at her teary eyes. "'kay."

"Okay." Taylor gently coaxed her toward the bed. "Now, the quicker you go to sleep, the sooner it will be morning and the sooner we'll be able to read that book."

Ava let out a shuddering sigh, but she got under the covers and Taylor perched on the bed beside her, smoothing her hair off her face.

"I'll see you in the morning, okay?"

"I'm still mad we can't have a sleepover," she said, pouting. Relief washed through Jamie. *Oh.* This meltdown wasn't because she was upset about them dating, but that she'd been excluded from something fun.

"How about this?" Taylor offered. "Maybe for your birthday, you and me and Charlie can have a sleepover. We can play with makeup and have popcorn and everything."

Ava's eyes went wide. "Really? Could I do that, Daddy?"

Jamie shrugged. "If you show me you're responsible enough for it and Taylor and Charlie want it, sure."

"I'll be good," she said, pulling the covers up to her chin. "So good."

Jamie smiled. "*You* are always good. You just have to work on your behavior sometimes."

"'kay." Her eyes were beginning to droop. "G'night, Taylor. Night, Daddy."

"Night, sweetie," Taylor said, and Jamie's heart nearly turned to mush when Ava sleepily held her arms out for a hug.

"Night, Bear. Love you," Jamie said when they were done, brushing his lips across her forehead. Ava mumbled it back.

Jamie checked that the nightlight was on and left the door open a crack.

Taylor crept quietly down the hall behind him and neither of them spoke until they were curled up on the sofa in the living room, Jamie leaning against the arm of the sofa, Taylor tucked into the cradle of his outstretched legs.

"Okay, well, that went better than I thought it might," Jamie admitted, pulling Taylor's back against his chest. "You handled that *really* well."

"Did I?" Taylor craned his neck and bit his lip. "I'm never sure how much I should jump in."

"I get that." Jamie rubbed Taylor's shoulders and he let out a happy little noise, wiggling to get more comfortable. "But I like the way you approached it. It was a reasonable compromise. We can talk more about it in the future if you want."

"That would be great. It's going to take me a little while to figure out my role here."

"Well, I like where you fit so far." Jamie kissed the side of Taylor's neck and wrapped his arms tightly around him. "Seems perfect to me."

Taylor melted, his head falling to the side when Jamie flicked his tongue against his earlobe before gently tugging it into his mouth to nibble a little. Taylor let out a shaky groan.

"You like that, huh?" Jamie whispered.

"Yeah. It's really sensitive."

"Mmm, good to know." Jamie flicked at it again, using his teeth a little harder this time.

Taylor's hand bit into his thigh. "Fuck. Don't start something unless you plan to finish it."

"Who said I plan to stop?" Jamie purred. He slid a hand under Taylor's sweater and reached up to toy with his nipple. "I had someone come in to fix the lock on my bedroom door, by the way."

"Really?"

"Mm-hmm. We'll have to be quiet, of course, but I can promise there will be privacy."

Jamie lapped along the long, narrow curve of Taylor's neck, pinching his nipple between his thumb and his forefinger.

Taylor let out a shaky sigh. "Privacy's good."

"Thought you'd like that."

"I like you touching me." Taylor had begun to rock his hips and Jamie groaned, shifting until his cock was positioned between Taylor's cheeks.

"I plan to do a lot of that tonight," Jamie promised.

Taylor shuddered, then scrambled off the couch, breathless, his cock hard. "Take me to bed, Jamie. Please."

Jamie smiled and surged up, catching Taylor and using the momentum to throw him over his shoulder in a fireman's carry, pinning Taylor's thighs against his chest to keep him in place.

Taylor yelped quietly and drummed his fists against his back. "Oh my God. Your *shoulder*, Jamie."

"This one's fine," he said with a laugh, carrying him toward the stairs. "Now, don't wiggle or I'll drop you."

Taylor let out a muffled giggle against his back but he behaved, letting Jamie carry him up the stairs. Jamie was a little winded by the time they reached the top but he managed to toss Taylor onto his wide bed without making anything in his good shoulder hurt at all.

"Jamie!" Taylor scolded in a mock whisper, coming up onto one elbow to give him a glare. His face was very red but he hadn't stopped smiling. "You should be more careful."

Jamie gave him a smug little smile, then locked the bedroom door, hearing the satisfying noise of it clicking into place. "I can handle a little thing like you."

Taylor scoffed. "Oh, you think so, huh?"

"Mm-hmm. I know so." He sauntered over and yanked Taylor toward him.

Jamie peeled off Taylor's socks and leggings. He stared down at Taylor intently and he rubbed his thumbs against the crest of Taylor's hipbones, then dragged his snug underwear off too. He tossed them on the rug below.

He put one knee on the bed between Taylor's legs and pushed them farther apart.

Taylor let out a whimper.

"Do you think you can be quiet while I finger you and suck your cock?" he whispered, stretching out over the length of Taylor's body to kiss him.

"Yeah. Yeah, I'll try."

"Good." Jamie gave him a hard, deep kiss, then slid back and reached for the lube in the drawer.

He tossed a pillow down to kneel on, then settled between Taylor's thighs, hooking them over his shoulders. Taylor trembled.

Jamie pressed a kiss to his inner thigh, then licked the spot. Taylor squirmed. So Jamie kept it up, sucking lightly until Taylor let out a quiet whimper. Encouraged, he kept going, using his teeth a little, worrying the skin until a satisfying dark mark appeared.

He glanced up to be sure Taylor was enjoying himself and was greeted with the sight of Taylor's head lifted and his huge eyes filled with need.

"Fingers, Jamie," he hissed impatiently. "I need them so bad."

"Mmm." Jamie reached for the lube. "Is that so?"

"Yes!"

Jamie slicked two fingers, then brushed them across Taylor's hole. His whole body shuddered in response. "Think you can take both or do you need me to work up to it?"

"Both. *Please.*"

Jamie eased forward, watching for any sign of pain, but although Taylor's legs quivered and he clenched around Jamie's fingers, he soon relaxed. Jamie pushed in, slowly but steadily until he was buried inside Taylor's body.

The angle gave him a closeup show and he used his free hand to lift Taylor's balls out of the way, cradling the smooth heft of them. Though there was a patch of soft, dark hair at the base of his cock, he shaved everything below it. Jamie dragged his nose along the inside of Taylor's thigh, breathing in the sweet musk of his skin before nuzzling into the crease of his hip.

So different from going down on a woman, but he loved this too. Loved the velvety skin along the shaft of Taylor's cock and the sticky head, already leaking at the tip. Jamie moved slow, slower than Taylor approved of if his urgent little whines were any indication.

Jamie teased Taylor with short thrusts of his fingers and laps of his tongue until Taylor writhed under him and his noises grew louder.

"*Shh,*" Jamie coaxed, lifting his head to meet Taylor's gaze.

Taylor glared down the length of his body, eyes glittering with need, but he obediently grabbed a pillow and covered his face.

Jamie rose to his knees and sank his mouth over Taylor's cock until he found a rhythm of deep but not too fast strokes inside him that made Taylor's hips lift and his abs tense. Spit trickled down the length of his cock as he sucked and Jamie worked him harder, trying to coordinate his hand stroking at the base too.

Taylor's whole body went tight. His quiet groans dissolved into a low moan of need, muffled against the pillow. He quivered through the orgasm, trembling as Jamie held him down and worked him through it, swallowing his release.

Eventually, Taylor tossed the pillow aside, slapping at Jamie's hands and lifting his head with a tug on his hair.

Taylor's face was red, and his hair disheveled as Jamie eased his fingers out of his body, pressing another kiss to the hickey he'd left on Taylor's inner thigh.

"*Ohmygod,* Jamie." Taylor panted. "That was intense."

"Good." Jamie rose to his feet, knees cracking a little. He stripped off his clothing, wiped his hand on his discarded shirt, then stretched out over Taylor's body, pushing his tongue into Taylor's mouth to taste him hungrily.

His cock was hard, aching as he slid across the defined groove of Taylor's hip, leaving a sticky trail behind.

Jamie was content just to get himself off that way or use the lube to stroke his cock but Taylor pushed him away after a few moments to fumble in the nightstand for a condom.

"Not too sensitive?" Jamie whispered, his fingers already shaking with anticipation as he took it from Taylor.

"No. Please, please, I need you."

Jamie rolled the latex over his dick, hissing at the brush of his fingers where his pulse throbbed, achingly turned on.

He swallowed Taylor's breathy moan with his mouth as he slipped inside, slow enough to be sure it wouldn't hurt. Taylor looped his strong thighs around Jamie's hips, digging his heels into the meat of Jamie's leg.

The snug, slick grip and Taylor's hands roaming across his arms and chest urged Jamie on and it wasn't long before he gasped, shuddering to control himself. It felt too good, his emotions too close to the surface to hold anything back. A bare handful of thrusts later, he eased out, stripping off the condom to come all over Taylor's cock and balls.

He struggled to draw in desperate, gasping breaths as he finished, less from exertion than sheer overwhelm, staggered by a need to show Taylor how much he meant to him.

When the haze finally cleared, all he could do was stand there, softening cock in his hand, staring at the stripes of cum decorating Taylor's body, a little of it landing right on the mark he'd left earlier. The sight of it seemed so right that Jamie bent down and kissed him, helpless to find the words he wanted to say.

Taylor awoke in the middle of the night, warm and relaxed. Jamie was curled up behind him, but he was definitely awake, his palm gently smoothing up and down Taylor's thigh.

Taylor murmured sleepily and Jamie kissed the spot under his ear in answer, whispering, "Why are you awake, baby? It's not morning."

Jamie's sleep-roughened voice sent a shiver through Taylor. Jamie must have thought he was cold, because he fitted their bodies more tightly together. He was hardening, his cock nudging at the lower curve of Taylor's ass.

"Why are *you* awake?" Taylor whispered back.

"Probably because I couldn't stop thinking about you."

Taylor closed his eyes, lips curving up in a smile. "Good things, I hope."

"Always." Jamie kissed the back of his neck, his lips leaving a shivery trail of warmth as he worked his way down to Taylor's shoulder. "But mostly how glad I am to have you in my life."

"Jamie," Taylor breathed, head swimming. He loved the quiet, whispered words and the way Jamie's big body curved around him, sheltering him. He loved how perfectly they fit together but not just physically. The way he had so easily slipped into Jamie's world like a missing puzzle piece Jamie and Ava had been waiting for.

It made Taylor feel like he belonged here in Jamie's bed, in his house, in his life.

Taylor let out a little sound, a quiet groan of contentment and Jamie let out a shaky breath.

"God, I want to be inside you again, baby."

"Please, Jamie."

Jamie flexed his hips, grinding against the curve of Taylor's ass, the movement feeling more like a reflex than a conscious choice. "You aren't too sore?"

"No." Taylor said breathlessly. "Want it. Want to feel you tomorrow."

In the dark, Jamie found the lube and condoms. Taylor gripped the covers when Jamie pressed slick fingers between his cheeks, licking and biting at his shoulder while he eased inside.

It didn't take much to open him up, not after their earlier sex, and Taylor let out a contented groan when Jamie's cock was deep within him.

"God, Taylor." Jamie sounded half delirious as he began to thrust, his hand splayed across Taylor's stomach. "You feel …"

But neither of them had words when Jamie rocked in and out. It was so slow it made Taylor want to beg him to go harder and faster but it was so sweet to be pinned between Jamie's palm and his hips, hot breath against his ear.

When Taylor whimpered, Jamie shifted, getting his arm underneath Taylor's neck so he could settle his palm against Taylor's mouth.

Taylor flicked his tongue out, teasing Jamie's fingers until he took the hint and slid two thick digits into Taylor's mouth.

Taylor hungrily swirled his tongue around them, loving the feel of Jamie filling his mouth and his ass at the same time. Taylor had never experienced anything like it before, surrounded and wrapped up tight, warm, and treasured. He wanted to drown in Jamie but how could he when Jamie would always be there to keep his head above water.

Taylor softened, let Jamie rock in and out while Taylor lapped at his fingers with quiet little groans and soft sucking sounds. The whoosh of Jamie's breath in his ear, Jamie's lips pursing occasionally to press half-distracted kisses to his neck, were almost too much, threatening to tip Taylor over the edge without a hand on his cock.

Under the sheets, the heat built between them. Sweat slicked their skin making every shift of their bodies smooth and frictionless.

Taylor had spent years searching for this, looking for the man he could trust, the one who would keep him safe. The one who saw a future and didn't flinch from the challenges, only set his jaw and went after what he wanted anyway.

The one who would fight for Taylor, despite the hardships.

Emotion welled up, threatening to spill over in a hot press of tears behind Taylor's eyelids. He sucked harder on Jamie's fingers, his noises muffled as Jamie moved, slow and sweet. The heat threatened to overwhelm him, fiery and filling him with desperation.

Two more breaths and Jamie groaned in his ear, body shaking with helpless shudders as he ground against Taylor. When he smoothed his palm up the length of Taylor's shaft, Taylor was done for too, tears and his release spilling over simultaneously in a rush of intensity that made him tremble in Jamie's arms.

When they were both still and spent, Taylor felt weak and shaky. Jamie eased his fingers from his mouth but when he shifted to pull out, Taylor clamped around him, not ready for that empty ache that would linger when he was gone.

Jamie nuzzled into his cheek. "Taylor, I …"

Taylor shifted, twisting his shoulders so he could look up at him in the dim bedroom. "I know, Jamie. I know."

"It's so soon." Jamie sounded surprised, his movements tender as he wiped the tears from Taylor's cheeks. "But I … God, I'm falling in love with you."

There was a reverence in his tone and Taylor knew instinctively that those weren't words Jamie used lightly. They meant something to him, something powerful and profound.

They were a promise.

"I'm falling in love with you too," Taylor whispered back, and though the words weren't new, they felt different from anything he'd ever said to anyone else before.

Jamie buried his head against Taylor's neck and sighed, body going soft and pliant, and Taylor was dazzled by the visions of the future that lay before them.

CHAPTER TWENTY-THREE

The team had away games in Detroit and Columbus. By the time they touched down in Illinois, Jamie knew he couldn't put off talking to Coach Daniels any longer. He spoke with Coach Tate, and when the three of them were holed up in a conference room with coffees before practice, he blurted it out.

"I'm dating Taylor Hollis."

Coach Daniels seemed to instantly age ten years as the news hit and he scrubbed his hands over his face. "Christ. I thought maybe we could get through the rest of this season without another guy coming out on this goddamn team."

Jamie gave Coach Tate a worried look but his expression was reassuring. "Thank you for telling us, Jamie."

He gave the head coach a pointed look. "C'mon, Ken, that's not exactly the reaction a guy who's coming out wants to hear."

"Sorry." Daniels managed a weak smile. "I appreciate that you told us, Walsh. I think you know I'm supportive."

"I do." Jamie had never doubted *that.* "But I get that this will be a huge hassle for the organization."

"Sure will." Daniels sat back in his chair, expression weary. "How'd your old man take it?"

"Pretty well. We haven't told Taylor's dad yet though."

Both coaches winced.

"Yeah." Jamie laughed humorlessly. "We're doing it in stages but I didn't want to blindside the head office or anything."

"Like Gabriel and I did?" Tate asked, his pale blue eyes amused. He tipped his coffee mug up to take a long drink.

Jamie shrugged but didn't deny it.

"Don't suppose you want to wait until the off-season?" Daniels asked. "I mean, a quiet social media post or something? Or do you want to go the full presser route?"

"It shouldn't wait," Jamie admitted. "The odds of my kid staying quiet about it are not great. And I can't say my relationship with my ex-wife is the best. There's a chance she could spread the news."

Daniels nodded but when he didn't say anything, Jamie continued.

"I definitely don't want to do a full press conference. I spoke with my agent and Taylor had a long talk with Samantha about how to break the news and we have an idea."

"What's that?" Daniels asked gruffly.

"Well, we already have fans invested in the videos the team did with Taylor, right? We have another week or so of that to wrap up but there's no reason it couldn't finish with a video of Taylor and my daughter and I all skating together and a couple of short interviews with Taylor and me talking about our relationship."

Daniels considered the idea. "Samantha knows her stuff. If she thinks that's a good angle, I'm not opposed."

Jamie set down his mug. He hadn't even touched the coffee. "I hope you know the last thing I want is for my relationship to be a distraction from the game. And I know that we're at a crucial point in the season. I don't want to be a liability to the team."

Daniels and Tate exchanged glances and Tate was the one who spoke. "We know that, Jamie. And you shouldn't feel like you are one."

"Can I be blunt?" Daniels asked.

Jamie had never really known Daniels to be anything else, but maybe he held back more than Jamie knew. "Of course."

"The truth is, I'd be way fucking happier if I never had to answer another question from a reporter about how a player's relationship will impact their play. Gay, straight, or anything else under the sun. Not because I give a shit who you're dating but because I think it's a damn distraction from the game. But that's not on you guys."

Jamie nodded.

"And I know there's going to be extra attention on players when they come out and it's going to be a while before we get to a point where it doesn't matter to the media. After Tate and Theriault came out, my wife reminded me that you guys don't have the luxury of choosing if this turns into a big deal or not and I can't argue that. The timing isn't great, and I'd rather be thinking about how Underhill's going to fit into our PK unit than how our GM is going to feel about your relationship, but that's not on you." He let out a tired sigh. "I've got your back with the head office; I hope that goes without saying."

"Thank you, Coach," Jamie said, surprisingly touched.

Daniels was gruff. He always had been and presumably always would be. But his heart was in the right place and not only had he given Jamie a chance right when he thought he might quit skating altogether, he was willing to stand up for him now. Jamie couldn't ask for more.

"Anything else?" Daniels asked, a hint of amusement lurking in his tone.

"I sincerely hope not," Jamie said.

Daniels snorted and rose to his feet, holding out a hand. "Good man. Now, I expect I'll be seeing a lot more of you in the next few weeks while we hammer out the details of how we're going to handle this but thank you for being upfront. Getting ahead of this makes it easier."

"Just let me know what you need from me," Jamie said.

"How about some more of that action I saw against Columbus? That long-range goal that tied us up at the end of the second was a beaut."

Jamie flushed. "Wasn't enough to get us a win."

"No, but it was enough to make it a respectable one-goal loss. Do that a few more times a game and we'll be sittin' pretty." He clapped Jamie on the arm.

Jamie laughed. "I'll see what I can do, Coach."

They wrapped up their meeting and Jamie let out a shaky breath as he walked down the hall, simultaneously relieved and a little overwhelmed. He wasn't surprised when he heard Tate call his name though, and he turned to see him jogging to catch up.

"Hey, I just wanted to check in. How are you feeling?"

"Good. Mostly relieved, but it's a lot, you know?"

"It is." Tate gave him a sympathetic look. "I want you to know that if you need to talk, I'm around, okay?"

"Thanks, Coach," he said sincerely. "That means a lot."

"The one thing we didn't discuss was when you want to tell the team."

"Oh. Soon, I think? I'm going to talk to my ex the next time I see her, so I want the team to hear it from me before there's a chance of it going public."

"Perfect. You choose whatever time feels right."

"Okay. Thank you."

"Yeah, of course. And I mean it, my door is always open, Jamie. Don't hesitate if you need to talk."

Jamie headed straight for the workout room and hopped on the treadmill, needing to burn off some of the shaky energy coursing through his body.

He'd done it.

He was one step closer to proving to Taylor that he was ready for this relationship.

Taylor scrubbed his body, smiling at one of the purple hickies Jamie had left on his hip the night before. That was getting to be a habit.

Taylor's smile widened when the bathroom door opened and a few moments later, the shower curtain rustled.

"Hey, you." Jamie's voice was soft, and a little sleep roughened.

Taylor sank back against him, sighing at the feel of Jamie's big warm body against his back and the hot water pelting down on his chest. "Hey yourself."

"Why didn't you wake me up?"

Taylor laughed, turning in Jamie's arms to look at him. "I *tried.* You were dead to the world."

Jamie wrinkled his nose. "Your fault. You wore me out last night."

"*My* fault?" Taylor sputtered. "*You* were the one who showed up here all fired up after your game and fucked me six ways until Sunday."

Jamie silently ticked things off on his fingers, expression thoughtful before he shook his head. "I think it was at least seven but the last two were all you."

Taylor laughed and pressed a kiss to Jamie's collarbone. "Okay. Can't argue that."

He winced when the water hitting his ass cooled. "You want to wash? We're about to lose the hot water."

He was already spoiled by the endless hot water at Jamie's place. Someday he'd be calling that gorgeous house his own too, though, and the thought filled him with happiness that had nothing to do with ample square footage and marble countertops.

"Sure, just need to rinse off and dunk my head under." Jamie squeezed Taylor's hips and carefully shuffled past. "My hair was wet when I went to sleep and it's doing weird things now."

It was, in fact, sticking straight up. But Taylor liked that he was beginning to see the less-than-perfect side of Jamie. The wild morning hair and his grumpiness after a bad game. The way he hogged the bed and wrapped around Taylor like a particularly cuddly octopus when they slept.

With a quick kiss, Taylor ducked out and left Jamie to shower. He dried off and wrapped himself in his robe, deciding to get breakfast going before he got dressed.

Charlie was out—*again*—and Taylor and Jamie would be leaving for practice soon.

Taylor still got warm little flutters when he thought about Jamie coming out to his coaches a few days ago.

Step by step, they were getting there.

Jamie was *proud* to be with him, not ashamed or trying to hide him.

Taylor had most of their scrambled egg and spinach breakfast burritos assembled by the time Jamie appeared. Taylor looked him up and down, enjoying the view of him shirtless in low-slung gray sweats with wet hair dripping down onto the collarbone Taylor had definitely left a hickey on. Maybe they'd both been feeling fired up last night.

They ate breakfast at the small table, smiling at each other over the food, Jamie's big feet casually pinning Taylor's to the floor like he had to be touching him *somewhere*.

They had a few bites left on their plates when there was a knock on the front door.

"Hmm, wonder who that is?" Taylor got up to answer it, wiping his fingers on a napkin. "Maybe the neighbor. She gets grumpy when they put my letters in her mailbox."

He caught a glimpse of Jamie stealthily reaching for the food on Taylor's plate.

"Hey! I saw that! Don't eat the rest of my breakfast," he called back. He fumbled for the lock and pulled the door open. "I'm starving and I need my strength after last night."

His eyes widened at the sight of his parents on the other side of the door.

"Hey, sweetie." His mom beamed at him and held out a bag. "We had a meeting in the area this morning, so I thought we'd drop off some of the apple oat muffins that you and Charlie like so much."

"Uhh," was all Taylor could manage. He tightened the belt on his robe, scrambling to think of a way to get his parents out of there immediately. "I've, uh, gotta get to practice and—"

"Taylor, do you want me to make you a second burrito?" Jamie called to him.

His parents blinked and they all stood frozen for a moment, staring at one another. There was the soft pad of bare feet behind him.

"Baby? Everything okay?" There was nothing but warm concern in Jamie's voice. He slid a hand around his waist in a comforting gesture.

Oh fuck, oh fuck, oh fuck was all Taylor could think as he watched his father's gaze rake over Jamie, undoubtedly taking in all the little incriminating details. The wet hair. The hickies. Their state of undress.

Jamie tightened his grip.

"What in the hell is going on here, Taylor?" Rick Hollis snarled as he looked between the two of them.

Taylor backed up against Jamie, who wrapped both arms protectively around him.

"Umm," was all Taylor could manage. He had a sudden wash of sympathy for Jamie's reaction when Charlie had walked in on them. "Uh, Dad," Taylor said faintly. "Fuck. I …"

"Answer me, Taylor. What in the hell are you doing with the Walsh boy?"

"For fuck's sake!" Taylor snapped, finally shaking himself out of his stupor. "His name is *Jamie*. And he's my boyfriend."

There, bandage ripped off.

Rick's jaw tightened. "Taylor, I suggest you ask him to leave."

Jamie sputtered. "Sir, I'm—"

Rick held up a hand. "I don't have anything to say to you. This is between my wife and me and our son."

"With all due respect, you're upset at him because of me. And I love your son very much," Jamie said hotly. "If he wants me to be here, I'm going to be here for him."

Rick let out an aggravated sound, his nostrils flaring.

Taylor's mom reached out and gripped his shoulder. "Rick, please take a deep breath before you have a stroke."

"Wouldn't be the first time a Walsh put me in the hospital!" he snapped.

"Jesus Christ! Can you set aside the grudge for ten fucking minutes so we can have a civil conversation about this, Dad?" Taylor begged. "Please!"

"You damn well know my feelings about that family, but it's clear that you're only thinking of yourself."

"Rick, stop it! This isn't helpful," Taylor's mom said, her tone firm.

"Fine. I'm leaving." He turned to go, walking down the hallway like he'd lost game seven in the Cup Finals.

Lindsey let out a sigh. "Taylor, sweetheart, I think it would be best if we head out. Maybe a cooling-off period will help us gather our thoughts so we can have a productive discussion about this. I'm sorry your father is being so hard-headed."

"What else is new?" Taylor muttered.

She gave him a rueful smile, pecked his cheek, and left without another word. After Taylor closed and locked the door, he turned and buried his head against Jamie's chest. "Oh God. That was not how I wanted that to go."

"I know." Jamie wrapped his arms tightly around Taylor. "I'm sorry, baby. I didn't mean to—"

"It's not your fault." Taylor sighed and lifted his head. "Neither of us knew they were going to stop by this morning, and I could have at least looked through the peephole before I opened the door."

"C'mon. Let's sit down and talk for a minute," Jamie coaxed.

After they took seats on the couch, Taylor curled up in a ball tucked under Jamie's arm.

"Are you okay?" Jamie asked.

"Not really."

"I get why your dad's pissed about discovering we're together," Jamie said with a frown, "but this seems like a bit of an overreaction."

"Yeah, well … this is the one thing he's never been particularly rational about." Taylor scrubbed a hand over his face.

"So how are we going to deal with this?"

"*We*?" Taylor looked up at him.

"Well, I'm not going anywhere unless you tell me to," Jamie promised, his expression determined.

Those words made warmth fill Taylor's chest. He sat up and wrapped his arms around Jamie's neck. "Thank you."

"You never have to thank me for loving and supporting you," Jamie whispered against his hair. "Never."

CHAPTER TWENTY-FOUR

Two days later, Taylor sat in his living room, staring at the bank balance on his laptop screen with a knot in his stomach that refused to go away. His dad was still furious and along with the mounting tension of his dwindling bank account and bills coming due, Taylor was overwhelmed.

He'd called in every extension he could get and asked for a loan, but he'd been denied. This was the final notice, and he was *going* to have to pay the bill for Charlie's rehab stay or they'd send it to collections.

Now that Taylor could no longer delay payment, he was in a horrible spot he had no idea how to extricate himself from.

He felt a little faint. He'd worked so hard to be a grown-ass adult and prove to his parents that he'd made the right decision to stop competing. He couldn't ask them for a loan, or he'd be admitting that he'd made a mistake. That he couldn't handle his life as well as he thought.

And right now, with his dad furious and barely speaking to him? There was no way he'd beg them for money.

The paycheck from the Otters had been a huge help but no matter how he juggled his budget, it wouldn't cover the bill in full.

There was no denying it. Taylor was in deep trouble.

Jamie had offered to help a while back. Taylor briefly considered telling him he'd changed his mind and could use the help, but he knew he'd been right. If they were going to make this relationship work, Taylor couldn't be beholden to him financially. Not this soon.

And for God's sake, Jamie had a kid.

Their age difference didn't bother Taylor much, but if he was going to prove to Jamie that he was a responsible adult who could be an equal partner and be a good influence in Ava's life, Taylor had to have his shit together.

Begging for a big chunk of money would do more to hurt their new relationship than help it.

Taylor nibbled on the edge of his nail before remembering he'd painted them this morning. *Gross.*

He flopped back with a sigh and rubbed his eyes. There had to be some solution, damn it.

The sound of Charlie's bedroom door opening made Taylor sit upright. He hastily closed the lid on his laptop and stuffed the bill under the computer, face down. Charlie didn't know what bad shape Taylor's finances were in and if Taylor had his way, he'd never find out. The last thing Charlie needed was more stress in his life.

"Ready to go?" Taylor asked brightly. He hopped to his feet, hoping Charlie hadn't seen his furtive moves as he walked into the living room.

Charlie wrinkled his nose. "What on earth are you wearing?"

Taylor glanced down at the teal and black fabric with the rainbow Otter logo, glad Charlie was easily distracted by his sartorial choices. "A Pride jersey?"

"An *Otters* jersey. You've always been an Auto Wrench fan."

"Yeah well, Evanston has been paying my bills lately," he said tartly. "Detroit hasn't."

"You sure it doesn't have anything to do with a certain winger you're dating?"

Taylor flushed, his cheeks suddenly hot. "Well, it doesn't *hurt*. But it's not exactly great PR if people see me in Detroit stuff when I work with the team here."

"Not to mention it'll get brought up once you two go public. That *is* a thing that's going to happen, right?"

"It is," Taylor said confidently. "One step at a time. Now, are you ready to go or what?"

He turned away but Charlie let out a horrified noise. "Oh my God, you're wearing Zane Murphy's jersey?"

"Well, I didn't want to be *obvious*." Taylor frowned and he pulled on his winter jacket. "I mean, I thought about wearing Jamie's but he doesn't even know we're going to the game tonight and I feel weird about it without his okay."

"So, you're wearing his hot bisexual captain's instead?" Charlie sounded scandalized. "Are you trying to make him jealous?"

"What? No!" Taylor protested. "Of course not."

"Sure, honey." Charlie shot him a skeptical look as he slipped his boots on. "You keep telling yourself that."

"Can we drop it?" Taylor muttered. "*Please* focus or we'll never get out of here. You spent forever doing your makeup."

"You should have spent more time," Charlie retorted. "Your eyeliner on the left is atrocious. That is not a crisp wing."

Taylor ignored the snarky comment in favor of holding out Charlie's puffy coat for him to put on, but after he shoved his feet into boots, he wobbled unsteadily.

"Dude, have you been pre-gaming without me or something?" Taylor asked with a laugh but when he caught a glimpse of Charlie's pale face, his stomach dropped, and he grabbed Charlie's elbow to steady him. "Hey, seriously, you okay, Charlie?"

"Just a head rush." He pasted on a completely fake smile.

"Did you—"

"Yes, Taylor, I ate today," he snapped.

"Whoa." Taylor held up his hands. "What's with the sudden 'tude?"

Charlie closed his eyes. "Sorry. I—I have a bit of a headache, okay? I think I need some water. I probably didn't drink enough after hot yoga this morning."

"Okay. I'll go grab some you can drink on the drive over. Unless you don't want to go—I know the games get pretty loud and with a headache—"

Charlie smacked at Taylor's hands, which were still clutching his elbow. "Quit mothering me, you worrywart. I'm fine. I'm a little dehydrated is all. Get the water and we can go. I thought you were worried about being late!"

But although Taylor fretted on the way there—more about Charlie's well-being than being late—Charlie obediently downed two waters and they made it to their seats in plenty of time. That was mostly thanks to the badge Taylor had, which allowed them to park in the staff lot instead of general parking.

He'd been offered tickets when he'd agreed to work with the Otters, and his time with the team was nearly over. Charlie had been bugging him about it for weeks so he figured he should cash in before it was too late.

"I still can't believe you talked me into this," Taylor muttered as they took their seats.

Charlie wiggled excitedly. "What? A hockey game? You *like* hockey."

"Yes, but …" Taylor flailed for an answer.

It felt *weird* all of a sudden, like he was spying on Jamie. Maybe he should have talked to him about it first.

The team came out on the ice for warmups and Taylor saw the moment Jamie spotted him. He'd been skating slowly, scanning the crowd.

His gaze swept past Taylor before he jerked his head back for a second glance. His hand lifted like he was going to wave before he stilled and his face did something complicated before he gave Taylor a little nod.

Charlie, of course, waved back like a lunatic.

"Would you quit it?" Taylor hissed, tugging his arm down, mildly irked by Charlie's showiness but relieved to see him acting normally. It must have been the dehydration earlier.

After Jamie passed them, he slowed to a stop, his face lighting up. Taylor felt the strangest twinge, wondering who had made him smile so big. He caught a glimpse of a woman with long blonde hair and a jersey with *Walsh* on the back. Taylor had a painful, momentary flicker of doubt and mistrust before he spotted familiar blonde curls and he realized it was *Ava* that Jamie was smiling so brightly at and the woman was Jamie's *mother*.

Jesus, of course it was. How could Taylor have doubted?

He'd dated some shitheads in the past but Jamie was incredibly loyal.

It was a good first period. The Otters pulled out a 2-1 lead and Jamie got the assist on the first goal that Truro sniped in and Taylor was so damn proud of him. Taylor hoped no one got him on cam because the heart eyes he had going on were probably visible from space.

"See, aren't you having fun?" Charlie asked brightly as they returned to their seats during the first intermission.

They'd agreed to split an order of pork tacos. Charlie was munching on some chips and salsa which put Taylor's mind at ease. He'd probably been worrying about Charlie unnecessarily. Taylor took a big bite of the tacos, the flavors of salsa verde and cilantro bright on his tongue.

"Yeah, I am," Taylor admitted, finishing the taco in a few more big bites. He nudged Charlie's thigh to get his attention and they traded food containers. "Hey, what's going on with you lately, by the way? You're hardly home."

"Well, the new job is keeping me pretty busy. We're doing a huge condo reno for some corporate lady bigwig and I am awash in creamy neutrals and blush pink."

Jamie dunked a chip into the salsa and opened his mouth to ask about Charlie's love life—or at least his sex life—when he heard a shriek.

"Taylor!"

He turned his head to see Ava barreling up the steps toward them. She threw her arms around him, and he reflexively clutched at the container of tortilla chips. "You came to see Daddy play."

"Well, I came to cheer for his whole team, yeah," he lied, feeling guilty as he patted her with his free hand.

"Hi, Charlie!"

Ava let out a little squeal and squeezed in past Taylor, causing him to bump into Charlie, which sent the taco container tumbling out of his hand with a messy splat. Taylor tried not to sigh. That was money he didn't have going to waste. And Charlie hadn't even had a chance to eat one. A funny little feeling squirmed through Taylor's stomach. Had that been intentional?

But Ava drew his attention before he could dwell on that thought.

"Whoops." Ava's eyes got really big, and her lip quivered. "I'm sorry. I didn't mean to do that."

"It's okay, sweetie," Charlie soothed. "It was all Taylor's fault. He bumped me."

Taylor sputtered but Charlie wasn't exactly wrong, and Taylor certainly didn't want Ava to feel bad, so he let it be.

"I love your bows, sweetie!" Charlie continued. "You look so cute."

She had accessorized with teal bows that matched her mini jersey and teal sneakers. She beamed at Charlie; all thoughts of spilled food forgotten. "Thanks! I like your eye makeup. It's so sparkly!"

"Sparkles are the best," Charlie said brightly. He'd gone for some exceptionally dramatic makeup with contouring that highlighted the hollows of his cheekbones. Taylor was a little more subdued. Though they still were probably the only guys in the entire stadium wearing makeup.

"Ava Grace Walsh!" Jodi stood a few steps below, shaking her head. "We've talked about you running off like this."

A guilty look crossed her face. "Sorry, Gramma."

Jodi gave Taylor a "what can you do?" look as she walked up the stairs to greet them. She was well into her fifties, but still fit and trim with long blonde hair and the same ocean-blue eyes Jamie had.

"Jodi, this is my roommate, Charlie Monaghan. Charlie, this is Ava Walsh's grandma."

Charlie's eyes gleamed. "Why *hello*. It's lovely to meet you."

Intermission was nearly over so Jodi coaxed Ava back to their seats.

"So that's the future mother-in-law, huh?" Charlie muttered when they were gone.

Taylor whacked his arm. "Would you shut up?" he hissed. The arena wasn't packed tonight and there were some empty seats around them but Jesus.

"I'm just saying …"

"I'm saying you need to shut your mouth before I shut it for you," Taylor whispered.

"Baby." Charlie sounded scandalized. "I didn't know you were into that."

———

"Helloooo, gentlemen."

Jamie looked up from unlacing his skates to see the locker room doors open and Charlie posed dramatically between them. Media had finally left so they were down to players and the equipment managers who had to deal with their stinky, sweaty gear.

Jamie was still buzzing after his game-winning goal against Detroit and he blinked a few times, momentarily wondering if he was hallucinating as Charlie pranced into the room.

"Who the fuck is that?" Jack Malone asked under his breath.

"Taylor Hollis's roommate," Jamie said automatically. A couple of guys turned to him with identical puzzled looks, like they couldn't figure out how the fuck *he* knew that. Jamie shrugged because he was terrible at lying on the spot.

Charlie rose on his tiptoes, craning his neck and trying to see around a couple of guys stripping out of their gear. That or to get a better look at them. Jamie wasn't quite sure.

"Oh, hey there, Jamie! Great game tonight." He gave a cheery wave as he approached.

Jamie smiled at him. "Thanks. What are you doing here, Charlie?"

He looked at Jamie like he was an idiot. "Watching the game with Taylor?"

"Right." Jamie shook his head and peeled his skate off. "I … yeah. Obviously. He should have let me know you two were coming. I could have gotten you tickets."

Charlie's mouth curved up in a little smile. "That's what *I* told him. But he said the team had offered him some."

"What the hell are you doing in here, Charlie?" Taylor hissed from the doorway. "You're not supposed to be in the locker room. I *told* you to wait in the lounge. How the fuck did you get in here, anyway?"

Charlie gave him a sheepish smile. "Umm, I snuck in?"

Taylor grimaced and slipped between O'Shea and Cooper who were watching the proceedings with amused smiles.

Zane Murphy looked mildly concerned. "Everything okay, Taylor?"

He looked at Zane. "Oh my God. I'm sorry about this. This is my nosy roommate, Charlie Monaghan."

"It's fine," Murphy said with an easy smile. "Good to know he's not a dangerous stalker though."

"Well, I wouldn't swear to *that*," Taylor muttered. "They're not supposed to let any fans back here, are they?"

"No, not usually," Murphy said with a little laugh. "How did you manage to get by security, Charlie?"

"Dude, I had this." Charlie waved the lounge pass he wore on a lanyard around his neck. "The guards got distracted for a minute and I snuck past."

"Yeah, you might want to talk to someone and get your security beefed up," Taylor said to Murphy with a sigh.

Charlie made a face. "I'm wounded, Tay. Wounded. I'm not some *riffraff*, you know?"

"Are you going to introduce your friend to the rest of us, Taylor?" Hartinger asked, looking delighted by the whole exchange.

"No need, I can introduce myself. I'm Charlie Monaghan." He sauntered over to Ryan with a grin. "That was quite a goal you scored tonight in the third period. Verrry impressive."

"Why thank you," Ryan said with a grin, towering over him. He ruffled Charlie's hair playfully, who absolutely preened at the attention. "And I don't blame you for being impressed. I mean, I *am* pretty damn impressive."

"Yeah, you are." Charlie blatantly looked him up and down. "On *and* off the ice."

Ryan grinned at him, shirtless and sweaty and clearly enjoying the attention.

Zane rolled his eyes. "Please don't encourage him."

Charlie smirked and batted his lashes at Zane. "Aww, do you need some love too, Captain Hot Pants? Because if you two are interested in some three-way action, I promise I can be very discreet."

"Ahh, no. Sorry bud," Hartinger said with a laugh. "We like to keep it just the two of us. But we are flattered."

"Oh, sweet Jesus, will you shut your damn mouth?" Taylor looked mortified and he yanked on Charlie's hand, tugging him toward the door.

"Well, if you ever change your mind, boys, you know how to find me," Charlie said with a little waggle of his fingers.

Taylor shoved him out the door, then turned back to stare at the team. "I'm very sorry for everything he's said." His sigh was heartfelt. "I hope you can accept my most sincere apologies and please, um, forget everything that happened in the past ten minutes or however long this lunatic has been running off his mouth."

He turned and disappeared through the door with another shake of his head but all Jamie could see was Murphy's name and number in rainbow letters across his back.

Jealousy flared hot in Jamie's chest. That wasn't right. He could guess why Taylor had chosen it but he hated it. He hated everything about it and he wanted *his* name and number to be the only one Taylor wore.

And Jamie couldn't do that until everyone knew they were together.

He was on his feet before he realized it.

"Hey, guys!" he called. The room quieted.

"What's up, Walshy?" Hartinger asked with a quizzical smile.

"I have an announcement to make."

Theriault, who had returned from the showers and was dressed in a towel, raised an eyebrow.

"Taylor and I are dating," Jamie said, glad his voice came out steady and sure.

The room went silent, the upbeat music Cooper had put on earlier the only sound until he fumbled for his phone and turned it off.

Murphy blinked at him. "Congrats?" He sounded a little tentative and Jamie cursed himself for not telling his captain first.

"Thanks." Jamie rubbed the back of his neck, his skin gritty with dried sweat. "Sorry I didn't give you a heads-up but I uh, hadn't planned on telling you quite yet. It, um, felt like the right time, I guess?"

"Hey, that's cool." Hartinger grinned and slapped Jamie on the back. "Welcome to the club. Taylor seems like a great guy and his friend Charlie is a fucking riot."

"Taylor is great," Jamie agreed. "I feel really lucky, to be honest."

Zane gave him a sincere smile as he regained his composure. "No worries about the lack of heads-up. Honestly, it's a lot and I know sometimes the timing doesn't always work out the way we plan."

He shot a pointed glance at Hartinger, whose expression turned sheepish.

Jamie wasn't quite sure what that was about but he hadn't been with the team when Murphy and Hartinger came out, so maybe it was some inside joke or something.

That seemed to shake everyone out of their shock though, and Jamie got sincere congratulations from most of the guys.

O'Shea gave him a knowing look and punched him in the arm. "Dude, you could have said something the other night when we were hanging out. I thought maybe something was going on but you blew it off and I didn't want to pry. I would have been fine with it though."

"I know." Jamie pulled him in for a one-armed hug. "Appreciate it, man. I just wasn't ready then, you know?"

Understanding flickered in his gaze. "I get it."

Underhill only gave Jamie a small nod and there was a noticeable coolness from two of the rookies but Jamie was beginning to think it might all go down without any fuss when Malone spoke up. He was talking to Underhill but he didn't bother to keep his voice down.

"You know, I'm starting to think this team is full of guys more interested in dick than winning," Malone said venomously.

"What was that, Malone?" Murphy went from relaxed to on edge in an instant.

Malone stood slowly and crossed his arms. "I'm just saying, I don't know what the fuck is going on with this team but we're not exactly burning up the league at the moment. Want to guess when that losing streak started? Hmm, must have been right around the time Theriault and Coach got found out. I fucking told you it was going to hurt the team."

"You might want to watch your mouth," Murphy said, his tone even but clearly filled with warning.

"It's fuckin' ridiculous!" Malone snapped. "Do you pay any attention to the shit that gets said on social media? And now we're about to have another goddamn player come out. I'm sick of answering questions about who my teammates are screwing."

Jamie stepped forward. "If you have a problem with me, say it to my face, Malone."

He wasn't a fighter, never had been, but holy shit he was sick of this guy.

"C'mon, leave it," Underhill said, tugging on Malone's shoulder. "I don't give a fuck if Walsh or anyone else is dating a dude."

Malone looked around. "So, we're fine that everyone and their brother is fucking gay now? Who else on the team is gonna come out? How many of you have been hiding shit?"

Lindholm rose to his feet and even in bare feet, he was half a head taller than Malone, his expression grave. "Me. You have a problem with that?"

Jamie blinked and O'Shea made a weird little wheezing noise as he whispered Lindy's name.

Lindholm glanced at O'Shea with a concerned expression, but he quickly turned back to Malone. "I'm serious. I'm bisexual. Do you have a problem playing hockey with me?"

Anders Lindholm's record was legendary. After nearly two decades in the league, his points total was staggering and the fact that he was still performing at such a high level at almost forty was a legacy that would be difficult to beat.

Even guys like Malone respected that.

Malone tossed his bag over his shoulder. "Jesus. This team is turning into a goddamn gay joke."

He left before anyone else could reply.

Jamie turned to look at his captain but before he could open his mouth to apologize, Murphy shook his head.

"Don't, Walsh. You did nothing wrong. Malone has a problem with some of us but you don't need to apologize for anything. This team will support you. Now, go get your guy. And Jesus, get him one of your jerseys. I'm flattered and all, but he should have your sweater on."

Jamie laughed and dragged Murphy in for a hug. "Thanks, man."

Murphy pulled back to look him in the eye. "Great game tonight too, bud. We're glad to have you on the team. I hope you know that."

CHAPTER TWENTY-FIVE

"Are you *sure* you have to go?" Jamie begged and Taylor hid a smile, wondering if he realized he sounded a bit like his five-year-old at the moment. It was rather cute actually. "We should spend the day in bed. Mom's watching Ava and I'd rather spend today getting you naked and sweaty."

Taylor laughed and sat up, his sheets a tangled mess around his lower half. "You've done nothing *but* that since we got home from the game last night."

"Have any complaints?" Jamie curled around him, pressing a kiss to the nape of his neck and sending a shiver down his spine.

"No." Taylor sighed, goosebumps breaking out over his body.

Jamie had been fired up last night after his beautiful goal, the team's win, and coming out to the guys.

They'd barely made it in the door of Taylor and Charlie's apartment before Jamie had ripped Murphy's jersey off, replaced it with his own, and bent him over the bed, his hands hot and possessive as he reminded Taylor who he was with.

Taylor still felt a little dizzy remembering it.

The middle-of-the-night sex and the first-thing-in-the-morning sex had been amazing too and Taylor could still feel the sweet ache of the toy Jamie had used on him at one point. But he did need to do something today other than get screwed silly.

Taylor turned and pressed a kiss to Jamie's mouth. "You have blown my mind. But man cannot live on sex alone. I have a rehearsal for my new show, and I *can't* miss it," he said. "And you have an afternoon practice."

Jamie let out a grumbly sigh and adjusted his glasses. "I've been plenty athletic this morning."

Taylor thought about the positions they'd gotten into earlier and nodded. "Not sure that's gonna please your coach though. C'mon. You've gotta go. You can't slack now."

Jamie's look was pouty. "I know. I need to prove to the guys that I'm not going to let this distract me."

"I'm sure most of them know it," Taylor assured him, turning to untangle himself from the sheets wrapped around his legs.

Though Taylor had an even greater dislike for Jack Malone after what Jamie had told him about his comments last night. Jesus, what was that guy's problem?

"I hate to be the source of conflict," Jamie said with a sigh, hooking his chin on Taylor's shoulder. "I already drove a wedge into the middle of one team."

Taylor finally wrestled himself free, then turned to face Jamie straight on, cupping his face in his hands. "No, you didn't. You did nothing wrong when you were in Chicago. Boyd and Kara made their choices. And you coming out last night didn't drive a wedge into anything else either. You said it yourself, Malone's had an issue with guys coming out from the beginning and we know he's a prick all around."

"He is." Jamie still looked a bit hangdog though. "He definitely is. I just don't want—"

"Jamie," Taylor said, not meanly but sharp enough to get his attention. "You don't have to sacrifice your happiness to make everyone else happy."

Jamie's swallow was audible, and he blinked at Taylor a few times. "I … yeah. You're right. I have done that a lot, haven't I?"

"More than is probably healthy." Taylor kissed Jamie's forehead to soften the blow. "Just … talk to your therapist about it, okay?"

"Yeah, I will," he promised.

This time, Taylor pressed a kiss to his cheek. "Now, let's get some food in our bodies before we both starve to death and pass out on the ice this afternoon."

"Definitely." Jamie pulled him in for a quick hug. "Thanks for the pep talk."

"Any time," Taylor said with a smile. "Now, let me get dressed."

Jamie pulled on a pair of sweatpants. "I'm ready."

Taylor eyeballed him as he dragged on a pair of underwear. "Great look but aren't you missing something for your upper half?"

Jamie shrugged, a smile playing around the corners of his mouth. "I'd rather you wear it. At least during breakfast." He held up his jersey and Taylor shook his head with a wry grin.

"You're a possessive motherfucker, aren't you?" Taylor joked. He took it, rather than pointing out that Jamie had plenty of shirts in his overnight bag.

Jamie sobered. "Is it too much?"

Taylor slipped the fabric over his head and walked toward the door, stopping to glance behind him with a coy smile. "I didn't say I minded."

Laughing, Jamie grabbed for him but Taylor took off giggling, skidding around the corner as he beat him to the living room. He stopped dead when he spotted papers scattered on the floor. He bent down to pick them up, a cold pit of dread building in his stomach. They were the bills he'd tucked under his laptop last night. Had Charlie been home this morning and seen them? There was no way they'd ended up there on their own.

Jamie turned the corner and ran into Taylor with a muffled 'oof'. He grabbed his hips to steady them both. "Hey, two minutes for tripping!"

The words rushed past Taylor without sinking in and he went white when he realized what it meant if Charlie had seen the bills.

"Shit, shit, shit," Taylor whispered, the dread deepening.

"Hey what is it?" Jamie asked, his voice going deep and serious. "What's going on, Taylor?"

"Charlie," he said in a strangled tone. "Shit. I have to call him."

Taylor patted himself down, looking for his phone before realizing it was still on the coffee table where it had been tossed last night when Jamie had his way with him. He called Charlie as quickly as his fumbling fingers could manage.

"C'mon, pick up," Taylor begged. When it switched to voicemail, he ended the call and threw his phone on the couch. "Fuck."

"Hey, what's going on?" Jamie asked, brows drawn together with concern.

"So, you know how I told you that I'm struggling financially? It's really bad," he choked out.

Jamie gently took the papers from his hand and scanned them. "*Ooof*. That's a lot of money, Taylor."

"Yeah. I'm down to the wire on getting these bills paid." He gestured helplessly. "I … Charlie doesn't know I took out the loan to pay for his rehab. But I think he came home sometime last night or this morning and saw them."

Charlie had been in a good mood when he said goodbye at the arena, so Taylor rode home from the arena with Jamie. They'd offered to go to Jamie's place but Charlie assured them he had a date and wouldn't be home anyway. Taylor should have had plenty of time to hide the bills, but he'd been too wrapped up in Jamie to remember.

Fuck. This was all his fault.

"I'm really fucking scared," he continued. "I know if Charlie saw these bills, he'd be really upset knowing I kept this from him. He has so many trust issues from his family and if he's already not in a good headspace, I worry it'll make it worse. He's seemed off lately. He's been gone a lot and we haven't really talked much but I saw a few signs lately that he might be restricting his eating. I'm worried. What if he's relapsing?"

Jamie rubbed his hands up and down Taylor's arms for a moment before hugging him close. "He'll be okay, baby. I mean, I'm concerned too, I'm not trying to downplay that it's serious. But it's not like drugs or something, right? Not eating for a short while isn't going to cause an immediate crisis."

"I know." Taylor tucked himself against Jamie's chest. "I'm just terrified. I keep thinking about how many signs I missed last time, and …"

So much depended on how long this had been going on. Weeks, maybe? Taylor tried to think back. Had something triggered a relapse? For Charlie, it was usually his family or relationship issues. But God, had Taylor been so distracted by Jamie he'd missed the signs?

"Is there anywhere else he'd go? Mutual friends he'd stay with if he was in a rough place and upset with you or something?"

"Maybe?" Taylor said doubtfully. "We have lots of friends in the skating community."

Though Charlie had cut most of them out of his life during his recovery.

With a sick, sinking feeling Taylor realized he had no idea *who* Charlie would turn to now.

But although Taylor wanted to tear apart the city to find Charlie, there was no getting out of the commitments he and Jamie both had.

After they both choked down breakfast, too worried to really enjoy it, Jamie went off to his practice with the team in Evanston and Taylor drove farther south to the arena near Garfield Park where his ice show rehearsals were held.

It was good to see his friends and Taylor tried to put his usual level of enthusiasm into his rehearsal but by the time it was over, he had a pounding headache and no messages from Charlie waiting on his phone. None from his parents either.

Taylor returned to his apartment but there were no signs of Charlie having been by.

Exhausted and worried, he sank onto the sofa and dialed Charlie's number again. This time, it went immediately to voice mail.

"Charlie, it's Tay. Please talk to me," he choked out. "I know you're upset but I'm really worried about you. I want to talk but mostly I want to be sure you're okay. Send me a message when you get this even if it's only a text saying you're fine. *Please.*"

Taylor hung up the phone with trembling fingers and buried his head in his hands.

God, what a mess he'd made of things.

"Do you have a moment?" Jamie asked. He'd said goodbye to Ava, who tore into Boyd and Kara's house with an excited whoop, in search of their dog who she hadn't seen while they were on vacation.

Kara squinted at him and pulled the front door closed behind her, wrapping her sweater more tightly around her. "Uh, sure. What is it, Jamie? Everything okay with Ava?"

"Ava is doing great. I know she missed you a lot but we had a fun time together."

"It sounded like it when we Skyped." Kara's brow furrowed. "What is this about you hanging out with Taylor Hollis?"

Jamie cleared his throat and stuffed his hands in his pockets. "So, I don't really know how to tell you this but, uh, I'm dating him."

Kara blinked. "I'm sorry, I thought I heard you saying you're dating a *man*."

"I am."

"What the fuck, Jamie?"

He tensed. "Do you have a problem with it?"

She stared blankly at him. "I mean, it's not really my call anymore, is it?"

"No. But if you're going to say homoph—"

"Whoa." She held up a hand. "Don't put words in my mouth. I'm not fucking homophobic. I'm confused. Since when are you …"

She didn't seem to know how to finish that sentence, so he swallowed hard and finished it for her. "I'm bi."

"Since *when*?"

About four years ago, he thought wildly, *when I got my first glimpse of Taylor skating.*

But that probably wasn't true. That wasn't really how it worked. He'd always been bi or at least the potential had been there but he had yet to meet another man who lit him up inside the way Taylor did.

"Since … always, I guess?" He swallowed again.

"Right." Her lips pursed. "So, were you, like, hooking up with your teammates this whole time or …?"

"Jesus Fucking Christ, Kara," he snapped. "No. Of course not. And have you forgotten that it's your boyfriend who was one of my former teammates? *I'm* not the one who cheated with Boyd."

She flinched. The reaction felt good but he forced himself to take a deep breath because he didn't want this to turn into a huge argument.

"I'm sorry. That was unnecessary. Look, I just wanted to be upfront about what's going on with me. Now that Ava knows, Taylor will be around a lot more in the future. You and I agreed we'd keep each other up to date on the people we bring into Ava's life so I'm trying to do that."

"I appreciate that." She frowned at him. "Are you planning to come out? Like to the public?"

"Eventually, yeah, but I don't have an exact timeline yet and I'd really appreciate it if you wouldn't spread this around until I give you the all-clear."

"You want me to keep your little secret for you?" There was something snide in her tone.

"Well, I didn't trash you in the press after I found out you were cheating so yeah, I kinda feel like you owe me one." He couldn't disguise the snark in his words either.

Her mouth tightened. "You still don't get it, do you?"

"Get what, Kara? Why you fucked Boyd? No, I don't." His throat went thick. "And I never will."

"Jesus, Jamie. Do you know what it was like? Feeling like you *only* married me because I got knocked up? Knowing that Ava was the only reason you stayed with me? God, it was like she was the center of your world, and I was just the means to what you really wanted." Her tone was bitter and hurt, eyes welling up.

Jamie reeled back. "Kara … I never …"

"I know, Jamie, okay?" She closed her eyes, tears glittering on her lashes. "Looking back, I know you probably didn't mean it that way but at the time that's how it felt and it fucking *hurt.* I was so lonely. You came home and you had no time for me. It was always all about Ava. I loved that you were such a good father but I felt invisible to you."

"I was trying to be a good father and husband," he said, stricken. "I wanted you to have a break. I was gone so much and—"

"I—I know that too. I do. I … God. I was lonely all the fucking time. I just wanted to be *seen*."

"And Boyd gave you what I couldn't," he rasped.

She nodded. "He did."

"You could have talked to me."

"I *tried*." Her chin quivered. "I never felt like you heard me."

Jamie stuffed his hands in his pockets and nodded. At this point, he didn't know which one of them was more at fault. Clearly, they'd both fucked up. He didn't think there was any excuse for what she and Boyd had done behind his back. But this conversation had given Jamie some things to think about, that was for sure.

"I am truly sorry for making you feel that way but we're here now," he said after a long, awkward pause. "And I'm with Taylor. I'd appreciate it if you were willing to keep things quiet until we make it official to the public."

"I'll do that." Her tone was a little softer than he'd expected.

"Thanks." He nodded and turned away. There wasn't much else to say and at this point, there was only so much living in the past he could do. He'd spent the past year feeling angry and betrayed and now there was nothing but a numb, distant frustration.

After all that hurt, it now felt oddly unimportant in the face of the future he was focusing on with Taylor.

Maybe that meant he was actually putting his past behind him.

He could only hope.

CHAPTER TWENTY-SIX

Unfortunately, Taylor's phone remained silent all day except for a few texts from Jamie checking in to be sure he was okay.

Later that evening, they lay curled up in each other's arms, talking about the conversation Jamie'd had with Kara earlier.

When Taylor's phone rang, he bolted upright and answered it, disappointed it wasn't Charlie but glad to see his mom calling. He'd texted her earlier letting her know he was worried and to let him know if she heard anything.

"Honey, I don't know how to tell you this, but Charlie's in the hospital. We had to take him to the ER."

"What?" Taylor said, his throat strangled so tight he could barely force the words out. Jamie settled a hand on his back, rubbing softly. "What happened?"

"He came over this evening and he was very upset. Crying like his heart was breaking. We could hardly understand what he was saying but after a few minutes he just slumped over and passed out in the hallway. We called 9-1-1 and we're here at the hospital with him. He's … well, it looks like he had a relapse."

Taylor felt a little faint himself. "How serious?"

"He's dehydrated and his electrolytes are off. They're concerned because his pulse is erratic. It's nothing *critical* at this point but they're keeping him for observation overnight because of the heart issues he had in the past."

"Fuck," Taylor swore. "Okay, what hospital?"

"North Shore Medical Center."

"Okay, I'm on my way."

"Honey, I'm not sure that's such a great idea," she said carefully. "Earlier, he said you'd lied to him about his rehab bills. I don't understand what's going on."

Taylor closed his eyes. "I'll explain everything to you later. I screwed up, I … I have to see with my own eyes that he's okay. I promise I won't stay long."

She hesitated. "Well, I suppose he won't mind if you stop by for a few minutes. I don't want you upsetting him further though. He needs his rest."

"Of course. And I'll pack an overnight bag for him."

"That would be good." She hesitated. "You should come alone though. I'm not sure bringing Jamie would help this situation."

Taylor sighed. He wanted Jamie to be there but he could see where she was coming from. "Okay. See you soon?"

"Drive safe. I love you, Taylor."

"Love you too, Mom."

When Taylor hung up, he rose to his feet. Jamie looked at him with a concerned frown. "I heard most of that. Charlie's in the hospital?"

"Yeah," he said numbly. "I'm going to take a bag over to him."

"And you're going alone?" Jamie looked torn.

Taylor swallowed hard. "I think I need to. My mom's right. I don't need my father getting all riled up and making an already stressful situation worse."

Jamie sighed but nodded. "If that's what you want."

"Well, no, it's not what I want. But I think it's for the best."

"Okay, baby." Jamie pressed a lingering kiss to his forehead. "What about a compromise? I could drive you over there and wait outside if you want."

"I … yeah, I'd like that," he said through a lump in his throat. "Thank you."

Taylor was a jittery mess by the time he walked into the ER, carrying the bag he'd packed.

"Mom," he said, the moment he spotted her in the waiting room. She leapt to her feet and wrapped her arms around him immediately. His dad got up more slowly but he hugged Taylor too. "How's Charlie?"

"He's resting. They're giving him fluids and monitoring his heart."

"No feeding tube?"

She shook her head. "He's flirting with being underweight but he's not like he was a year ago."

"So, a setback but not a full relapse?"

She shrugged helplessly. “I’m not sure. You’ll have to talk to Charlie about that when he’s ready.”

“But I can go back to him?”

“Yeah, they have him in a private observation room. You need to get a visitor badge at the desk.”

Taylor broke into a cold sweat at the thought of what this all would cost but he nodded and followed his mom to the check-in area. He’d … figure it out somehow. Fuck, he’d donate plasma or sell his sperm or fucking compete in the goddamn Olympics again if that’s what it took to pay for this.

Charlie was dozing when Taylor peeked his head in the room but his lashes fluttered open as Taylor walked toward the bed. Charlie looked small under the blanket. Too thin.

That was the problem with someone built like Charlie though. Ten or fifteen pounds made a huge difference.

“Hi,” Charlie rasped, sliding so he sat upright.

“Hey,” Taylor said tentatively. He held out his bag. “I um, brought you some stuff.”

“Thanks.”

Taylor set it on the floor, then took a seat in the chair near the bed. “I’m sorry.”

Charlie closed his eyes, lashes thick against his cheek, though all his makeup was scrubbed off. “I don’t want to talk about it, Tay. I can’t right now.”

“Okay.” Taylor reached out. “When you’re feeling better.”

“Thanks.” Charlie chewed at his lip for a second but he took Taylor’s hand. “I didn’t mean to worry you, you know?”

"I know. I just get really scared I'm going to lose you."

"I know. I, uh, think once I'm released, I'm going to stay with your parents for a few days though."

"Oh." Taylor swallowed down the hurt. "If you think that would be better."

"I know you want to take care of me, Tay, but I'm hurt you lied to me."

Guilt washed over him. "I know. I get that."

They were both silent a few minutes.

"Um, Jamie said hi, by the way," Taylor added. "He sends his get-well wishes."

"Great, more people who know what a mess I am." Charlie's pale cheeks had two bright spots of color on them.

"More people who care about you," Taylor pointed out.

Charlie sighed. "I know. And thank him. It's just … embarrassing to admit what a mess I am."

"You're not a mess." Taylor reached out and hugged him. "Or at least no more than the rest of us. It comes out in different ways but I fuck up too."

"Yeah, maybe." Charlie patted his back half-heartedly and yawned. "Now scram. I'm exhausted and I need my rest."

Taylor pulled away. "Okay. Um, let me know if you want me to come here to visit or to my parents' house or whatever. Whenever you're ready."

Charlie nodded and shifted so he was lying flat. "I will. I need a few days to get my head together again first."

"I understand." Taylor bent over and kissed his forehead, his heart clenching at the sight of the IV in Charlie's arm. It brought back too many memories of the last time. "Love you."

But Charlie was already asleep. That or pretending to be. Taylor couldn't be quite sure, and he hated that. But he tiptoed out of the room and quietly closed the door behind him anyway.

He found his parents waiting in the hallway.

"He's sleeping," Taylor said quietly.

"That's good." His mom looked tired, with dark circles under her eyes.

"He said he'll be staying with you?"

"Yes. Of course."

That stung. Taylor had always been there for Charlie.

Of course, he'd utterly failed to help him either of the two times he'd been in really bad shape so maybe it was better if someone else did it. Apparently, Taylor had done a terrible job.

His parents walked with him toward the exit.

"What is this about the bills?" his dad asked when they were in a quiet hallway with no one around.

"Um, Charlie's hospitalization and rehab were pretty expensive last time. I knew he couldn't afford it all so I covered what I could, but I'm not in a great spot financially now. The bills are coming due," he admitted, his shoulders slumping. It was humiliating but there was no point in hiding it now.

"Why did you lie to us?" his mom asked, clearly hurt. "Last year we asked if Charlie needed help and—"

"I wanted to take care of him!" Taylor argued.

"Well, you went about it poorly."

Taylor dropped his head, staring down at his toes. "I know."

"And we still need to talk about this thing with the Walsh boy."

Taylor closed his eyes and prayed for strength. "Not now, Dad. *Please*."

"Let's focus on Charlie and getting him well now," his mom said. "That's what really matters."

Exhausted, Taylor nodded and said goodbye to his parents before trudging out to the parking lot where Jamie waited.

The second he approached, Jamie hopped out of the Range Rover and wrapped him in a huge hug. "You okay, baby?"

"No," he said thickly. "But it's better with your arms around me."

"Can I take you home? To my place?"

"Yeah," Taylor said with a sigh. "Yeah, I'd like that."

CHAPTER TWENTY-SEVEN

The following week passed in a blur. Jamie had meetings with what felt like everyone in the Otters' organization. Samantha and his agent and the GM and owner and … it felt endless.

But he slogged through them and went to practice and played in two games and tried to be there for Taylor, who had been staying at his place.

Jamie knew Taylor felt cut off from both his family and Charlie and there was only so much Jamie could do to help him.

It wasn't until Jamie got home from the two-game roadie in Anaheim and Los Angeles that they had a bit of a breakthrough.

"Can we hang out with Charlie?" Ava asked as they made homemade pizza for dinner. "He was fun!"

Taylor's face crumpled. "Um, I can tell him you miss him," he said, clearly trying to put on a brave face for Ava. "But he's kind of mad at me. I did something that hurt him."

"Did you say you're sorry?" Ava carefully pressed pepperoni into the circle of dough.

"I tried," Taylor said with a sigh. "He doesn't want to listen."

"Maybe you should do something nice for him to show that you mean it. Daddy says that's important."

Taylor looked up at Jamie and he shrugged because it was true. He had said that in the past.

"I haven't," Taylor said slowly. "But that's a good idea. He's been feeling kinda sad, I think."

"Maybe you should draw him a picture," Ava suggested. "Daddy says that cheers him up when I draw for him."

"Would you like to help me with that?" Taylor asked. "And do one for him too? He might like that."

"Course!"

Ava beamed at Taylor and Jamie fell a little bit more in love with him.

After pizza and salad for dinner, they all drew pictures until it was Ava's bedtime.

Jamie stood in the doorway, watching Taylor read to Ava, his voice animated as he read her current favorite story and she snuggled close.

The three of them were so good together.

Maybe Jamie had failed to tell Kara how much she meant to him. Maybe he'd neglected her and put too much of his focus on their daughter. Unfortunately, he couldn't go back in time and fix it.

But he knew he could do a better job with his relationship with Taylor from here on out.

Jamie's priority was to figure out how to help Taylor fix the rift in his family. Because even if Charlie wasn't Taylor's brother by blood, he was in every other way.

And Jamie hated the thought of how much they were both hurting right now.

CHAPTER TWENTY-EIGHT

"Hi! I'm here to see Charlie Mona-mona—" Ava glanced up at Taylor as if begging for help.

"Monaghan," Taylor supplied.

Taylor's dad looked between the two of them, ignoring Jamie completely. His expression wasn't hostile but when it landed on Taylor, it was filled with that look that said, 'I know what you're up to, son'.

And yes, Taylor was unashamedly hoping to use Ava's adorable friendliness to soften his father and his best friend.

"Who might you be?" Rick Hollis asked Ava, his tone surprisingly gentle.

"Ava Grace Walsh!" she said proudly.

There was a flicker of something in his expression that was gone before Taylor could identify it.

"You're a friend of Charlie's?"

"Yes. And my daddy and Taylor are boyfriends." She beamed up at Taylor. "I like him *so much*."

Rick did smile then. Not a big smile, but the first crack in his armor had appeared. "I like him too. He's my son."

"Oh!" Ava had finally put the pieces together although Jamie had explained that on the way over.

"Well for goodness' sake, let them in, Rick!" Taylor's mom gently scolded. "It's warming up out there but it's still winter."

Rick let out a little *hmmph*, but he did so.

"Thank you, Mrs. Hollis," Jamie said politely when they were inside.

"Please, call me Lindsey."

They stood around awkwardly for a minute before Ava spoke up. "Is Charlie here?" She held out the papers clutched in her hand. "We drawed him pictures!"

"Drew," Jamie corrected softly. "You drew him pictures."

"Charlie is here. Would you like to come with me to see him, Ava?" Lindsey held out a hand and after Ava checked in with Jamie and he gave her a nod, she took it.

"Yes, please."

After they disappeared, Rick cleared his throat and looked at Taylor. "Well, I suppose you want to talk."

"Yes," Taylor said. "And I know you aren't happy about Jamie being around but he cares about Charlie, too. I'd like him to be a part of the conversation."

Rick merely grunted, but he turned and led them farther into the house.

When they were in the living room, they all fell silent. Taylor took a deep breath. "Dad, I'm sorry I blindsided you with the relationship with Jamie and lied about the bills."

Rick sighed heavily. "I don't know why you feel like you can't talk to me."

Taylor swallowed. "I lied about the bills because I wanted to prove to you I could manage my own life. You and mom acted like I'd done something childish by not wanting to skate competitively anymore."

"We were afraid you were throwing away a lifetime of work for nothing."

"But it wasn't for nothing!" he burst out. "It was *hurting* me. Maybe not so obviously as it did Charlie, but every competition made me more miserable. I was hurting and exhausted and disillusioned and I needed to find something healthier for myself."

"You never told us you were hurting," Rick said, worry creasing his face.

Taylor opened his mouth and then closed it, realizing he was right. "I should have. I just … things with Charlie seemed so much bigger and—"

Jamie covered Taylor's hand with his and Taylor clung to it. He saw his dad's gaze track the motion and something in the set of his shoulders seemed to soften.

"And I didn't want to let you down," Taylor admitted. "You were so proud of my skating, and I wanted to keep making you proud. I know you were disappointed when I quit hockey as a kid but you were so supportive of my figure skating and I wanted to do my best and win for you and—"

Rick blanched. "Taylor, your mom and I, we never wanted you to be miserable to *please* us. We were proud of you no matter what."

"I know that. But I still felt like I was letting you down." He looked down at the floor, tracing the pattern of the rug with his sock-covered toes. "And I tried really hard not to fall for Jamie because I knew it would upset you but …" His throat went thick. "I love him and Ava too much. I want a future with them."

"I can see as much," Rick said gruffly. "I just wish we'd found another way."

"Sir, we were going to tell you," Jamie said softly. "We were trying to figure out *how* when you stopped by."

Rick nodded.

"Honestly, Dad," Taylor said with a sigh. "Sometimes I think you want to hold on to the grudge you have against Adam Walsh more than you want anything else."

Rick's gaze flicked to Jamie again but when he stayed silent, he looked back at Taylor. "That's not true, son. I want you to be happy more than anything in the world. You should know that."

"And if Jamie makes me happy?"

He cleared his throat. "I guess I'll have to live with it."

"Dad." Taylor leaned forward. "Maybe it's asking too much but I'd like a little more than you *tolerating* our relationship. I want you to get to know Jamie. See what a good man he is. See what an amazing little girl his daughter is. I want you to treat them like family because, well, someday I hope we all will be."

Rick nodded. "I … I know. Give me a little time to adjust, okay? I've … well, I've hated Adam Walsh for a damn long time."

"You shouldn't," Taylor said bluntly. "I watched the footage, Dad, and you're wrong. Jamie's father wasn't at fault for your accident."

"Taylor—"

"No, hear me out," Taylor argued. "Please. *Listen* for once. Don't let this decade-old grudge get in the way of you hearing the truth. I'm begging you."

His nostrils flared but he took a deep breath. "I'll listen."

"Have you watched the full clip?"

"Not …" He cleared his throat. "Not in years."

"I watched the whole thing recently. It was a chain reaction that started with *your* teammate."

"I … that's not true." He looked between Taylor and Jamie. "That's not true, is it?"

"It's what my dad has always maintained," Jamie said softly. "And the league agreed. I know that's not easy to hear, sir, but it's right there in the footage if you're willing to watch it. The media … they usually only show the short clip but the uncut one shows the truth of what happened."

"You don't have to do it now, Dad," Taylor said. "But will you watch it with me sometime? Promise to have an open mind?"

His lips flattened into a thin line, and he was silent so long Taylor was sure he was going to say no, but eventually he nodded. "I'll try my best."

"Thank you." Taylor rose to his feet and Rick did too. "Thank you, Dad." His voice was choked as he threw himself into his dad's arms.

"You're my son," he said gruffly, hugging him tight. "If this is what you need me to do, I'll do it. I want you to be happy, okay? Even if it's with the Walsh boy here."

Jamie stepped away with the excuse that he wanted to check on Ava, but it was mostly to give Taylor some time alone with his dad.

He found Ava putting tiny ponytails throughout Charlie's hair while Taylor's mom looked on, clearly amused.

"Wow. I look so pretty," Charlie said flashing a grin when she finished, but his smile didn't quite reach his eyes. "Thank you, Ava."

"Would it be all right if I gave Ava a snack?" Lindsey asked when she noticed Jamie lurking in the doorway of the guest bedroom.

"Sure," Jamie said easily. "We'll do dinner fairly soon, I think, but she doesn't have any allergies, so as long the snack's not too huge, whatever you have will be fine."

Ava was already on her feet, wide-eyed and eager. Jamie patted her shoulder as she walked past, following Taylor's mom, chattering on about how much she loved celery with peanut butter but *only* if it was the smooth kind.

"Hey, Charlie," Jamie said softly when they were gone.

Charlie glanced up and managed a weak smile. "Hey, Jamie."

"You doing okay?"

He listlessly shrugged. "Not great. I mean, physically I'm okay but …"

"Is there anything I can do?"

Charlie's face spasmed with something that looked like an attempt to hide tears. "Not really. I'm pretty hurt by what Taylor did."

"I know," Jamie said. "And I get that."

"You're not on his side?"

"I'll always support Taylor," he said carefully. "But I don't think there are any sides in this case. He did something that hurt you. He thought he did it for the right reasons and maybe he was wrong. But I do know there are a lot of people who are worried about you and that's the important part."

"I know." Charlie picked at the sparkly nail polish on his fingers. "I feel like things are out of control again."

"That's an awful feeling," Jamie said, moving into the room to lean against the low dresser that faced the bed where Charlie sat.

"You've felt like that before?" Charlie looked genuinely surprised.

"Oh boy." Jamie laughed. "I have, yeah. I was a pretty big mess last year after I found out my wife cheated on me. And I recently did some damage after a game I played against the guy who she cheated on me with. Who happened to be my best friend, by the way, so yeah, I definitely know something about feeling like my life is spinning out of my control."

Charlie grimaced but he looked almost impressed. "You punch him out?"

Jamie chuckled and walked over to the bed. Charlie scooted over so he could sit next to him.

"No. I didn't. But I *have* broken things around me. Lamps. A hockey stick. And I don't really like that feeling. Like I'm not in control of my own life."

"I don't like feeling this way either," Charlie admitted in a small voice.

On instinct, Jamie held out an arm and Charlie tucked himself under it, curling up against Jamie's side with a tired sigh.

"So how can we help you feel like your life is more in control?" Jamie asked after Charlie's stiff frame softened.

"I don't know."

"Well, do you think you'd be willing to talk to Taylor and come up with some ideas together? Because he wants to help you."

"I can't afford to go back to rehab," Charlie said, sniffling like he was maybe trying not to cry. "And Taylor can't afford to pay. I saw how bad the bills are."

"I can afford it," Jamie offered but Charlie shook his head.

"I can't. I can't take it."

Jamie wanted to shake him because it was just fucking money and what did it matter when he had more than he knew what to do with and he could see how narrow Charlie's wrists were.

"Have you been … not eating lately?" he asked. He didn't know a lot about eating disorders and wasn't sure if that was really the right question but he had to ask.

"Sometimes," Charlie whispered and Jamie could tell he was crying now. "Not like it was before but it could get really bad if I let it."

"There would be a lot of very sad people if it did," Jamie said. "Including my daughter. And trust me, you *don't* want to see her sad face turned on you."

Charlie snuffled wetly, wiping his arm across his eyes. "I really don't."

"So … I don't know how to help you but I really want to. I know Taylor does too, and Taylor's parents do as well. Will you at least try to figure out a plan with us?"

"Yeah," Charlie said in a small voice. "I think I can do that."

"Good." Jamie gave him a kiss on the top of the head because damn it, he liked Charlie and the thought of him starving himself to fix whatever was going on inside him made Jamie ache too.

"You know, I had my doubts about you at first," Charlie said slowly, sitting up.

"And now?"

"I think I'm glad Taylor found you."

Jamie smiled. "Me too."

After that, there wasn't much more Jamie could do so he gently pried Ava away with the bribe of going to the park for a little bit so the Hollis family and Charlie could have some time alone.

It was a dreary late February day but not cold or raining and he let her play on the swings and hang off the monkey bars until she was drooping from exhaustion.

Jamie checked in with Taylor who said he could come back whenever, and he offered to pick up dinner on the way back.

It wasn't much, but it was the best he had to offer.

"I'm mad at you, you know," Charlie said, his nose smushed against Taylor's chest.

"I know." Taylor squeezed him a little tighter. "You should be."

"Yeah?"

"Yeah." Taylor sighed. "I shouldn't have lied to you about the bills."

Charlie pushed at his shoulder, and he flopped onto the bed, looking up at Charlie. His eyes were red, and his makeup was smeared. "Why did you?"

"I was trying to *protect* you," he said miserably.

"Lying and hiding shit from me is a crappy way to do it."

"I know. I just … you were already struggling and under so much stress and I felt so helpless. I needed to do *something*. I was afraid you wouldn't go to rehab, and you'd waste away and *die* on me because you were too stubborn to get help because you couldn't afford it."

Charlie froze. "Fuck. I …" A conflicted expression crossed his face. "Maybe."

"So, I *know* it was bad to lie but it also seemed better than letting you keep hurting yourself."

"Damn it," Charlie grumbled. "I want to be so mad at you but it's getting harder. And dude, using Ava to soften me up? Low blow, man."

"I won't apologize for that," Taylor said with a small smile. "She's my secret weapon."

"Seriously. That kid is awesome." Charlie heaved out a big sigh and tucked his head under Taylor's chin. "Her dad gives great hugs too."

Taylor's lips twitched in a smile. "Are you trying to make me jealous?"

Charlie held his fingers up in front of Taylor's face, less than an inch apart. "Little bit?"

Taylor dug his hands into Charlie's side, making him squeal and wriggle away. "Asshole."

When they were both out of breath and lying on the bed side by side, Taylor turned his head to look at Charlie. "Please get help."

"Okay." Charlie swallowed, his lashes dipping to cover his sad blue eyes. "I will."

"What was it this time?" Taylor asked. "The trigger?"

"A guy. A stupid asshole guy who was shitty to me. And then I had a client in the same building my parents are in and I—I started to spiral."

"You know you're supposed to reach out for help when that happens."

"I know." Charlie's voice got very small. "But you were so happy with Jamie and …"

Ouch. That hurt.

"Okay, but what about your therapist?" he asked.

"I don't think they're helping anymore."

"Then we have to find you a new one. A better one."

Charlie heaved out a sigh. "I know. But I can't afford it and you're already about to go broke. And no, I won't take money from your fucking boyfriend."

"He offered it to you too, huh?"

"Yes."

Taylor flipped on his side and grabbed Charlie's hand. "What about my parents? You know they offered."

"Yeah." Charlie stared back at Taylor, eyes wide, fragile and vulnerable looking. "They said they'd pay off the debt you have and I could pay *them* back in installments. Interest free."

"It's not a bad solution for any of us," Taylor said gently. "They love you a lot."

"And if I do that you won't be stressed about money anymore."

"I won't."

"And maybe I can drum up some good clients soon and get a couple of big fat commission checks." Charlie looked a little hopeful.

"*While* you take care of yourself," Taylor said forcefully. "That comes first."

"Yes." Charlie poked at his sternum. "But maybe I need to do this without you hovering this time. I know you wanted to keep an eye on me but I think I need to know I can manage without that. Someday you're gonna move in with your hot hockey player and have more babies and I'll need to be able to take care of myself."

Taylor took a deep breath and nodded. "Yeah, okay. I understand that. Do we have a plan though?"

"Yeah, we have a plan," Charlie agreed.

"Good."

Taylor pulled him into a hug because hearing that was like having a million-pound weight lifted off him.

"You're smothering me," Charlie muttered against his chest.

"Get used to it," Taylor said brightly. "You have so many people who love you."

"Ugh, gross." Charlie said, wiggling away and wrinkling his nose. "Do you think maybe Jamie's going to be back soon with food? I'm actually pretty hungry now."

"Probably." Taylor glanced at the clock as he got off the bed. "If not, I have it on good authority that my mom makes delicious peanut butter and celery snacks."

"Well, if Ava approves …"

"Exactly." Taylor held out a hand to Charlie. "We okay?"

"Yeah, we're okay," Charlie said. "I promise. Just … pinkie swear you'll never lie to me again. You know how much that hurts me. I've had more than enough people do that in my life."

Taylor hooked their pinkies together. "Never again. I swear it."

Charlie looked into his eyes and Taylor realized he'd gotten it all wrong. Being an adult wasn't about hiding the truth, it was about being up front about the mistakes you made, apologizing for them, and trying to do better.

"Okay." Charlie slung an arm around Taylor's shoulders. "Let's go tell your parents we have a plan."

Taylor rested his temple against Charlie's. "They're your family too, you know?"

Charlie let out a choked little noise and wiped at his eyes. "Yeah, I know."

Jamie and Ava reappeared a short while later bearing bags of food.

As they sat down to dinner, Taylor forced himself to not watch Charlie put food on his plate.

Charlie was right. It wasn't his job to monitor that. Charlie had to do it for himself this time.

And while Taylor's dad was clearly still wary of Jamie and his mom seemed determined to talk about anything and everything under the sun to keep the peace, Ava was the best icebreaker around, filling the air with her enthusiastic chatter as they ate their dinner.

While they cleared the dishes, Taylor felt pretty hopeful that with time, they could all get through this.

And best of all, they were in it together.

One big, complicated family.

Enemies to Lovers at Its Best: The Jamie Walsh and Taylor Hollis Story

While it was impossible to watch the Evanston River Otters' latest media campaign, On the Edge, *without a dash of cynicism (we here at* JockGossip *have seen more than our share of blatant media manipulation tactics over the years) even we had to admit that we enjoyed watching gold medal Olympian Taylor Hollis teach a handful of the Otters' finest how to figure skate.*

Though not all players were equally skilled, the on-ice shenanigans were worth a few laughs and served their purpose as a feel-good media piece after the shocking news last December that Coach Lance Tate was involved with two-way defenseman Gabriel Theriault.

What we didn't expect was the final video, highlighting the brand-new relationship between the feisty figure skater and the Otters' 2nd line forward. While Jamie Walsh took a beating in the public last season after his messy divorce, it appears he's found new love in none other than Taylor Hollis.

For those not aware of the family history, Jamie's and Taylor's fathers were bitter rivals when they played pro hockey and, in fact, Rick Hollis has always maintained that Adam Walsh was to blame for his career-ending injury.

Although a minor spat between the younger Hollis and Walsh at the Olympics occurred four years ago, it appears the sons have more than mended fences.

Jamie Walsh's sweet coming-out story was expertly filmed and released by the Otters' media crew. The skating lesson montage was overlaid with a voiceover by Walsh about how he and his five-year-old daughter, Ava, fell in love with Hollis.

While there's no doubt the feel-good piece was skillfully crafted, there was also no denying the sincerity in Walsh's voice or the feelings between the men.

Walsh's ex-wife Kara Humboldt, currently dating Chicago Windstorm's center Boyd Marsh, declined to comment on how she feels about her former husband's announcement concerning his bisexuality and new relationship.

Then again, if rumors are to be believed, she was involved with Marsh well before the ink on her divorce was dry so perhaps she's concerned about the focus turning to her indiscretions.

The coming-out video concluded with footage of the entire team on the ice with their families. Even our frosty hearts melted a fraction as cute-as-a-button Ava skated between her father and his new boyfriend, all wearing matching Walsh *jerseys.*

But with less than two months to go in the regular season, the team is going to need to buckle down and focus less on romance and more on hockey. It'll take more than media spin and feel-good stories to get the Evanston River Otters to the Cup Final this year.

CHAPTER TWENTY-NINE

"You need help with anything else?" Taylor asked. "People will be getting here soon."

Jamie looked around his house.

Both of their moms had done a thorough job of decorating yesterday and Jamie and Taylor had picked up the catered food this morning. It was still too cold for them to do anything outside in the backyard, but Jamie was looking forward to having people over this summer.

And Ava was *very* excited about her slightly belated birthday party.

Charlie was helping her get ready, so Jamie took advantage of the peace and quiet to give Taylor a long, thorough kiss. He cupped Taylor's cheek in his hand, looking into his beautiful eyes, even more striking with the makeup he wore.

"Nah. Just need you."

Taylor smiled. "You big softie."

"That's not what you said this morning." Jamie slid his hands down Taylor's back, smoothing over the soft swell of his ass.

Taylor smiled coyly. "No, you were very, very hard for me, weren't you?"

"*Always.*" Jamie crouched a little and hoisted Taylor up onto the counter, making him flail and giggle.

Jamie's shoulder gave a little twinge of protest but it hardly mattered, not when he pressed between Taylor's splayed knees and gently mouthed at his neck.

"Love you, baby," he whispered.

Taylor let his head fall back, sighing as Jamie kissed along his collarbone. "Love you too. So much."

"I can't wait to get my hands all over you again. Fuck."

Jamie nipped at Taylor's mouth. He rubbed his palms across his lean, strong thighs and kissed him more deeply, desperately hungry for him even though in the past few weeks, they'd spent every free minute they could in bed.

Taylor let out that little whimper that Jamie knew meant he was very turned on and he kissed him harder, sweeping his tongue into Taylor's mouth. Taylor grabbed for the front of his shirt and hauled him in tighter.

The doorbell startled them both and Taylor pulled back with a pouty sigh. His lips were slightly swollen and very red and his gaze was a little unfocused as his hands fluttered to his hair to smooth it down.

Jamie helped him down and they answered the door together, smiling at the sight of the Tremblay family on the other side. Naomi shot Jamie a knowing look as if she knew exactly what they'd been up to but he only had to endure a little of Dean's chirping while he and Taylor greeted the kids, ushered them into the house, then showed them where to put the presents they brought.

They'd already picked up a cake and several flavors of cupcakes from Naomi's bakery this morning.

Ava tromped up the stairs, shouting with joy and talking a mile a minute at Andre about a toy she wanted to show him. Charlie appeared in the kitchen soon after, smiling as he tucked his arm through Taylor's.

Jamie was glad to see him looking so relaxed.

The Hollises had paid off Taylor's loans and Charlie had drawn up a repayment plan. He was seeing a new therapist—also someone Lowell Prescott had recommended—and while it was much too early to be sure if it would stick, all they could do was be supportive while Charlie did the work.

Jamie's parents arrived soon after, and then some of the other guys from the team, the house growing exponentially louder with their addition. Kara and Boyd arrived, looking distinctly uncomfortable.

Everyone was excruciatingly polite as they were introduced, though Kara could hardly meet Taylor's gaze. It would be a while before that situation wasn't weird and fraught.

Boyd had reached out after his coming-out video went live, wanting to talk. Jamie had listened to him but there was nothing Boyd could say that would undo the hurt he'd caused.

Boyd had made his choices and he'd have to live with them.

Besides, Jamie didn't want to think about his past any more than he had to. He'd talk about it with his therapist because it was important for the sake of not fucking up his relationship with Taylor, but beyond that he wanted to focus on the future.

Although Boyd was never going to be someone Jamie wanted in his life any more than necessary, he couldn't deny that Boyd was good to his daughter, and it wasn't fair to punish Ava over their broken friendship. For her sake, they could be cordial.

Someday when Ava was older, she'd realize the truth about how Boyd and Kara's relationship had begun, and she could make her own choices about how she felt about it.

Thankfully, some of Ava's friends arrived then and she immediately dragged them to the play area in the basement. Taylor's parents knocked on the door after that. Jamie passed them off to Taylor, then greeted Dustin Fowler, who was coming up the walk behind them.

"Damn, it's good to see you, man." Jamie hugged Dustin warmly. "I'm so glad you could make it today."

The Toronto Fisher Cats were in town for the weekend. Evanston had beaten them in a 5-0 shutout the night before and they played Chicago tomorrow.

He shrugged as he stepped into Jamie's house. "I mean, I think it's pretty generous of me to show up after you guys beat the pants off us last night but we don't fly out until Monday, so I figured why not? Gotta say, man, I did not see this relationship with Taylor coming. Pretty sure you owe me for introducing the two of you at the Olympics."

Jamie laughed and held out a hand to take the wrapped gift Dustin had brought Ava. "I think that might be stretching it to say you introduced us, but I'll keep it in mind."

People kept coming after that. Teammates. Ava's friends and their parents. The house was noisy, filled with running kids, and people eating and catching up.

Jamie's mom had put herself in charge of refilling platters and answering questions about where the bathroom was so Jamie could enjoy himself with Taylor tucked up under his arm, laughing at the ridiculous shenanigans of his teammates.

It was hard to believe it was mid-March already. The coming-out video released by the organization had blown up on social media. Jamie still felt a little dizzy at the number of views. According to Taylor, the response had been overwhelmingly positive, and the haters had been thoroughly shut down by a handful of vocal fans who were fiercely protective of the out members of the team.

Jamie had avoided most of the coverage when he could, limited comments on his social media accounts, and let someone from the team's PR handle the responses for him. He didn't need to see the negativity that did exist. He was too happy with Taylor to let anything else creep in.

He'd always treasure the video though.

Samantha had done a great job with it. She'd wrapped up the media campaign with a few final lessons from Taylor to the team, and then a small, choreographed "performance" of what they'd all learned. Cooper had managed to stay upright at least, and Hajek could probably muster up a second career as a figure skater if the goalie thing didn't pan out for him.

And Jamie, well, he'd done okay. He wasn't the best or the worst of the group and that was probably how it was always going to be, but he had a place on this team that felt unshakeable.

Best of all, even the rivalry between Rick Hollis and Adam Walsh had been put to rest.

Rick had finally sat down to watch the accident footage with his wife and Taylor. Jamie hadn't wanted to intrude, so he'd stayed home. Taylor had come back to Jamie's place drained. Apparently, it had been very emotional but Jamie had been happy to provide a lot of hugs after.

Rick had admitted he'd been wrong about the accident. He hadn't apologized to Jamie's father or spoken to the media about it, but Adam seemed okay with that.

"Look, he's been pissed at me for over a decade," he'd said to Jamie. "I'll take the fact that he was willing to admit he was wrong as a win. Maybe someday we can talk more but for now, this is enough."

Their dads were both here for Ava's birthday party today and all Jamie wanted was for no fights to break out. He was hopeful that everyone was more concerned about a six-year-old's happiness than petty grudges and longstanding hurts.

"Thanks for the invite," Coach Tate said a while later, as Jamie cleared away a few discarded plates.

"Glad you and Gabriel could make it." He nodded toward their defenseman who was busy catching up with Dustin, his former teammate from Toronto.

"This is more our speed than going to the bar."

"Yeah, mine too," Jamie agreed.

"Sure, I bet that's what you say to all the coaches."

Jamie laughed, his gaze drifting over to where Ava was crawling into Taylor's lap. "Nah, I'm pretty good with the quiet home life."

"It suits you." Coach tapped him on the arm and Jamie smiled.

Not all the team had come. Malone wasn't there—big shocker—and a few of the other guys had claimed prior commitments. Some legit. Some probably not. But most of them were here and most of them were supportive of Taylor and Jamie's relationship.

Jamie hoped that the rest of the season would go smoothly because while Taylor had been right that his coming out wasn't to blame for the rocky past few months, he wanted nothing more than to be a part of the team's future success.

———

After 'Happy Birthday' was sung, candles were blown out, and the presents were opened, Jamie and Taylor cleaned up some of the mess, sorting it into trash and recycling bags. Charlie fell into step beside Taylor as he carried the bags toward the garage.

"So, I guess you got everything you wanted." Charlie smiled and opened the door, revealing Taylor's car parked beside Jamie's Range Rover.

Taylor gave him a perplexed smile in return. "What do you mean?"

"The man, the children, and the cute little house in the 'burbs."

"I have the man, a child, and a gorgeous *big* house in the 'burbs, for sure. I'm lucky."

"Well, I'm sure if you and Jamie keep trying hard enough, he'll put a bun in your oven eventually." Charlie gave him a cheeky wink.

Taylor laughed and stuffed the bags into their respective cans. "Pretty sure that's not how it works and we're definitely not going to rush anything but yeah, someday."

"Someday you'll be Mrs. Jamie Walsh," Charlie said, clutching his hands to his chest and pretending to swoon.

"Fuck off," Taylor said playfully. "It'll be Mr. Taylor Walsh, thank you."

"But you want that?" Charlie asked, suddenly serious.

"Yeah, yeah I do," Taylor said, his voice coming out a little thick. "I'm really happy."

Charlie hugged him. "Good. I'm glad."

"How about you?"

"I have zero desire to procreate or live in the 'burbs."

"What about a relationship? I know you're taking a break from the hookups."

"Yeah, my therapist thinks it would be for the best and well, she's probably right." He made a face. "Six months with no sex, Taylor. Why did I agree to this?"

"Because you want to get better."

Charlie's expression grew serious, his swallow audible. "Yeah, I do."

"Good."

"Now, enough of that. I believe you promised me more of that delicious sangria you made for the grownups."

"Oh, I did, did I?" Taylor asked, shutting the garage door behind him.

"Yes." Charlie held out a hand, tugging him along

"Well, that excludes you, doesn't it?" Taylor teased.

Charlie sputtered but they both fell silent as they approached a cluster of blondes in the kitchen. Taylor didn't know them well. They were the moms of some of Ava's friends. From what Taylor could tell, they were all pretty tight with Kara.

"Well, I guess we know now why Kara and Jamie got divorced, huh?" one of them said snidely.

A second woman giggled. "Seriously. Guess he had a preference for *something else*. Poor Kara. Sucks to be married to someone who can't even satisfy you in bed."

Charlie let out a peal of laughter as he stepped closer, reaching between them to snag a glass of the sangria. "Oh, sweetie, if there were problems there, it wasn't because the man doesn't know what to do in the bedroom. Trust me, I've heard how loud he makes his partner scream."

The first woman turned, her jaw dropping open. "Well, that was rude. Butting into our private conversation."

"Maybe you shouldn't have your private conversations in public then," Charlie said with a purse of his lips. "And I swear to God, if you say one more nasty thing about either Taylor or Jamie, I will rip that ratty blonde weave out so hard, your natural hair will never grow back."

Taylor snorted out a laugh, feeling guilty for it, but too amused to really tell Charlie to behave. It was good to see him feeling feisty.

"Easy there, tiger," someone said, and Charlie whipped around, raking his gaze over Dustin Fowler.

"What did you call me?" Charlie snapped, bristling.

Dustin smirked at Charlie and Taylor shook his head, hiding a smile. Oh, that man was so dead. He just didn't know it yet.

"I said, retract the claws, kitten. No need to start a cat fight at a child's birthday party."

"For your information, I was merely standing up for people I care about," Charlie snarled, drawing himself up to his full height. Which wasn't saying much since he was only about 5'6" and Dustin had nearly half a foot on him.

"Admirable and all, but I suspect Jamie's had about enough drama in his life."

"And who the hell are you?"

"Uh, Charlie," Taylor interjected, amused by their interaction but Dustin *did* have a point. "This is Dustin Fowler. Emily Fowler's sister. You remember her from our training facility, right?"

"Oh." Charlie looked startled. He gave Dustin a quick up and down. "I do remember she had a hockey-playing brother. I thought you were in Canada or something though."

"Toronto, yeah." He smirked at Charlie. "But I was in town for a game and Jamie and I go way back."

Charlie's eyes got big. "Whoops." He glanced guiltily over his shoulder but the little gaggle of blondes had disappeared.

Ahh well. They probably wouldn't be gossiping about Jamie's prowess in bed anymore. At least not where anyone could hear them.

"Charlie, Taylor!" Ava said, tearing into the kitchen. "We're gonna play mini sticks! You wanna watch?"

"Mini sticks?" Charlie looked confused.

"Street hockey," Dustin clarified. "With short sticks. For children."

“You don’t have to treat me like I’m an idiot.” Charlie’s nostril’s flared.

“It’s fine. You’re a cute idiot. C’mon.” Dustin held out his arm. “I’ll teach you the finer points of the game.”

“You most certainly will not,” Charlie said tartly, pointedly ignoring his offer and following Ava who was attempting to herd them toward the basement where Jamie had set up a little area for the kids to play.

“Aww, don’t be mad, tiger,” Dustin said following him down the stairs. “I’ll even use small words so you understand.”

Taylor snickered and left them to it, figuring he’d make one round of the house to see if anyone needed anything before he went to watch the mini sticks game. He’d be worried about Charlie starting something he shouldn’t—because a good argument was absolutely Charlie’s favorite form of foreplay—but Dustin was heading back to Toronto tomorrow night.

And besides, Taylor had to trust Charlie to take care of himself.

“I was wrong, you know.” Taylor’s dad gently snagged his sleeve as they passed in the hallway a few minutes later.

Taylor blinked at him. “About?”

“Jamie. I’ve never seen you so happy, son.”

Taylor swallowed and hugged him. “Thanks for giving us a chance.”

His dad squeezed tightly before he let go. “Not gonna lie, it was that little girl who did it. Ava’s something else, huh?”

“Yeah, she really is,” Taylor said with a smile. “Now, do you want to go see small, adorable children play hockey?”

"Pfftt," Rick Hollis said with a laugh. "Is that ever really a question?"

"Nah, not really," Taylor said with a grin. "C'mon, Dad."

"Think I could get in on this?" Adam Walsh said with a small smile, his expression wary but open.

Taylor blinked in surprise and held his breath but his dad merely nodded. "Sure. You never know, they might need some pointers from some of us veterans."

Taylor let out a quiet sigh of relief and led the way through the kitchen, swiping a glass of sangria on the way through.

"Mind if I join you?" Taylor asked a few minutes later as he spotted an empty seat on the couch between Naomi and Charlie, who was studiously ignoring Dustin. The Toronto player stood behind him, chatting with Zane Murphy about something hockey related.

Naomi patted the cushion with a grin. "Welcome to the WAGs, by the way."

Taylor tried not to choke on his drink. "Oh God. I am officially one now, aren't I?"

Naomi shrugged. "Well, Murphy and Hartinger are both players. Theriault is dating Coach Tate … you're the first for this team. We'll have to come up with a more inclusive title now though, eh?"

Charlie patted his thigh. "You could always go with Wives and Partners," he said with a grin.

"Hmm. W-A-P," Taylor spelled out without thinking before it clicked. "Damn it, Charlie!"

He snickered. "Sorry. Couldn't resist."

"It's a good thing I love you," Taylor muttered with a sniff.

Jamie's chest warmed as he scanned the crowded basement. He'd thought the rec area was pretty spacious but with so many people here, it was a bit tight. He loved it though. Loved seeing friends and family mingling.

He squeezed between Gabriel and Coach Tate, who were talking to Taylor's mom.

"Oh, congratulations on the new house!" she said to them. "I'm so flattered you asked but I think my design firm is fully booked for the next six months. You might consider talking to Charlie Monaghan though. He was recently hired by another great firm downtown. He's new but he has an incredible eye for design and I'm sure he'd be delighted to work with you. I'd be happy to introduce you."

"That sounds great," Coach said. "What do you think, Gabriel?"

"*Oui*. Sounds perfect. Neither of us will have the time to think about it and we'd like to get settled in the new place by the time the off-season starts. I'm sure you've heard about my father's condition but we're trying to ease him through the transition of moving as smoothly as we're able."

"Oh yes. I'm so sorry to hear about that," Lindsey Hollis said. "I do love what you've done talking about player safety though. You should consider discussing that with my husband too. He's quite passionate about the subject."

Jamie smiled to himself as he moved out of earshot, winding his way toward Taylor.

He was surprised to see Lindholm and O'Shea speaking intently, Lindy's head bent to listen to him.

"You're sure you're okay?" their defenseman asked, his tone earnest in a way Jamie had never heard from him before.

"I'm fine, Kelly," Lindy said softly. "You worry too much."

"I know this must be hard. At a six-year-old's birthday party when Elia will never have one."

Lindy let out a sigh. "It is. Not a day goes by that I don't miss her though. No matter where I am or what I'm doing."

Jamie sucked in a breath, thinking about the horrific accident that had taken both Lindholm's wife and daughter from him. He couldn't even fathom the pain Lindy felt. The thought of anything happening to Ava or Taylor was excruciating.

"I know. I'm just saying, if you want to duck out, you can blame it on me." O'Shea's voice was still so earnest and unlike his usual playful, sarcastic tone.

"I appreciate it. But weren't you the one who reminded me I can't stay buried in the past forever?"

Their gazes caught and met, and Jamie looked away, afraid he was intruding on a private moment.

He squeezed past, glad they were too intent on each other to notice him, slipping through the crowd watching the kids battling for the puck.

He reached the large sectional at last, and Taylor stood long enough to give Jamie his seat. Jamie immediately pulled him into his lap. "Love you, baby," he whispered.

Taylor settled back, turning his head to press a kiss to Jamie's cheek. "Love you too."

"God I'm glad I found you," Jamie said with a heartfelt sigh. "Without you, I wouldn't have all this."

"Ugh. Would you two shut up? You're nauseating," Charlie snarked.

Jamie snorted against Taylor's hair, his attention half on Ava. She had a fierce expression on her face as she dove onto the floor to cover the puck Andre had shot toward the goal.

"Hey, Hajs!" Ryan Hartinger called out. "At this rate, I think we might put her in net instead of you!"

Hajek laughed and said something back that Jamie couldn't hear.

But his heart was too full to care.

These guys, this team … these people. They all mattered to him so much.

He glanced over at Kara and Boyd who sat a little apart, tense and uncomfortable as they watched the kids.

For the first time, Jamie felt gratitude. He was *glad* their lives had played out this way.

He hugged Taylor close, promising to never let him go.

How could he feel anything but gratitude when he'd ended up with the life he'd always wanted?

Even if it did look different from what he'd originally imagined.

THE END

I hope you loved reading Jamie and Taylor's story as much as I loved telling it.

Rules of Engagement is next, featuring Anders Lindholm, a grieving Swedish center, and Kelly O'Shea, a snarky red-haired defenseman from Boston.

Anders isn't ready to move past the loss of his beloved wife and daughter but Kelly's determined to show Anders there is still a future to look forward to. They just have to hope Kelly's protective older brothers don't find out ...

Learn more here.

BRIGHAM'S BOOKS

Rules of the Game

Join the pro hockey players who fight hard and love hard in the Rules of the Game Universe.

The chronological reading order is *Road Rules, Bending the Rules, Changing the Rules, Unwritten Rules, Rules of Engagement, and Breaking the Rules.*

Road Rules: Rule #1: Don't fall in love with your best friend.

(A 45 k series prequel. Available exclusively through Prolific Works.)

Bending the Rules: Rule #1: Never give up on love.

Changing the Rules: Rule #1: Don't fall in love with your coach.

Unwritten Rules: Rule #1: Don't fall in love with your family's sworn enemy.

Rules of Engagement: Rule #1: Don't fall in love with your brother's best friend.

Breaking the Rules: Rule #1: Don't fall in love with your agent. Coming November 2022.

All titles coming soon in audio.

Pendleton Bay Books

Visit the fictional small town of Pendleton Bay on the shores of Lake Michigan. All books set in this universe can be read as standalones but characters from other books/series may appear from time to time.

There are currently two series set within the Pendleton Bay Universe.

Naughty in Pendleton Series

A complete m/m romance series set in the town of Pendleton Bay with characters exploring the kinkier side of romance. BDSM elements will appear in all books.

Date in a Pinch: When chemistry teacher Neil gets an unexpected delivery at the high school where he works, he's mortified when his crush, Alexander, sees the contents. Curious but inexperienced with kink, Neil has no idea how to live out his fantasies until the hot lit teacher offers a helping hand.

***Embracing His Shame*:** Forrest, the town's accountant, may look uptight but he's anything but. When he offers the local mechanic, Jarod, an indecent proposal to fulfill his shameful fantasies, Forrest will have to decide if he's willing to give Jarod a chance to show him that he can have love *and* the kink he longs for.

Made to Order: Donovan, head chef at the Hawk Point Tavern, loves to be in charge in the kitchen *and* in the bedroom. Tyler, a former solider, is pretty sure he's straight and definitely only into kink if he's the one dishing it out. Until he and Donovan start butting heads about who is calling the shots …

Flipping the Switch: When Logan, a silver fox Dom looking for *experience* on a kinky app, stumbles across Jude, a flirty switch who just so happens to be best friend's son, *and* introduces him to a sweet cinnamon roll of a sub named Tony, they heat between them will sizzle hotter than Jude's kitchen. But they'll have to decide if three is the perfect number.

Preston's Christmas Escape: When Hollywood actor Preston gets caught by the paparazzi in a compromising position, he flees to his home state of Michigan to hide out with his former best friend and ex. Reclusive potter Blake is reluctant to let Preston invade his quiet home in the woods but the heat between them can only be denied for so long … (BDSM)

Poly in Pendleton Series

An ongoing m/m/f romance series set in the town of Pendleton Bay.

Three Shots: Reeve, a local musician, and Grant, a computer designer, have fun in bed together but pursuing a relationship never feels quite right until they meet tavern owner Rachael and try to figure out how to be poly in the small town of Pendleton Bay.

Between the Studs: Coming soon

Peachtree Books

Visit the real life city of Atlanta, Georgia. All books in this universe can be read as standalone but characters from both series do crossover.

There are two series set with the Peachtree Universe.

The Peachtree Series

Complete, continuous m/m series featuring an age gap, light kink, and found family. *Also available in Italian.*

Off-Balance: Coworkers Russ & Stephen meet over a spilled cup of coffee and navigate the complexities of a nineteen-year age gap, a big difference in income, and the death of Stephen's estranged father.

Love in the Balance: Their story continues as Russ introduces Stephen to his family, searches for his absent mother, and asks Stephen to marry him.

Full Balance: They navigate new challenges as they take in a teenage foster boy named Austin and decide to make him a permanent part of their family.

Peachtree Place

Standalone m/m books in the same universe as The Peachtree Series

Trust the Connection: Evan & Jeremy find a love that will heal both their scars in this slow-burn, age-gap romance about living with a disability, believing in yourself, and building the family you always wanted.

The Midwest Series

Complete m/m series featuring four couples. Stories intertwine but can be read as standalones. Opposites attract m/m sports romance with numerous bisexual characters.

Bully & Exit: Drama geek Caleb is sure he'll never forgive Nathan, the hockey player who dumped him in high school, until he learns the real reason why in this slow-burn, second-chance new adult romance. Now available in audio.

Push & Pull: Lowell & Brent have nothing in common when they leave on a summer road trip, but by the end, the makeup-wearing fashionista and the macho hockey player will realize they're perfect for each other in this enemies to lovers, slow-burn story about acceptance. Now available in audio.

Touch & Go: Micah, a closeted pro pitcher, and Justin, a laid-back physical therapist, have nothing in common but when Micah blows out his shoulder, he'll have to choose which he wants more: baseball or love? An enemies to lovers, out for you romance. Now available in audio.

Advance & Retreat: When fate brings Ian and Ricky together, a college swimmer will have to figure out how to reached for the gold without losing the sweet hotel manager who lights up the stage as sizzling drag queen Rosie Riveting. An age gap sports romance with a gender fluid character. Now available in audio.

The West Hills

Standalone m/m series featuring three different couples

The Ghosts Between Us: Losing his brother in a devastating accident sends Chris spiraling into grief. The last person he expects to find comfort in is his brother's secret boyfriend, Elliot, in this slow burn, hurt/comfort romance.

Tidal Series – Co-authored with K Evan Coles

A complete, continuous m/m duology that takes Riley & Carter from best friends to lovers in this slow-burn romance featuring the sons of two wealthy Manhattan families.

Wake: After a decade and a half of lying to himself and everyone around him, Riley slowly come to terms with his sexuality and his feelings for his best friend, Carter, shattering their friendship.

Calm: Carter reaches his own realization and they slowly build the relationship they've been denying for so long.

Speakeasy Series – Co-authored with K Evan Coles

Complete, standalone m/m series featuring characters from the Tidal universe

With a Twist: After Will learns of his estranged father's cancer diagnosis, he returns home and slowly mends fences with him and falls in love with his father's colleague, David. Enemies to lovers, opposites attract, interracial romance.

Extra Dirty: Wealthy, pansexual businessman Jesse is perfectly happy living his life to the fullest with no strings attached, but when he meets Cam, a music teacher and DJ, he'll find that some strings are worth hanging onto in this age-gap, opposites-attract romance.

Behind the Stick: Speakeasy owner and bartender Kyle has taken a break from dating when he's rescued by Harlem firefighter Luka. Interracial romance and hurt/comfort.

Straight Up: When hot, tattooed biker chef Stuart meets quiet and serious Malcolm, they both have secrets they're hiding. Gray ace, bisexual awakening, lingerie kink.

The Williamsville Inn

Standalone m/m holiday romances in a shared universe with Hank Edwards

Snowstorms and Second Chances: Erik and Seth don't hit it off at first, but when a snowstorm leads to them sharing a room at a hotel, Erik discovers a whole new side of himself and his feelings about the holidays. A forced-proximity, bisexual-awakening romance with a second chance at happiness.

The Cupcake Conundrum: Adrian comes face to face with the biggest mistake of his past, Ajay, a hookup who he ghosted on. He'll have to make amends and win Jay's heart back in this single dad, second-chance interracial romance.

Colors Series

A continuous f/f series featuring a bisexual character and opposites attract trope

A Brighter Palette: When Annie, a struggling American freelance writer, meets Siobhán, a successful Irish painter living in Boston, the heat between them is undeniable, but is it enough to build something that will last?

The Greenest Isle: After Siobhán's father has a heart attack, she and Annie travel to Ireland to care for him. Their relationship is tested as they navigate living in a new place and healing old wounds.

Standalone Books

Baby, It's Cold Inside: Meeting Nate's parents doesn't go at all like Emerson planned. But there might be a Christmas miracle for the two of them before the visit is through in this sweet and funny m/m holiday romance.

Bromantic Getaway: Spencer is sure he's straight. But when an off-hand comment sends him tumbling into the realization he's in love with his best friend Devin, he'll have to turn a romantic vacation meant for his ex into the perfect opportunity to grab the love that's always been right in front of them in this best friends to lovers bi awakening m/m romance.

Cabin Fever: Kevin's best friend's dad is definitely off-limits. But he and Drew are about to spend a week alone in a cabin the week before Christmas. And Kevin's never been any good at resisting temptation. An age gap, best friend's father m/m holiday romance.

Also available in audio and in Italian.

Corked: A sommelier and a wine distributor clash in this enemies to lovers, age-gap m/m romance that takes Sean & Lucas from a restaurant in Chicago to owning a winery in Traverse City.

Inked in Blood: **Co-Authored with K Evan Coles** An unexpected event changes the life and death of a sexy, tattooed vampire named Jeff and Santiago, a tattoo artist with a secret. A paranormal, age-gap m/m romance.

Seeking Warmth: When Benny gets out of juvie, he's lost all hope for a future for him or his sister, but the help of his ex-boyfriend Scott will show him that hope and love still exist in this m/m YA novel about second chances.

The Soldier Next Door: When Travis agrees to keep an eye on the guy next door for a few weeks while his parents are out of town, he never expects to fall in love with a soldier heading off to war. An age-gap m/m novella.

ABOUT THE AUTHOR

Brigham Vaughn is on the adventure of a lifetime as a full-time author. She devours books at an alarming rate and hasn't let her short arms and long torso stop her from doing yoga. She makes a killer key lime pie, hates green peppers, and loves wine tasting tours. A collector of vintage Nancy Drew books and green glassware, she enjoys poking around in antique shops and refinishing thrift store furniture. An avid photographer, she dreams of traveling the world and she can't wait to discover everything else life has to offer her.

Her books range from short stories to novellas to novels. They explore gay, bisexual, lesbian, and polyamorous romance in contemporary settings.

Want to read more of her work? Check it out on BookBub!

For news of new releases and sales, follow on Amazon or BookBub!

If you'd like to become an ARC reader, take part in giveaways, and get all of the latest news, please join her reader group, Brigham's Book Nerds. She'd love to have you there!

Made in the USA
Monee, IL
14 January 2023